PRAISE FOR BROTHERHOOD OF THE MAMLUKS

"Graft nimbly inserts the reader into the world and mindset of the medieval jihadi. From the Russian steppe to inside the citadel walls, he takes us where Mamluks are made and loyalty between comrades is sealed."
— Steven Pressfield, bestselling author of
The Legend of Bagger Vance, The Warrior Ethos, and *Gates of Fire*

"*Chains of Nobility* is a harrowing tale of comradeship and combat, providing an in-the-saddle look at the process of creating Mamluks—early Islam's military elite. A great piece of work."
— Nathaniel Fick, former Marine Officer and
New York Times bestselling author of *One Bullet Away:*
The Making of a Marine Officer

"A gripping saga of brotherhood and devotion, *Chains of Nobility* is a must-read for military history buffs. Author Brad Graft enlightens us on the little-known reason behind Medieval Islam's triumphs during the Middle Ages: nomadic youth enslaved by the descendants of Saladin and sharpened into the spear tip of Muslim armies."
— Michael Franzak, author of *A Nightmare's Prayer*,
winner of the 2012 Colby Award

Book I of the *Brotherhood of the Mamluks* trilogy,
Chains of Nobility, was a finalist for the 2019 Colby Award
for first-time fiction that has made "a major contribution
to the understanding of military history, intelligence opera-
tions, or international affairs."

Also awarded a silver medal by the Military Writers Society
of America: "The author has created an intriguing and believable
world from ancient ideas, settings and characters, a masterful job
of both history and fiction."

Kingdom of
England

German
Empire

Kingdom of
France

Kingdom of
Hungary

VENICE ●
GENOA ●

Bulgarian
Empire

Latin Empire

Mediterranean Sea

1230 AD

BASHKIRS

BULGARS

Volga River

Rus Kingdoms

Dnieper River

KIPCHAK KHANATES

Don River

Ural River

MONGOL
KHANATE

Sea of
Azov

ALANS

Black Sea

Caspian Sea

Empire of Nicaea

SELJUK SULTANATE

Kingdom of Armenia

Detail Map
Area

SHAHDOM OF KHWARIZM

Crusader Kingdoms

AYYUBID SULTANATE

ABBASID CALIPHATE

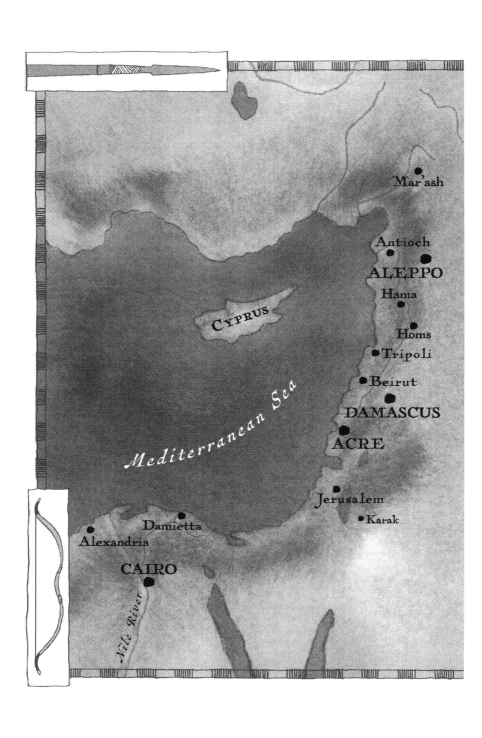

Mar'ash

Antioch

ALEPPO

Hama

Homs

CYPRUS

Tripoli

Beirut

Mediterranean Sea

DAMASCUS

ACRE

Jerusalem

Karak

Damietta

Alexandria

CAIRO

Nile River

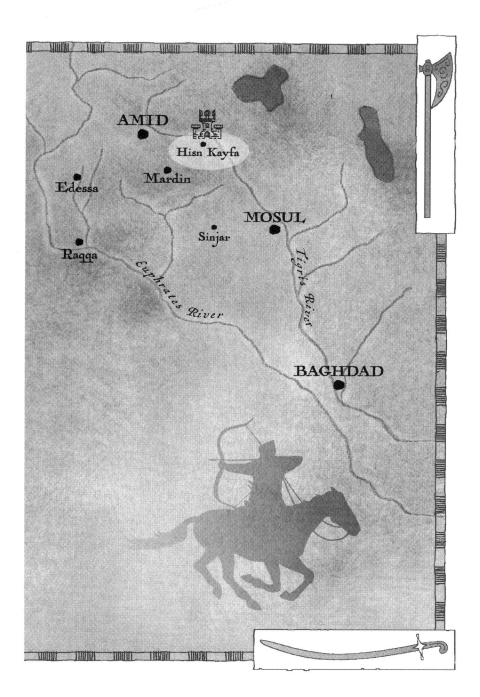

BROTHERHOOD OF THE MAMLVKS

·BOOK ONE·
CHAINS OF NOBILITY
A Novel

THE SAGER GROUP

Artifex Te Adiuva

Cover illustration and design by Steven Novak,
novakillustration@gmail.com
Cover design by Siori Kitajima for SF AppWorks LLC
Maps by Jenifer Thomas of Draw Big Design

Interior Design by Siori Kitajima for SF AppWorks LLC
Formatting by Ovidiu Vlad for SF AppWorks LLC
E-Book Formatted by Ovidiu Vlad

Cataloging-in-Publication data for this book is
available from the Library of Congress.

ISBN-13: 978-0-9996338-5-4
ISBN-10: 0-9996338-5-6

Published by The Sager Group LLC
www.TheSagerGroup.Net info@TheSagerGroup.net
info@MikeSager.com

BROTHERHOOD OF THE MAMLUKS

·BOOK ONE·
CHAINS OF NOBILITY
A Novel

BRAD GRAFT

THE SAGER GROUP

Artifex Te Adiuva

To my brother Marines. One hundred percent of the author's income from the sales of this book will be donated to screened charities that support wounded veterans and families of the fallen.

O ne obedient slave is better than three hundred sons; for the latter desire their father's death, the former long life for his master.

—Nizam al-Mulk, eleventh century statesman

AUTHOR'S NOTE

If I asked you, my reader, to name some of the most impressive warrior cultures in ancient times—in regard to historical influence, tactical proficiency, success on the battlefield, longevity, and dedication to their code—I am sure I would hear names like the Romans, Mongols, Vikings, Spartans, even the Samurai. All good answers. I am equally certain of one military caste that would elude most lists: a group of pagan steppe nomads turned lethal knights of Islam in the Middle East, men originating from the humblest of roots, yet whose professionalism and competence rivaled some of the most elite forces to ever take the battlefield; a band of fighters practically unknown to the average history buff in the west, despite having made a staggering impact upon world history.

Their name: the Mamluks, Arabic for "owned slaves." Their lasting effect: several historians cite that without the Mamluks, Islam likely would never have become a world religion on the grand scale it is today. For in the thirteenth century, the Mamluks—specifically those of the Mamluk Sultanate in Cairo—turned Egypt into an unconquerable fortress against all foes of Islam for nearly three centuries. And the enemies facing both the religion and the Mamluks could only be described as formidable. From their east, the Mamluks confronted the Mongols, invaders already ruling the largest contiguous land empire in history, a force generally unbeaten until that point. From their north and west, they defied the Crusaders from Europe, who for two centuries maintained a foothold in the Holy Land, largely due to their control of the sea. In time and against the odds, the Mamluks would cleverly and violently expel them both.

The shame, perhaps irony, from my perspective is too many of us in the West know too little of these military societies that formed the backbone of Muslim armies for so long. Too few of us know the plights of the young men, who were torn from their families and forged into these fine warriors. Even I, grateful to have carried a "Mamluk Sword" in another life as an officer in the US Marine Corps, knew only that this ceremonial weapon, with curved blade and ivory handle, represented a token of our corps' history—a war gift bestowed upon a brave Marine lieutenant, after a battle against the Barbary pirates in the early 1800s. I, and I presume most of my comrades, knew very little of the sword's namesake.

The haziness surrounding both the Mamluks and one of their primary "feeder tribes," the Kipchaks, is somewhat explainable: heavy-handed rulers have a way of rewriting real history, of obscuring the relevancy of historical figures, when they do not meet nationalistic agendas. One could argue that despite differing political agendas, governments in both the Middle East and Russia masked the role played by both the Turkish tribes and the Mamluks in the late Middle Ages. Fortunately, a collection of scholars have mined enough historical jewels—in the forms of war manuals, biographies, and artifacts—to reconstruct the deeds and methods of this impressive group of warriors.

Regarding the fiction that follows, all of the characters contained herein were spawned from my mind, save Aqtay and the host of Mongol khans and Ayyubid princes revealed. Very rarely did I veer from the exact dates of the historical events presented, doing so only when forced by the logic of story flow. For simplicity and ease of reading, I abbreviated the names of the royalty mentioned throughout this text. For example, al-Adil Abu Bakr II is referred to as the customary, al-Adil II. Units of measurement and time, Turkish names, Kipchak terms, etc. all take forms more understandable for the targeted Western reader.

In addition to museums, a tall stack of history books, and numerous academic publications, which filled my reading for years, this lengthy project compelled me to travel in the Middle East, where I traced routes and climbed through the ruins of fortresses, once inhabited by both Mamluk and Crusader. I was also drawn to the Far East—an equestrian greenhorn bouncing for weeks on horseback across the steppe of Mongolia, where I met nomadic hunters in the hinterlands, ate fatty sheep, and drank fermented mare's milk under hot felt with kind herders—at times hunkering down in their felt-walled shelters to escape the cold wind and snow.

Where I found gaps in knowledge, which could not be filled via observation with my own eyes, or pulled from text, I replaced them with material I thought "true in essence," or within the spirit of this incredible time. Any shortfalls in historical accuracy fall on me alone. I sincerely hope you enjoy this tale.

LIST OF CHARACTERS
(with English meaning)

DUYAL'S KIPCHAK FAMILY
- *Baris* (peace): younger brother
- *Gozde* (favorite): older brother
- *Bora* (storm): younger sister
- *Besim* (friendly): uncle
- *Gunes* (sun): father

"SINGER'S" KIPCHAK FAMILY AND
MONGOL COMMAND HE SERVED
- *Nergis* (daffodil): younger Kipchak sister
- *Baki*: younger Kipchak brother
- *Ferdi* (individual): Kipchak youth serving
  Mongols with Singer
- *"Stiff"*: friend; old Mongol warrior,
  who took Kipchak bride
- *Suren* (charm): Mongol squad leader
- *Chuluun* (stone): Mongol company commander
- *Vachir* (thunderbolt): Mongol battalion commander

NOVICES OF TULB NINE

- *Duyal* (perceptive person)
- *"Singer,"* nickname for *Halis* (pure/clear/real): Duyal's best friend
- *"Ox,"* nickname for *Balaban* (robust): biggest of the novices
- *Demir* (iron): thick-backed brawler; Ox's friend
- *Erol* (be a brave man): smallest of the novices; best bow shot
- *Ilker* (first son): served Mongols with Singer; old-looking novice
- *Ichami* (inspiration): exceptionally gifted novice
- *Galip* (victor): lanky novice; partnered with Singer and Duyal on navigation course
- *Bulut* (cloud): one of the weaker of novices
- *Umit* (hope): another of the weaker novices

INSTRUCTORS AND MEN OF HISN KAYFA CITADEL

- *Cenk* (combat): Tulb Nine's *furusiyya* instructor
- *Turkmani*: Cenk's former patron; amir killed near Aleppo
- *Safir* (mediator): head eunuch
- *Ekrem* (magnanimous): archery master
- *Koray* (ember moon): sword master
- *Aslan* (lion): lance master
- *Ishak* (a prophet): Bedouin groom at horse stalls
- *Bozkurt* (grey wolf): slave trader

AYYUBID ROYALTY REFERENCE
(Dates refer to reigns)

- *Salah ad-Din*, or *Saladin*: Sultan of Egypt (1169–1193); founder of Ayyubid dynasty
- *al-Kamil*: Sultan of Egypt (1218–1238); nephew of Saladin; son of al-Adil I, Sultan of Egypt
- *al-Salih*: Governor/Prince of Hisn Kayfa and Amid (1232–1239); son of Sultan al-Kamil
- *al-Adil II*: Sultan of Egypt (1238–1240); son of Sultan al-Kamil; younger brother of al-Salih
- *al-Asharaf*: Governor of Damascus (1229–1237); brother of Sultan al-Kamil
- *Isma'il*: Governor of Damascus (1237) and (1239–1245); younger brother of al-Asharaf
- *al-Mujahid*: Governor of Homs (1186–1240); second cousin of Saladin
- *al-Muzaffar*: Governor of Hama (1219) & (1229–1244); nephew of Saladin
- *Dayfa Khatun*: Regent of Aleppo (1236 to 1242); grandmother serving on behalf of al Nasir Yusof, a minor
- *al-Nasir Da'ud*: Governor of Karak (1229–1248); grandson of Sultan al-Adil I, Sultan of Egypt
- *al-Nasir*: nephew of Sultan al-Kamil; claimant to Damascus in 1238
- *al-Jawad*: another nephew of Sultan al-Kamil; also claimant to Damascus in 1238

MONGOL ROYAL FAMILY REFERENCE
(Dates refer to reigns as "Great Kahn")

- *Genghis Khan*: (1206–1227); consolidator of the tribes
- *Ogodei*: (1229–1241); son of Genghis Khan
- *Batu*: son of Jochi; grandson of Genghis Khan
- *Mongke*: (1251–1259); son of Tolui; grandson of Genghis Khan

SECTION 1

THE DEPARTED

CHAPTER

I

Duyal
The upper Volga River country
July 9, 1236

D uyal swings his scythe with machine-like efficiency, each
stroke adding a tidy clump of hay to his row. Blood oozes
from the cracks in his fingers, adding a gloss to his weathered
grip—crimson trickling down the maple shaft and into the
splits, mixing with the black stains from his people's earlier
toils. When his hands begin to cramp, he halts. Shrugging to
ease the tightness in his neck, he looks up to the cloudless sky
and then forward to the waving grassland, where the wind
ripples bristled spikelets as far as he can see across the vast
steppe.

His life, their life, had always been about the grass. It
fed their animals and the game they hunted. Its dried, melded
strands in gathered cow dung fueled their fires, kept them
warm. Its nutrients and moisture became the milk they drank,
the meat they ate, and the wool and felt that kept out the

winter wind. They moved always in search of the best of it, passing by the thin shanks growing in sandy soil, yet staying for moons in rich floodplains, where its sheaths grew stout. They were happiest when its blades were thick, green, and abundant, anxious when it was scarce or snow-covered; they thanked the Great Sky when the spirit doused it. It had always been this way for the Kipchaks.

A dozen men work nearby, engrossed in their rhythmic task. They advance as one, each whoosh from their sharp edges adding length to the parallel ribbons of scythed grass snaking across the rolling steppe. Those men not cutting hay work honing stones across their curved blades, from beard to toe, sweat from their chins helping to lubricate the metal.

Ten paces away, Duyal's Uncle Besim rotates his body with straight arms, releasing his powerful stroke with no apparent effort, the toppled stalks falling cleanly behind his steel in wide swathes. The lanky man leans the tool against his ribs, raises his leather flask, draining the last swig.

Before he can set down the container, Duyal grabs the vessel and those belonging to the other men, placing their straps around his neck. His uncle smiles and winks as Duyal passes him. He runs to the stream and fills them. After he returns each, his uncle walks over on pigeon toes, gazing at their morning's work.

"You drink first," Besim says, stooping to grab a handful of grass and crushing it in his hand. "The Saman spoke true. The Great Sky smiles upon us. By tonight, even this grass can be stacked." He smiles, jutting out his pointed chin. He chugs the water, pats his nephew on the back, and resumes his task.

As the sun shifts farther into the southern sky, there is nothing but the swish of blade, the grunt of men around him, and the fresh scent of hay. Sweat drenches his tunic. He concentrates on maximizing each swipe, making certain the entire blade is employed.

A scythe goes silent behind him. Another. He turns, follows his uncle's eyes. Dust rises in the distant hills. Nearer now, a flash in the dirt screen around them. Another spark from a rider's head. Helmet. A second one, then a dozen emerge from the dust, black figures in column.

His uncle's tool strikes the earth with a thud. Three whistle blasts.

Women scream. A baby wails. Men run to their shelters, exiting with bows and quivers. Some wiggle into chain mail shirts on the run; others plunk the odd Rus helmet on their heads. Warriors sprint to the herd, jump on barebacked ponies, pulling fists of mane toward the enemy.

His uncle grabs him, pulls Duyal's chin to face him. "Grab Baris, scatter the flock into the woods, hide yourselves in the spot."

"I will stay and fight alongside you."

He backhands Duyal across the face. "Do as I say! The flock—they mustn't get the animals."

Duyal pulls loose and rushes toward his younger brother, grass whipping against his trousers. Baris and the others are already yipping and waving their arms about the black-headed sheep. He finds the family's most valuable possessions, slapping each ox hard on the ass, causing both to run in opposite directions.

"How many riders?" Baris asks.

"Too many."

Duyal turns. The first of the Mongol warriors has already topped the hill. He runs, his feet pounding the uneven meadow, Baris beside him, pumping his arms wildly to keep his brother's pace. Downhill to the rocky draw. Baris falls forward, skidding to a halt, the force of his body breaking the string of his bow.

Duyal pulls him up by the arm, turning frantically to see if they follow. Reaching the hiding place—a crevasse surrounded by three huge rocks—he pushes Baris in it.

He tries to slide in, but no longer fits. He sucks in, ramming his body sideways into the cranny, scraping flesh from his shoulder blades and sternum as he pops through. They collapse inside, panting like dogs. The distant beat of hooves, the howl of wounded men. Baris moves toward the opening.

Duyal pushes him back down. "You won't save them. Stay as we were told."

Baris covers his ears to block the bugling neigh from their ponies, the choppy orders blurted, and the screams from kin.

Then silence. They wait, pulling the clammy air into lungs with rapid breaths.

A woman's whine. The clank of metal over the hill.

"You stay," Duyal says, slamming his way back through the opening. He scampers up the hill.

He crests and stops. Four Kipchaks lie on the open steppe, arrows protruding from their bodies. A group of mounted invaders circles the tower's sheep and goats. A Black Tartar chases Duyal's older cousin, bringing his pony alongside to hack him down in an almost lazy slash. Women huddle in small groups holding the youngest to their breasts. His uncle lies face down before them. Beside him, Duyal's father, Gunes, tugs on an arrow buried in his shoulder.

Rage consumes him. Duyal charges down the hill. His father takes another arrow to his thigh, a third to his back. Embracing his fate, Gunes grins, snapping all but the arrow in his back. He draws, shoots at a Mongol moving across his front. The surprised Mongol falls from his horse.

Two more arrows plunge into his father's chest, felling him. With eyes wide and his shoulder propped up by the broken arrow in his back, his father smiles up at the Great Sky.

Duyal screams. Nearly blind with tears, he charges a Mongol archer. Time and space and fear cease to exist. He will die with the others.

Something catches his left foot. He takes another stride and is instantly upended. The rope goes taut about his ankle. Mongol laughter fills his ears. From behind, "Choo!"

He is slammed to the ground, spun to his back. A single puff of cloud floats in the sky. He attempts to take a breath, yet is unable. A yank. Now skidding across the grass, he fights to keep his tunic from pulling up around his head. His arms become pinned. Hoof beats at the gallop. A dusty powder packs his nostrils, covers his tongue. The earth speeding beneath him strips the skin from his back and buttocks. A burn, then numbness.

He struggles to his butt, frees his arms, and grabs the rope with one hand to reduce the tension, fumbling with the slip at his ankle with the other. The stalks slap his face and arms, like a torrent of water rushing over him. He gasps for air. He wonders if he will drown in this raging river of grass. His ass pounds a hard lump, throwing him back. A hit to his ribs, another to his head…

He awakens, struggling to breathe in small bursts. The blur of two dark figures in leather chestplates, bickering over his body. He closes his eyes, feels a lump growing on the back of his head, blood seeping down his forehead. A surging pulse throbs through his temples. He tries to clear his head, slowly moving his left foot, realizing the rope around his ankle is loose.

"You killed him. What will we tell them?" a Mongol asks the other.

Duyal rolls to his feet and lunges for the closest one. The tall Mongol turns in his saddle, lifts a club and cracks Duyal with an offhand swipe across the skull.

Blackness.

CHAPTER

2

Duyal
The upper Volga River country
July 9, 1236

With his right eye socket swollen nearly shut, Duyal peers down with his good eye. A pair of wasps land on the animal skin before him, the crumpled hide turned inside out, exposing its slimy tissue. Treading on the white surface, the two insects push through clumps of flies, until finding a sliver of pink muscle. The wasps scissor pieces of flesh, wrap their legs about the morsels, and depart for the nest. Duyal wishes he could take flight with them.

A gray encompasses both sky and steppe. Nearly one hundred fly-speckled sheep hides lie scattered about Duyal and the other four boys. The tinny smell of blood on grass now owns what was their summer camp. A heap of skinned heads stare at him, their unblinking eyes holding a perpetual look of shock, disbelief that he did not do more to save them. Their pale tongues protrude through closed mouths, as if each sheep died disgusted with him.

Flies find their way through the rips in his tunic and trousers, biting at his oozing abrasions and the gash across his back. He occasionally pinches his shoulder blades and tenses his skin as would a cow, but he mostly lets them feed. An ache thumps inside his skull.

The Mongols had led his people's ponies over the hill, while they took the boys and most of the sheep and goats down to the river. There they pulled stakes and leather straps from their saddlebags and secured the animals' rear legs to make the skinning easier. Pulling daggers, they made their incisions behind the shoulder and reached bloody right arms into sheep after sheep, tearing vein from heart. Penned sheep downwind bawled, hearing the screams and smelling the fate of the others. With his own feet secured by the same stake and strap, for a time Duyal pondered if they would skin him and the other boys as well. They still may. He does not care.

Most of the butchered animals went on the backs of ponies, departing in every direction, while the remaining livestock was driven northeast.

"Tonight we break loose. They don't know our land like us," Duyal whispers to his brother, only half believing his own words.

"It looks to be their land now," Baris says without looking back, his glazed eyes fixed on the fur-brimmed hats and slant eyes of those who set their bivouac.

"No speak!" the guard says in broken Turkish, looking up from his pony's bit ring, which he attempts to bend back into form. He is the youngest among them and has grown his thin mustache long to make up for its lack of thickness.

Duyal looks away. He makes a fist to encourage circulation past his bound wrists. His foot goes numb. Despite the warm weather, he begins to shiver. His teeth clank together, as do those of his brother and another youth. Two more remain curled in the grass, lumps of worn flesh and tattered garments.

He runs his tongue across a split lip, letting the taste of iron linger. He grinds his teeth. His eyes swell, tearful. The animals' cries and moans will always ring in his ears. He is a coward. This is how he repaid his family, his elders, at their time of need. His mother—he hid while they slew his sweet mother. Tears soak the collar of his tunic.

The sun dips. He rolls the day's events over in his head. He had followed his uncle's instructions, yet the twisted hides and curled wool adorning the bank serve as reminders of his ineptness. He was given but a boy's task and could not even properly execute that duty. He prays for the Great Sky to take his miserable life. As he does, the wind changes, blowing the scent of cooked mutton across his nose. The smell turns his stomach. He stops his prayer short. He won't insult the spirits of his parents and uncle by making any wish related to himself.

He tells himself he must remain aware, ready if a chance presents itself. He counts the number of short-legged men stuffing meat in their faces—thirteen, their saddles staged in neat rows beneath the aspen. Two men wander about their pony herd, guarding nearly forty animals.

An iron-helmeted trooper approaches the five youths, cupping his wooden bowl with short fingers, his round face bronzed by the sun, his eyebrows so long they nearly trap his lashes when blinking. His dark mustache beads sheep juice, looking like a mink just leaving the river. Clad in long jacket and black-scaled armor, he shakes his head and raises the fur on his lip, as if he had just drunk from a cup of rotten milk. "Why do they spare these scamps?" he asks, turning to an older man who now joins him.

"Young and sweet like Russian honey, more dear than Chinese silk," the old man chuckles, slurping a piece of stray flesh into his mouth. He waves his greasy mutton leg at the prisoners to confirm his words and saunters back to his fire, looking over his shoulder to growl his commands. "Get the girls some fleece. Feed them—or it will be our asses," he says.

Two deep-chested troopers snap to their feet and approach on stiff, bowed legs. One tosses hunks of half-cooked shank meat to the boys, as one would to dogs. The other dumps a heap of fleece at their feet. They walk away.

"Their hands," the old man says with one open palm.

The troopers turn on their heels. They kick awake the sleeping boys. Untying the hemp from the boys' wrists, they bring the captives' hands in front and rebind them. Duyal winces as his arms are brought forward. He considers flinging his bound wrists over the man's neck and choking him, but such an attempt would be futile.

A second warrior joins the young guard, laying his bow across his knees, leaning back against a scrawny pine. He pulls a file from his leather sack and begins working an iron head drawn from his quiver. The warrior looks up. Duyal looks down, before their eyes meet.

Duyal eyes the camp, taking in their weapons. Axes, clubs, leather-handled swords. He makes out the c-shaped form of composite bows lying across their saddles, cased in waxed skins. An arm's reach away from each man, a second bow, strung and ready. A mass of buzzard-feather fletching extends from quiver openings. Arrows encircle a rock, straight willow rods stacked neatly to dry, the grass concealing the likely assortment of deadly blades. A dread fills him.

"Don't even think of it," the young warrior says with a scowl, seeing Duyal's eyes upon the projectiles. "Just eat, so you don't die."

Duyal leans forward to spit at him, but again he thinks better, swallowing the thick saliva he prepared for launch. Squinting in the low light, he memorizes where each bow rests. His brother tips over and immediately begins to snore.

When dusk creeps upon them, the soldiers return to secure the boys' arms behind their backs for the evening. One man weaves another long rope around the neck of each boy and leaves the running end in the hand of the watchman. The lads remain seated, facing the invaders with indifference. Before them sits the untouched meat, the last of the flies finishing their dance upon its withered surface.

Squinty-eyed men ladle fermented mare's milk, *koumis*, from his people's gut bags into wooden cups. Their smiles break only long enough to allow a gulp of the spirit and then return again, even broader.

He bites his cracked lips. This morning, things were as they had always been. Just over the hill, thirty-eight ponies belonging to his tribe, or what the Kipchaks called a "tower," munched on half-brown grass, gracefully hopping on hobbled legs. Underneath nine of the sixteen mares, young foals suckled.

Koumis hung from the support beams of every shelter, as they had entered the season when milk was becoming plentiful, when the colts were nearly old enough to nourish themselves by grazing, when pairs of women milked the mares day and night, using a foal to start the flow of milk and then reaching around both sides of the mare's rear leg with bucket on knee to milk her properly. And by candlelight in the gers, the felt-covered lodgings of the Kipchaks, young children learned their numbers by counting each stroke, as they churned the fermenting liquid.

Their sheep had been healthy, and all was set for a fine breeding season this fall. They had already begun the late summer regimen, drinking mare's milk and eating yogurt curds to spare their sheep and goats for the leaner months ahead. But their livestock is no more. Their lives are no more.

The pine snaps and sizzles in their fires. The black-clad men squat about the flames, some still cutting flesh from the spitted animals with long knives. The *koumis* works upon them. Their tallest man laughs hard and often, the kind of merriment seeded from a satisfying day's work. One releases a long, deep belch, sounding in tone much like that produced by his drunken father.

> *Outside the ger, the scuff of boot heel on dirt, and then a stumble. Duyal roused from his sleep inside. His father's belch, followed by his cursing at the entrance flap.*
>
> *His older brother, Gozde, clicked his tongue and scampered on all fours to the wall opposite the entry flap. He burrowed his head beneath the felt of their shelter.*
>
> *Duyal followed, pushing his brother's butt through, waiting with the heavy material upon his back until Baris also vacated their expedient escape hole.*
>
> *Then iron fingers latched to his ankle. A shot of adrenaline ran through him. The grip tightened, like an owl's talons upon the neck of a hare. He rammed his knee forward. It went nowhere. The leg then jerked backward. His brothers gripped each of his arms, yanking in the opposite direction, their butts skidding on the dew-covered grass, reversing any gain.*
>
> *Duyal looked up to their faces, his eyes white in the night. "No, run... you run," he said calmly, knowing it was no use. His father would only get to beat one of them this time.*
>
> *His siblings persisted, but the second hand found him, wadding the back of his tunic into a fist. Back into the family dwelling he went, sprawled and scratching the turf in defiance, the felt up around his neck.*
>
> *"Run, hide," he whispered to his brothers, the sound of tearing grass in hand spelling his fate.*

The hollow sound of ponies ripping grass is muffled by the lapping of river over stone. The crickets begin their melody. His eyelids grow heavy, becoming lost in the nearest blaze. He is beyond tired but cannot sleep. The wind picks up, pushing the hissing licks of flame sideways, flapping them like a child's blanket.

Their smoke drifts into the boys' faces, causing the youths to bow in reverence and suck in their captors' fumes. Flecks of gray ash fuse to raw skin, leaving them speckled ghosts of their extinct towers.

With head down and fingers locked, he thinks back to his mother's ger and the voice of an elder, barely heard over the crack of fire and felt-muted patter of the rainfall. The oft-recited verbal history whistled through the gaps in the old man's teeth.

It was five generations ago, when Duyal's line of Kipchaks moved down from the northern country in search of a kinder climate, better hunting, and improved grazing lands for growing flocks. Legend had it that for weeks many towers traveled south and west, through the country of both ally and enemy, eventually reaching the lush grasslands between the Volga and Ural Rivers. There, the Kipchaks met fierce resistance from the nomadic Oguz— herders, hunters, not so different from Duyal's own people. Every Oguz band united, fighting to protect their lands.

Yet they were no match for multitudes of Kipchaks and their accurate arrow fire. In only days, the Oguz were driven out. Over the decades, the Kipchaks pushed farther toward the setting sun, dominating all the steppe between the Black and Caspian Seas, settling on the drainages of four major river systems: the Dnieper, Don, Volga, and Ural. The lineage of many ponies in the Kipchak towers could still be traced back to stock taken as plunder from the war with the Oguz. Dances and chants, festivals and tales were created as tribute to his brave predecessors.

He had always been thankful for his ancestors, those Kipchaks with the resilience to endure the trek from the

Tobol River and the courage to push the enemy from this land. Yet he had never given much thought to the Oguz. Still bleeding and staked like a pony, he thinks of them now. A dark smile fractures the mask of crusted blood upon his face.

They change guards. Their flames fall off to breathing mounds of coals, like the gills of newly spawned beasts living beneath the soil. Beasts. In these fires, whatever child was left within him burns to ashes; whatever man he was meant to be drifts away in their smoke. The raiders disperse into the murk with leather bags over shoulder to occupy the gullies, pulling skins over their hardened bodies, seeming to slink back into the crevasses of hell from which they must have come.

Duyal rolls his shoulders, a vain attempt to loosen the knot about his neck. He lies on his side, fights the fleece over him. Staring into the darkness, he shivers.

CHAPTER

3

Duyal
The upper Volga River country
July 10, 1236

Duyal awakens. Moving his arm, he expects the soft felt wall of his ger against his elbow, but it is not there. He reaches to wipe his face, yet is halted by the cut of hemp on wrist. The past day's events slowly sink into his mind, like a pebble tumbling to the bottom of a deep pool. The sting returns to his heart. No. He must still be dreaming. He must have dreamt it all.

He digs a thumbnail into the back of his hand, breaking skin, but he does not wake among his family as hoped. He attempts to sit up, but is stopped short by stabs of pain in his ribs and legs. Struggling, he finally rocks himself to a rest on sore buttocks, a setting crescent moon throwing faint shadows about his wretched form. The Mongol watchman turns, letting Duyal know that he is alert.

His head pounds, the pressure feeling as if it will crack his skull. He feels his gut push upward and leans to puke, wiping the lingering string of mucous upon his shoulder. The last coils of smoke from their embers seep into his lungs, stinging his nose and throat. He shrugs to lose the sheepskin from his shoulders, yet the fleece sticks to his back, a layer of dried pus and blood bonding tunic to fleece. A forced swallow and blow of thick snot to the ground.

In time, he raises his eyes to the dawn. A violet hue cast wide across the rolling sea of grass. Swollen clouds float across the fading specks in the night sky. What was only a gurgle in the vast darkness transforms into the meandering ribbon below, a steady purr of current. River scrub awakens with the chatter of sparrows and chickadees. His brother still sleeps, blotched with mud and covered in hair-like cinders from their fires. A breeze goes through him, a shudder.

The first rays of sun break the horizon gloriously, the beams pushing the invaders from their hasty bivouacs, like a stick jammed into an ant mound. They go from sleep to action instantly, stowing skin covers under leather flaps and saddling ponies, while chewing on dried meat and yogurt curds. Men head riverside with their comrades' leather flasks slung over shoulders, the hollow knocks of hard leather marking their steps.

Their leader calls them in with only a raise of his hand. Speaking over a model of the terrain, he points with riding stick at the boot heel-constructed valleys and mountains, occasionally turning to indicate the actual territory before them.

Duyal nods off. He dreams of wild dogs feeding on his tower's lambs, of him and Baris carving through the drooping plumes of grass atop their ponies, methodically shooting the livestock killers. On the run, the pack's alpha male looks up at him with yellow eyes, exposing a soaking bib of red about his neck and chest.

He stirs, the hoof strikes in dream stomping him into consciousness. A band of ponies, more than twenty, Duyal guesses, thunder into camp, dripping water beneath curved bellies, their thick legs plastered in mud, their shoeless hooves clacking over river rock and hammering the turf in resounding thumps. Bays and grays and chestnuts, some spotted white. All are twelve to fourteen hands tall; some with untrimmed manes in black and white, splayed in wild elegance, engulfing their rippled necks. Several nicker as they near, toting with them the smell of damp leather and churned river bottom. Others stomp their hooves, jerk their heads, upset to be halted.

Most of their riders are cloaked in padded long coats, wrapped at the waist by silk sashes in blues and reds. Their trousers are wool; their thick-soled boots crafted from cow leather. A few wear armor, covering their chest with hardened scales like fish skin, but void of protection upon their backs. Some sport helmets of iron, or hardened leather. Others are in strange felt hats with two or three flaps tied up to the crown of their heads, like ger entrances. One bears a wound on his head, a bandage wrapped diagonally above his ears. Another wears a tunic stained red-brown, a soiled cloth snugged around his forearm.

Half the riders dismount and hobble their ponies, all the while hurling smiling barbs in foreign tongue at their mates. These are received with insults, soft chuckles, and smirking nods from the others.

Yet those pulled behind the riders on bareback do not laugh. Nine more Kipchak boys, secured by horsehair rope to the invaders' mounts. These captives, red- and blond-haired adolescents, are unbound, free of marks and injury. One coughs nearly continuously. Their ponies bunch, and the boys whisper among themselves, eventually looking in the direction of Duyal and the other youths.

Duyal glares at them, and then at the man at the front of the formation. He must be their khan.

This man leaps from his mount with the spryness of an eight-year-old. His braided hair, long and shiny-black, dangles about his shoulders. His nose spreads flat across his face. His eyes are no more than slits, and these dart around camp, taking stock of the situation. Swaggering on short legs to the restrained youth, he looks over each from head to toe.

For a while, he paces behind the boys, swinging a wooden riding stick from a leather strap around his wrist. With great speed he alternates between single and double rotations, each time catching the gnarled oak in his palm with a slap. He talks to himself, agreeing with only some of his own counsel.

The khan calls over last night's leader and another warrior. They confer, occasionally looking and pointing to various Kipchak boys. The mounted warriors wait in silence upon saddles laden with maces and battle-axes, their blades and pikes pounded into deathly shapes unfamiliar. From wooden frames hang quivers and cased bows and the same leather bags. Their ponies rip at tall grass and sample branch tips from riverside alders. Several men lean far to one side, leaving only one thigh on saddle, providing relief to worn asses.

The three break from their meeting, nodding in agreement. Their khan crosses his arms and strokes his thin beard, while the other two shout orders to the troops. The men pull six of the new boys off their ponies, as if they were baggage, leading the Kipchaks to Duyal and the others. They then untie the older boy behind him, along with Baris. Two warriors push the coughing boy upon another pony and lead him over the hill.

A man motions for Baris to mount a pony among the warriors. Baris hesitates. The brute reaches for his club. Baris jumps on.

"Can my brother and I stay together—he's right there," Baris says, pointing at Duyal.

"Shut up," the warrior says without looking back.

"He's able, a hard worker. Please," Baris says.

The warrior turns, placing a hand to his club, but then eases it back to his side after catching a scowl from his superior. Baris looks to his brother with wide eyes, mouth ajar.

Several warriors run to the shade tree, where piles of wrapped meat sit. They snatch several, tying the bundles to their saddles, while others fill water flasks. The Mongols then depart with their boys packed into the center of the column. Baris turns back to his brother, hopeless tears streaming down his face.

Duyal fails to fight back his own tears. Through blurry eyes, he watches his brother's outline on a thick-legged gray fade into the dusty eastern horizon.

The five newcomers exchange glances, eyebrows drawing tight when their eyes pass over their new companions. The clean Kipchak faces go long, as the Mongols bind them to the human chain.

"Why? We will not run," a boy says.

A strong-necked Mongol finishes his knot. He slowly turns his head to check his commander's location and then throws a quick elbow across the Kipchak's face.

Duyal bites his lip. He wishes to strangle them. If these boys had not arrived, maybe Baris would have been allowed to stay. In one day he has lost everything. He wrestles the woolskin with chin and shoulder, pressing his head in the dirty fleece to muffle his sobs.

He hates himself, weeping, as would a young girl. He is a disgrace to his bloodline. He reconstructs his father's and uncle's final moments. Can he not muster even a fraction of their courage? How could he think he was on the verge of manhood? He will give the Mongols a reason to slay him. If the spirits wish to punish him for his weakness, this is fine. But they can choose only the form of punishment; Duyal surmises that he has a say in its duration. He wipes his eyes, turns to watch the pair of warriors trot back over the hill, trailing the coughing boy's empty-saddled pony behind them.

CHAPTER

4

Duyal
The upper Volga River country
July 12, 1236

"Schwack!" The bite from the Mongol's riding stick sends a jolt of adrenalin pumping through Duyal's limbs. The surge lifts his head, compressing the sunburned skin on the back of his neck. His eyes pop open.

A multitude of silvery plumes ripple in the sun, blinding him. He turns away, squints to ease his eyes' adjustment. The tanned hills of the steppe stretch before him, blunt-topped ridges and curvaceous fingers interrupted only by cut ravines and clusters of pine and scrub bunched in the depth of its drainages.

"No sleep," the Mongol behind him growls.

Duyal corrects his seat on the bare back of the pony, sliding easily on the grunge, which coats his backside to the knees. The pale slime has formed each afternoon, the rubbing between his and the pony's flesh tearing at the sores on his buttocks and thighs, until his blood is churned frothy with the pony's sweat. The Mongol in front of him turns, peering over Duyal's head to shoot a warning glare at the assailant.

They have assigned a warrior to each lad, this guard responsible for every aspect of their boy's upkeep. When his youth eats, pisses, or shits, the Mongol sponsor is obliged to supervise. At night, Duyal cannot roll over in sleep without the joined leather straps awakening his personal escort. Under bow point last evening, he was made to strip and wash, his sentry's motivation less about concern for the boy's health or comfort, more about his commodity surviving the trip south.

No Mongol has bothered to ask the name of his boy, probably for the same reason that Kipchak boys do not trouble themselves in naming their sheep. Instead, the Black Tartars identify each of the eight boys by distinguishing marks or behaviors. Those names that seem to have stuck: "the tall one," "one with splinted arm," "stupid boy," "tiny," "one who won't shit," "wild-faced boy," "orange-hair," and for Duyal, "puffy-eyes."

They ride, the adolescents led by rope procession, the Mongols looking like a string of protective fathers pulling in tow their family of oversized tots, or perhaps a gaggle of captured wives. Those Mongols unburdened by a youth work the front, rear, and flank security, all riding with bows strung across their thighs, quivers flopped open.

The man to his front is Duyal's Mongol. While no taller than the youth, beneath his lamellar armor is a chest as broad as a barrel; on each shoulder are straps of muscle the size of goat legs. Under his thick boot leather flex calves chunky from life in the saddle. His cheekbones sit high and plump, covered in dark skin, which turns into premature wrinkles near his goateed chin. His face tapers to lips thin with no expression. He rarely shows his teeth, yet when he does, they gleam sharp and yellow. While this duty seems beneath him, his eyes alone give indication that he takes this and probably every assignment seriously.

For three days they have stuck to the west bank of the endless Volga, pushing downstream, some of the boys astride ponies that once belonged to their tower's warriors. The Mongols ride hard, starting just before sunrise and stopping at dusk.

The sun beats upon the column. Sweat pours into Duyal's eyes. He can do nothing but blink the sting from them. Those Mongols with helmets have stowed them, preferring their brimless felt hats, made by their women from four identical sections sewn together to form a point at the top. Some now fold the sides down to protect their ears and necks, while the Kipchaks endure with bare heads, their hats long since taken or lost.

The khan points his finger. They push their horses uphill. His keepers are not foolish. They trod the upland country, far above the dense groves of aspen and colonies of bush willows, which thrive in the river bottom. They continue, staying higher than the abundant feather grasses, which dominate the hillsides, not wishing to risk their precious cargo in flopping tussocks, tall enough to swallow both horse and rider.

They drop back down with hardly a word passed between them, only the clank of tack and thuds of hoof on dry grass telling their presence. They move through spindling stalks of labiate, the last of their purple-eared flowers peeking among the stipa grass at the riders like curious mice. Through a meadow, they part striking cornflowers with mops of floppy yellow hair and white-headed umbellifers, looking, as Duyal's mother often said, "like Kipchak gers must when viewed far above by the Great Sky."

Rounding a bend, they clomp over circular patches of dark soil, where over one hundred gers once stood. Turf-pocked shadows, gloomy silhouettes mocking towers once large and strong. They weave around old Mongol fires, charred stubs of ger frames and goat bone relics edging the charcoaled beds. More livestock bones gleam where the slaughtering took place, tossed by the new lords of this land, each limb stripped successively cleaner by Mongol, then wolf, then ant. Above them, rain-pitted mounds of dirt dot the hillside, the graves of kin being the wives', sisters', and mothers' last chore, before the women were led away.

Each day they have passed such places, those upriver only recently devastated or abandoned, while most of those farther downstream laid to waste moons ago, the dung from their departed herds bleached white and hard, shoots of new grass pushing up where nomads once slept.

They continue for most of the day, eventually topping a hill. In the valley bottom, a tower seems to hum with surprising normalcy, women going about their chores, unaffected by the occasional Mongol patrol, which ride up and down both sides of the river. Duyal figures there is only one way these Kipchaks were spared, their khan having taken the often unpopular path of submitting to Mongol rule. He is beginning to wish his small tower had done the same.

They drop down, the Mongols keeping their distance from the tower. A woman mending trousers looks up from her work. Seeing the roped boys, she shakes her head and spits on the ground. Her face returns to the gray mass on her lap.

Two lads, toting reed baskets on their backs, collect dried dung with pronged sticks. One of them, upon seeing the white skin of the riders, releases his load and walks toward the column. Able to see the Kipchak faces, he halts atop a small knob. He squats, sitting upon his heels, his arms wrapped about his knees. Seeming to recognize none, he drops to his ass, his eyes now riveted to the grass at his feet.

Two whistle blasts pierce the air. An old man tending a tiny herd watches the boy. He makes no sign, leaning on his staff. The boy turns to him, takes to his feet, and returns the basket to his back.

The column moves away from the water for some time, eventually cutting across an oxbow in the river's course. The familiar stench of death fills a depression in the terrain. Duyal buries his nose in his tunic.

Movement above grabs his attention. A slim woman drags a twisted corpse uphill, using its bare foot as her handle. Lowering her butt, she lurches the body upward, the stiff man's bent elbow collecting grass at its bend like a human hoe.

The file of riders startles her. She pauses, her gaunt chest heaving, her deep breaths sucking in the fabric tied neatly across her face. The cloth conceals her attributes, disclosing only dark bags below empty, green eyes. She brings the neck of her dress up to wipe the sweat from her forehead.

Seeming to know better, she averts her gaze, looking over her shoulder to the location of three more warriors in the grass, dead Kipchaks fixed at strange angles, a Rus shovel leaning against the contorted leg of one. Lean limbs protrude from bloated torsos; strong arms that once drew bows to provide and protect have now gone rigid and decayed. She continues to pull on the man, up and up, to a height where the spirits may aid his transition. Rotting men, going underground without weapons or ponies, slain in this world and soon to arrive without protection when they get to the next.

Duyal figures he would have been better off like those on the hill, his body decomposing, but his spirit with those of his family. But that didn't happen, and he and the other boys know their fate—it is no mystery to any of them where they will go.

For many moons, Kipchak Khans had harassed the southern and western principalities of the Rus, raiding settlements and whenever possible taking captives down to the slave markets. At least thirteen trading hubs dotted the Volga, places where traders would gather to deal and then organize strings of slaves to be carted south to the Black Sea ports. All khans preferred this trade to any, as even in bad times a healthy boy could yield a dozen ponies or maybe thirty metal pots. And such bartering was not limited to the Rus, as plenty of Kipchak youth also ended up on the slave blocks, living goods sold by hungry families or threatened fathers.

The scent of wet pony and human stench radiates beneath Duyal. Drips of perspiration trickle over his ribcage and down his buttocks, stinging his wounds. He becomes entranced by the sway of the tasseled mane cinched between his pony's ears, the black hair bound atop the beast's forelock with thin cord, the tress swinging in a steady rhythm. The even rock of the pony again causes his head to bob. A spasm snaps him awake. They ride, the sun in his face dipping farther in the sky.

Before descending into the lower country, half the Mongols on each flank canter over the crest of the nearest hill to reconnoiter. Resuming their trek, they enter a deserted basin. Heaps of dried grass, mounded chin-high by the nomads, half-built pens, tools left where they were dropped. He recalls piles from his younger years, late-night safe havens for him and his brothers. Grass sanctuaries, clawed out caverns, where the three huddled in the cold, weathering their father's unwarranted storms.

Duyal stretches his shoulders forward, drawing tight scar tissue on his shoulders, remnants from years of his elder's drunken work with a willow branch, well applied mostly during the autumn, when the intoxicating *koumis* was too plentiful. He takes a deep pull of sweet air into his lungs, the wind at his back pushing the aroma of hay down the valley. Some green still in the cut stalks—fresh piles. Just three days prior he had held a scythe himself, proud to work it with the tower's men rather than carrying the herding staff of a boy. Tears roll down his cheeks.

A single lamb appears from behind a pile. Seeing the riders, it cries. A hollowness forms in his gut, Duyal sympathizing with the lost animal that surely returned to find his kin gone. A Mongol on the flank tosses a rope about the lamb's neck, securing the end to the back of his saddle. A tug from his rope adds the lamb to the file.

They pass more haystacks, Duyal trying to guess the size of the flock once owned by these Lower Valley Kipchaks. Of course they would have nearly had their winter's work done, as to be lazy in the summer was not an option for the Kipchaks. Like an ant, the nomad thinks winter all summer long. Survival of their animals meant survival for the tower, and the open steppe in winter was an unforgiving place. While a pony could scrape away snow with its hooves to expose the grass underneath, a sheep used its nose. When the snow became ice-crusted, a sheep's face could become bloody and raw.

Left alone, ewes might starve in a field with ample forage right beneath their feet. Hence, nearly all steppe people mounded cut grass, not only to make the feed easier for the sheep to access in the snow, but also to protect the hay. While the top layer in a stack would spoil in the elements, this blemished grass would act much like the thatched grass roofs used by the Rus—protecting the loose hay beneath, and allowing the sheep to simply nose away the bad and eat on the good fodder under it.

Of course the hay was only good if it had been stacked when properly dried. Despite Besim's nearly constant grin, Duyal knew his uncle had always stewed about their vulnerability if heavy rain should sweep in while the grass was spread to dry. Such moisture could render their work useless and ruin the winter feed. But his uncle always held such thoughts inside. Pleasantness was his nature, regardless of circumstance.

Aside from his brothers, perhaps he will miss his uncle the most. For all of Duyal's fourteen years, his Uncle Besim had been the patient teacher and skilled hunting mentor that Duyal's father was not. Quick with a compliment and slow to anger, Besim's demeanor drew Duyal and his brothers to him. He gave a kind hand and the fatherly advice their own father could not. And while their uncle was practically the opposite of their father, Besim defended his only brother to the end. "People just don't understand him, don't understand what he's been through, that's all. Just remember you boys are everything to your father. He has nothing else," Besim would say.

Perhaps their uncle had known their father best, had known something the boys did not. Or perhaps it was only Besim's loyalty and tolerance for misery that allowed him to put up with such a man, when most others could not. Besim could indeed endure abuse.

Duyal's aunt often told a story of Besim's childhood, of their parents attempting to correct her brother's pigeon toes by putting him in a restraining device that forced his feet outward. His parents would fasten toeless boots to oak at the heels and make the youngster wear them at night. But each night Besim would somehow destroy the contraption, without waking a soul. In the mornings he would hand the heap of strap, oak, and boot to his astonished mother with a grin, earning him a thrashing almost daily.

Duyal had inherited his uncle's build, Besim not possessing the thick limbs of Duyal's father, but the misleading, lanky strength of a whitetail. And like a wise buck, his uncle's nose was always to the wind, his big ears practically swiveling at any snap of a twig. Yet unlike a buck, tempered to run at danger's first sign, his uncle had proven himself one of the tower's fiercest warriors, never failing to turn his pony's head toward the enemy. On foot, his pigeon toes were unrivaled for speed, often making him the first to meet the enemy, but also the last to leave a man behind.

Such was the case in the raid this past spring, Duyal's first. While Duyal and four other boys filled water skins and tended the camp and ponies, the tower's warriors snuck into a Rus village to snatch candles, knives, tools, and rigging from the soft-handed people in the wooden shelters. The raiders were found out and forced to beat a hasty retreat. In the process a warrior's leg was broken. The wounded man refused help, certain more would be killed trying to save him. Yet Besim went back, carrying the man across his back into the night, occasionally hiding under shrubs from the pitchfork-toting Rus.

Duyal's pony twists, nearly throwing him backward. He squeezes his thighs to keep from falling.

A Mongol shouts from the rear, "Stop, you fool!"

Duyal flinches, anticipating another crack from the stick. Receiving none, he turns.

A lad breaks free, the knot on his lead somehow failing. With his hands still secured behind his back, he heads for a gap on the Mongol flank, where the feather grass is thick and high. The youth buries his heels under the pony, lies flat against the pony's neck, the mane clutched between his teeth. The boy wrenches his mount's head right. Through a mouthful of coarse hair, he blurts in the way of the Mongol, "Choo! Choo!"

On the left, a pair of Mongols put their ponies to the gallop, almost casually taking the perfect angle of pursuit to head off the youth. One nocks an arrow, draws, and punches the shaft into the Kipchak's flank, knocking the boy from his mount. Upon hitting the ground on his side, the boy springs to his feet. He sprints toward the gully, the fletching in his side flapping on each step.

"Hold that shot!" the khan says.

The second shooter ignores the command, perhaps not hearing over the sound of hoof beats. He closes and releases his projectile, hitting the boy with a "whop" in his upper back. The youth drops, scrabbling the turf with hand and toe toward the tall grass.

Duyal begins to eye the flanks. This distraction could be his opportunity. He wonders how fast he could run with his hands tied behind his back. His Mongol in front watches the crawling boy, shaking his felt-covered head. Duyal looks behind to see if the stick bearer's attention is diverted.

"Don't try. I'd be glad to shoot," the Mongol says, grinning from behind his bow.

Duyal looks the man in the eye. The Mongol slides his arrow down and home in response, the bow at his thigh, but his hands in shooting position. Unflustered, Duyal returns his gaze forward.

Why not? He pictures his zigzagging tack to the long grass and battering through trees, upriver to the ford site. He could hide in the thickness long enough to get his hands untied. Darkness would be here soon. Then maybe he could swim across the wide expanse. They would expect him to head north, but he would go east.

Or would they just fill him full of arrows within his first ten steps? Fuck it—wasn't that the idea anyhow? He feels his heart race, as his body prepares for the flight his mind conjures. But from somewhere within, a calming force takes him by surprise. An inner voice tells him, "Don't go." His body responds, a loosening in his chest, his shoulders slump forward. The tingle fades from his limbs, as if cold water were being poured upon death's glowing embers.

"Your pony is secured, there is nowhere for you to go," his Mongol says, twisting at the waist, the tight knot held in his palm.

Duyal sneers at him. Maybe there will be a point to all of this someday. Why give his life so cheaply? If only some of the other boys had attempted to flee, he would have run.

Instead, the boys stare at the escapee with stone faces, the crawling boy having been stopped just short of the high scrub, the burst of a scarlet bubble from his mouth concluding his folly.

"If you want to die, follow him," the khan says, riding slowly down the line, stabbing the air with one short arm in the direction of the blood-soaked boy. "We have no problem killing you all, one by one. All of you!"

The khan spins his pony, riding straight to the second Mongol shooter. Upon reaching him, he tilts sidewise in his saddle to get into the young man's face. He circles the trooper, hissing obscenities unheard. The shooter looks on sheepishly, nodding in confirmation, periodically looking down at the grass and over at his kill.

The leader returns to the column, a thick vein having risen on the squat man's neck. A warrior breaks the formation to retrieve the boy's pony, which tromped upwind of the blood to walk circles, until eventually settling in to munch on the tall grass. The pigtailed end of his lead droops from his tack, evidence of his owner's neglect.

"Check your knots," the khan snorts. "Each of them!"

The shooter pouts his way to the corpse and dismounts. He pulls a dagger from his sheath and stands there. Kneeling on his reins, he places his hand underneath the boy's chin and slits the Kipchak's throat. He stands, kicking the boy over to his back, revealing both wounds.

He pulls loose the arrow in the boy's side, cutting away the fleshy fiber that grabs at the arrow's barbs. He drops the bloody shaft on the grass. He stares at the second, his own arrow snapped midshaft. He then commences to save the head, gripping the broken willow and again slicing at the stubborn tissue to free the iron blade. Finished, he wipes his dagger on the grass and then on the boy's trousers, before sliding it back into its sheath.

CHAPTER
5

Ox
Lower Dnieper country
July 14, 1236

"Don't do it," Ox says.

Two ravens caw overhead, chiming annoyingly with the bleat of his animals. A kiss of wind whispers through the seed heads, bowing an endless blanket of bronzed stalks before him. With hands on hips, he watches.

Two rams eye each other from their peripheral vision. They separate, each dragging a leather-banded wood chunk secured on right forelegs. They turn and rumble forward on a collision course, a rickety three-legged charge. They rear back in near unison and butt with lowered heads, sending a crack across the valley. Black head on black head, they grind the base of their broad horns, the bone protruding from just above the eyes and curling back in tapered shades of tan, grooved and striated like dirty icicles.

They huff with wide eyes, the larger shredding turf as he pushes the three-year-old. The smaller goes to his knees, blood dripping around his bulbous eye socket. Eighty-four others observe with a vacant interest, continuing their sideways mince of grass, stray strands hanging below their jaws. Heads looks over backs, necks stretch around butts to get a view of the duel.

Ox shakes his head. "Silly bastards."

The rams have been separated from the ewes for weeks and have their pecking order figured, but these two dominants persist in their brawls. He can't have them crippling one another, or he will be thrashed himself.

He approaches the panting victor from straight behind, being careful to stay in the beast's blind spot. He reaches over the top, slipping his thumb into the ram's mouth, behind the incisors. With this grip, he jams his knee into the sheep's rump and bends the animal's head back across his leg. The sheep balks.

He lowers the beast to the ground, pinning the ram with his knee to its loin, with a wet boot lodged under its flank. He reaches into his side pouch and pulls out a leather facemask. He slides on the nosepiece and then secures a buckle behind the sheep's ears. He and the sheep rise, the ram's frontal vision now restricted, though it retains the ability to see down to feed and backward to spot predators.

"Maybe both this and the clog will suit you, you stupid prick."

He looks to the loser. While this ram is still groggy, he kneels on him and hobbles a fore and rear leg just above the pastern joint with a leather cinch, leaving a natural distance between legs.

"I told you to give this shit up."

He yawns, unsure if the drowsiness is from his sleepless night or boredom in tending the animals. He looks down to the lower valley, toward the distant chirp of whistles and yap of hounds. The morning sun begins to devour the rolling mist below, exposing several boys tending the tower's massive flock of ewes. From afar, the Karakul's cream and black torsos appear to glide across the steppe, their black legs lost in the fog and tufts of brown grass. Behind many of the sheep, tiny black flecks in singles and pairs follow on tail.

Most of the lambs are solid black at birth, retaining this color for moons. Early on, they stay in their mothers' shadows, perhaps nature's hand in helping to fool the eyes of wolves, hawks, and eagles. Each spring the boys were expected to keep their bows in hand, as the larger raptors were wise enough to use the contour of the hillsides as cover, and then swoop in to snatch the newborns. With the lambs now over three moons old and weaned from their ewes' teats, wolves have become the more lethal threat, these predators traversing the scrub cover on the edge of the pastures, searching for lambs lost or separated.

The breeze picks up, pulling apart the remnants of vapor which had settled in the familiar saddles and draws of Ox's Kipchak homeland. Sixteen boys and their dew-soaked dogs are gradually revealed. They lead the flock to fresh grass in a loose spearhead formation. "Flankers," those dispersed down either side of the tip, carry long staffs, minding the herd's periphery with the dogs.

Clad in an oversized tunic, handed down from his brother and fixed at the waist with a thick belt, the youngest of them pokes the damp air with a finger. He counts black dots, mindful that losing even one lamb will leave him with no dinner and an ass full of switch marks. Another, with a strung bow slung over his shoulder, ambles toward a stray lamb and pats the beast on the rear with his staff, pushing the animal back toward the others. Sprinkled among the sheep is a smattering of goats, grazers both brown and white.

The fog burns off farther up the valley, unveiling dozens of white-domed shelters, appearing like a gray-stubbled beard upon the morning face of the steppe. From here, two armed boys, his relief, begin their trudge up the hill toward him. He hopes they have brought plenty of snuff. As they near, he checks to see if any warriors observe from their watch. The best of the warriors rarely made trouble with the boys, but of course the frailest of the men often did.

"Useless bastards," he says to himself, contemplating how he will one day get even with two recent weaklings.

Shearing in sleep-deprived delirium, he nicked the ewe's belly. "Shit," he said. Two sheep later, he did it again, this one dripping blood clear down to its foot. A small man in the tower saw it and in a short time, he and another weakling showed up with switches.

"It was a mistake. It will heal before fly season," Ox said to them.

When they tightened the grip on their sticks, he knew his penalty had already been set. "I see you women come in a pair. Afraid coming alone might cause the switch to be turned on you by a mere boy?" He laughed, taking two steps forward, patting the meat of his arm.

They hit him extra hard that day, even across the head, but he did not care. He could kick their asses and they knew it.

The entire tower calls him "Ox," save his mother, who still calls him Balaban. His own father gave him the nickname early, astonished that at only three years the boy was already wearing the hand-me-downs of chaps more than twice his age. Most men in the tower give the boy little time, the lad being a freak of sorts. All refuse to trade grips with him, unwilling to have their hands dwarfed in that of a boy's.

The two youth head straight for him. With staff propped under his arm, Ox chuckles, looking down at the tops of the felt-brimmed hats of his mates. He calls out to them, "Have you come again to be parted from your fathers' snuff this fine day?"

The bolder of the two looks up at the giant boy's neck, the stiff edge of his hat preventing him from meeting Ox's eyes. "You won't be so lucky this time."

"Hah, we'll see. Yep, your timing is good. My tin is getting a bit light," Ox says, shaking the small box attached to his belt for show, the weather-beaten receptacle acquired long ago by his father, during a bartering session with the Rus.

"Enough talk."

"I believe I'm up," Ox says.

They pull arrows from quivers patched with calf hide, each shaft inside bearing the three-feather hawk fletching of their tower. Out of habit, Ox strokes the vane of each feather with rough fingers, neatly aligning the barbs, before nocking home an arrow. He senses his competitors' impatience and draws back slowly, feigning a shot high and to his right. He then pops to one knee, quickly releasing an arrow to his left that skims across the waving seedheads.

Knowing their shots will not count unless launched before Ox's arrow reaches the ground, the boys respond with rapid shots from the offhand, aiming at a point sixty paces away, where they think the arrow from the thick-chested shooter will land. The shortest of the Kipchaks smiles, as the three walk over to the iron-tipped arrows sticking in the turf.

"You lose," the shortest boy says to his pal, his arrow the closest to Ox's yellow-striped shaft, only four feet away. The youth opens his tin and carefully places a scoop of the fine powder into the tin of the winner. The three retrieve their arrows.

Ox chuckles. "Watch for the rams, though I can't see you hitting any target, aimed for or not."

"Yeah," the short boy says, releasing an arrow high in the air.

Nearly simultaneously, the other two shoot theirs, attempting to mirror the prior boy's direction and trajectory. The three twangs from their gut strings sing in succession; their arrows whistle through the air.

"Ah, a sound sweeter than music from Etkin's lute," Ox says.

Before the arrows strike the ground, the three are off at a jog. Both boys moan as they see the yellow-striped arrow closer to the first shooter's.

"What I meant was, it's not like notes from the lute—more like the sound of coin jingling in purse. The sound of victory and spoils, my friends," Ox says, withdrawing his arrow and wiping the soiled iron across his thigh.

The shortest boy becomes melancholic.

"Don't worry, your father won't notice a few pinches missing," Ox says, smiling. Sensing the lost snuff is not the boy's worry, he turns to find its cause.

Below them riders trot in from the east, one being their tower's khan on his prized gray mare. The trio dismount, tossing their reins to young boys, who throw elbows for the privilege of watering their leaders' ponies. The khan and his kinsmen step off in the direction of the gers, not even taking the time to loosen the girth of their saddles.

Ox grimaces. "I'm one up on you girls," he nods to his replacements. "But I'm out till tomorrow." He chucks his staff to the nearest one. He steps off and then catches himself, turning to the loser. "Thought I'd forget my prize?"

The boy opens his tin. Raising his eyebrows, Ox takes a dip. With powerful strides, he pushes toward the tower's sixty-odd gers, swooshing through the saturated grass, chopped shin-high by the tower's flock. Adjacent to the round-walled dwellings, smoke rises from cooking fires, sending wavy tails of gray dissipating into the southern hills. He sees the haze rising from behind his mother's ger and acknowledges the grumble in his gut. He hopes she has a pot on.

Approaching the gers, he moves past groups of women placing the leather straps from their drying racks in pouches attached to their waists and stacking hand-worn sticks into neat piles at their feet. Two men sit with their backs against the felt. One laces a hardened leather arm guard, while another replaces damaged leather scale on his body armor. Neither looks up as Ox passes. In stride, he peers through an open flap to see a woman stuffing clothes into leather bags. He groans. Dirt-faced children, oblivious to all around them, giggle and chase each other in and out of the south-facing entrances.

Three days past, Kipchak scouts from the east returned with somber news. The Mongol's Great Khan, Ogodei, had sent a large army from the distant Mongol capital. In its charge, Ogodei placed Batu Khan, one of the grandsons of legendary Genghis Khan. Batu had split his force, sending a portion of his large horde west to the lands northeast of the Kipchaks, under a senior warrior named Subodei.

Renowned as the Mongol's best warrior mind, Subodei had ridden for years with the legendary Genghis Khan, taking part in numerous campaigns. Yet now into his sixties and rumored to be as fat as an overgrazed cow, Subodei could not even mount a pony. And despite being blind in one eye and toted around by his troops in a metal chariot like some Chinese aristocrat, the Mongol's greatest living general had already routed the Kipchak's Bulgar neighbors and was only a six-day ride to the east. The Mongols now had complete control of the eastern Volga country and uncontested access all the way to where the sun rose on the Mongolian steppe.

Yet of more immediate concern to the Lower Dnieper Kipchaks: the remainder of the Mongol horde, under Mongke Khan, the second grandson of Genghis Khan. Rumor was this khan was only a day's ride to the east. And it was this man, Mongke, who had called a meeting yesterday with the leadership of all the adjacent Kipchak towers.

The khan and his kinsmen weave through the scattering of gers. Both warriors and women examine their khan's face for any sign of their fate. Ox walks ahead of them, his approach hidden along the back side of the shelters. He must know the unfiltered word of what they say. At the khan's ger, he looks about and then dives under a fold of unburied felt at the bottom of a shaded wall. Expecting the men to enter the ger at any moment, his heart races. But they do not.

Soon the clouds part in earnest, heating the felt and soaking his tunic. Working a rock from the turf, he props up the heavy woolen crease and slowly turns over to suck in the air that seeps beneath the covering. Picturing the warriors finding him here and beating him senseless, he decides to vacate, while it is quiet. He raises the felt with his elbow, just as men enter their khan's ger opposite him. He freezes. Undetected, he slowly lowers his elbow.

"We were well received. Mongke said his Mongols would soon move southwest into the lower Dnieper," the elder Kipchak says.

"What were his demands?" a younger warrior asks anxiously.

"He didn't come with threats. He spoke mostly of what we have in common, said the Kipchak steppe reminds him of his own lands. Our shelters, our ways, are like theirs. He wishes to not fight us—only fought those Kipchaks in the upper valley who resisted."

A silence fills the ger.

"And I believe him. I see in his eyes the wisdom passed down by Genghis Khan. Mongke wants us to join forces against the Rus," the khan says.

Several of the Kipchaks mumble among themselves.

"Ally with those who come to take our animals and en-
slave our women? Then fight those who trade for our goods?
Why wouldn't we ride east and join the Alans in pushing
these devils from our land?" another warrior asks.

This brings a clicking of tongues from several men.

"Listen. Mongke said any Kipchaks who join the Alans
will be destroyed. The Mongol Saman has seen a vision—all
the steppe people, every blade of grass, united under the
Mongols. A golden horde. He wishes us to become part of
their empire," the khan says.

"If we join with both the Alans and the Kievan Princes,
couldn't we defeat the Mongols—and keep alive the trade for
our sheep and skins?" an older warrior asks.

A clicking of tongues from three or four more.

"The Mongols would become our allies, our trading
partners. They have many more warriors than the Alans and
access to more trade goods than the Rus. There may not be any
Rus states left, once the Mongols arrive in force," the khan says.

The ger stays silent for several moments.

"What will become of our people, our grazing lands?
We'll just roll over—let the Mongol wolves take our sheep, our
lives?" the young warrior asks.

The elder khan sighs. "You understand little. For this
invasion alone, the Mongols have fifty-thousand warriors,
three times as many horses and thousands of allies from the
east. We're fortunate Mongke treats us with dignity. If he
wished, they could ride down and crush us all!"

"I won't hear it! Your words burn my ears. They bring
shame to the spirit of my father and yours," the young warrior says. Something falls to the ground. A man storms out of
the shelter.

Again silence.

"We've never lived under another's rule. What if
Mongke Khan exaggerates the forces he has? I'd rather we

split and fight them on the run, than cower at their feet," another warrior says.

"While the four of you were pups, still in your mother's gers, I met Subodei in his prime. Thirteen years ago," the khan says, his voice dropping to a monotone. "I heard nearly the same Mongol speech from Subodei himself and witnessed the consequences. Do you not take heart in the chronicle passed from your elders? Or perhaps since you didn't ride that day, it feels like nothing more than a tale? Well, I rode with thousands of Kipchaks and Rus against the Mongols, and I'll not make the same mistake twice."

Ox tries to control his breathing. Sweat drips across his forehead. He ponders the oral history, a dozen versions repeated by the old warriors.

The khan deepens his voice. "I tell you, I was there. Twenty-thousand Mongols, under Subodei, came from the east to put eyes on the Kipchak Steppe and then the Rus provinces to the west. Hmmph. And the Kipchaks chose not to ally with the Mongols, but instead partnered with the arrogant Rus, princes from the west and north—Galich, Smolensk, Chernigov, Kieve, Volhynia, Kursk, Suzdal. All of them!"

A table or stool is kicked.

He continues. "Then, just as now, the Rus princes were fools—disorderly, more concerned with rivalry among themselves than the proper training of their armies."

"But my Khan, aren't the Rus now better armed? The Franj, the Rum—don't they feed weapons and armor to the princes?" a warrior asks.

"Bah! We join those fools now and just as before, they'll bring peasants, armed with farm tools, not warriors with weapons. Most of those Rus troops will be in rags and straw hats, not the boots and armor of infantry. Believe me!"

A clicking of tongues from several.

"Listen. Time can water down the hard lessons of war. Don't think I look back contented in my actions all those years ago. I'm khan today because several braver than me died on the Kalka River Valley—following Rus princes, on the heels of Mongol rabbits in feigned retreat. Stupid Rus, blinded by ambition and competition among each other. Fools! Believing the sooner they caught the Mongols, the sooner they would get hold of the Black Tartar's plunder, swag pillaged from the Georgians. You all know the ending—when the Rus and Kipchak armies were stretched out, the Mongol main force appeared, tearing us to shreds with arrowshot. Less than half of us made it back, riding for our lives."

"Wouldn't the allies be wiser now to Mongke's tactics?" a young man asks.

The khan's tone turns somber. "The Tartars wouldn't need any hint of surprise... no grand strategy. This time, the Mongols come not with a reconnaissance force, but with an invasion force five times larger. Half your fathers and uncles still lie on that Kalka River Valley. Thirteen years ago the Tartars rolled in like a dust storm and then disappeared like shadows. My brothers, they are back now not to take a look, but to increase their territory and pull booty from the Rus cities. I had no choice but to seek the best terms I could. I wouldn't let them destroy our tower. I couldn't face burying the best of our warriors again."

"And what were those terms?" a young warrior asks.

"Our men will join the Mongol invasion westward. Two thirds of our boys of thirteen to fifteen summers will be taken by the Mongols and sold at the south market. We'll split these takings with the Mongols. We'll turn over a third of our flock," the khan says with a sigh.

Ox licks the salt from his lips. From underneath the felt he smiles. Surely he will be one of the boys sold. Finally the Great Sky has heard him.

CHAPTER
6

Duyal
The Azaq
July 25, 1236

With his back against an alder, Duyal dangles his feet over the riverbank, his eyes to the eastern sky. Lightning forks the horizon, illuminating the dark belly of clouds in pinks and yellows. A belch of thunder rumbles. The dark curtain creeps toward them, seemingly strengthened by the fair sky it devours.

He rubs the sore on his wrist, from where the hemp digs in. Sensing the Kipchaks knew the futility of escape, especially when traveling through the shorter grass, the Mongols had loosened the ties some days ago, placing the captives' hands across their fronts, so that all could eat and mount their horses without assistance.

He grinds away on a hard yogurt curd, although he is not hungry. He thinks of Baris and how far east they would have taken him; he recollects their hunts, his brother's hackled hair, deliberates how long before time will steal his face from memory. Pressing a hand into his pocket, he fumbles the remaining curds he must finish before their rest expires. As his Mongol looks away, he chucks one down the bank, moving his foot simultaneously to mask its landing with the slide of pebbles.

For nine days the Mongols led the captives south along the winding Volga, downstream through country Duyal had only heard about around evening fires. "There's as many gers on the lower Volga as rocks on a beach," his uncle once said. Duyal did not see it as such.

Where the lower course of the Volga neared the Don, the Mongols stayed west, following the east bank of the Don for seven more days, toward the Azaq, or "lowlands," inhabited by the Coastal Kipchaks. These towers had seized the land from the Slavic princedom almost two hundred years ago, the nomads valuing the lucrative trade spawned from its location on the northeast coast of the Sea of Azov, inlet to the great Black Sea.

A Mongol approaches, dragging his Kipchak behind him. The man nods to Duyal's keeper, tossing his end of the rope to him. He moves into the scrub, pulling up his longcoat to unbuckle his belt. Erol, or "Tiny" as his Mongol call him, sits down near Duyal.

"Eat," his Mongol says, noticing Duyal does not chew.

Duyal jams the last curd into his mouth and turns to the youth, whose features resemble a frail antelope.

"Bah-hahhh," Erol moans, raising his head as would a sheep.

The small boy is right. They must be nearing their destination. Since reaching the Don, the Mongols forced upon their captives fistfuls of dried meat on the move and at night ample quantities of mutton off the spit. When the throng stopped midmornings and late afternoons, the youth were made to drink from the river and devour yogurt curds. The

Mongols intended to add some weight back to their pathetic flock, just as Kipchak shepherds fatten their sheep when approaching a Rus settlement, shortening the distance covered per day and increasing the graze time. "Never smart to trade away a bony sheep," Duyal's father always said.

"Shut your mouth," his Mongol says to Erol, taking a step toward the river. He clambers down the embankment, dips his cup and gulps. He sinks his flask into the water. Waiting for the air bubbles to cease, he looks up to meet the pierce of Duyal's almond eyes. The Tartar raises a lip. He snugs his stopper and flings the excess water from his hands in Duyal's direction.

Duyal looks away. If only free of the rope, and with a bow and quiver full of arrows, he would find gratification in trailing this formation, picking off the Mongols one by one. But such thoughts are mere fantasy.

With a snort, the mustached man clambers up the edge, stones tumbling at each boot-plant. He ties their ropes to a tree and leaves them to stow gear on his saddle.

"Do you think there's a chance we'll ever see our towers again?" Erol asks, raising his thin eyebrows, leaning toward him.

Duyal looks him in the eyes. "No."

"Do you worry what will become of you?"

"I used to."

Erol pulls upward on a stalk of grass. He flicks the seeds downslope, one at a time. "Becoming a slave didn't sound so bad in the freeze of winter, or when there was no food. We figured at least the slaves down south got fed. But the idea of it now—it doesn't feel so good."

"Well, we'll soon be into it."

"Yeah." Erol sighs, kicking a rock down to the river's edge. "My mother was sick. I was taking care of her. The Mongols left her. I don't know who will look after her now."

"I'm sorry."

"Your mother. Did they take her away with the children?"
Duyal looks into the lazy current. Swirls of light sedi-
ment rising in the column, falling. A yellow leaf spinning in
a whirlpool. He pictures his last vision of her—the pale face,
broken nose, the diagonal slit beneath her throat. Her blonde
hair, soaked in blood, tangled about her shoulders. He bites
his lip, holding back a wave of emotion. He turns to Erol. "No."

"We go!" the khan says.

Duyal rises. Reaching his pony, he loosens the hobble,
setting the leather strap atop the pony's hips for his Mongol
to stow. He pats his pony's neck, latches a fistful of mane and
leaps upon his back.

"Thwack!" He turns toward the sound. The "boy with
splinted arm" struggles to mount his pony.

"His father never taught him," the Mongol says to his
mate. They laugh.

Duyal's pony kicks a rear leg back, his hoof landing with
a thud on the shoulder of the stallion behind him, just missing his Mongol's knee. The man moves forward, pulls out his
whip, and cracks the belligerent animal across the head twice
with the handle, swearing in his native tongue.

Duyal leans back to avoid the flogging. When his
Mongol turns, Duyal rubs his pony's forehead, whispers calmly in his ear, "It's all right, it's all right."

They trod for half the day. With the rich soil of the
northern steppe having long diminished into the rockier mix
of the Don River basin, patches of barren crag now mark the
landscape. The taller feather grasses of his homeland have
given way to wind-swept dunes and the short stipa grass, its
shiny-haired awns flipping, looking like spray blown from the
tips of whitecaps on some endless lake.

They cross a tributary, heading for two dark figures and
a scattering of feeding goats. As they near, the opaque forms
become two gray-haired shepherds. The grubby men squat in

silence among the white clover, careful not to look up at the passing riders.

Over the hill, one of their women scrapes a deer hide, while others place neatly cut strips of meat on drying racks. Four women tussle to return the large felt blanket across the top of their shelter—two half-hidden forms pushing blunt-ended branches under the heavy felt, inching it over the rounded framework, while women on the opposite side receive it with their poles, occasionally looking up to the threatening sky. The felt.

Leaning on his scythe, Duyal glanced down the hill. The wooden skeletons of his family's two gers stood bare upon the open grassland among the others, exposing their possessions through stout ribs of willow. Near the frames of their dwellings, inch-thick sections of cream-colored felt covered the grass like stubborn patches of snow on a mountain's north face.

With one hand, his aunt dipped her lashed clump of grass into a wooden bucket and then shook sprinkles of water on the felt in a cadenced motion. With her other hand, she grabbed a wad of wool from a basket, applying the precise amount to thin spots marked with chalk. Meanwhile, his mother, on all fours, scrubbed the moistened wool into the felt with a rough-surfaced rock, while Duyal's cousin whacked the repaired areas with a v-shaped stick to meld it with the old wool.

Turning to her sister, Duyal's mother laughed in response to some jest, her sweet voice ricocheting through the hills.

The two sisters were inseparable, sharing not only every waking moment, but also the same high cheeks, long hair, and dimpled chins. And of course the identical giggle, which now became contagious. The eldest in the tower, braiding yak hair into rope from her ancient stool, chimed in too, with a toothless cackle. His cousin shook her head and smiled, accustomed to the pairs' eruptions.

Those felt sections, made by Duyal's grandmother and her sisters, were perhaps the Kipchaks' most precious creation. Many years ago, his kin had measured the raw fleece and then beaten it into the proper thickness on stout pine frames, finishing the felt's compaction by rolling the stick-pounded sections around a wooden rod, dragging the device by pony across the clean grass.

Yet since this original production, successive female generations had repaired the bulky felt enough times that these seamless patches became numerous, so numerous that the initial covering became less his grandmother's and more an accumulation of the sweat and spirit of every woman who'd ever lived under the felt's protection. Just as the mounded hay could not be separated and clearly identified as the work of this man or that man, so the felt coverings were a compilation of the women's efforts.

As they drop over a hill, the putrid scent of sea-washed algae and swamp hits Duyal at the same instant as the flash of sun on faraway water. Below them spreads the alluvial plain, terrain dominated by numerous channels cut during annual flooding, draining their way haphazardly to the flat river mouth. In their wake stand small towers of sand and gravel, stacked in sweeping forms by the constant rise and fall of moving water.

They crest another rise. In the distance, a smattering of gers and wooden shacks occupies the high ground and sandstone bluffs, above pockets of brackish water. The greatest concentration of shelters is near a harbor within the giant bay, where large slabs of flat stone extend a natural rock jetty, protruding far into the sun-dappled water. Teeny people scurry about the place. Cargo litters the docks; boats are tied off, some with sail and oars secured.

While all knew of the big water at the end of all rivers, most of the boys had never seen the sea, or the vessels that ply it. They look now indifferently at the scene below. Each boy likely amends his mind's picture of the country, previously gained only through tales from elders and passing travelers, with the reality of their situation and the place now set before their eyes.

Duyal had always envisioned what it would be like seeing the great water. An excitement to share with his brothers and uncle. Looking at it now with strangers, a wave of nausea passes through him, moistening his pits. Where will they go from here? Farther and farther from their territory, until it is but a faded remembrance.

A sheet of black overhead gradually overwhelms the last patches of blue sky, leaving the shallow sea a fickle tone of turquoise. The metallic scent of rain sets in. Lucent tentacles blow sideways beneath the dark horizon.

For the first time he fully realizes he will never again see his homeland. He has nothing; he belongs to nothing; he is nothing. He does not blink for a time, letting the silty-green water blur into a vast grayness. He leans his elbows upon his pony's neck and stares down at the beast's hoof, the bone striated in a dismal rainbow of blacks and grays and browns.

He raises to again look upon the vast expanse of water stretching before him, pondering the tiny dots of sail far out in the sea and those ships tied to the shore.

A heavy drop hits his nose, then another upon his arm, and then comes the deluge of cold upon their backs and heads. The grease from his hair and the salt from his face wash down to coat sun-split lips.

CHAPTER

7

Singer
Steppe, between the Volga and Ural Rivers
July 25, 1236

"How's the knee, Singer?" Ferdi asks, his friend noticing the boot hanging free at the pony's side.

"Ah, fine, fine," Halis says, forcing a bend in the swollen joint. He slips his boot back into the heavy stirrup to push the conversation away from himself.

Both the Mongols he now serves and his fellow Kipchak mates have begun calling him "Singer"—surely because they have overheard the tunes he often hums or sings to himself during the lulls in duty, or when events become chaotic. Halis did not realize how often he did it; sometimes did not even realize he was doing it. Ah well, he does not care what they call him. He figures he comes about the habit honestly; the songs just come to him, just as they had seemed to come naturally to his mother, when she was working.

"Horseshit," Ilker says, spitting cleanly between his teeth. He, like Ferdi, is looking at the swell in Singer's leg.

"We moving soon?" Ferdi asks.

"No, they said there's another push of them behind this one," Singer says.

"Unbelievable," Ferdi says.

Singer leans over his mount, taking in the span of pale brown hills before him. Where pockets of shade pervade, silky-gray wormwood dangle golden blooms. Suspended on sturdy stems, compact clusters of purple flowers appear as bunches of tiny grapes, waving in the wind. He scans for any movement on the skyline. Nothing. In the shadowed draws and stubby fingers that reach off the ridge and down into the valley—quiet. He looks east.

All the way to the horizon, the pack train snakes across the mounded steppe, its carts heaped with iron pots, garments, brass kettles, furniture, curved blades stripped from tools, and all other things Rus. They plow through what was once Kipchak grass, its stems doubled over from the burden of their flowering spikelets, the plants appearing as weary as the travelers who move in the direction of the Mongolian capital.

Stubble-chinned men, dressed in the shabby rags of peasants, hold the ropes to their rib-bearing oxen in open hands. The beasts need no drivers, mindlessly following the cart to their front, the oxen seeming to have also succumbed to the squinty-eyed invaders. Stretched high upon the odd cart of household goods are Rus clerks, tradesman, translators, and other civilians of Raizan who happened to catch the eye of the hordes pillaging about a twenty-day ride to the west.

For nearly a year, Mongol units have systematically conquered the people of the Volga River Valley—every strain and tower of the Bulgars and Kipchaks to the north and west. But the Mongols now begin to push their attack even farther west into the cities of the Rus, as evidenced by the line of laden carts stretching below Singer. It is this cargo and selected human prize that he now guards, alongside his unit, Mongols handpicked by old General Subodei for their knowledge in the languages of the beaten peoples.

Accustomed to raids, Singer was unsurprised that booty, goods reaped from the sedentary societies, was the main target of the Mongol campaign. Orphaned and caring for his young brother and sister for years, he would come down from the Ural Mountains to steal the occasional sheep when game was lean, or perhaps filch the odd pot, knife, or metal bridle from nomadic bands on the move. But mostly he hunted, his daily stalks to kill deer, antelope, marmot, and birds being his young family's primary means of survival. Incompetence or bad luck on the hunt meant empty bellies; getting caught or shot on a raid meant untold misery and likely death for his young kin. He had avoided both.

Yet it is the scale of the Mongol operation that boggles his Kipchak mind. With his own people's raids, warriors brought a spare pony or two, swooped in to pilfer and then vanished. But the Mongols are not the Kipchaks. He reckons the entirety of the Kipchaks have been just a minor obstacle for the Mongols, one to be stepped over or squashed, as the Black Tartars push farther west to the lands reconnoitered nearly thirteen years ago by Subodei. The old man. Subodei knew the real treasure lay in the Rus cities and in the lands even farther west. Singer hopes to one day meet the great one.

Having put at bay every competing army all the way east to Mongolia, the Mongols now have an open route home. The complex system of local taxes and extortion once found along the entire route—gone. Rus goods now flow to the heart of the empire, as efficiently as drainage off the mountains. Booty and livestock trickle down this pass and dozens more like it, feeding the larger river of goods like tributaries to a giant river, eventually discharging a thirty-day ride east into the ocean of goods which is Karakorum, the Mongol capital.

Singer winces, again pulling his boot from stirrup to lessen the pain in his knee. Wooden wheels of every size creak their disgust on strained axles, their multi-pitched whines drowned out by the constant thud of hoof on turf. Atop one load a scrawny Rus wife sits cockeyed in her rocker. Wedged between a bureau and bundle of coats, she clutches the rail, determined to accompany her man and dusty household on their forced journey. A musician sprawls barebacked, his shirt wrapped about his future, knowing that death may be his alternative if any damage comes to the polished maple and taut strings clutched across his knees.

"Oh, here we go," Ferdi says to his friends, nodding to a swiftly approaching rider.

Singer and Ilker turn in their saddles. They smirk.

A rosy-cheeked Mongol bounces in at the trot, smiling. The Mongols call this gregarious old man "Stiff," for the permanent crook in his left elbow, a lingering injury he sustained as a five-year-old, when chosen to represent his tribe in a horse race at the important *Naadam* games. The most fluent of the Mongols in the Kipchak's Turkish dialect, Stiff is a favorite of the Kipchaks attached to this Mongol unit, a man who rode with Subodei during the Mongol recon, even taking a Kipchak bride on the trip home thirteen years ago.

Stiff winks at Singer. "There's a brown-haired Rus in a cart up there that says she wants to talk with the balding Kipchak over here. Says she can't resist his scent."

"Wouldn't surprise me. That's the same thing your lady said before we left," Ilker jokes.

"No, no. My Kipchak woman bathes most every day. She only sleeps with a clean man, a Mongol man. No stinky Kipchak."

"Shit," Ilker says.

They all laugh.

A grin remains on Stiff's face. He strokes his gray-streaked beard while eying a cart-bed packed with wine skins and jugs of lamp oil and bouncing barrels of honey—all goods seized by Mongol troopers on the outskirts of Riazan, the first Rus city targeted by the eastern conquerors.

"Stiff, have you ever seen so many carts?" Singer asks.

"No. My father used to tell of goods moving like this far south, beyond the great desert. When Genghis ruled, it was an endless river heading north. Both men would be pleased to see plunder funneling in now from the west," the Mongol says, propping his rigidly bent arm on the splintered frame of his saddle.

"I didn't know there were so many goods in all the world," Ferdi says.

Stiff smiles.

"How can they possibly keep track of all this stuff, once it gets to the capital?" Singer asks.

"Why do you think Subodei makes sure his men throw a few scribes atop the loads? We aren't heartless; we at least let a few Rus count the things we take from them."

They chuckle.

Stiff waves his hand. "All these goods—they'll eventually be dished out from the capital, based on the Great Khan's wishes. Already common Mongol herders have the finest bridles and ropes woven with silk. Our women? They're happy. Inside their gers are flower-printed silks and Chinese vases painted with scenes of tiny animals. Plus more. It's very important to keep the women happy—you know this, right?" he beams, looking directly at Ferdi.

"Uhh… I don't know too much of those things," Ferdi says.

Again, chortles between them.

Seeing the approach of Mongol drivers, Stiff's face goes somber. Silver-haired men in black cuirasses sit erect and straight-faced at the bench, the elder Mongols looking out of place not astride their high-saddled ponies. Stacked in neat rows on their cart-beds are rawhide bags, six feet long and tightly sewn at both ends.

"They take the fallen home?" Singer asks.

Stiff nods, letting the carts pass in silence. "The command always reminds the men that each is unbeatable in combat, even forbids any Mongol to speak of being killed… but many troopers make it known to comrades where they wish their remains to be laid."

Singer nods in respect to the old man, his lips pursed.

"I don't blame them. Who wants to be left in some cultivated field of the Rus or upon a stranger's knoll, where peasants can loot their kit or defile their bodies?" Stiff asks.

Ilker turns to his mates. "The Mongols don't bury their dead like us. Most Mongols wish only to go back to earth purely in their homelands—with weather, the fangs of wolves, and the beaks of birds bringing them back to the land proper." He nods to Stiff.

The old man bows, turns his pony toward his own security sector and gives his pony the heel.

"You've heard them say that Genghis hated luxury and material possessions—sure seems his people back east don't share the great one's view, or at least not his son," Ferdi says, watching the old man trot away.

"Yeah, Ogodei may be the Great Khan—blood of the legend—but he's no Genghis. They won't come out and say it, but it sounds like Ogodei is fonder of wine and chasing women than leading his army," Ilker says. "Sitting back in his black stone house… surrounded by black stone walls… that protect his black stone warehouses."

"If I were a Mongol in Karakorum swimming in all this loot, I'd put my ger outside the walls, nowhere near Genghis Khan's spirit banner. Living soft amid the great one's essence just has to be a bad omen," Ferdi adds.

"Shush. You both best keep your keen observations to yourselves," Singer says, turning to assure no other Mongols approach.

Ilker snorts, showing both rows of teeth, stained yellow-brown. While the same age as Singer, he figures Ilker might be the oldest fifteen-year-old he has ever met. Ilker's orange hair shows tinges of gray and thins prematurely at the crown, receding high up his freckled forehead. His eyesight is poor. Through old teeth, he tells bitter, timeworn tales. His breath is as foul as the old man smell that emits from his body. He even sits upon his horse with the rounded back of the elderly. But the Kipchak lad does not have the senility of an old man—he is bright and picked up the Mongol language and ways quickly.

Like the handful of other Kipchaks here, Ilker was driven from his homeland and bargained off to the Mongols with other youth of fighting age in return for lenient treatment for his tower, often in payment for unpaid tribute to the Mongols. For more than a year, Ilker has served within this Mongol unit, his most useful charge thus far being the rough translation of the Mongol's Altaic tongue for those Kipchaks about to lose their goats and sheep.

Ferdi, on the other hand, has only been with the Mongols about half as long, nearly the same as Singer. With the face of a hawk and the compact frame of a mountain goat, Ferdi is in his fourteenth year. A couple of years ago, Ferdi's old man had given his boy a pony and bow, kicking him to the steppe to fend for himself. One less mouth to feed; one less young buck to beat down. From what Singer understands, Ferdi roamed for just over eight moons, surviving mostly on marmots and mice with another boy he came across. Yet with his friend dead and tired of being tracked by the Mongols, Ferdi eventually wandered hungry and palms forward into the winter camp of the enemy. Former enemy, that is.

Heading in the opposite direction behind them, a woeful moan erupts, a brute whining its displeasure, or perhaps simply making its bloodlust known. A giant whirlwind catapult, built into a high-walled cart, wobbles across the grassland. Like a pretty girl knowing appreciative eyes are upon her, the creature shakes the high head of her timbered throw arm, causing the dozens of traction ropes to dangle and wrap about the device's lever.

"At least we won't be on the wrong end of that rig," Ferdi says.

"Like my father used to say, you don't have to look very far to find somebody worse off than you," Singer says.

"Yeah, I guess I'd rather be with the guys feeding that thing, than catching what it throws," Ilker says.

Escorting this war lass is a chain of supplies also heading west. Leather, canvas, coins, ponies, bundled silk from China, and *airag*—the Mongols' fermented mare's milk. Things not readily scavenged from the Rus, yet needed by the warriors spread far across the grassland. Shorter-armed mangonels, lashed with wide leather bands and attended by their flat-hatted keepers, seem to crawl menacingly, their bulky wheels masked by the knee-high grass.

Accompanying these machines are numerous carts of Bulgar design, these having been emptied of tribute and sent back for the front, filled with kegs of gunpowder, plus empty earthenware pots and ready-made smoke bombs. The pots, wrapped in fleece covers, appear as orderly lambs of death, rocking patiently until permitted to unleash their choking sheet of doom.

Following these come doubled-tarped loads holding the fiery ingredients for Chinese "naphtha." Once reaching a besieged city, the Chinese will mix these together and pour this devil's brew into vessels. After training up legions of conscripted Rus, the Chinese allies will then force these poor souls to deploy the flaming canisters against their own countrymen during the siege of the walls.

While the Mongols wisely keep this westward column close to the eastbound traffic to minimize the number of troopers needed for protection, Singer figures they also want the Raizan commoners to see firsthand the wisdom in their decision to surrender.

A woman slides from the back of a load with a girl in hand. Singer turns in his saddle to see if Suren has noticed them. His Arban commander is already on them. In jest, Suren points two fingers at his eyes and then at the Rus woman, the signal for "enemy sighted." Singer and Ilker look at each other and then put their ponies to the canter, with bows at the ready. Better safe than sorry, as who knows if their jocular boss is serious this time?

The girl shakes loose her mother's grip, bounds several feet from the cart and promptly crouches to urinate. Her mother spreads her skirt to cover the child and scowls at the riders with hands on hips. Singer reins in and turns his head away, as he hopes any other would do if his own sister were squatting. He looks back at his boss, who is now laughing. Singer smiles back, but thoughts of his own sister cut his grin short.

Ah, Nergis. The image of her, clear-eyed and bouncy-stepped, sends a twinge of pain. Just over a year ago, both of his siblings were killed by Mongol club. More like his children than younger brother and sister, it was one of the few times they ignored his words. Know when to fight, know when to flee, know when to listen. He found them bludgeoned along a stream bank, in hunting ground that Singer had forbidden them to enter, where the Tartars often traveled.

He buried them. Forced their whole lives to scrap in the mountain scrub, his brother and sister were laid to rest on a hillside far southwest of the peaks, overlooking the easier existence he had wished for them on the rolling steppe. He did not mark the grave, yet placed the bodies beside each other, bows made from his own hand slid between their callused fingers for use in the afterlife. The responsibility of raising them was off him, but not the burden of guilt in failing to prevent their deaths. He should not have let them hunt alone that day. He would have steered them away from the danger. He hums a song, pushing the incident into the back of his mind, which is where it belongs.

The wind shifts, sending across his nostrils a waft of soap scent from the Rus girl, cutting short his solemn tune. Singer wonders what his own mother would think of him now. If alive, she would have begged him years ago to find an alliance, find a tower who would take them in. Yet he did not. For seven years he kept his siblings safe, without the assistance of anyone. Hiding in the rugged hills, they remarkably stayed one step ahead of moving game, wandering bands of thieves, and toward the end, ceaseless Mongol patrols. Yet as is life in that harsh forest country, all can change in one day.

It is past. But the pain of culpability sits like a heavy rock in his heart, only accentuated by the consequent hospitality of his siblings' killers. Since being taken in by the Mongols seven moons ago, he tries to recall a day of hunger, or even one when his unit was more than a half day's ride from a flock of sheep or scattering of goats. He cannot. He reaches down and pinches his abdomen. Incredible. A thin layer of fat. He cannot recall ever being able to grip anything between his fingers, except opposing layers of skin.

He remembers being awestruck upon arriving at the Mongol camp. After answering a line of questions, shooting his bow at a moving target and getting a nod from their company commander, Chuluun, three Mongols from the squad fanned across the unit, rounding up a spare bag, two water skins, flints for fire, and needles for mending clothes. They gathered from each man a few strips of dried meat and chunks of milk paste, placing the grub in two saddlebags. Then the three descended upon him. Suren, his squad leader, thrust the lead to a young roan into his hands, while the other two secured the bags to his new mount. Singer could only stand with mouth agape.

Later, when Stiff saw Singer's old dagger at his side, with three inches broken off the tip, he replaced it with one from his own sheath, silver handled and razor sharp. More surprisingly, once seeing that Singer only possessed his father's short-range bow, the Mongols provided a second more powerful one, plus arrows made to penetrate armor. Crafted from the horn of the Ibex and stout hardwood, his new weapon could shoot nearly twice the distance of his old one.

In time, they clothed him in attire like their own, Chuluun himself pulling garments from a westward-heading cart. In place of his grimy tunic, his commander tossed him a long Mongol deel, or woolen overcoat, which doubled as his blanket at night. His disintegrating boots were swapped with calf leathers that came nearly to his knees. Now also hanging from his saddle, a chestplate of scaled leather, not surprisingly absent of armor across the backstraps. With little ceremony, his few Kipchak possessions (save his trousers and smaller bow) were tossed to rot on the steppe.

As was likely Mongol design, Singer and the other Kipchaks have returned the invaders' generosity with loyalty to the unit and to the old man, Chuluun. While the Mongols do not yet treat him as a brother—and he wouldn't trust them if they did—they have certainly made an effort to pull him and the other Kipchaks into their fold. He wonders if he is possibly here on some unspoken trial basis. This seems sensible to him. Regardless, having never allied himself with anyone, Singer feels thankful to have stumbled upon a group so well supplied. He wishes only the opportunity to prove himself.

Still turned away from the Rus daughter, he looks farther south, where freshly sheared lambs feed. Each bears a red slash of paint across their rump, evidence of their inspection and cataloging by clerks impressed into duty. Mongols in crescent moon formation push the flock and their Rus shepherds away from the river, the warriors treating both four- and two-legged creatures in like fashion. Most will be driven northward to the vast grasslands of the occupied Bulgar Steppe, where they will join the ponies, sheep, goats, and oxen captured from the Bulgars and Kipchaks. One Rus shepherd with a thick beard uses his staff as a crutch, gimping on bound feet to keep up with the others.

The sun beams gold through the thin clouds, dancing on the riffled water. The river—so similar to his old water in the upper Ural country. The summers to the north. Tossing his braided line upstream in successively greater arcs to cover the dark-watered runs, adding just enough weight to bounce his gut wad on the bottom, or spin his shell lure through the freestone waters. Setting the carved nasal bone hook gently when feeling the smack of a high-finned *Alabalik*, so as not to stress his line of ponytail hair strands, a thousand times mended. And once having eased the silver fish ashore, smashing its head before slipping it in the pouch sewn into the back of his tunic. Then back upstream to feed his hungry siblings with the satisfying wet mound thumping his shoulder blades.

And the winters. Walking the ice-shelved banks for miles to check his marked line of desman and mink traps, into the icy water to pull up by stout tail the soaking mounds of black or brown pelts to be dressed for spring trade. Along the river's flats, spearing porcupines from bark-stripped trees and following wolf tracks along the rocky banks downstream to wintering herds of elk and deer.

Mother and child pull themselves back atop the rolling cart, their entranced driver oblivious to both their departure and reembarkation. The man drives, but his mind surely drifts elsewhere. Singer imagines this Rus father must feel a remorse parallel to his own, the man moving in the opposite direction of his besieged city, just as Singer walked away from the death of his relations.

"These peasants from Raizan… this is only some of them. The Mongols let many scatter to the walled city," Ilker says.

"On purpose?" Ferdi asks.

"Yeah."

"In through the gates, where the ousted thought themselves safe," Singer says.

Ilker leans on his saddle. "Yeah, carrying tales of slaughter about those Rus who wouldn't give up their goods or pledge their oath of capitulation to the Tartars. Inside the walls—scaring the shit out of everyone and eating more and more of the city's precious stock."

"All of it working to only speed the city's fall," Ferdi says.

"Right."

"It's keen, you have to admit," Singer says. "Ruthless, but keen."

Ilker chuckles. "The Mongols seem to care little what strategy is used to achieve victory, as long as triumph is won with the least of their own killed. Honor on the battlefield . . . that is something they leave for Rus princes to savor. A Mongol leader's reputation is elevated with conquests and spoils gotten. That's it."

And shielding these spoils has been his unit's only thought the past seven moons. Chuluun passed their current mission in one sentence last month: "Along your sector of responsibility, protect the two-way flow of goods from disorder and would-be thieves." Their unit is just one cog in the greater machine, as the Mongols have spread units along the entire route to Karakorum, with a higher density of forces dispatched to the newly secured areas around the Volga country and also farther east at the pass, which runs south of the big mountains, skirting the last major barrier to Mongolia.

The thousand-man unit, which Singer serves within, is tasked with patrolling a stretch that runs east-west along the upper Ural River, maybe a five-day ride from end to end. Within this sector, the Mongols have further subdivided the task, assigning subordinate units to specific areas, taking into account terrain and the number of north-south spokes feeding into the main stream of goods. The last few moons, most of the action was on these vulnerable spurs, where occasionally Singer helped chase off the odd rogues or rebel nomads, those trying to pick off a sheep or loot a cart. Yet mainly the battalion fought boredom. Few insurgents were foolish enough to hit during the day, and the nights, while long, were mostly uneventful.

For Singer's squad of ten, most of their days have been spent riding back and forth along their zone, with a focus on guiding Rus shepherds and small caravans of gear south along a thin pass the locals call "craggy gap" for the monoliths that mark its route. Before the Rus, they merely watched over the Kipchak herders, who already knew the way—bitter men leading their livestock, sneering at the guards, especially the white-skinned traitors in the enemy's long coats.

Unlike most of the other Kipchaks in the unit, Singer has felt very little grief in seeing what was once the only symbol of Kipchak wealth being led away from their territory. With every moment of the last few years occupied with worry about protecting his small herd from raiders and feeding his siblings, he feels no loss of pride with the confederacy's fall and the affluence lost by the individual towers. But he is the oddity, the ties and obligations of the tribe lost to him many years ago.

"Crack!" An axle snaps on a cart, digging box into turf, causing the driver and rider to claw their way to the opposite corner to keep the load from tipping. The bed teeters before crashing to a rest. The Rus pair sit wide-eyed, straddling a barrel apiece. The supply train offers no sympathy, slithering around the busted cart like a snake navigating a rock.

In short time, a beleaguered wheelwright arrives with his Mongol escort, his tools and spare parts clanging to a stop beside the tilted heap. Those in the bed sit, watching the hairy-armed man reach over the rail and dig through his bed full of implements.

"Will you sit there like sparrows on a perch? Get off your asses and start unloading her," the wheelwright says, tossing metal parts aside.

One Mongol lets loose a high-pitched laugh, while a serious-faced one beside him pulls his bow from its skin case and sets it across his thighs for further effect. The two Rus look to each other and then scramble off the steep load.

CHAPTER
8

Duyal
Azaq, on Sea of Azov
July 25, 1236

The Mongols bear left on the path skirting around the harbor of Azaq. Just upstream from the mouth of the Don, fifty-odd Kipchak gers stretch along the river, under the shade of towering pines. A handful of kids tussle nearby in a patch of wild strawberry plants, while a solitary man in the dale fits a log into the pen he builds. Duyal's own father had also worked alone. As they near, he tries to make his father appear in this man's form.

Below, with a pine log pinned between strong thighs, his burly father pulled the draw blade toward him methodically, curls of cinnamon bark tumbling over his thick forearms—pull, pull, pull, rotate, pull, pull, pull, rotate. Beside him, a half-built log shed, fresh cow dung recently packed between the dried logs by the tower's children to keep the winter winds off livestock.

The children seemed to always start this work near dark, slinking in when he left to take his dinner, afraid of the man who was not a Saman, but talked to the spirits anyhow.

Finished with another, he kicked the bare log aside, as if brushing a fly from his plate. He rose, strips of bark falling off him. He muttered something, pulling another stout timber from his pile with a single hairy paw.

Whom did he hear in that head that knew no peace? He likely scorned the Mongols, those who had disfigured his face so long ago. Perhaps he spoke with Subodei, the great Mongol commander. Maybe he told the khan how the spirits of his fallen Kipchak mates would torment the Mongol for not just this life, but for eternity.

The lone worker peers over his shoulder at the advance of stringed ponies, exposing a stranger's features. Duyal chides himself for the disappointment he feels. "Fool, none in your family is alive." The void again consumes him. He tries to fill it with better memories of them.

He had always been baffled that his father and Uncle Besim were brothers. Although they shared the attribute of courage, there the similarities ended. While Duyal's uncle had been all ears and affable, his father was grit and fire. A wounded animal, backed up to a cliff of mental torment. Most in the tower kept their distance from the man, who wore serrated scars across his knuckles, his elder's way of settling most arguments.

Apparently there was a time when his father shared the jovial nature of his brother. His parents gave him the name Gunes, meaning "sun," but the demeanor earning him that name left him at about the same time the tower began to fragment. This was in the spring of 1223, when the entire confederation of Kipchak towers also disintegrated. That year, his father lost forty ponies, essentially his entire wealth, and too many of his lifelong friends.

He wore the loss on his scarred face, a mask of anguish, the crosswise slice having severed the muscles on the right side, slurring his speech and stealing his ability to smile. But Duyal doubted Gunes would have used these facial muscles, even if they were still functional. For as long as he could remember, his father's mouth wore a constant scowl. He never recovered from that Mongol battle all those years past; for that matter, neither did many from the towers of Volga Kipchaks.

The string of riders continues along the path, the way churned thick in the center from the hooves of oxen and scored thin on the edges from carts rounded full. The reek of decomposing seaweed fights the smell of dried pine needles under hoof for primacy, the blend mixed fleetingly with the smoke from roasting goat.

They enter an alley, squeezing past a sparse marketplace. Three racks on a slant, half-covered with apricots, the odd vegetable, and two large fish, curved stiff and with eyes glazed white. A young Kipchak woman with tangled hair down her back tends the stand. Her cobalt eyes flip from boy to boy. She crosses her arms with shawl, her jaw dropping slightly, her lips tightening. As they pass, his Mongol gropes her with his eyes.

They close on the jetty, each stomp nearer the harbor bringing more people, more activity, a strengthening of energy emitting from the port. Under the dominion of dark-haired scribes, pairs of Kipchaks and Turks, with tunics wide open, load barrels and bundles of grain and goods onto smaller pushcarts.

These clunk over the rutted hardpack, moving steadily in two-way traffic from the wide staging area to the jetty, where six ships line the rock platform, waves lapping their long hulls. There, more clerks guide the goods, using nets, ropes, and three-poled contraptions to set the swinging loads on ship decks.

But the men of money show little concern for these supplies, focusing their attention on cargo more valuable. Turks, Mongols, Genovese, and Seljuqs, dressed in a variety of long coat and robe, squeeze into alleyways and deliberate in the open spaces, some hunkered about thin tables with cross-legged supports. Other vendors in turbans and cotton-fleeced *kalpaks* gesture at their dusty-haired wares, the boys sitting mute and absent in the cart beds, each appearing alone despite their packed quarters.

Straight lines of carts cleave the staging area, splintering into ever-more jumbled veins of traffic, as they stretch away from the harbor and into adjacent streets and alleys, where their drivers snore and grumble and nod off to sleep. Kipchak boys pile over the sides of two carts. Forty or more funnel toward the gangplanks of two ships, the oar-driven galleys sitting like giant insects kicked into the sea, kept afloat by their multitude of gangling legs.

The khan orders Duyal and the others off their mounts. The security element sits their ponies, while out of habit the remaining Mongols fill in the gaps of the lazy perimeter surrounding the boys.

"You come with me. I make you happy forever," a Mongol says to a passing dame, patting the rump of his pony in offer.

"When hell freezes," the smooth-skinned Turk replies, continuing with the water jug atop her head, her left hand raised to grasp the lip of the jar, drawing her *entari* tightly across luscious breasts in an unwanted pose.

His mates explode, some leaning forearms on wooden saddles to contain their laughter. In sham astonishment the Mongol turns his pony with knee and heel, elevating his palms upward for comic effect, watching her sleek behind as she passes.

Erol leans toward Duyal, breathing in quick huffs. "Will they put us on these boats?"

"Starting to look like it."

"I won't go. I can't."

"I don't think we'll have much say."

"If we are to be sold, why can't they keep us here on land?"

Duyal sighs. "Go tell your Mongol how you would like this all to work and let's see how that goes."

"Uhh. If the boat sinks, I cannot swim."

He turns to Erol. "If the boat sinks, then maybe we'll all be freed from this scrape."

Erol shakes his head, his eyes flittering.

Starting to feel bad for his coldness, Duyal puts his hand on Erol's shoulder. "Listen, just relax. We've got no choice. It can't be a long voyage. We'll be all right."

A tall man with a well-shaven face and floppy hat approaches. Clothed in tan robe and purple sash, he stands erect, a brass-handled cane mashed into the meat of his palm helping to prop up his girth. His lifted chin seems to indicate his position among the merchants; his strange shoes with pointed toes seem to entrance the boys. The man scans the mob of Tartars. He scowls, apparently unable to pick out the most important looking. "Who's in charge?"

The khan raises a finger.

"Your scroll."

The Mongol leader pulls the rolled paper from his leather pouch and hands it over.

The merchant skims it, while lowering it on occasion to view the Kipchaks. "Did you drag half of them behind your ponies?" the merchant asks with raised lip.

The Mongol troopers turn their ears toward the conversation. The khan looks over his motley collection of captives, as if noticing for the first time their dark-stained clothes, the filth about their faces and the scabs on their arms and necks. He shrugs and then leans down to the man. "They're here safely, fat man—make your mark and shut your mutton hole." Again, chortles from the Tartars.

The merchant turns his back, grumbling. He dips his feather into the well and scribbles. He hands it back. The khan holds the merchant's symbol to the light and then nods to his men.

Those Mongols responsible for individual lads now dismount, tossing their reins to the security men. Each of these Mongols grabs his boy's tunic and follows their khan toward the jetty, pushing the Kipchaks into a single column across the open space. They slow, allowing a pair of porters to cross, a timber between the workers' shoulders, dangling a roped crate just above the ground.

The galleys to their front grow larger with each step forward, the first ship likely over forty paces in length. They head to the nearest one on the north side, where a line of boys is already forming. One Mongol cracks his boy across the neck twice with his riding stick for no reason, perhaps his way of saying good riddance. Reaching the gangplank, the Mongols depart without word or gesture.

At the entrance stands a gap-toothed Turk with a knife slid into the belt of his threadbare trousers. As each boy steps forward, the Turk dips a thick brush into a bucket of red, slopping a streak of paint from the back of the head to shoulder blades. He then unties their hands and points up the plank. For those with knots too tight, he pulls his blade and cuts the rope, a pile of stinking hemp already at his feet.

"Enjoy your journey," he says mockingly to one. The Turk turns to watch the boy reach the end of the bouncing plank, before sending another. "This is only the start of your fun," he says to a strong-backed youth, the one the boys call Demir.

"Blade or no blade, make another crack and I'll show you some real fun," the adolescent says with low voice and clenched fist, stopping to eye the man before scurrying up the two-foot wide board in bounds. The Turk laughs with raised eyebrows.

Erol steps forward. He ignores the knife, the blade sawing only inches from his wrists. With red dripping to his calves, he peers warily over the edge to the echoing sea below and then back toward Duyal, who gives him a reassuring nod. Erol starts up the plank, vacillating halfway, preoccupied with the slosh of sea between dock and galley.

"Go!" the Turk says.

The boy grimaces, then squats and scampers across the remaining stretch of plank on all fours like a primate, bringing a chuckle from the ship's crew, stretched about the nets and barrels on break.

Sensing movement from the corner of his eyes, Duyal looks up. A spindly-limbed sailor prances up a rope ladder along the foremast, the spar looking tall as firs in the mountain country. The sailor shimmies across a tilted yardarm to loosen the hemp that binds the cloth sail.

Tingles prick Duyal's fingertips and toes. Atop the foremast, a flag with red cross on white field waves in lazy ripples. The same colors fly on two other galleys, while both ships on the north side of the jetty boast a blue flag with yellow-winged lion in center.

Duyal moves forward. The smack of bristles against the back of his head. A warm dribble of paint down his butt crack. The Turk cuts the hemp and Duyal rubs the sores on his wrists as he plods up the board, unable to see bottom through the silty-blue water. Green algae hugs the pier rocks. Men were not meant to live upon bent boards, floating on the sea.

A raised forearm from an olive-skinned sailor stops him. "Down and forward." He grabs Duyal by the tunic, turning him a half circle so he can climb down a ladder. Eight steps down, the sweet air blowing across the deck disappears, replaced by the wet scent of urine-soaked pine and rancid breath. Near the bottom, the sharp bite of mold predominates.

Into the darkness, Duyal tests for the last rung by foot and then enters the hold. All is damp. He turns and takes a blind step forward, feeling the squish of shit beneath his boot. A dull echo fills the chamber from a dozen hushed conversations. He takes another step and bumps into Erol.

The line moves, his eyes adjust. He steps forward on strips of planking, running narrowly atop the keel. Whites of eyes shift in hollow faces, watching the passers. Dark-haired sailors in thick-cloth dungarees push indecisive boys to benches. Nearly every seat is occupied. Only several benches from the bow, he comes to face a sailor. "There," he says, pointing left.

A giant man sits with his elbows on thighs, legs spread across the entire bench; nothing but muscle exists between the base of his skull and where his thick shoulders begin. His feet are the size of beaver tails. They must be taking grown men across the sea as well. A prisoner being punished for some crime?

The goon turns his head, exposing the features of a Kipchak. Boy. Duyal turns to the sailor, his expression begging for another seat.

"That's right. There. Go," the sailor says.

The giant lad clamps his legs together slightly and scoots in. Duyal slides onto the sliver of open wood, stumbling on the chain between benches. He sits, keeping half his ass hanging off the bench, so as not to upset the ogre. The large boy ignores him, exhaling through his nose like a bull that ponders a goring. In time, he looks Duyal up and down with small blue eyes, and then goes back to looking out a tiny porthole.

From their bench, they face aft. From the southwest, sunrays stream through the twenty-odd holes cut into the hull of the craft, frowns of yellow casting downward on angle, sneaking into the ship over the thick-handled oars. The staggered beams of light reveal particulates of hanging moisture, and the brown and blond heads seated on the port side galley benches. The thick shafts of the oars cross their bodies, coming out their shoulders, as if the pairs had been spitted together like animals before cooking.

On the starboard side, the muted sun sulks through the oarholes, fanning dull light on the profile of empty faces. Necks crane, casting eyes aft at the north shore, a last look at lands once Kipchak. Three sailors, in thick leather belts and gray uniforms, work their way down the line of benches, securing shackles around Kipchak ankles. One stops to face an opposite bench.

"I won't wear one. How will we swim, if it fills with water?" the Kipchak asks.

The sailor backs away from the bench and his assistants step up, pulling clubs from hoops on their belts. They flail at the youth, hitting as often the benchmate of the troublemaker, who cowers near the wooden wall with his arms overhead.

"No, no! Stop!" The Kipchak screams, standing to grab at one of the clubs. As he does so, the second club comes down across his skull, dropping him across the lap of the other boy. He slinks to the deck. Two sailors pull the unconscious objector back onto his bench, where he falls backward to the knees of those behind him, blood dripping from his brow. The first sailor then steps forward and shackles the now-cooperative Kipchak.

CHAPTER

9

Cenk
The citadel, Hisn Kayfa
July 25, 1236

Cenk nudges a runner with his forearm to keep from being pushed into the limestone block wall. He lengthens his gait, targeting the broad-backed coats of white in front. These Mamluks, fellow slave soldiers, move in a quick cadence of squeaks and thuds, their leather armor stretched by muscled torsos, their boots drubbing the earthen floor. He looks about him, wonders how men so big can move so fast. He tells himself to stop thinking, just stay with them, just keep going.

Slowing, he reaches down and scoops up a sword from among those staged on the deck. A wash of sweat pours down from inside his helmet. He flips the heavy blade under his armpit and resumes his stride. He passes another instructor candidate, his thick thighs churning past the burly man. He grins, gaining confidence, passing another and then another.

With no others to catch, he focuses on the staggered seating of the hippodrome, the Mamluk's training arena. He concentrates on the rhythmic pounding of the round shield strapped on his back, the drum of brass on lamellar body armor akin to the beat of hooves on hard ground. That song of the horse always brought him comfort, taking him back to his childhood and the freedom felt latched to the neck of his sweating mare as she galloped along the winding trails of his Bashkir homeland. He takes a deep breath, recalling his young mare's earthy scent, his drenched leather cuirass matching closely the smell of saddle on horse.

On his eighth pass around the outer loop of the stadium, he is first among his classmates to pick up a heavy-headed mace from the staged pile. He lets the handle slide through his gloved fingers, until the weight of the iron-spiked weapon rests atop his fist. With the last piece of gear gathered, he concentrates on slowing his breathing, lowering his swinging hands down near his waist to save energy.

He must move like his horse. He imagines the animal's fluid movements as she negotiated the scraggy routes, high up in the Ural Mountain Range. He locks his lips, forcing himself to evenly push and pull the air through his thick-bridged nose. In, in, out. In, in, out. He must keep this pace, meet the time limit, maybe even win this event.

If he can pass the last of the graded events this coming week, he will graduate as a *Mu'allim,* a *Furusiyya* instructor, one of the few tasked with teaching Mamluk novices every technical and moral skill necessary to become the most elite mounted warriors in the world. He knows that when he is finally assigned a tulb of novices to train, he will make certain the young cavalrymen in his possession will not just meet but exceed the requirements needed to earn the title *al-Salihiyya,* Mamluk in the service of his patron al-Salih Ayyub, governor of Amid and Hisn Kayfa, and prince to the Sultan of Egypt, al-Kamil.

He is determined to excel in serving his prince because he truly owes the man everything. As was common practice with military slaves, after the death of Cenk's former patron Amir Turkmani, al-Salih wrestled with how to divide this deceased amir's Mamluks. The prince eventually redistributed most to newly promoted amirs, yet al-Salih kept five for himself. Cenk was one of these fortunate men. To Cenk, this outcome was beyond luck—it was the hand of God.

He passes the timekeeper, the amir squinting as he watches the hourglass. There is little time left and still four laps to go. Two broad-shouldered candidates pass him on either side, this event giving advantage to those built like workhorses, those able to maintain speed with heavy loads. He feels a tightness in his chest. His legs become burdensome. His cuirass, or chest armor, looking like the shell of an armadillo, begins to dig into his trapezius muscles. For the first time, he can feel his boots sinking into the soft floor on each step; his shoulders and arms ache from the weapons' weight.

He begins to worry. If he fails this event, he will not graduate. Al-Salih would frown on such an outcome, the prince keeping at the front of his mind the responsibility that comes with Saladin the Great's blood flowing through him. His prince refuses to surround himself with the mediocre. Cenk loves him for this.

But while al-Salih's position is solid because of his bloodline, Cenk realizes his own fortunate status is tenuous. Anything but success here at the citadel would be a disgrace, a permanent black mark on his record from which he would never recover. A failure at the instructor school would give his patron reason to consider passing him on to one of his senior amirs, or sending him to his lesser possession in Amid, or worse yet kicking him back into the scrub on patrol. Although al-Salih made obligations to the town's merchants, promises to keep the trade routes open, Cenk feels he has already done his part. Let others in the regiment do their share of the patrolling. Let them deal with the Khwarazmians, the continued mess in the south and west—the place where he lost his beloved former patron, Amir Turkmani.

The compression in his chest moves up into his throat. Selfish. He deserves the discomfort he now feels. He curses himself for thinking of his own interest. He must graduate not to improve his own situation: he must finish the training to best serve his new patron and maximize his impact on the regiment. Through his prince's success he will succeed. He huffs. Self-centered fool. So soon he forgets the promise. He must never forget the promise, never break his promise.

His mind wanders. He loses the calm in his breathing. He resorts to panting heavily from his mouth, as would an antelope when chased. He hates the lack of control, but must push on. He has to push on. Another candidate passes him at a full sprint. He tries to swallow, but cannot, every drip of moisture having left his throat.

His ears ring, his mind twirls, rushing him six moons prior to the rolling hills and rock faces between the upper stretches of the Tigris and Euphrates Rivers.

He pulled up his collar to fend off the winter wind, leaned into the sleet and sand pecking at his cheeks. About him, men held themselves in a manner uncharacteristic of the Mamluks, slumping a little in their saddles, cold and tired. Too many days patrolling the upper stretches of the Patriarch Route, as Amir Turkmani and his forty Mamluks trailed a small band of robbers through the sprawling acacia and thick grasses, their scouts following a set of old horse tracks.

Pushing through the brushwood, they came upon a small water hole. And there they were. Not a few, but many: Khwarazmians, filling their skins and tightening down their camels' bulging loads.

The thieves turned. Sun caught a single piece of silver in their khan's mouth, as the leader flashed the black-toothed grin of a man who sensed advantage. And then, as if flicking a spark into the driest grass, saddled boredom turned to mayhem, with both sides scrambling to assemble.

Another runner passes him. He pulls for air in hoarse gasps. His feet, earlier blessed with the bounce of fresh energy, now feel as if encased in boots of stone. His heart pounds against his armor, a giant davul drum hammering its message of despair. A frantic call for help, sounded among the cliffs and long grasses; a plea amid the blood and beating hooves on the frozen soil south of Hisn Kayfa. He grimaces as the blurry images smash together in his mind, those moments pulsing in rapid succession, until like two spinning gears whose giant teeth finally engage, it clicks and he is again there.

The whiz of Khwarazmian arrows rushed past his ears like enraged wasps kicked from their nest. The head of a brother slammed sideways as an arrow passed through both cheeks, bulging his eyes and forming lips into a contorted pucker of agony—a final kiss of death.

His beloved Turkmani hollered orders, which failed to rise above the screams of his wounded. He and his brothers disregarded the natural flight reflex, embracing their training, turning the unwilling heads of their Arabians toward the source of danger, spurs digging deep.

Then that arrow, arriving like a blind punch to the head, bounced harmlessly from his helmet, bringing forth a fire inside that quickly rose to a fury. Buckets of oil poured onto a flicker of flame in his core, combusting into a blazing inferno of rage and lust for revenge.

He feels no pain. His eyes glaze. Those visions, which fill his nights with terror, are now harnessed like fire-drafted wind caught in sail. Is it Turkmani? It must be. His former patron's spirit returns now to assist him. He welcomes the push, accepts the throbbing in his limbs. He no longer forces his short legs to drive harder, his limbs seeming to catch the craze-driven gale, powering themselves along the final stretch of dirt.

The timekeeper raises the hourglass up to his eye, while watching the approach of the final runner in his peripheral. The last grains of sand in his glass fall evenly, tumbling onto the pile below. Cenk swings the sword and mace with arms gone numb. Passing the timekeeper, he falls across the finish in a heap of iron, sweat, and leather. He sucks in the air, his heavy draws pulling sand across the rawhide his tongue has become. Four brawny arms raise him to quivering legs by leather shoulder straps.

"By Allah, you made it!" a candidate says with wide smile, his nose nearly touching Cenk's. The Mamluk embraces him, then pushes him back, only two hands now holding him up by the shoulders.

Cenk looks through him, wobbling, wild in the eyes. His brother-in-training looks into his eyes, but seems to sense the Bashkir is not home. He slaps Cenk on the back, likely figuring the fatigue of the event has made the man dopey. He keeps his arm across Cenk's shoulders, grasping his tunic to keep him upright. They hobble across the dirt, trying to get their legs back. "You run like a madman," the Mamluk says to him.

Cenk wheezes. He has not the energy to wipe from his face the tears that push down his sand-covered cheeks. When Cenk is able to stand on his own, the Mamluk moves away from him. He is not surprised. He looks up to the sky and mutters, "My Turkmani, I will keep the promise. One step closer to keeping the promise."

CHAPTER

10

Duyal
Sea of Azov
July 25, 1236

D uyal rests his head against the oar. Muffled waves slap
the hull in a cyclic knock. He tries to sleep, but the heat
radiating from above is too much. He pulls off his tunic and
wrings the sweat at his feet. He wipes his face. The giant's
head fills the oarhole, his chin resting on the oar's salted
sleeve, his mouth sucking air in gasps. Fifty others do like-
wise, their heads acting like corks, trapping the sun's heat
within the hold. A barrel rolls overhead. The slide of a large
net. The hollow pound of boot heel and voices, but fewer
than hours earlier.

The giant bends to rest elbows on knees, releasing a
slight gust through the leathered lips of their oarhole. Duyal
leans toward the opening, positions his face to catch the puff
of air. Atop the hole, a slot has been cut on slant to allow the
oar, blade and all, to be pulled into the ship. Hinged by rivet, a
wooden cover sits above and right, waiting to be rotated over

the opening during rough seas. He envisions waves bashing the hull, the ship tossing in the sea. He glances beside him at the boy's forearms and biceps. They are bigger than the legs of most men.

A creak. Light floods in from behind. Two hatches slam on the deck in succession. Warm air floods in through the cavity; a breeze sucks through the oarholes and aft toward the laddered hatch eighty steps away. A collective groan of relief.

"Cap'n be bent if we suffocate his rats," a sailor says to another, standing atop the opening.

"Ah, they're but babes. They expect to win battles with those?"

The older one snickers. "Heh, it don't happen overnight. They're sold to sultans and princes and such, up and down the Mediterranean. They train 'em up. Make 'em into soldiers. Isn't somethin' new."

"Who'd be dumb enough to fight for somebody who just enslaved yah?"

"Them."

"You'd think they'd at least buy 'em old enough to fight."

"Hmmph. Peek your head down there. Look how many of the pups we fit in the hold. Cap'n's no fool. Those bigger galleys cost twice this one. We can move a hundred a crack. Plus, this size of Saracen is easier for the Mongols to round up."

"But they're just boys."

"Boys… but not like ours in Genoa. These rats grew up harsh. Each could knock a hawk out of the sky with bow-shot—every damn shot. And war in the holy land, it's mostly on horseback. These boys were on ponies while still pissin' their knickers. They're young enough to where these princes can make what they want 'em to be. Like a dog—who wants to train an old soldier?"

"Hmmm."

The pair stands, inspecting their cargo.

"Almost pitiful to look at."

"Yeah... but these won't be riding against armies for a long damn time. The nobility's been training others for years who are ready. Who cares anyhow? Pay's been steady. Just need fair winds, so that we can dump these and get back for the next run. Then home for a stretch. That's it."

"Right."

Duyal sighs. Slave soldiers. Princes. The Mediterranean. He stares at the planking around him in disbelief. He deliberates his fate, while half-inspecting the ribbed guts of the vessel, just divulged by the sun. Soft amber between the musty planked walls; cotton driven in the gaps and smothered with a dark pitch. A carpet of short green fur, where the deck meets up to running planks. His mother had warned him of the stuff and the sickness that followed its presence.

The giant turns. "My oldest cousin made this same voyage across the Black Sea. South and west through Constantinople. He sent us back messages, became an amir in the service of al-Kamil—the Sultan of Egypt."

"An amir?" Duyal asks.

"An officer, a leader of horsemen. A man of wealth and prestige," Ox says, the words putting a wide, white smile on his mouth, causing the youth to straighten his massive shoulders.

"Oh," Duyal says, looking away.

"I'm Ox—from the lower Dnieper country, west. Who are you?"

Duyal attempts to hide his disdain. "More Rus than Kipchak" was how his uncle had always put it, describing those towers close in proximity to the sedentary towns in the south and west. No wonder the boy is so large, he has likely lived fat off the trade from his tower's huge flock. Shit, he was probably beef-fed. Duyal wishes he had not even opened his mouth.

"I am Duyal, from the upper Volga."

"Ah, well then, you're lucky."

Duyal stares at his boots for a few moments, then looks Ox in the eyes. "My folks are dead, my tower is gone, my brother was led away by the Mongols. We sit in shackles. Lucky?"

"Yeah, I mean, I'm sorry for your family, but you're not odd among this lot. I mean really we're all lucky, probably heading to Egypt—Cairo. They'll turn us into soldiers." Ox smirks with the naiveté of a child.

"I already dread a land where it's custom to put their new soldiers in chains."

"We won't stay in 'em for long."

Duyal tries to change the subject. "Did your family survive?"

"Yeah, my parents. And my younger brother was chosen by our khan to stay with the flocks. Was it your only brother that was taken by the Mongols?"

"No, well yeah. But there were four of us. My sister, Bora, died in her fourth year. My older brother, Gozde, was snatched about three years ago, we figured by Armenian traders."

"He should've been back by now," his father said. They contin-ued the search, Gozde's tracks leading to the armful of branches dropped, peeling off into the high-toed tracks of a sprint. Then they came upon the intersection of large boot prints, those also dug deep into the snow.

The wind picked up. Back to camp they ran, fumbling the tack back onto weary ponies with shaking hands. Snow had al-ready drifted over the trio of tracks, but not before terminating at the signs of a scuffle.

His father cried when his son's prints disappeared into those of the Armenians' ponies, staged in a nearby wood.

"We'll find him," Duyal said. Those blank eyes in return, long bereft of their optimism, just another twist in his curse. The kidnappers' trail ran southward, snow blanketing the last traces of them.

Under a wide-branched cedar they stopped, Duyal backing between those muscular legs to sleep. Often he was awoken by his father's shudders, never knowing if they were shivers from the biting cold or silent sobs.

"Ah," the Ox says.

A sailor blurts from above, "He comes. Turn to."

The chatter up top drops off, in its place the scuff of wood and metal rail on deck and the thump of boots and crate. Then two pairs of hard-heeled shoes clack the deck, their sharp clicks increasing the pace of work from the others. The pair moves to the open hatch above them. Duyal senses them peering down.

"Good, good," an older man says. "Let's get underway."

A gray-whiskered sailor descends from the aft hatch. He turns clumsily on a bad leg, leaning on a cane. Two others climb down to his side. All eyes are upon him. "Do as I say and there will be no trouble."

The old sailor hobbles down the planking, inspecting their chains, a sailor in tow. He stops at Duyal's bench, gazes at Ox with a look of wonder upon his face. "Move the big one inboard," he says to the sailor.

The sailor puts the key into Duyal's shackle, releasing the metal band, and pulls him off the bench. He removes Ox's irons and steps aside. "Smaller one in first," the sailor says. As Ox moves near him, he chokes up on his club, fear filling his eyes. The Kipchaks switch places and the sailor affixes their restraints.

"Loose the hawser!" sounds from above. The nose of the galley is pulled away from the jetty in yanks matching the faint slosh of distant blades pulling water. Another vessel moves them from the dock.

The old sailor eases his way aft. He turns. "Eyes here! We'll soon be rowing. Rats on the inboard will keep both hands on the oar grip at all times. Outboard man will do the same with the grips carved in the loom." He raises a leather strap, dangling a metal loop. "Oarloops will be freed upon my orders only. Lose 'n oar at sea and we'll be hauling you topside and tossin' both of yah after it."

CHAPTER
II

Singer
Lower Volga River
July 27, 1236

The sun bakes the wool across Singer's back, the warmth slowing his breathing, dropping heavy eyelids across bloodshot eyes. His head dips forward, twitching to a stop. His eyes pop open. He looks to see if anyone notices.

"You best cut that shit out," Ilker says, heaving a water jug to his friend. Singer uncorks it and takes a long swig of warm water. He silently reprimands himself for his inattention. Lifting his hat, he dumps some of the water upon his head. "They should've been back."

"Yeah."

He seats the cork with the heel of his hand and chucks it back to his friend. Struggling to rise on his good knee, he peers through the gaps of sagging bush willow branches and thick clumps of twitch grass. No movement.

In the center of their perimeter, ponies tear at the blanket of grass. Shimmering leaves sprinkle broken sun onto their backs of cream and chestnut and mottled gray. To their flank, a handful of Rus craftsmen work in the shade of sprawling trees, repairing Mongol gear. Pots and stacked hides lay staged in good order. Four skinned sheep hang under the cool of branches by single rear legs, the white-backed carcasses slowly turning in the breeze.

A tailor picks the curly handled shears from his lap, snips a thread and cinches a knot with hands skilled from his repetitive work. He carefully folds the trousers and places them on a pile to his left. He shifts on his stool, looks down at another pair and three coats at his feet. He mutters something in his language. Grasping the neckline of his shirt, he wipes the grime from his brow. Slump-shouldered, he heaves a sigh.

A Mongol swaggers past him on chunky, bowed legs and then stops suddenly, as if compelled by afterthought. He turns. As his head comes around, the beads on his braids snap against the hardened leather scales covering his chest.

The white animal fat spread on his face and across the back of his shaven head glistens in the sun, futile protection from the tormenting lice and fleas. Clumps of it, smeared high into the tufts of black hair at each ear, collect dust and bits of grass like filings to a magnet: dirt-flecked horns, tapering downward to the tight wraps that terminate his woven tresses.

"You're slower than a knotty-handed biddy," he says. "Pick up the pace, old woman, or we'll find another."

"Yes, yes," the Rus says, snatching a torn deel from the ground, squinting to thread his needle with quivering hands.

The Mongol raises his pointed chin, a look between doubt and revulsion moving across his face. "I told them a girl would be better." He stomps off.

The Rus lowers his sunburned head, a thick wave of hair on each side flaring like turbulent water in opposite directions, specked in brown and gray. He chews his lip in likely disbelief at how he could be so far from his shop, forced to serve these barbarians.

The Rus. Singer is glad not to be one of them. To the west, their wooden shacks sit empty, their spaces soon to be occupied by varmints. Their crops—trampled by the Mongols to encourage the regeneration of pasture to feed pony herds during the follow-up campaign, farther into the heart of Europe.

"Wonder where that tailor's family is?" Singer asks.

Ilker turns to the Rus and scowls. "In Raizan... or likely farther east on the trail to Karakorum."

Singer nods. The poor man's family would probably be accompanying those unfortunate hundreds destined to off-load the goods from their and their neighbors' homes and then be judged by their overlords for usefulness.

"And what happens to those Rus with skills unneeded in the capital?" Singer asks.

"They'll be marched back west on foot. The fit pressed to man the siege engines, others serving on foot in front of the mounted Mongols against another city's Rus."

"Hmm. The Mongols value infantry that little, huh?"

Ilker laughs. "Yeah. And those Rus killed, their bodies will be dumped into moats, cheap fill for the Mongols. The healthiest of the women and children can mostly look forward to the slave market."

Singer winces, switches back to his bad knee. He scans the distant scrub for any movement. "I suppose if we were a couple of years younger, we might have been joining them."

Ilker raises his thin eyebrows. "Eh, I think the Mongols saw in us riding and shooting skills that could be put to use now."

"Or maybe the unit being shorthanded saved us."

Ilker raises his thin eyebrows. "Yeah, maybe."

Regardless, Singer knows he should be grateful for being assigned to his Mongol *arban*, or squad of ten men. He appreciates the simplicity of the Mongol military structure.

The *arban* is the base tier of the giant Mongol horde: ten squads forming a company of one hundred, what the Mongols term a *zagun;* ten companies making a battalion of a thousand, the Mongol *mingan*; ten battalions comprising a *tumen* of ten thousand warriors, the leader of each of these largest units chosen by Ogodei, the Great Khan. Singer has not been told the exact number, but is under the impression that the Mongols field in excess of a dozen *tumen.*

Singer's *arban* takes on the outlook of its leader, Suren. Quick with a laugh and fast to act. They all can shoot. In fact, Singer feels most of the troopers in the bigger *zagun* of one hundred are good men, their soldiering skills and tactics in the field attained not from formal training but through their experience in herding animals and hunting game across the wide Mongolian steppe. Perhaps these men are really not too different from himself.

They are certainly men of one purpose, even if not men of one blood. Sprinkled among the company are mostly Tartars, Merkid, and Tayichiud. And in their *mingan* of one thousand are men with roots to these tribes, plus many more peoples. While most of the men were not directly assimilated into the unit as Singer was, many of their fathers were. As young boys, some here probably watched with initial horror as warriors from their various tribes were sent away to join different outfits across Mongolia.

"Stiff said that Genghis was the greatest of all khans—the one who united all their people. Can you imagine that task?" Singer asks.

"I think it took many years, one tribe at a time."

"The conquering of tribes is one thing, but to mix the warriors and even the families from every tribe on the Mongolian Steppe…"

Ilker grins. "Stiff told me that after each victory, Genghis made sure the beaten weren't treated as defeated tribes of the past—looted, caged, enslaved—with the survivors left to reorganize."

"Left with nothing but the fire of revenge pumping through their veins," Singer says.

"Right. He broke that ancient chain of events. By spreading each conquered tribe's warriors to standing Mongol units, old enemies were forced to live and fight beside one another."

Singer nods. "I suppose Genghis knew in time that intermarriage and bonds forged by men training and bleeding together would turn his vision for the steppe people from idea to reality."

"Yep. One Mongol tribe. 'The people of the felt walls.'"

Having witnessed the camaraderie among them, Singer finds it difficult to conceive that the fathers, and in some cases grandfathers, of the men in his unit once fought each other. For this *zagun* eats, sleeps, and shits as one unit. Word of one man's poor health or tragedy is felt in earnest among them all. Their oneness has even begun to take shape physically. In just a generation or two of mixing, Singer can see only subtle variations in facial color and the shape of short noses, the traits of their various home tribes being slowly melted into the look of a single race.

"Must be what Genghis' grandson has envisioned for the Kipchaks, eh?" Singer asks.

"I hope so. Hope Genghis' prophecy didn't die with the man." Ilker looks to the sky for inspiration. "Sure seems like Ogodei and the other khans are continuing with the plan."

"Let's hope so," Singer says.

"Yeah, I see no shame in being a member of the latest swallowed tribe."

Singer smiles. Eventually, he feels there may be some privilege in being absorbed into the ever-expanding Mongol horde. While he cares little about whatever share of the material goods filling the large warehouses in Karakorum will be his, he longs for the sense of belonging that has been absent from his life for so long. Each day he is around these men, the more he also wishes to be part of their contagious vision.

And while the yellow-skinned warriors do not yet call him or the other Kipchaks *aga*, or brother, as they do each other, he feels if he just keeps his head down and does his job, all will be well. He will work, execute each mission, until his tacit status of stepbrother is elevated. And he will encourage the same course for his friends, Ilker and Ferdi. For what seems to matter in the *zagun* is not the origin of the warrior, or even the color of his skin, but how well he performs his duty. Singer respects this.

A Mongol in the perimeter pops up, cups his short fingers, makes the warning squawk of a crow and pats the top of his helmet twice—the signal for friendly forces inbound. All rise from their assigned positions, standing to nock arrows. The Mongol's eyes grow round, then intense.

Ilker peers over Singer's shoulder. "Ah, shit."

The clack of hoof on rock follows the snap of dead branches. A Mongol from the main body plows through feather-leaved willows and into the center of the perimeter, the arrow in his arm flopping at each hoof strike. His pony bears a shaft in the thigh and one in the shoulder. The rush of adrenaline, which has fueled her sprint back to the rally point, has also pried her eyes wide and white.

Her rider leaps off and backhands the visor of his helmet, sending it tumbling. He curses, circling to her right side with the protruding arrow in his arm scraping unintentionally across his girl. He pats her neck, speaking softly in her ear. He inspects the depth of her wounds.

In comes another man, leading the reins of a third, who lies heavy over his beast's neck, his hands interlocked in a death grip across the pony's throat. Blood runs red and diluted over the sweating chest of his gray mount. With the scent of his master's blood about him, the pony prances irritably with nostrils flared, testing the lead with short tugs. The horses in the center grow anxious, sending Mongol watchmen snatching for bridled heads.

The lead rider dismounts and begins to lever open his mate's fingers. The injured man's eyes crack open. Once seeing he is inside the friendly encirclement, he allows his friend to help him off the pony. He looks down at the arrow in his side, the shaft clean through his abdomen, the head pushing outward from his deel. He crumples to his back and begins to fumble for the clasps on his blood-soaked garment. His friend grips this maroon-crusted hand and opens the coat with his free hand.

The clank of steel on rock as two more battered Mongols dismount, dumping their gear. Before Singer can think, his legs are moving. He runs over to one of the injured, who plops on his ass, grimacing as he wiggles an arrow from his calf, the iron-barbed head clinging to a strand of tissue on its stubborn exit.

Singer drops to his knees, dismayed to recognize the fletching pattern on the arrow as that of his own people. He pulls a clump of felt from his pouch and reaches for the dagger at his hip to assist. The Mongol recoils, frightened at the knife or possibly the white-skinned hand that holds it.

"Leave him! Back to your place in the perimeter," Chuluun snaps, he and his chestnut pony sharing the same splattered blood across their foreheads and cheeks.

"I was only going to crush the barb and treat his wound," Singer says, surprised to see that his company commander has rumbled into the center with a dozen more troops.

Chuluun leans forward in his saddle. "Go!"

Singer looks up confusedly, sheathes his dagger and trots back to his position. He picks up his bow and faces outboard on knee.

"If these are just the wounded, how many are dead?" Ilker asks.

Singer just shakes his head, scanning the bush line for enemy. More Mongols from the main body pour in. He hums a song of his mother's, attempting to drown out the escalating disorder behind him. He pictures her, straight-backed and clear-skinned, a fistful of coat holding a bulging load of dung beneath her breasts for the evening fire, singing the same tune through a smile soft and content.

He sighs. All of this was so predictable. Just an hour earlier, as their unit of light cavalry was moving south, the *zagun* came upon six Kipchak men filling their skins at a creek in the distance. Upon being spotted, the Kipchaks jumped on their ponies and charged up the steeper grade and over the top, never looking back.

Chuluun sensed an easy kill, ordering two *arban* to stay at this rally point to guard the extra ponies and supplies while the main body pursued the enemy. As the hasty preparations were made, Singer had pulled Suren aside, mentioning to his superior that he did not think those Kipchaks had actually been surprised, but were baiting the Mongols into a trap.

His squad leader smiled. "Feel no sympathy for your people who evade Mongol rule—not all were wise as you. They'll now pay for their actions."

"But over the ridge, the valley walls are steep. They…" Singer said, before being cut off, pointed to his position in the perimeter.

The Mongols had not put together those fleeing Kipchaks with the evolving circumstances. With the flow of wares moving eastward in greater quantity, the higher command had dedicated more resources to defending the long supply trains than to finishing off the recently conquered towers. Using this opportunity, those Kipchaks who refused submission to Mongol rule now embraced all who wished to fight the invaders. They trickled in by pairs and by entire towers.

While loyalty to the confederation of Kipchak towers had been dubious for years, this all changed with Mongol occupiers now on Kipchak land. Even remnants of the outlying Bulgars, those who preferred death in battle to living under the Mongol yoke, moved southwest under the cover of night to join the fight. Mongol intelligence revealed that in the past week, resistance forces had grown exponentially, the rebels hiding in the mountains until their numbers had grown great enough to attack the Mongols in force.

And just yesterday, Chuluun had received the word. Kipchak-Bulgar dissenters had just decimated the ranks of a Mongol *zagun*, three units to the east. Would Batu Khan, overall commander of the Rus campaign, have detached two thousand troopers from Raizan to return east and crush the last of the renegades, if the threat were not real? Perhaps Chuluun had been lulled asleep by their easy caravan security duty. Perhaps his company commander felt his new mission of disrupting the insurgents was going to be just as simple. Chuluun had underestimated his enemy, and his *zagun* now pays the price.

Singer counts the wounded, the line of bodies laid side by side, hands over chest. A crying Mongol grabs the shoulders of an unresponsive mate, trying to shake open eyes that will never again see, trying to rattle a start to a friend's heart that will no longer pump. Chuluun has six of his leaders in a semicircle, the remaining four still in the gorge, likely dead or fighting their way out. The commander waves off the words of one man and points to three others, while digging his heel in the dirt to create the faux terrain for his expedient plan. The tailor has pulled himself and the mended garments under a cart. The man buries his head in a deel, shielding his ears from the screaming horses and curt orders shouted at those around him.

Another squad leader rides in with two others, both bearing dead Mongols over the asses of their ponies. The troopers peel off as Chuluun approaches, leaving the leader of their *arban* to face him.

"Where are the rest of your men?" Chuluun asks.

"They, I, I have seven—three went down in the draw. I needed to get my men out of that gorge, or we would have lost more," the shaken Mongol replies.

"Is this our way? Get your men ready, we'll be going back to retrieve your dead, before those Kipchak dogs strip them and steal their ponies. Now!"

The Mongol looks through his commander with glassed eyes. "Yes, Chuluun."

Seeing a gap in the perimeter, one arriving Mongol rides up next to Singer with a corpse slumped behind his saddle. The man dismounts and leans his forehead against his dead friend's back. He makes a fist with his reins, then begins untying the wraps, which had hastily secured his comrade to the saddleback.

He notices Singer. "I'm surprised you and the other Kipchaks did not run off and join your brothers, during the skirmish." He hefts the body over his shoulder.

Singer rises to grab the flopping legs, but the Mongol lays his friend down gently in one motion. Singer looks into the Mongol's eyes. "Run? My *arban* was here on guard."

The Mongol nods in bogus approval. "A few more of us dead and your loyalty might have been tested." The dark-haired man tosses a stirrup atop the seat of his saddle to expose the strap.

Singer bites his tongue, tells himself to keep calm. "Our orders were to stay here with the gear. But if they'd been to attack those fleeing men, then those Kipchak arrows would have been aimed at me as well as you."

The Mongol turns back toward his mount, ripping downward angrily on the worn leather strap, tightening his saddle. "Maybe."

CHAPTER
12

Duyal
The Black Sea
July 27, 1236

The galley rolls under a setting quarter moon, the ship's long planks moaning against their wooden pegs. Pulleys with hemp stretched between them and metal collars wedged on the mast alternately whine their disgust with limp sails hanging in the salty dark. Below deck, a chorus of snores. Two Kipchaks trade hoarse coughs, one spitting dislodged mucous to the deck. Another boy whimpers.

Duyal sleeps doubled over his oar, his cheek pressed hard between molars and curved pine, his shoulder wet against the hull. The grate of boot heel against ladder rung to the aft—his eyes open. A swaying lantern throws its quivering light across beams and oars and crumpled Kipchaks.

A groan. Certainly their rest time has not expired. He straightens, working the ache from his jaw and stiffness from forearms and back. With palms together, he bends swollen knuckles, stretches his arms, nearly touching the boy in front of him. He slumps back over the oar, the hard wood lodged in his armpits. The acidic rank of vomit still fills the hold, the puke produced shortly after leaving the harbor's protection, a chain reaction of spewing that at first rippled through the boys, but eventually subsided into sporadic aftershocks of dry heaves by the time they passed between the narrow spits of land and emerged into the open Black Sea.

The briny wind of the Azov filled the sails that first day at sea, pushing the galley upon its southern course. Yet since midday yesterday, the breeze fell off, leaving the dark water like glass, the salty air as dead as it was foreign. Their oars had been in the water since, save the short spells of sleep given to the neophyte rowers.

The flicker brightens, illuminating tawny hulls dotted with moisture, casting gold upon the red-striped heads, the surrounding hair matted in auburn and creams. A scuff of heel and tap of cane on deck confirm the presence of the first mate. An elongated shadow hides his thick hair and bushy eyebrows; the candlelight reveals the gray in his beard, the wart protruding through his whiskers. "Wake up na', or we'll bob here for 'ternity!" The sailor pokes Ox, yielding no response.

A small Kipchak chases the light, stepping over stowed oars, lowering one piss-filled bucket with a slosh to stoop and shovel shit into another. He is the slightest among them, the only one without metal on his ankle, permitted to climb the ladder and dump his buckets to sea, once filled. Perhaps his size makes him the most expendable, the lad being the cheapest item of cargo onboard, the smallest loss in case he wished to fling himself overboard.

The damp air hangs. More boys awaken, hacking up phlegm, blowing noses into fists and tunics. With thumb and forefinger, Duyal works an inflamed tendon in his elbow. The Ox snores, his knees open wide, his head buried in crossed arms upon the oar.

The lantern's glow exits the hatch. Another man makes his way down in the dark, stopping three quarters of the way forward between rows. Duyal knows it is the piper, even before the three legs of his stool touch the deck. The pair of sailors with clubs descend, hanging smaller lanterns fore and aft.

Duyal elbows Ox. "Wake up."

"Deploy your oars," the piper says.

Duyal pulls the oar toward the sea, startling his bench-mate as the hefty rod slides beneath his arms. All fifty shafts hum a deepening note across the oarholes' hammered metal. When the oars are two thirds out, the boys lift them to pass the stitched leather sleeves, bound tightly about the loom to prevent abrading where pine meets bronze.

"Refasten oarloops!"

Duyal feels in the dark for the iron ring hanging by riveted leather. He slips the hoop over the grip, dropping the oar to let gravity seat it home. The club bearers stroll the passage as the sliding rings terminate their glide in a communal chime. Three rings aft clink their tardiness. Duyal pulls the wooden collar from the bench and slides it over the handle, securing it with three turns of the thumbscrew. The Ox rubs the sleep from his eyes, grabs the oar.

"To work now, lads," the piper says.

Duyal props his feet against the oak rib of the vessel, feeling with his feet for the two rounded footholds worn into the wood. He reaches the limit of his chain, the shackle on his right ankle digging into flesh, already worn pink.

"Ready to row!"

Chains clink as they leave the deck, complimented by a communal grunt as the boys push oar grips down and forward. The pairs of rowers stay hunched, like cats ready to pounce. The drips from their oar blades are lost in the blackness. They wait, as the last of them gets into position. Duyal closes his eyes, listening for that dreaded pitch.

The pipe yelps. He and Ox dip their oar into the sea and push against the timber at their feet, while pulling back against the wood in their grip. Their buried spoon hardly moves. His lower back screams; the tendon in his elbow burns in retaliation. The groan of oar blends with that from the boys. The mass of floating wood and limp canvas defies their exertions, fighting against the water, as if her bow was flat and driving through a sea of mud.

They lean forward. Another long blare from the pipe. She starts to concede. Forward again they lean and a blast of pipe, shorter than the last. A slosh on the wood opposite him, as the bow begins to push water.

Pull by pull their tempo quickens, the faintest of breezes moving against their necks and faces. The pipe falls into its usual peeps as the galley finds its sweet spot. Duyal imagines punching the pipe, lodging the device deep into the piper's throat. He pushes the air from his lungs and drives his legs.

The piper's dreaded voice. "Legs and pull." Tweet. "Legs and pull." Tweet. "Together now." Tweet. "Pull now." Tweet. "Drive it." Tweet. "Hard on starboard." Tweet.

He pushes his chest against fists, concentrating to relax going forward, fixing his arms to use his legs when pulling back. He must save his arms. Save the arms.

"Inside hand." Tweet. "Feather 'em now." Tweet. "Settle." Tweet. "Settle." Tweet. He lets his mind drift, trying to ignore the pain. Pain in his elbow. Pain in his back. Pain in his forearms. The twist of wrists on forward stroke feathers oars, so the spoons will not catch the wind they wish was there. Let it rise. The splash of blades catching water, the throaty moan of pine in oarhole, the whoosh of water pulsating across long planks in steady time. And then again the pipe.

For what seems like forever, it is nothing but the monotonous harmony of boys plying oars and the chirp of the pipe. Like an enormous creature just hatched from the deep, the galley cuts the sea's surface, reaching back with synchronized arms, lurching the torso of the wooden beast across the windless plane of sea, maybe fifteen paces per stroke.

His stomach churns. It has been minimal water and scarce rations of mold-covered bread and half-rotten beans for two days. His thighs and forearms burn. Anything to forget the ache.

"They steer us south and east," Duyal says. Tweet. "Not south and west." Tweet. "Maybe they have something else planned for us." Tweet.

The giant shakes his head. "It has to be Egypt." Tweet. "It will be better." Tweet. "We will become soldiers." Tweet. "Finally done with the damn sheep." Tweet.

"I'd rather be back on the grassland." Tweet.

"No more freezing winters." Tweet. "No more running from Mongols." Tweet.

Duyal sighs. Has the baby-faced giant ever really experienced a hungry winter down in the south country? Has he no loyalty to his tower, or the land his ancestors bled for? "Yeah, no more running from the Mongols." Tweet. "They have us in fucking chains." Tweet.

The Ox laughs.

They row. Soon the sun begins to peek through their holes.

"How many in your tower's flock?" Duyal asks. Tweet.

"Fourteen hundred plus—sheep and goat." Tweet. "Three hundred horses." Tweet.

Duyal frowns. Just as he thought. Then he chuckles. What's the point in being jealous? Here and now, the affluent and lowly share the same oar, the orphan and khan's nephew pull the same ship.

"Did the Mongols take your animals?" Ox asks.

Duyal looks through the crescent-shaped opening above his oarhole, the hazy moonlight now shimmering on the black water rushing by. He recalls the mound of skinned sheep heads, their jutted tongues and glazed eyes staring in every direction; his tower's warriors hacked and arrow-ridden; the heap of throat-slit women, the red-lipped smiles below their chins wide and open and dribbling blood.

"Yes, they took everything," Duyal says. Tweet. Tweet. Tweet. Tweet...

CHAPTER
13

Cenk
The citadel, Hisn Kayfa
July 28, 1236

Cenk moves down the line amid the clunk of metal on wood and scrape of sliding plates. A plop of pale vegetable. The smell of roasted meat fills his nostrils. His stomach grumbles. Across the scraped counter, a baby-faced novice with serving fork looks down at the black belt about Cenk's waist, likely not noticing the white band on the right side, which designates Cenk only a *Furusiyya* instructor candidate, not an official *Mu'allim* yet. The boy shakes the small piece of meat from the long tines and stabs a bigger one from his serving platter. He places it gently upon Cenk's plate without looking up.

Cenk turns from the line with wooden plate and cup and searches for a seat. He wishes to find one where he will not have to speak, ideally one near the end of a table, where a novice sits, another boy too terrified of the black belt to say a word. He has no time for, no interest in, idle chatter.

He scans over the top of seated heads, avoiding any eyes in the overcrowded room that may meet his in invitation. The tables are full. He grunts his frustration. Finally, he spots a small table against the far wall with an empty chair. Seated there is a lone man. Cenk's eyes are drawn to the old sage's red beard, so long it covers the top three buttons on his coat. A smile from him, a raise of his chin. Ekrem, the archery master. Well, if he must share a table, it may as well be with another recluse. He heads for the table.

Having been acquired by al-Salih after the death of their patrons, both Ekrem and Cenk are what the Mamluks call *Sayfiya,* a status akin to being orphans of the military order, second-class citizens in the eyes of al-Salih's personal Mamluks.

Reaching the table, Cenk nods. "Good afternoon, amir."

"Afternoon. Please sit. I trust your improved release is here to stay?" Ekrem says.

Cenk meets his eyes, grins. "I've been meaning to thank you since the test. Without your assist, I wasn't going to clean up that twitch and find the black again."

"That's what I'm here for," Ekrem says, grinning and waving his hand in dismissal, but surely knowing that it was he alone who solved Cenk's minor flaw in archery technique. It was Ekrem who helped put Cenk's arrows back into the center of the targets, securing him the score required for graduation.

Cenk is grateful, as there were other candidates who also needed instruction that day, but Ekrem kept circling back to help him. Cenk feels perhaps the grizzled archer's deed was part of the unspoken bond between him and the handful of other *Sayfiya* in the regiment. With both of their initial masters dead and a majority of their own surviving brothers-in-arms spread among many units across the empire, both Cenk and Ekrem were now alone, exposed. Rank was irrelevant—the outcasts simply had to look out for one another.

For a while, Ekrem's future looked more dismal than Cenk's. For after losing his patron in battle, Ekrem was forced into retirement, the sultan undervaluing this Mamluk's worth to the corps. But al-Salih knew better than his father, wasting no time in pulling Ekrem back into service at his current duty as head of all archery instructors.

Cenk stuffs a wad of meat in his mouth, looks down at Ekrem's empty plate. "Please, don't let me keep you, amir."

"No, I have some time. I enjoy the company. It's not like you or I have our brothers to lean on anymore. Although given our circumstances, neither of us has much to gripe about, eh? Seems we couldn't have landed in a better place, maybe as fortunate as the prince himself." Ekrem looks over his shoulder.

Surprised at the comment, Cenk stops chewing, looks left and right to see the tables beside them are starting to clear. He straightens himself in the chair. He supposes it is known to the entire Ayyubid Empire that the sultan shifted al-Salih, his ambitious son, to this remote part of the domain for no other reason than to push him as far away from the power center in Cairo as possible. And that maybe not so un-expectedly, al-Salih had taken full advantage of the situation.

Cenk looks the amir in the eyes. "Yes, my Amir. I feel Allah has blessed us both—and our prince too—but like a cat, there was no doubt al-Salih was going to land on his feet."

"Well, what's it been—three years since al-Salih re-ceived the governorship of Amid and Hisn Kayfa? And he's already built a new mosque in Hisn Kayfa, renovated another in Amid to win favor with the masses. Any of the clerics who didn't adore him for that have since come around after he restored the tomb of Imam Abdullah (uncle of the Prophet Mohammad)."

Ekrem smiles, leans forward, puts his elbows on the table. "And of course who doesn't love the man here in the citadel?"

Cenk nods his head. Ekrem does not try to lead him into a ruinous comment. His words are genuine. In the last several years, al-Salih has nearly doubled the size of the citadel. Since, his army of already dedicated horsemen have only become more loyal; the builders and merchants in Hisn Kayfa hold the prince in greater esteem. As the town now feels safe, the area has hummed with trade and growth. "No surprise— our prince was born to lead."

"Yes. Even more so now that he has been freed of all... hindrances."

Cenk looks at him confusedly.

"You know, since Shams al-Din died last year."

Cenk grins. "Yes. Yes, I see." He assumes the amir means that once the sultan's adviser to al-Salih died, this planted mole was no longer able to forward word of the prince's doings to the father in Cairo. Since the sultan, al-Kamil, never replaced Shams al-Din, al-Salih had indeed acted with even greater skill and cunning. Cenk supposes that al-Salih was just following the path he knew. A scorpion will always be a scorpion.

As had happened when al-Kamil assigned his son the position of vicegerent, or second in command, in Cairo seven years ago, al-Salih was now making the most of his current duty, using the distance from the sultan as an opportunity to build up his treasury and then subsequently spend it on growing his forces in the thriving town. The sultan's son was where he wanted to be for the time being: on the periphery, where his ambition and creativity went unbridled.

Cenk figures that perhaps not so ironically, al-Salih's father also has a vital interest in his son's ambition. For both Hisn Kayfa and Amid are not just commercially, but also strategically important to the Ayyubids. The towns sit precariously on the edge of enemy territory, their fortifications acting as northern buffers to possible invasion from the Rum, Seljukids, and even from the Mongols, farther to the northeast. The possession of both towns seals Ayyubid control of the upper Tigris valley, leaving only the southern town of Mardin in the hands of a non-Ayyubid prince. Cenk can only imagine the wariness the sultan must feel in tasking al-Salih, his renegade prince, to protect the empire's vulnerable northern flank. But who cares of the sultan and his worries? Cenk's only concern is for al-Salih.

Ekrem sits back. "Well, enough of the intrigue in the realm, you must feel some relief. You've made it. Will pick up your tulb soon, eh?"

"Yes. Again, thanks to you."

Again Ekrem shakes his head, refusing to acknowledge the compliment. "Training worms has to be better than being down in the south—what a tangle."

"I will go where assigned, my Amir, but I'd be lying if I said I look forward to going back there ever again."

"Of course. You were just there, weren't you?"

"Yes, my Amir. Well, about six moons ago."

"So the trade route was secure between Damascus and Aleppo, the trouble was between Aleppo and here, right?"

Cenk sighs, looks down while nodding. "Right. Unfortunately, our sector. The Khwarazmians were mostly hitting caravans in the tight sections of the route. They knew the steep country, were hell to find. On good horses and well-armed."

Ekrem tightens his lips. "Squeezed west by the Mongols and south by the Seljukids, they had to go somewhere, didn't they? Were going to find their silver somehow…"

Cenk furls his lip. "The bastards will work for anyone who will flip them a coin. Will steal anything—we chased them once and they were dumping plants destined for Hisn Kayfa as they rode away. They don't care."

Ekrem sighs. "I'm a... sorry about Amir Turkmani. He was a good man."

"He was. I, we lost too many good men to those pricks."

Ekrem shakes his head. "I hear they're still working out of Diyar Bakr."

"The Khwarazmians?"

Ekrem nods.

"Oh, I'm sure they're still there. Too close."

Ekrem leans nearer. "We can't have it. We need every spur of that route open. Our prince—he's hiked the merchants' taxes in Hisn Kayfa, just like he did in Cairo when the sultan was away. Amir Aqtay says the bigger traders have already started objecting."

Cenk clenches his fists. "I've heard."

"If the wealthy can't hawk their wares, they can't pay their taxes. No tax silver flowing means no pay for us," Ekrem says with one raised eyebrow.

Cenk looks him in the wrinkled face. "That's it. No tax silver, no purchase of fresh Kipchaks, no growth of the regiment."

Ekrem leans back in his chair, stretches his legs and sighs. "Well, our prince will find a way. He's committed to bringing in new novices, to building the regiment. He wouldn't be pushing up new instructors like you, if there was nobody arriving to train."

Cenk runs his hands through his hair. "Yes. Yes, my Amir."

CHAPTER

14

Ox
Black Sea
July 28, 1236

E vening creeps over a ginger sky. A whoosh of sea surges over barnacled planks, in perfect time with the monotonous call of the piper. Ox's head aches. If the pipe's chirp were from a bird, he would drop it with an arrow, stomp its head, and wring its neck. But it is not, and he has no choice but to endure its squawk and pull the oar.

The boy at his side slumps over the grip, his elbows wrapped about the shaft, his hands clutching fists of puke-stained tunic. Although resting his lanky arms, the Kipchak from the mountain country still puts shoulder to pine, continues to pump his thick legs.

Ox leans to him. "Back off some. I got it for a while." Tweet.

"I'm all right," Duyal mutters. Tweet.

Ox shakes his head. "You're a hard thing." Tweet.

A boy four rows aft falls to the deck. His fingers draw

in to his wrists, as if slowly cranked by a winch. His chest convulses, knocking shoulder blades against wood. Slowly released from their trance of thoughtless tempo, rowers near-by turn to watch, their rounded backs still rolling in unison. Some look over their shoulders to the club-toting sailors in silent, half-hearted requests for help. The piper continues his cadence, keeping time despite the clatter of the boy's chains and the hollow pounding of elbows and skull on deck.

"We have a boy down!" Duyal shouts. He stands, receiving vacant stares from his fellows. The crew ignores him.

Ox pulls him back down to his seat. "Like they don't know. Shut up, or they'll put the rod to us both."

"Hey! We have a rower down!" Duyal screams.

The sailors saunter down the narrow passage, reaching the crumpled boy as his tremors lessen to quivers. The boy's fingertips involuntarily tap upon his forearms, as if he were plucking a tune on his tambour back in the north country. His eyes roll back, until only the whites stare blankly at the dripping planks overhead.

"Unlock me and I will help him," Duyal says.

One sailor glares at him. The other takes a step closer to the downed lad and crosses his arms. The boy lies on his side, a grotesque quiver in his lower jaw. The sailors stoop over him with hands on knees and look at each other. One pulls a key from his belt.

"Let her run," the piper calls.

The boys rest sweaty chests atop their oars. The galley sloshes to a lazy stop. Hot air seeps in through every crevice, making the sweat pour from their bodies.

"Detach oarings!"

He loosens the thumbscrews. The familiar clink of metal. "Oars in!"

The sweeps buzz, ending their short song with a thud of grips hitting the deck. Ox rubs a sleeve across his forehead and bends until his torso arches across the oar shaft. He sucks in the sour reek of bile and body odor. The spasms subside in his lower back. He peers out the oarhole at the blazoned ribs of cirrus clouds curling over the featureless skyline, and then back down to the yellow slime at his feet. He wonders how many more days it will be, if they will ever see land.

"Give 'em some damn water!" the first mate shouts down from the tiller.

The sailors unlock the downed Kipchak from his shackles and stand with hands on their hips, thumbs locked into their belts. The boy does not move. They whisper, ending their words with a mutual shrug of shoulders. They unlock two boys from the bench beside them.

"Don't do anything stupid. Just take him up and then you come straight back down," one sailor says.

The two teenagers rise from their benches like old men and drag the boy to the ladder by his arms. They prop him against a beam. They each look up the ladder and then down at the limp boy. The sailors pull out their clubs and move toward them.

The Kipchaks place shoulders under armpit and crotch and wrestle the wilted body upward, the corpse's boot tips ticking each rung as they climb. Some of the Kipchaks stick their noses outside the craft, most face forward in a glassy-eyed daze, their minds numb with indifference.

A slender-faced sailor approaches with the water bucket hanging by a strap from his neck. He dips his long-handled ladle and reaches the dripping bowl across the bench. Ox cups it in his hands, pulling the water down in two swallows.

His oarmate is already asleep, maybe passed out. As the sailor redips, Ox palms Duyal by the back of the head with one giant paw and steadies the bowl with the other, tilting the weary head to accept the precious liquid. Duyal takes three swallows, but then stops with a choke. Ox wonders how the boy lives. No food or water has gone into him in a day, only the bile coming up.

The sailor turns to the next pair.

"Another," Ox growls.

The sailor stops, wincing from the slave boy's grip on his elbow. He dips the ladle once again and turns to see if he is noticed by his club-toting mates. Duyal pulls his head away in refusal. Ox grabs the bowl and downs it.

A grunt overhead and a splash. The young rower plunges unceremoniously into his ink-black grave, the second to die so far. A cask thumps the deck above Ox. The click of sharp heels.

"Ah, we'll always lose a few… uh yeah, tap this one too," the old man slurs, his voice clearly heard through the hatch.

A rap of hammer on oak. "Well, if you told me twenty-five years ago that I'd be running slaves, I'd a laughed in your face," the old man says, belching an exclamation. "Hell, my grandfather married into the Della Volta family and became a man of privilege. Ship owner, running Genoa to Acre. Back then, five families owned trade in the Levant—about all of it. My father bumbled in and grew his lot to six ships. Your father and I… we met on the *Padrona*, as young men like you, after my time in the navy. Gold and silver going east, spices, cloth, and dyes coming back home. God, I still hate the smell of nutmeg."

"The *Padrona*. I think I remember hearing that name," a younger voice says.

"Yep, yep—fill it all the way up. Yeah, your father and I would talk at the rail each night, just like this. Just like this… scheme of how we were going to run our own ship. Heh, heh. Well, we ended up doing just that. Saladin's romp through the coastal towns put an end to the advantage given my grandpa's favored class. From then forward, any lummox with a dream and the charm to convince investors was in the game. That competition nearly put my father into his grave. He eventually gave up the sea and became an agent in Cairo—that's where I met al-Salih, probably eight years ago."

He slaps the rail. "But your father and I. Hell, we weren't afraid. Took our shot, got our ship. Mostly moved Stamford wool, dyed in Genoa. Brought back brazilwood, pepper, cotton, indigo, incense, cinnamon. Anything. Everything. But it was al-Salih that got us into running military slaves."

"Al-Salih… right, right. I remember my father speaking his name. Why slaves?"

"Because the damn Venetians locked up most of the Eastern Med. Bastards. Your father and I were only about a month away from losing our ship to creditors, when al-Salih convinced us to start moving slaves across the Black Sea. Sold the big ship and bought three galleys. Pure luck that al-Salih was pushed to Hisn Kayfa—with another vault of silver to spend on Kipchaks. His merchants already knew us. We were in. Their preferred source. Our sunset tour."

"Do you see a future in it?"

He belches. "The slave trade?"

"Yeah."

"Tsst. Even if the Syrian princes stop fighting each other, it's only a matter of time before they turn their Mamluks on the crusading armies. No truce will last. The Mamluks are the backbone of every army in the Levant. And the princes only put the first generation of Kipchaks into their royal regiments—so they need a constant supply of them. I suppose the princes figure Mamluk offspring in Syria and Egypt grow up too much like their own people—a little soft. It's brilliant, really. Fill your elite ranks with those raised harshly. Well, it's worked for us—hell, we haven't carried ballast heading south in four years. So much silver to be made."

Ox nudges Duyal. "Are you hearing this?"

His benchmate snores.

Ox sighs. "Ehh, I'm on the wrong side of this business."

"But why would the princes go to the trouble and expense of bringing these boys all the way from the Asian steppe, when they have boys in their own lands who could be trained?" the young man asks.

The old man laughs. "Why hope you can train the soft to be hard, when you can buy the hardy on the relative cheap? Listen, most Muslims on the Med distance themselves from politics, from their rulers. Their faith is mainly in the *umma*, the community of Islam and its ideals. Even if the princes wanted to fill their ranks with their own people, these folks wouldn't willingly send their sons to the military—to be slaughtered in petty wars waged more against fellow Muslims than infidels, like you and me. With the spread of Islam north and east to the steppe, the Islamic royals have access to better stock. Kipchaks. Lots of 'em. These boys below—even when full grown men—they'll endure unthinkable miseries for their prince. Miseries your typical Arab soldier would never consider."

"But wouldn't allies, or even hired mercenaries still win battles for less silver spent?"

"Well sure, and that happens. But think about it... any ally has at heart largely his own country's interests. And mercenaries—they can't see much past the jingle in their purses. Are these the men you would want surrounding you in battle? Are these the men you would place in your royal guard?"

"I suppose not."

"The Kurds, even the Bedouin auxiliaries, they can't always be relied upon when things get the ugliest. But the slave soldier, the lad born on the steppe is a different animal. Most in Genoa have no comprehension."

He lowers his voice. A cup clanks the rail. "It's frightening what these boys will become, how devoted they will eventually be to their patrons... I sometimes wonder if I drink to deaden the reality of my sin. That I grew rich while arming the wrong religion with the most lethal of weapons. Kipchaks. Hopefully God has his head turned the other way."

"Yeah, hopefully for both of us… and my father. God rest his soul."

"Yeah. All the while, the Muslim princes hold their places in heaven. You see, Islam not only provides Jihad as justification to take up arms, but also holy laws to validate enslavement. The Sharia forbids Muslims from enslaving Muslims and Christians both. But the Kipchak boys. Hell, they're nonbelievers. Pagans. The princes can chain 'em en masse, without even raising Allah's eyebrow. I'm telling you, the whole thing is genius. Really."

The old man forces a fake chuckle. "Must be nice to arm yourself with the best of weapons to destroy the enemy of your religion, while saving your soul in the process… we have no such luck. But no matter. Remember, it was the crusaders who pushed us out of the Levant. We had to trade somewhere."

"That's right. You think the silver will stay with this trade, right?"

"There he is… your father showing through. Enough of the philosophy, the theology, the musings of an old man. The trade, back to the trade… we pulled more dinars nine years ago, but it's still hard to beat. Your father and I used to pay thirty, even sixty percent on the routes to Syria. On this route, I'm only paying eighteen. Less risk means lower interest on sea loans and fewer shareholders, cheaper insurance. Your father might have told you—lenders like the boring runs, the short routes. I can see the end of my career. But you could double our fleet—fill that damn harbor before the Venetians do."

"What about the Mongols?"

"What about them?"

"They control every port on the north shore now. Will they always be so cooperative?"

"I don't know they're that cooperative now. They abolish the port duties, want every market wide open. The Great Kahn, Ogodei. He knows he has to keep a steady flow of goods eastward to stay in power. Problem for us is open markets cause more Venetians to slither into the Black Sea, driving down our prices. Mongols don't care much about price."

"Why would the—"

"Main thing right now—the Mongols are just capturing too many Kipchaks. I guess they figure each Kipchak boy sold into the Middle East is one less adult they may have to beat down years later on the steppe. Take the older ones into their own army, sell some... kill some. Yeah."

A long burp. Scuffing heels back to the keg.

"The Mongols aren't the problem. The true crooks in the business are the Turkish and Syrian merchants on the south side of the sea," the old man says.

"How's that?"

"I'm forced to smell this lot of pigs day in and day out and deal with the Mongols, while the middlemen just cater to the whims of the sultanate. And shuffle scrolls. All they have is the relationship with al-Salih's amirs. It was better when we dealt with al-Salih directly. That's the downside of him being in Hisn Kayfa. He's too far away. These merchants add little, only shrink our takings."

"Hmm... what will we make on these?"

"It's set. Eighty dinars apiece. Below is a prime lot—most will become military slaves. If they were sick... or older, or not from the steppe, they'd be sold farther south as ordinary slaves and we might only get thirty. It pays to know your type of Saracen and how to spot one that's ailing, or they'll fleece you on the south shore. Stick with Kipchaks—damn good stock."

"So the future… should we plan to make up for the low prices in greater quantity?"

He chuckles. "Not we. My days are numbered. Low price is another reason for this old salt to get out. But if I was you, I'd look at another galley or two soon. Price won't be low forever. That's what your father would've done. That's probably what he'd want you to do." The old man grunts, then belches. "I miss him."

"Yes… who do we meet in Trabzon?"

"The Turk—Bozkurt." The old man spits. "He thinks he outsmarts me. He's mostly a thief."

"Hmm."

"Just another who's in with the amirs. Al-Salih has gotten where he puts too much faith in these peddlers. No matter… I already have Bozkurt's silver for this load. I'll be giving him a little surprise to get his attention."

"Surprise?"

"Let's just say I doubt he'll be making his markup on this lot. We'll let him squirm in front of al-Salih's amirs with a ship full of skinnies… by God, haven't they rested long enough? Piper!"

Silver. Ox lingers on the word. He yearns for it. He remembers the dusty rider from the west arriving at his aunt's ger. The man raising the scuffed flap to reveal a leather bag filled with it. Upon the coins, the simple letter from his cousin. The smiles. The tears, shed in realization of needed goods that would soon be theirs, of sheep and cattle to be bought and bred. He tries to grasp all that was said topside.

"Deploy your oars!" the piper says. "Refasten oarloops!"

His stomach protests. He is ravenous, feels his body eating away at itself. The bastards again did not bring them an evening meal. He eyes the thin-armed boy across the passage. When the hard bread is passed out next, he will take this boy's, daring him to snitch. And then beside him, the pathetic youth sharing his own oar. Good chance that Duyal will be too sick to finish his next meal. More bread. How is this boy still able to pump his legs. Ox had never met one of these wretches in person, those ragged boys occasionally shot on the edge of the herds; those of little means from over the hills, tempted to snake a sheep or two at low light.

He recollects a young bandit from a year or so ago. The one who took two arrows at nightfall, but managed to crawl away in the dark. Tracking the next morning was easy work. They followed the beaver trail of blood, a chest-wide alley of matted grass and crimson, preserved by the night air. Over each hill, they expected to find the body bloating in the sun, but the beaten grass eventually turned to the bent stalks made by footsteps, until once reaching the river, the sign of tracks and blood disappeared altogether to the north.

He had hated those raiders, more clever than wolves, known also to sneak in close and slit the throat of a watch-man. And now he is surrounded by them. How could louses like these become soldiers, much less amirs, or part of a royal guard? Ah well, perhaps the future payoff in silver and land and stature will be worth the poor company. He looks down at the matted hair beside him, strangely hoping this one will survive.

"Ready to row!" the piper calls.

"Just rest on the oar for a bit, or I'll smash your melon," Ox says to Duyal.

Duyal leans forward, arches his back in preparation for the command. "Fuck yourself. I'll pull my share."

Ox fixes his grip on the oar. He shakes his head and smiles. For some reason he likes this scoundrel.

CHAPTER
15

Duyal
South coast of Black Sea, port town of Trabzon
July 29, 1236

Duyal climbs the ladder on shaky knees, grasping the rungs with swollen fingers, his knuckles feeling as if filled with the same putrid salt water that slops against the galley's sides. Nearing the top, the sunshine scorches his eyes. He buries his head in the soaked shirt to his front, placing his hand on a shoulder to shuffle forward. The drum of weary feet on deck.

He draws deep breaths, wishing to purge the nausea from his gut. A breeze blows across his wet hair and salt-crusted rags, his temporary blindness only accentuating the sweetness of grass mixed with the air's brackish scent. Sailors line the rails, prodding the edges of the bunched mass as they would mindless sheep, keeping them tight, driving the Kipchaks starboard. He shields his eyes, squints to see.

Sheer cliffs and rounded hills surround the circular bay, with wood and mud-built structures dotting the higher ground in all directions. A sand-colored building with high rounded tower dominates the thickest conglomerate of them. Dots of people pour out of the place, making their way down a beaten walkway, dust from their feet pushing west. Farther yet are steep hills of white pine and birch, patched with sun-burnt grass.

The gangplank drops on a flat piece of ground, the galley docked along a rock-strewn spit protecting the harbor town. Ships of the red cross on one side, opposed by galleys of the blue-lioned flag on the other. He feels the push from behind, the flock of boys anxious to be rid of the ship and sea. One at a time, they wobble down. A boy trips and falls on his side, his leg dangling above the sloshing sea; another grasps his belt and pulls him to his feet.

At the bottom, a man counts them with the point of his stick. With sailors on their flanks, they straggle across a cargo-laden pier, clogged with men moving crates and bundles of fine cloth. The white-capped men move drearily, unloading goods from the holds of two ships.

The first full light in days reveals in earnest the entire lot of his fellow Kipchaks for the first time. Their cheeks suck into faces, their arms hang thin from tattered tunics. The red slashes of worn paint on heads and shoulders appear as if each boy absorbed an identical blow on the back of the skull. Most wear no boots and filthy trousers. Nearly all share a maroon stain on the bottom of their right pant legs, where the shackles broke skin.

A boy still possessing boots steps on skin soles, his leather uppers flapping as he walks. Another wears a deep wound on his upper arm, leaking thick cherry-black blood into his tunic. Beside him, a youth bears a wide slit across his forehead, his matted hair embedded deep into the wound. An emptiness swells inside of Duyal. He sees little of the warrior in them, nothing but broken sons of once-proud nomads.

A white-bearded man in a turban arrives out of breath. Reaching them, he stops, his mouth dropping open. Following the lead sailor, they glide past him like a slow current around a boulder. Most seem to notice little more than the man's leather shoes and clean white stockings, their eyes resolved to convey meekness.

Duyal looks up at the wrong time, meeting the man's attentive eyes. They fix upon him, reading of pity. Duyal wants none of it from him. The man raises a lip, narrows his left eye, the sad blue in it transforming to fire. Not wanting to challenge him, Duyal averts his glare, setting his eyes upon his own bile-splattered tunic and tattered trousers.

When all have passed the gray-cloaked merchant, the man moves quickly back to their front, motioning for the captives to make their way to the shade of four great pines, where several covered carts sit. As the boys settle under the trees, the man turns and with purposeful strides of a man twenty years his junior, stomps his way across the pier and up the bowed ramp of the ship.

Red-faced, he reaches the captain and business partner on the top deck, squaring himself between the two. The merchant rants, flailing his arms and pointing back at the boys under the trees. Unfazed, the drunk captain smiles, looks to the young man beside him, laughs. The old men exchange heated words, mostly muted by the distance and splash of wave on rock. All sixty-one Kipchaks in the shade observe the tirade indifferently.

"What's the use in screaming, bearded one? Throw a punch," a boy says, seated with arms over knees.

"Yeah, beat the ass of the prick who starved your precious goods," Ox says.

"Better yet, just give me the chance and I will do it for you," Demir says.

Ox looks at Demir blankly for a moment and then breaks into a hearty laugh, patting the thick-armed Kipchak on the back.

Most sit straight-faced, taking in their surroundings. They stare at the carts nearby, where three barefooted boys and two leather-faced men sit with their backs against the wheels, uninterested in the Kipchaks' arrival. Only the men speak to each other in soft voices, their lips hardly moving. An old woman sits separately, atop a cart, looking over the newly arrived with forgiving eyes. A group of Turks sit farther back, strung bows in hand. Ten sailors encircle the boys, some tapping clubs in palms, daring the youth to run. Several without clubs scan the faces that pass nearby, nodding, waving on occasion to acquaintances.

Duyal eyes the skinny alleys, traces a route up to a saddle in the mountains, using the cover of the buildings and suitable terrain. A way congested with people and cargo. He must seek the right time. Perhaps at night, or maybe whenever this place is busiest. He memorizes his chosen course, the lay of the paths, the mountain tips in all directions that would remain visible at night to help guide him. The sky looks to remain clear; the moon would already be high in the sky by nightfall.

He tries to calculate the number of days since he was captured, but is unable. So many enemies between here and the Volga country, even if he could find his way back. But surely he could disappear from this place. The sailors would not stay here. There would be bread to pilfer; a stray dog to kill and eat. He could pummel a local boy and take his clothes to better blend with the natives. If he was lucky, there would be a pony to steal. He could escape to the grassland, far from the port. There had to be others in the hills like himself, those who'd also made a break.

On the galley, the young man standing beside the elder Genoese takes a step forward, fumbling with a scroll.

He makes calming motions with hands as he speaks, tracing symbols on the scroll for the older men to see. The conversation takes on the youth's politeness for several moments, but then erupts again. The young man rolls up the document and mopes his way aft to sit on a crate.

The merchant steps away in anger. "Just keep the silver! Get out of my slip, you worthless louse!"

The old captain cracks a sloppy smile. "You think you're the only trader in Trabzon? The arrogance!"

"Bah! None will deal with you when I'm finished!" The merchant descends the gangplank, griping to himself.

The captain raises his mug in a mock toast from the rail, smirking, while the merchant returns to the tree line. Upon the gray beard's approach, the workers around the carts get to their feet, stand with hands behind their backs. The frazzled man nods to them. They remove the tarps from the carts, spreading two on the ground. The young workers remove buckets and reach for wooden ladles. The old Turks set crates and baskets atop the tarps. The woman eases down from her cart, putting a leather bag across her back.

The merchant motions with his hands for the Kipchaks to gather around him. "Come, Come." Seeming to detect the sailors' wish to leave, he says, "Yes, yes go ahead. We're fine here, thank you." His eyes narrow, sending an unspoken order of vigilance to the archers, who now move closer. He takes a deep breath and looks at the Kipchaks with furled brow, as if trying to recall the faces of long-lost relatives. "Please. Come closer."

Duyal examines the deep wrinkles scored below the man's turban, the pattern emerging again on his tanned neck. Folded across his chest are large hands, but strangely free of dirt or grime under nail. His thick beard is coarse as the tail of a deer and nearly as white. Most of the boys ignore him, engrossed with the growing feast being spread upon the tarps behind him.

"My sons, you are in the port of Trabzon, in the Empire of Trebizond. My name is Bozkurt. I work with the amirs of al-Salih, a fine prince south of here, in providing recruits for their military regiment. I'm here to look after you. We'll talk more later. For now, eat, drink, rest. We must be well for the final leg of your trip." He opens one arm, motioning for them to move toward the Turks, their round bread loaves and fruit baskets evenly spaced across the edge of the covers.

Noticing the Kipchaks' apprehension, Bozkurt dips a bowl into the water and drinks, wiping his sleeve across his beard. He then grabs an apricot from a handcart and takes a bite. He nods at them. "It's good. All of it. Please eat."

One Kipchak steps forward. Another. Then in mass they descend upon the goods.

Duyal heads for the water and drinks a full bowl. He looks above the hills and thanks the Great Sky for getting them to dry ground. He drinks another bowl and shambles to the back of the mob, which surrounds the food. As the line dwindles, he moves toward a cart heaped with loaves. A young boy atop the rail breaks a loaf in half and hands it to Duyal, as if feeding a wild animal. Beside the fruit cart, only two bruised apricots remain in the last basket. He grabs them both and turns. The tiny Kipchak, Erol, steps forward, peering into the empty baskets.

Ignoring the grumble in his stomach, Duyal throws him an apricot.

"Thanks," Erol says. "I don't think I can eat yet anyhow. Half my gut is on the bottom of that ship."

"Yeah. I hope ship is not the way this al-Salih moves his army," Duyal says.

Erol smiles. "Yeah, I hope he has a large herd of ponies."

Duyal nods.

Erol's lips tighten. "Are you scared?"

Duyal takes his eyes off the treetops, looks about the feeding boys, and meets Erol's eyes.

"Yes, my friend. I'm scared. Anyone saying different is a fool or liar." He walks away, picking the farthest pine, where the giant Ox munches an apple, a full loaf of bread stuffed under the big boy's arm. Accustomed to sitting next to no other, Duyal joins him. Demir, also wandering about the mass of boys, comes over to them. He throws himself to the ground with a groan.

Ox spits out a seed. "You see? They will now begin feeding us like soldiers deserve to be fed." He palms the loaf and rips off a large piece with his teeth, smiling with a half-chewed wad in his cheek.

"Seems to me a soldier's meal would be meat, not bread. This meal is fitting for the slaves they aim to make of us," Demir says.

"You wish to be back on that galley eating nothing? Or on the steppe trapping rats? This will be the best thing that ever happened to you," Ox blurts through a mouthful. "Soldier, not slave."

"Slave soldier. You enjoy your bread, slave—there'll be more of it to come," Demir says.

Ox snorts through the hard crust, shaking his head. "A bunch of worrywarts. A bunch of damn girls."

Duyal watches Bozkurt. He tries to read the man. The bearded one puts his hand on the old woman's back and then points out five or six Kipchaks from the group. She nods and then walks to the first with her bag and a smaller bucket of water. She sits beside the Kipchak with the infected arm and speaks to him, points at her bag. He removes his tunic with a grimace and she begins to clean his wound. She blots it dry and then scrapes salve from a small board, smearing the thick oil upon his gash. She finishes by tying off the end of a wrapped bandage.

Another cart rolls up, towed by a fine ox. Bozkurt directs its contents to be offloaded. He grinds a fist into his palm and looks over the heads of the boys like a nervous hen. A robed herder arrives with seven goats. Bozkurt looks over each animal before reaching into his purse to pay him.

"Meat? You asked for meat, grumbler? There's your meat," Ox says.

Demir, lying flat with hands laced behind his head, opens one eye. Duyal forces down the bread, hoping it will settle his queasiness, knowing that he must eat to gain strength for his escape. He grows tired. He must rest for a short while. Just a small nap to sharpen his mind. He leans his head against the rough bark and closes his eyes.

The rock of the ship will not leave his head, still moves the ground beneath his buttocks. Is this some scourge of the great sea? Will this miserable sensation ever leave him? He breathes in the familiar smell of dried pine needles. It soothes him, calms his stomach.

Duyal tossed the rope over the stout pine branch and flipped the tail end to his brother. He and Gozde then hauled the dressed buck up by his antlers. They stood back, admiring their morning's work.

"You're a lucky little prick. You couldn't make that shot again to save your life," Gozde said.

"Shit, somebody had to take it."

"You mean steal the shot."

Duyal laughed. "Right, right. You felt that breeze switching from the east and didn't raise your bow. Scared, I figured. If I had waited any longer for you, he'd still be running with our scent in his nostrils."

"Those branches blocked any shot I had."

"Of course. Of course."

Gozde smacked him across the back of the head.

Duyal laughed, walked around the animal. He grabbed a leg to steady it, ran his hand across the stubbly coat, just turning prime. He lay down, propped up by elbow, looking up at the open ribs. He belched the taste of the animal's blood, smiled contently. "You better sleep for a bit. You'll need to be sharper tonight, if you want to match this animal."

"Shit."

"Doubt there's two like it. Girls see this one and it could be all over."

Gozde rolled over, chuckled. "Ride in with a buck like this, you might finally get a look from Husnu's daughter."

They both laughed. Duyal spun to his side, released one last chuckle, the scent of fresh pine needles beneath him.

A scream startles him. He reaches instinctively beside his right thigh for his bow. It is not there. A flood of alarm goes through him. Where is his weapon? Where did he leave his weapon? He sits up, his anxiety diminishing only gradually as he realizes where he is and the fact that he has not had his bow for many days.

Across from him, Erol's head moves as if on a swivel. The lad huffs. The tiny one closes his eyes and tries to compose himself, appearing also to have finally comprehended his true location. Whatever just happened was only a nightmare. His eyes fill with tears, and he shakes his head with pursed lips.

"It's all right, my friend. It was only a dream," Duyal says.

"No… I wish it had only been a bad dream," Erol says, shrinking back into a ball, turning his face to the tree bark.

Strangers. Miserable strangers sprawled all around him. Duyal's heart empties. The familiar unease percolates back into him. He mumbles to himself, "Lazy fool." He has slept the entire afternoon. About him most of the boys snooze;

several sit cross-legged, talking in small groups. On the edge of the pines, a group of men stand with their hands on hips, chatting as they occasionally rotate the line of goats simmering on individual spits over smoldering coals. A group of women dice fresh vegetables on the open end of their ox carts, four more having arrived while he slept. They shoo flies. His stomach gurgles.

The old woman with the bag approaches Duyal. She must have been waiting for him to awaken. Through stained teeth, she smiles and nods. Like most of her people, her skin and eyes are dark. Her high cheekbones narrow to a delicate chin. Only small folds of skin about her jowls and streaks of gray tell her age. As a younger woman, she must have been stunning. She points to his ankle and raises her eyebrows in question. Duyal nods. She dips her cloth into the clean basin, wrings out the excess, and begins washing the dirt from the torn skin around his ankle. He ignores the pain, noticing the fresh bandages on the wounds of his shipmates.

"What will they do with us?" Duyal asks.

She looks up from his abrasion, her eyes finding the location of Bozkurt. Seeing his back is turned, she squares her eyes on his. "Many different things will happen to each of you." She looks back down at her work.

"But will they make us soldiers, as the bearded man says?"

"That will not be your worry. Allah has already chosen those among you who will be his fighters." Her face grows stern with the words.

"Who?" Duyal asks.

She smiles, the patience of a mother coming back to her eyes. "God. The great one." She points upward with conviction. "It is already written. There is very little now for you to do."

CHAPTER
16

Cenk
The citadel, Hisn Kayfa
July 31, 1236

Cenk tips forward. On the front bench sit his fellow thirteen graduates. Tan, block-jawed faces. Rigid trunks shrouded in the white summer coats of the regiment. Palms resting identically on the gold-colored trousers of the *Salihiyya* Mamluks. He grins. They appear flawless in the dress uniform of those who serve al-Salih Ayyub.

He sits back, the taut summer wool and tightly bound threads holding his back straight, the stiff collar holding his head high. Yet he would have held himself as such without the assistance of the fabric, feeling content to be seated with a group as athletic and talented as these.

He reflects on those who did not graduate, more a result of recurring injuries than inability, as all forty-nine Mamluks invited to the elite class were handpicked by the senior amirs, all capable of passing the rigorous training. He reckons it was partly the will of God that pushed forward only fourteen, those now entrusted by al-Salih to soon lead as many new tulbs, units of fifty comprising the prince's *Mutaʿallim*, young Mamluks under training.

He looks forward to the next several moons, when Kipchak recruits will start trickling in, filling up the training tulbs, one by one. Once the boys from the steppe are finished with their initial indoctrination, he and his fellow *Muʿallim*, along with the weapons instructors, will teach them the *Furusiyya*—the Mamluk's cavalry doctrine. He knows the text nearly by heart, is able in many places to recite verbatim its guidance in employing the weapons of their craft. Aside from the Koran, no book is more revered by the *Salihiyya*.

A pair of Mamluks waddle into the assembly room on stiff knees, having just dusted off their woolen coats and put a brush to worn boots. Dirt remains etched into the lines of their brows; bags droop below their glassy eyes. They nod to mates not seen in several moons, taking seats behind the new instructors on aligned benches.

While all surely understand the importance of this event and the critical position the young men in the front bench will hold, Cenk knows that most come just to see their patron's face and to wisely keep theirs in front of him. And of course those who have been criticized for any lack of mission effectiveness surely want the prince to see fatigue in their faces and grime on their coats, proof of their diligence in executing his assigned security patrols.

Though it is extraordinary regarding those who make the effort to attend the graduation, it is equally as remarkable who is not in attendance—those from the prince's Kurdish cavalry. Incredibly, not a single Kurdish horseman resides at the citadel in Hisn Kayfa; no Kurd but the senior amir, Husam al-Din, and al-Salih will attend the ceremony today. Cenk sees this as a clear indication that the Kipchaks are truly the future of al-Salih's regiment.

But Cenk has no sympathy for the few Kurdish horse-men stashed in Amid, fully grasping what it feels like to be a foreigner. He is certain the other thirteen on his bench rep-resent the most capable of the junior ranks in the prince's regiment, yet he holds little attachment to his peers. Perhaps it is partly because he could not be more different than the others: they are mostly from the rolling grassland, whereas Cenk is from the mountains. Their skin is light, his is dark; they watched over flocks as youth, he hunted continuously. They grew up speaking the fast Turkish dialect of the Kipchak, while he spoke the thick tongue of the Bashkirs. Shit, he may as well be a Kurd.

Yet for the good of the corps, these disparities could be overlooked. They often were. As was the mantra during their training—"All *Salihiyya* Mamluks bleed the same scarlet of their master."

Needless to say, this motto does not hold up to a force more powerful. It always comes down to the *Khushdash,* the solidarity and loyalty among comrades in common servitude and manumission, the bond of those who shared both years of training and the same nominal release from slavery.

With the exception of Cenk, all in the instructor class received their initial training together at the best citadel in the land, built by Saladin and known as *Qal'at al-Jabal*, or "Fortress of the Mountain." Conversely, Cenk trained at a dilapidated citadel south of Cairo, nicknamed *Bok Deligi*, or "shithole," by the sultan's elite Mamluks. This was a place where amirs of lesser means sent their novices to acquire battle skills. Early on, this was all Turkmani could afford, and Cenk certainly had not held it against his master.

Further, all graduates present, apart from Cenk, were pulled from the Kipchak steppe nearly seven years ago and count al-Salih as their only patron. They are fortunate. As one unit, these Mamluks made the four-year transition from frightened boys to polished warriors. They know everything about each other—which mate's bow fits their own hand, who farts the loudest, who is weakest on lance, whose bladder can hold piss the longest, where to strike the killing blow on each in a sparring match with any weapon. More importantly, they have an unbreakable fidelity toward each other, second only to al-Salih himself.

Being a *Sayfiya*, only recently gotten by al-Salih after Turkmani's death, and also having not endured the years of mutual hardship and resultant bonding in the same initial training class, Cenk is simply not one of them. Perhaps in principle because he has toiled through the four-moon instructor course with them and now shares the same master, their bond has tightened. But he is not and will never be a *Khushdashiya*, or blood brother, with these thirteen on the bench. So instead, Cenk feels he is an outsider, more of a grudgingly admitted stepbrother, especially to most of those seated behind him. He is a realist, knowing that his status will likely remain as such. This binds him all the more tightly to al-Salih. The prince is all he has left.

And fortunately al-Salih is a wise man. He is not just their patron, but also a genius at getting the most from each of his Mamluks. Unlike many princes throughout the Levant who utilize military slaves, this son of the sultan knows that battle-tested *Sayfiya*, in the hands of a leader who respects them and their military talent, is the quickest way to gain men of unquestioned loyalty.

Cenk feel eyes upon him. He looks behind and right. Ekrem, the archery master, gives him a nod of congratulations. Cenk returns a tight-lipped smile of admiration, lowers his head slowly in thanks to the man who helped him tweak his form with the bow.

He closes his eyes feeling thankful, as he could have been discarded, tossed in a senior amir's ranks, buried forever in obscurity. Instead, he has been plucked by the best prince, one owning the charisma that draws in all men. Al-Salih. Should he be surprised of the prince's magnetism, considering al-Salih's great uncle was Saladin the Great, founder of the Ayyubid Dynasty? Due in large part to Saladin's effort, the empire now stretches across Egypt, Syria, part of Jazira, Lesser Armenia, and a good part of the North African Coast.

Sure, the domain is a little messy, the Sultan al-Kamil forced to act more like a big brother of sorts, collecting reluctant allegiance from his relatives in the various Ayyubid provinces. But compared to its neighbors, Ayyubid rule is still strong and established; they are the major force in the Middle East.

And of course al-Kamil will not live forever. Cenk figures that all present today feel their master represents the future leadership of the empire. Al-Salih is the strongest bull from the most royal blood. To a man, they would throw themselves from the citadel's ramparts without question if ordered to do so by their prince. Of this, he has little doubt.

"All rise for the glorious al-Salih Ayyub!" the personal scribe of the prince shouts. His master's name bounces off the vaulted stone ceiling, adding further eminence to the man. Bench legs yelp in unison, leaving only the soft patter of their master's soles as the prince strides across the cobbled aisle, bisecting his men, who stand straight, their hands locked to their sides.

"Please, please be seated," the prince says as he reaches the front bench. The tall man's warm eyes absorb the whole room in an instant.

Cenk smiles. His master appears vibrant, his eyebrows raised high, his jaw muscles tense in anticipation of addressing those most valuable to him. Aside from his close-cropped beard, his face is cleanly shaven, his bronze skin shining a healthy glow. Parallel creases from daily worries stripe his master's dark forehead, disappearing into a white turban.

Cenk surmises it was the black skin of al-Salih's slave mother that may have saved him, when Cenk was chosen to serve here, in the citadel. For surely only a prince with dark skin would overlook Cenk's color, pulling him into his fold at a time when all seemed grim. How many Mamluks of non-Kipchak origin can say they have been reeled back into the circle from obscurity not once, but twice in their lives? After Turkmani's death, Cenk's options were few. Only al-Salih and Allah's good graces allow him to be seated on this bench today. He will not let this opportunity be spoiled; he will not disappoint this prince, just as he never disappointed Amir Turkmani.

Just thinking of his name sends a twinge of pain to his soul. He misses the man dearly, his former patron, more a father than a commander. He pictures Turkmani. A yak's neck and thick skull, with those soft eyes set far into their sockets. Gentle eyes like al-Salih's, as if placed by God into a rugged warrior's face by mistake, by the creator who makes no mistakes.

He had always been astonished how a man so intense in battle, so bloodthirsty toward his enemies, could also be so kind, always knowing the right thing to say at the right time. "If they were all like you, Cenk, I would have little to worry about, eh, my son?" Turkmani had said in numerous instances, both of his hands set upon Cenk's shoulders. That sentence meant everything to Cenk, nearly made him cry each time he heard it. Never once in his childhood had he heard words like those. Every time, Cenk was forced to look down from his master's face, bite his lip to keep from blubbering. His previous patron was also dark-skinned and certainly spared Cenk from a life of misery five years ago, when Cenk was on the slave block. Without Turkmani, how easily Cenk could have become an animal tender or even a common slave, like most of the other dark-skinned captives gathered from the north. Yes, Turkmani, too, had rescued him. Somehow God was on his side.

"We gather to celebrate a graduation. Before us today are men who will soon be executing the critical task of making the next generation of God's warriors," the prince says.

All in attendance look down and murmur in private, "God is greater."

The prince raises his voice. "Within their training tulbs will not only be troops, who will shoulder lances and wield swords to destroy the enemies of Islam, but also amirs in the making, those who will guide this regiment into the future, securing the destiny of both Egypt and Syria. I ask all who sit behind these fourteen to embrace their crucial mission."

The prince looks directly at the graduates in the front row. "My sons, none will spend more time with our new brothers than you. None will do more to screen, train, and develop these youth. Always remember that I expect you to create not just warriors loyal to their patron, but warrior leaders, young men able and willing to step in and win battles, if their seniors should fall in the fight. Our Kipchak novices, future Mamluks, need to live up to the example of the brave who sit among us. How proud I am, as I look upon all in this chamber. Surely there is no better collection of warriors anywhere in the land of Islam." Al-Salih drops his head and clenches his lips, tries to hide from his Mamluks the tears in his eyes.

Cenk feels a surge of delight. These are not just words; their master speaks from the heart. Here is a man whose bloodline is second only to the Prophet Mohammad's in its contribution to the land of Islam, shedding tears for his own soldiers. Cenk loves it, loves him.

The prince looks up, the power returning to his speech. "For fifty-one moons we have been in the far north, detached from Mother Cairo. Lesser men would have pouted like children, or overindulged in the food, drink, and idle nature of this population. The irresolute would have sulked … yet in my sons the fire of the warrior glows as brightly as ever!"

Cenk whispers to himself, "My father, this is a tribute to your magic, not our discipline." He nods, as do those around him. What the prince says is true. Here is al-Salih's force, the *Salihiyya*, pushed more than a week's ride north of Aleppo by the sultan, steadily supporting their patron in the farthest reaches of the empire. And they do this eagerly, despite inadequate pay, monotonous patrol duty, and the stress of leaving their Egyptian fiefs, their *iqta*, at best unsupervised and at worst already in the hands of the sultan's own Mamluks. Cenk knows only a patron with al-Salih's magnetism could hold the unwavering confidence of his Mamluks in such conditions.

He realizes that while part of the Mamluks' conduct is pure loyalty, the *Salihiyya* are not completely selfless. They know that indirectly part of their monthly pay, or *Jamakiya,* goes straight to al-Salih's regular purchase of Kipchak slaves. Their father grows the family.

This sits well with the *Salihiyya*. They delay their greed, while the prince concurrently buys not only slaves of their own bloodline but also precious time, al-Salih waiting for his chance to exploit any instability in Cairo that would justify his pursuing the sultanate. Once back in Cairo as sultan, al-Salih would then elevate his Mamluks' status to "Royal Mamluk," rewarding them with not only the best assignments, but also with lofty pay from Cairo's fat treasury and vast grain-producing farms as *iqta*.

The prince treads before them, on the balls of his feet, eyes forward, as if stalking toward prey unseen. "The *Salihiyya* have shown their composition. You have held high our red-lioned pennant, not only protecting our gains in this land, but also improving our battle skills. You have shown trust in your father," al-Salih says to the dead-quiet room.

He turns, walks among them. "Keep faith, my sons. We will not be in the Jazira forever. Allah has picked us up and placed us here for a purpose. Here, God grants us gifts that we could not have possibly received in Cairo. Here, we operate independently, able to concentrate on training. We are closer to the steppe of your childhoods, the spawning ground of our regiment. In the next year, hundreds of raw Kipchaks will arrive to the citadel. And here, through the hands of these instructors, new Mamluks will be created."

Cenk looks again across his bench to the faces of his peers. Intensity fills their eyes. Resolve sets across their faces.

Pulling a stone arrowhead from his pocket, the prince holds it up for all to see. "Like those in your former towers, those skilled at turning rock blanks, crudely chipped by the hands of children, into sharpened arrow points, so we task these Mamluks before us in making Kipchak boys into Mamluks." The prince draws his hand across the row of new instructors. "I ask that you support each, for their chore will be as tedious as it is essential. Because when they have finished—from their pile of stones, they will have not just mounds of chipped rock flakes at their feet, but also baskets heaped with sharpened blades, which we will attach to our lances and arrows." He smiles.

Not one to water down his message, al-Salih nods to his scribe. The orange-robed man walks up with four others, two carrying over their arms fourteen black sashes, the sole designator of the *Furusiyya* instructor, or *Muallim*. The remaining men lug the gnarled staffs of the trade.

As the scribe calls forward each instructor, Cenk wishes his former patron could see him today. Amir Turkmani would have beamed with pride as once again his chance purchase from Bashkir country managed to overachieve. Clearly most present must recognize that today Cenk becomes the only Bashkir in memory to be given the honor of instructing young novices—an honor not only to himself, but also to his former people. Cenk feels he has defied the odds. He grinds his teeth. He will continue to outdo. Just as he outworked his peers in Cairo to gain prestige, advancement, and the approval of Turkmani, so he will do the same here—with double the fervor—for al-Salih.

To Cenk, regardless of its flaws, this is the true beauty of the Mamluk Corps—one of the key differences from a tribal life on the steppe. For with the *Salíhíyya* and most Mamluk armies, it is primarily one's ability and performance in battle which enables a man to gain wealth and prestige, not his bloodline. How many times in his homeland had he heard of a weak son inheriting the position as tower khan, only to stumble all over himself, to the demise of the tower? With the Mamluks, while good luck and the grace of God played their parts, it was nearly always the strong and talented who succeeded in the regiment. He only wanted a chance. And here it is in front of him, again.

Upon hearing his name, Cenk walks smartly and stops in front of al-Salih, locking his body at attention. He must exude confidence, look better than the rest of them. When indicated, he raises his arms. The scribe reaches around him, wraps the black piece of silk around his waist, the sash contrasting brilliantly with his white coat. The staff is thrust into his hand.

With sword clenched in hand, he pulled Turkmani into the protection of the jagged rock, the sleet blowing sideways. He cradled his amirate leader in trembling hands. His master smiled. "If only they could all be like you, my son." His patron again moved his lips, but this time his words were garbled.

Cenk pulled him close to his ear, so as to hear over the wind, the beat of hooves, the shouting. Only gurgles. He lowered the head of his master to his knee, looked at the ashen veil falling upon his patron's face. Amid the flying arrows, he glanced skyward and whispered, "No, no. What have we done?"

Turkmani's blood trickled across the dark hair on Cenk's forearms, saturating his yellow trousers with puddles of wet scarlet. Tears.

Their own ineptness had caused his death. While the arrows came not from Mamluk bows, it was his own men who had killed his father. And there, consecrated by his master's blood, he made the promise: "My father, oh, my father, I will make this right. I will make them better, cleanse the weak from our ranks."

Though the life had left Turkmani's eyes, Cenk knew his master heard him, if not in this life's form, then in the one drifting above him.

His eyes glass over as the silken knot is secured to his right hip. He faces left and marches away from al-Salih. He mumbles, "Oh my patron, oh my father. I will keep my promise, Amir Turkkmani. Now is my time. I will do this."

CHAPTER
17

Duyal
Anatolian steppe
August 3, 1236

A hawk banks and dives, tucking the tips of cream-streaked wings toward forked tail, hooked beak locked on target unseen. He flashes his back, a crescent of gray streaming toward earth. Spreading his wings, he hugs the slope on an invisible draft, his chestnut tail nearly ticking the yellowed kernels of grass. The hunter now motionless but speeding, silent save the hiss of air across feather. Death's shadow traversing the valley in oblique. He flares his wings, drops talons and snatches the wiggling fur. Laboriously climbing now, climbing.

Losing sight of the bird over the hill, Duyal returns his stare to the bobbing head of the captive opposite him. If only he too could be back hunting their own grass, his younger brother, Baris, at his side.

They sit with shoulders touching, the sweat from one soaking into the tunic of another. The musty odor of perspiration leaching through new cloth hangs in the air. Dust, stirred between the legs of the beasts, wells up into a floating powder, coating tan skin and hair with a layer of chalk, turning them into identical forms. Ashen-faced and at the mercy of the wrenching cart, they are but corpses, stacked upright to conserve space. Only mud sitting under swollen eyes gives indication that at least some of the silent cargo still carry a pulse.

"Haw!" The driver tugs his halter rope and cracks the lead animal low on the right shoulder with a wet slap, leaving a stain of cherry on the end of his lash. The ox succumbs, turning left to follow the other carts along the two-track. Duyal pushes backward against the weathered rail, providing some relief to his stiff back and battered ass. His action reminds the cadavers around him to take similar measures. Some sit on their hands, others cross legs, all in a futile attempt to buffer the jarring.

Up a hill. The groan of wheel. The clop of hoof on dirt. The ding of chain hook on staple. A dry cough. The front wheel slams into a rock, sending a boy catapulting over the rail. Duyal and three more are thrown forward onto the others. They unpile without a word.

A lad they call Ichami leaps over the side and takes a knee beside the motionless boy who landed flat on his back. He says a few words unheard, clasps the boy's hand, and brings him to his buttocks. Ichami makes a final remark, which makes the other boy shake his head and snicker. He brushes the grass from the stranger's tunic, rises and helps him to his feet. Reaching the cart, Ichami pushes the boy's ass back over the rail and takes his original place in the cart. Yawning, the thin-necked driver looks over his shoulder to check if his cart remains full. Seeing all is normal, he resumes his hunched position. They ramble southward.

"You know that skinny son of a bitch steers for the stones," Ox says, turning to Duyal.

Duyal leans forward to peer around the loud one's chest. To the front, four carts roll, jostling the heads of forty-plus Kipchaks side to side in ambivalent unity. Behind them, more carts, more boys and a train of bouncing cargo, secured with canvas and hemp. He licks the residue from his lips with dried tongue. The boy next to him blows snot into his hand, wiping the glob from palm to trouser leg.

On each flank of the caravan, six mounted Turks ride with bows stowed in leather cases. All on the west side have their backs to the carts, inspecting a flock of sheep and smattering of goats they pass. Earlier, when they had rumbled beside three teenage girls milking cows and another gathering dung, every guard had forgotten the train in their care.

He reaches down and peels the thick scab on his ankle from where the shackles once dug.

He should run off. He could hop the side and scurry to a hiding place without a single guard noticing. But like the others, he is no longer dragged south in chains or strapped to the carts with lashing, but rather teased into complicity. It does not sit well with him. He looks past the driver.

The muscles on the oxen's hindquarters expand and contract in dreary unison, entrancing him. Farther up the cart's dual tongues, swaying on its connecting rings, sits the round-edged beam, grinding necks to a raw pink. The rub of hard maple on sweating flesh churns a lather gone auburn from the rolling dust, this foam dribbling onto the bows clamped about the oxen's throats.

He sighs. Even the oxen would have the sense to flee, if freed from their restraints. But the riders they pull have lost this kind of judgment. The boys are like wild dogs, tossed just enough scraps near the women's fire to keep them following the moving camp. Just mongrels, preferring the easy meal provided by hand, rather than that gained by the hunt, until eventually they wander so far from their territory that there is no turning back. So it is.

He leans his shoulder against the rail and faces the direction of his homeland. Rocked drowsy by the sway of the cart, his head bobs, his vision blurs, turning the covered carts behind into brown blobs, until finally his eyes close. The cart drops into a hole, throwing Duyal's chin against another's shoulder. He spits out a small chip of tooth, rubs his tongue across the rough edge that remains.

Things could be much worse. He recalls the miserable winters and hungry springs on the steppe. How many times had he and Baris lay shivering for hours with bows, wishing a badger from his hole so his family could eat? But he would take that circumstance with no complaint right now. They at least had dictated their own destiny. Kill or starve.

Ever since they left the ship, Bozkurt has treated the boys well. During the two days at the port, he urged food and rest, like a caring mother. He took the time to speak with nearly every youth, trying to comfort each, as would a gentle grandfather. He even brought them to the pools of steaming water, enclosed in stone walls on the edge of town; there, he instructed them on bathing in the manner of the Turks. Upon departing the pools, they piled their clothes. A stinking mound of stained wool and chewed-up leather. In its place, each were given a pair of light trousers, soft-soled shoes, and an embroidered tunic, in the style of the local people. Duyal had turned to look at the pile of rags before leaving, a parting glance at the last shreds of Kipchak life. Gone.

Since winding over the roads southeast of Trabzon, past the tea plantations and up over the Pontics, every evening stop had been at a different tribe. In common to each was the reception given the gray-bearded slave trader.

Always there were smiles, tea, and the butchering of goats or sheep.

The new clothes on his back and consistently filled belly have put his mind off both survival and flight, leaving only thoughts of his extinct family and their grazing land to the far north. And he is probably not the only one with such thoughts. With long faces, the boys roll through landscape reminiscent of their homelands, their minds likely a twirl of decaying memories. For Duyal, every rolling hill and valley passed through in the Anatolian Plateau the last three days looks similar to another more adored feature back in their Volga country—*Net akis, Dik yuz, Ust duz.* He will never again see these cherished places, taste their waters, or see the bold rock faces.

He wonders what his family would be doing today if the Mongols had not come back. His folks would be making final preparations for the move to winter camp. He pictures his father and uncle up front on ponies, leading their small flock to the protected upland valley, a place where the roving bands would not suspect a tower to be wintering. Along with the yapping dogs, he and Baris would be working the flanks, pushing any stray sheep back toward the flock with long staff. His mother would be following with the other women, driving the ox cart filled with the family's possessions and the poles, frames, and felt sections for the family's gers.

The Mongols. Black Tartars. Before last moon, they were just specters, yellow-faced spirits from the past, who had unleashed their wrath over a decade ago, but disappeared eastward, as quickly as they had come. To Duyal, the Mongols had been only a distant subject of somber tales at fireside, rationale for why the younger Kipchaks must not shrug off their missed bow shots. Just a bundle in his mother's arms at the time of their first appearance, he had no recollection of them.

But his father, Gunes, and Uncle Besim never forgot. After 1223, the brothers vowed to never put themselves in

such a position again. They moved away from their traditional pastures. The tearless parting of the larger tower, as bands
of them dispersed across the grassland. From that point forward, Gunes' group was just six gers, what remained of two
close families. His father and uncle subsequently refused to
join their Kipchak allies in skirmishes against the southern
towers, or even take part in the larger western raids on the
Kievans. It was to be just them.

Duyal knew no differently. They lived always on the
fringes: the northern fringe of Volga territory; the fringe of
the steppe and mountain country. Living meal to meal, they
were often on the weary fringe between life and death. But
they knew which upland pastures held good grass, which distant neighbors would not act on a missing sheep or two. In
the summer, they hid higher in the mountains, where thin
topsoil made the grass sparse.

They fished, snared rabbits, ate mice, marmots—whatever bigger game they could stick.

As the Black Tartars preferred winter patrols, their
small tower made every effort to be an undesirable target.
Instead of making the fall season push downriver like most
nomads, toward milder climates, abundant game, and thinner
snow, Gunes' tower moved into upcountry plateaus, covered
in deep snow and too small for the larger Kipchak towers that
remained.

They splash across a small stream, taking him back to
the spring camp made by his small tower for two seasons.
Watered by a feeder stream of the mighty Volga and protected by a cliff from the northern wind, it was where the
survivors came after the winter camp. How they looked forward to that place, when the deadly winter was over and the
first green shoots of grass emerged from the snow-flattened
steppe. None of it matters now. They had been found, and
their tower is finished.

The carts bounce past a band of Turkish nomads. An olive-skinned girl in thin wool dress grabs her struggling brother by the shoulder to keep him from running toward the carts for a closer look. She pulls the giggling boy to the ground and lies on him. As the carts creak closer, the two sit up in the tall grass and gaze with wide eyes at the sixty-one light-skinned boys packed in like penned sheep. The kids lose their smiles. From the closed flap of a goat-skinned tent, a woman peers through an open sliver at the passing train. While the grass and animals of this country are much like the Volga country, the black-haired walls of their tents and dark skin of the people serve as stark reminders that this is not home.

If still alive, his mother and aunt would soon have been adding the second layer of felt, as autumn winds pushed a mix of rain and snow down from the high country, the felt then switching in function from provider of shade to insulator of heat. In just three moons, winter gales would bear down and the women would have added the third and maybe even the fourth wool layers to their rounded shelters. He yearns for the comfort of his ger, the smell of his mother's pot, the sound of a crackling fire, the cold wind blowing harmlessly against the tight wool walls.

He rekindles the faces of his mother and aunt. How long will the curves of their faces, the sound of their laughter stay fresh in his mind? The same hollowness fills him. Tears fill his eyes, and a sob bursts forth. Putting his head down between his legs, he pretends to cough roughly to disguise his weakness.

"No. I will become a Mamluk. I won't be holed up in some rich man's kitchen or be the sap digging tunnels under castle walls," Ox says, his massive thighs spread wide, unaware or unconcerned that he mashes a boy against the far rail. He slaps a cloud of dust from another Kipchak's shoulder.

Most ignore him. Ichami listens halfheartedly, the stout youth of such good spirit that even the most annoying fail to irritate him. Duyal raises his lip to the giant. He would throw an elbow across the Ox's face to shut him up, but realizes that such a blow would likely have no effect on the flatlander's thick skull. He considers it, caring little what damage the man-boy would inflict in retaliation. This goon acts as if being separated from his kin was a great prospect, that leaving his tower was somehow a burden lifted from his burly shoulders. Duyal does not understand it.

"Remember what the old man told us at the port? On board each galley are not only those who will protect the prince, but also some who will one day lead forty, or even an army of ten thousand," Ox says, leaning closer to keep Ichami's interest.

"Also on each ship are Kipchaks who will never again ride their ponies and hunt freely across the steppe, but instead will live in a mud house, serving food to a man of money and forced to wipe the asses of his offspring," Demir says, drawing the attention of several vacant faces near him.

The Ox laughs. "Mud house! Shit. Citadel, my friend. A citadel is where we will live."

"Slave in a small mud house, slave in a big stone house. What difference does it make?" Demir asks, dejectedly.

"Oh, here he goes again. It makes all the difference," Ox says.

"You seem to forget that we're gonna be slaves."

"Like you weren't already a slave to your father."

"At least there was an end to it."

"Shit. At least there will be soldiering to do, not sheep tending."

"So the misery will be over quickly."

"Tsst. Am I riding with future horsemen, or a bunch of whiny lasses?"

"We all might be doing girl's work before it's over."

Ox stands. "Hah! Look at the size of your arms, fool.

You think they haul your sorry ass across land and sea because they foresee your meat claws carrying goblets on silver platters? You won't think twice of your old pony, once you set eyes on the Mamluks' stallions." The giant shakes his head, examining a nugget dug from his nose before flicking it over his shoulder.

Demir looks down. Ichami reaches across to pat his thick arm, grins, and gives him a wink. Duyal lingers on the words. The spirit of his uncle would never rest if his nephew lived in house of mud or stone. Hopefully his uncle's spirit understood that each valley crossed, each day's progress south was another day's travel away from all that they and their ancestors knew. All going forward was to be strange lands and stranger people. It sits like a rock in his stomach.

He catches movement on the distant hillside. Three antelope lie hidden in the grass, each animal covering a different sector of vision. All three now stare at the carts through the brown stems. Will he ever go on another Saiga hunt? He drifts to those lessons learned with his uncle and brother, Gozde: of timing the antelope's migration pattern north to summer grazing, starting the hunts only when the gigantic herds dispersed into smaller family groups; of endless patience in scanning the distant grasslands for sign of cinnamon specks among the waving green; of plotting the day-long stalk, using every dip in the terrain, every bush, every bump in elevation to mask their slow pursuit, which always finished with a methodical crawl toward the male's pair of waxy-orange horns; of fall hunts and violent fights among rutting males for breeding rights; of winter hunts, draped in the white winter skins of the animals they shadowed; of fifty-pace shots made from their knees, or even seated on their buttocks; of bloody snow patches and slaps on the back; of self-punishment while searching for wayward arrows at dark; of high-pitched victory whoops when the hunters were first viewed from afar, carrying meat on their shoulders, Duyal suddenly forgetting his weary legs. Was it really all gone?

"You heard Bozkurt. The best of us will serve the son of the Sultan, al-Salih. Most of the others will be sold to the prince's amirs. We are slated to become horsemen, not housemaids. Remember, they came to find us. And I will be beaten dead before I am forced to serve some soft-handed merchant," Ox says.

"Maybe. But whether houseboy or slave to a prince, we will be the possession of a rich man for the rest of our lives," Demir says.

"Just let that rest. Damn… other boys in my tower have gone this path. Some sent back messages of cities visited, places conquered. A few fed their families from the booty for years. Like the gray beard said, Mamluks are royal slaves, part of the nobility," Ox says.

Nobility? Right. Duyal looks to the boys in their odd-fitting tunics, their empty, dust-covered faces. They seem more like vagrants, together cast upon the flow of a river over which they have no control. Each in the carts bets his life on the kind eyes and promising words of Bozkurt. Duyal hopes the silver-tongued elder speaks the truth.

The driver pushes through a flock of sheep, yielding a chorus of bawls from distressed lambs. He looks up, illogically expecting to see his brother, Baris, tending the flock. He sighs. Bozkurt gave him little hope.

"I have a brother named Baris. We were taken from the North Volga at the same time. Did he recently come through Trabzon?" Duyal asked.

Bozkurt squinted and looked up, trying to recollect what must have been thousands of Kipchak names and faces stored in his mind. He shook his head. "I am sorry. I have yet to come across a Kipchak since last moon with the name Baris. But that does not mean he is not at one of the other citadels." He raised his thick eyebrows in sincere hope. "You see, I'm not the only one carrying out this work."

The cart slams into a rut. He hears the crunch of flesh as his teeth inadvertently cut into his lower lip. As the warmth spreads across his tongue, he squints his eyes in thought. He must never forget these Mongols. It was they who killed his family and now occupy his people's land. It was they who separated him from his brother and took silver in exchange for his head. It was they who dealt with the Genoese and pushed him so far from his home.

He spits a red stream over the side. Maybe with these Mamluks he could get his revenge. With the tang of steel refilling his mouth, he wonders if the Great Sky chose this fate for him, the life of a soldier, a horseman. He sighs. He is a minder of sheep and shooter of varmints—what does he know of soldiering? And what other skills does he have that would be of use to those in the cities, if the prince does not want him? He is no tradesman, his hands incapable of crafting any good he has seen coming from the lands west.

He winces. Perhaps Ox is right. To those in the south, Duyal is at best a wicked bowshot and sturdy rider. At worst, he is a common laborer, suitable for use at any dismal task. If he is to be the property of another, he must find his way into the stone house, into this citadel. He must conceal the flaws in courage and skill he feels inside.

CHAPTER
18

Singer
Lower Volga River
August 4, 1236

Gray clouds hang low and damp over the valley, shrouding the hilltops around them, trapping the smoke that rises from sluggish Mongol fires. The mist that covered them all day with tiny droplets has lifted slightly, exposing in the west a glowing ball of orange burning its way among the dark-headed clouds. Far to the southwest, veins of lightning stab at the blackness in silence.

Singer limps to the fire of his mate and drops his saddlebag. Wet wood hisses its dissension in the oversized blaze. Beside the fire, three blackened pots sit half-filled, their dented covers leaking steam. He pulls off his deel and snaps the spray away from his friend. Folding the coat once, he sets it on the giant log beside his hat. Ferdi takes a sip, then hands him the steaming wooden cup. Raising his hands to the warmth, Singer sighs, sending a plume of smoke and mist curling. "Ah, you'll make someone a good woman one day."

"Piss off."

"Could almost stir this air."

"Yep."

Singer wraps both hands about the cup, savoring the bitter scent of the brew before sipping. He leans against the log and tries to rub the tenderness from his knee. "The nick getting worse on that mare?"

"Nah, looks to be healing up. Your salve worked."

"Good, good."

"She's still ornery as ever."

"Seems to run pure through them."

A breeze picks up. Ilker staggers in, dumps a load of half-rotted pine branches and plops down between his mates. Singer pushes the cup of tea into Ilker's hands.

"Thanks. Hope this wind pushes the wet away," Ilker says.

"Yeah."

Singer snaps off a branch and uses it to drag out the three stones positioned in the blushing coals. He pulls down his sleeve, grabs a hot rock, taps it to remove the heavy ash and slides it into the first pot. He repeats the process with each stone. He snatches two handfuls of dried meat from his saddlebag and dumps an even amount into each pot. He covers them, pushing them a touch closer to the embers.

Four fires away, a Mongol pretends to stir his broth, clanking his pot twice. The Kipchaks do not turn, but heed the warning, keeping the topic of conversation focused on their ponies and weather.

Through the hazy dusk, their barrel-chested company commander strolls behind the unit, his hands clenched behind his back, as if dutifully checking on the welfare of his men. While the crackling glow of a dozen fires, the aroma of stewing meat, and quiet banter of the men make for inviting stops, Chuluun stays to the edge of them, keeping his ear to the chatter about the fires. He passes behind the Kipchaks, looking in the opposite direction, continuing down the line.

"Look at the poor bastard," Ilker whispers.

"Yeah. Not exactly looking forward to his chat with Vachir, I'm guessing," Ferdi says.

Singer shakes his head. The events of last week have torn at the *zargun*. Murmurings of fault and "what-ifs" have drifted through the evening camps each night like the stench from a rotted carcass. "If Chuluun had not split the force, the rebel strike might not have been so effective. If our *arban* had not been held in reserve, none of it would have happened… "

As it was, last week the Mongols laid nine bodies on the rolling hills overlooking the Volga, the Mongols sickened that ravens from a foreign land would pick clean the bones of their brothers, rather than those creatures from their native country. Of the twelve Mongols who were injured, seven of the seriously wounded were piled into carts for a slow trip west to the large camp of Batu Kahn. There, Russians taken from their homes and skilled in the ways of medicine will be forced to treat their wounds.

The loss has been significant. The Mongols still mourn their dead comrades; the unit's fighting capacity has been diminished. One of Chuluun's squads of ten has but four men sitting by their fire this night, the spirit banners, or Mongol *sulde,* of each parted warrior now stand in their place. Against the blue-gray skyline, six staffs, wrapped in leather and bronze, rise in solemnity in front of this *arban's* bivouac. Clusters of tied ponytail catch a gust and flutter in unison, intertwining the hair from one warrior's favorite pony with that of his dead brother's.

Those in their *arban* will carry these spirit banners until the campaign is done, all the while welcoming the wind that transfers power from the *sulde* to the spirit of the deceased warrior. Once home, the banners will be given to the families of the fallen and posted in front of each warrior's ger. But home feels far away, and much work remains for this company of Mongols before they can start looking forward to seeing it and their families.

For days they have seen scant sign of the enemy, and when the trackers do point out the imprints of Kipchak ponies, Chuluun often finds a reason to move his remaining *zagun* of seventy-eight men away from the rival's sign. Singer wonders if the leader avoids battle for fear of being "plucked," Mongol slang for taking out a weak commander by friendly bowshot. Singer has some sympathy for Chuluun, as his boss's upcoming meeting with his *Mingan* commander, Vachir, will not be pleasant. Having already lost the better part of another company to the rebels, Vachir will investigate the details of the ambush and decide if Chuluun should be relieved. So Chuluun waits.

And this waiting seems to have not only eroded their leader's confidence, but also made him mistrustful of all those around him. While suspicious of his own Mongols, he is borderline obsessed with the dozen Kipchaks he impressed into his unit, apparently certain that at least one of them was responsible for tipping off the enemy attack. Singer has felt the contagious hate growing in his leader's eyes. Weeks prior, the Kipchaks were welcome to join the fire of any Mongols in their *arban*. Now an uncomfortable hush sets in whenever they join a group of Mongols.

"I fear what will happen to us the next time arrows fly," Ferdi says. "They already treat us like we have the fever. Suren saves the worst jobs for us. Hell, even Stiff stays away."

"That may change, if Vachir forces an election. With Chuluun gone, things might get back to what they were," Ilker says.

"Or they might get worse. He's right. They keep us riding point. I wonder when one of those seventy bows at our backs will loose an arrow at one of us," Singer says.

"Don't you encourage his drivel," Ilker says. "They'll get past it. We've done nothing but our duty. In time they'll realize it."

"I don't know," Ferdi says.

"You don't know what?" Ilker asks.

"Doesn't feel like it will ever go back to what it was," Ferdi says.

"Neither of you has been with them half as long as me. They'll get over it. We'll do our jobs and put their doubts to rest. That's all there is to it," Ilker says.

"Yeah, maybe. I can't help but think of bolting. I'm not sure we'll be around for the next new moon," Ferdi says.

"Shut your fool mouth," Ilker says, leaning toward him.

"I'm serious. What if we made for the Khazar Sea?" Ferdi says, his voice dropping, the firelight highlighting the shadows in his crinkled brow.

"You don't know shit. The Mongols crawl over every port," Ilker says, looking behind him and through the shrubs nearby. "And enough of it, they may have already heard you."

"We might be able to get aboard ship," Ferdi says.

"*You* might not. The runners would have the news of your desertion to the ports before you even arrived. They would greet you with the blade of their axes," Ilker says, heaving the stone from his broth, giving it a stir and placing the covered pot back to the coals with a stick through its handle.

A silence.

"What would they care for three of us gone?" Ferdi asks.

"That would be *you* gone," Ilker says. "And the command wouldn't care to lose an idiot, but they would care for an unpunished desertion to be witnessed by the others. The penalty is death—they would track you forever."

"They would expect us to head north, not south. We could stay to the river until light and by the time they were on our tracks, we hopefully would have put enough distance on them," Singer says.

Ilker grabs his temples. "Not you too. They would track you north. They would track you south." He looks up to the sky, shaking his head.

"I won't serve where my loyalty is repaid in contempt," Singer replies.

Ilker removes his hat, rakes his jagged fingernails through greasy hair. He replaces the stained felt to his balding head. He moans. "Oh, how righteous—you're both fucked in the head."

"Listen, the Ayyubids occupy the Jazira. We could push down to Hisn Kayfa. We would find men who could take us to our people," Ferdi says.

"Our people? Who's that?" Ilker asks.

"There's a citadel there filled with Kipchaks," Ferdi says.

"No. There's a citadel filled with Mamluks—there's a difference," Ilker says.

"My brother may be there," Ferdi says.

"*May* be there, or *is* there?" Ilker asks.

"Not sure. Doesn't matter. He made his way to the coast about a year ago and convinced a trader to put him in front of the Turkish amirs. We could do the same."

"That was before the Mongols arrived," Singer says.

Ilker puts his hat in hand and pulls his pot from the fire. He paces and then squats before Ferdi. "Let me get this right. You want to leave your place in an army that controls the entire steppe to risk your life in a journey through Seljuk country, in order to put yourself on the slave block?"

Ferdi shrugs his shoulders.

"While being chased by the Mongols," Singer says with a smirk.

"It ain't funny, Singer. Where's my club? His gray mush would be best used to green the grass." Ilker flings the wet from his hat into the fire.

"Yeah, it's grim. But what would you rather do, Ilker… hunt down and kill our own people for the coming year?" Singer asks.

"My people traded me off like a damn pony," Ilker says with protruded jaw. "These men took me in, took us in, keep us fed."

"These men also killed the last of my family and many like them," Singer says.

"Shut up."

They sit for a few moments, the sound of feeding ponies and crackling fire filling the silence between them.

A rumble of thunder groans its delayed satisfaction, bolts flashing in the southern darkness. Singer shivers, pulls his wet deel back on. He lifts the cover from his pot and dips the wooden spoon into the broth. He blows, then takes a mouthful, cautiously chewing the stringy meat.

"You've heard the briefs. There's no safe passage through any of that land down there, especially on the back of Mongol ponies," Ilker says. "You wish to have two, three different enemies tracking your asses at the same time?"

"If we are to fight and die, let it at least be with our native kinsman and not against them. The Mongols will never trust us. What do we really have to lose?" Ferdi asks.

Ilker drops his head. "Plenty. Unbelievable. Listen, you two make your grand plans. I want nothing to do with it. I know nothing about it." He flips off the lid to his pot and stomps toward the hobbled ponies to eat in better company.

They sit watching thin clouds pass over the stars. Singer lingers on thoughts of the mountain country and lean times spent with his siblings. He is in no hurry to again be back among the hunted, yet wonders if it is his destiny to live as such.

He and his kin. The young trio had been outcasts in lands on the far edge of Kipchak territory, where the rolling mountains butted into the steep country. There the grass grew in patches, yielding game less plentiful than those graced down south. Never owning more than a handful of sheep or goats at a time, they had been habituated to being hungry and cold; accustomed to enduring all that the upper stretches of the Ural River climate threw at them.

He had learned quickly when a chance was worth taking and when it was not, as a serious injury to him spelled certain death for all three. When stalking game, or when forced by hunger to prey upon humans for a sheep or goat, he had relied not just on his proficiency at the hunt for deer, but also on his engrained paranoia of where he placed each step, or when a shepherd's eyes could be upon him—all of the learned safeguards that prevented catastrophe. He had thought the toughest times were behind them, as in the last year his brother and sister had become assets, not just mouths to feed.

He sighs. As the oldest, he should have been more forceful in persuading them to surrender to the Mongols many moons ago. Yet the spirits saw otherwise. And here he is, contemplating bold action not much different than his young ones took—going where he should not. He had survived thus far by trusting his gut, but on this occasion, conflicting signals wrack him.

They have some time. He will not force it, but rather will invite the spirits to enter his mind tonight in hope of providing clarity. For after all, is it not always their will that guides him in a direction, not his own preference?

Snorts of water on flame bring him back, as down the line fires are kicked and drenched, the nightly ritual to keep their position from the eyes of ranging Kipchak patrols. The smoke billows against the last gray of daylight, blending with the mist, the moist scent of smoke from a dozen fires drifting over him and Ferdi.

CHAPTER
19

Duyal
Hisn Kayfa
August 7, 1236

The oxen snort their way through a saddle in the rocky
pass, alternately exhaling in deep huffs as they churn up
the rutted path. Across downed fir and windblown black pine,
they plod through the obstacles, breaking branches, stomping
them to mulch.

Duyal faces aft, sitting on one bent leg to absorb the
shock. The carts behind him lurch their way over exposed
roots, blond and red heads jerking from side to side in the cart
beds, as if in time to some music unheard. White-knuckled
hands clench to the sides.

The path flattens and he closes his eyes to enjoy the
smooth ride, the smell of dried pine needles stirred by the
beasts' hooves. Then up another switchback they jangle, the
way dotted with goat prints and strewn with loose rock.

Once atop, Bozkurt directs the drivers to stop the carts
on the barren summit. Walking on the flush top, he whistles,

waving his arms for all to join him. Duyal and the others spring over the rails and across the brown rockscape, the hazy violet peaks of the Taurus Mountains now far behind them.

With hands on hips, Bozkurt turns from the view below, beaming, to face the Kipchaks now at his heels. His smile narrows upon seeing them. Dried channels of sweat sprawl across their dusty faces, like ancient rivers long waterless. Fissures dissect swollen lips, some mouths painfully returning their keeper's grin.

"Bring up water!" Bozkurt hollers over the heads of the Kipchaks to his drivers, who laze with feet crossed and hands laced behind their heads. He snarls as these men dawdle to the water carts. He again turns to look at the view down the mountain. "My sons, come in closer. Below is your new home, the city of *Hasankeyf*, or as the Arabs say, Hisn Kayfa."

Duyal takes several steps forward. Expecting another dry valley and more summer scrub dotted with mud huts, the brightness instead forces him to look away. Below, the endless brown of mountains and rock-strewn plains bump into a scene of sun-parched white and shimmering river. Where the river bends hard south, the watercourse flattens into three prominent braids, the northern-most flow butting up to a gray-stoned cliff, appearing as if the ridge line had been cut clean in half by the gods. Upstream, the blue-muddied river winds its way through irrigated fields of green, the rich foliage eventually tapering to tan, every pace gaining in elevation away from the nurturing water.

"The Tigris," Bozkurt says.

At the highest white cliffs Duyal's eyes are drawn and kept. For atop this throne of rock a giant fortress sits prominently, its white-blocked walls matching in color the natural rock surrounding it. The stone house appears cleverly built into the contour of the mountain's rolling crest, making the two look as if they had been joined for eternity. Anchoring each corner of the sprawling compound, high rectangular towers loom menacingly into the sky. Atop poles on each, yellow flags fly, with miniature red lions wagging tails in taunting confidence—these pennants snapping an unneeded warning to steer clear of the men who live under them.

In the middle of the enclosure, a column rises high into the clouds, dark slits girdled by railing near its top. Its roof is domed gold, a spire protruding even loftier from it. Duyal recalls a regularly slurred comment from his drunken father: "The greater their buildings, the greater their desire for comforts, the more weak-willed their warriors." Perhaps his father would think differently if he saw this place.

"Across the river is of course the citadel and mosque. Next to it, the new palace of al-Salih," Bozkurt says, unnecessarily pointing to the structure that young faces already stare at, agape.

Downstream of the fortress, the remainder of the town seems to reside prostrate, inferior not only in the elevation, but also in the quality of structures. Hundreds of rock and mud-plastered buildings line the switchback paths—some stacked six high on both banks—only the odd juniper or pine finding root in the craggy ridgelines. Connecting the uppermost shelters are narrower paths, some chiseled into the smooth-faced rock. Everywhere along the ridge the rock is pocked, the deepest of these being oval-shaped caves speckling the ledges.

In these caverns, people have taken residence, using stacked rocks in futile attempts at privacy, filling ancient doorways and building chin-high walls between themselves. On thin ledges in front of their dwellings—a mishmash of clotheslines, hooded women feeding chickens, men peering out of shadows, like lazy sparrows waiting for an insect hatch.

"The Romans built this city," Bozkurt says. "They called it *Cephe* and used it as a border fortress against their Persian enemy. The Arabs eventually took the city—renamed it Hisn Kayfa. A hundred years or so ago, the Artukids captured it and it remained theirs... that is, until they were recently rousted by al-Salih and the other Ayyubids." He smiles.

Some of the Kipchaks point to the large crossing, magically suspended over the river's brilliant ripples, with five huge pillars rising from the water and its banks. The upstream side of each pillar forms the shape of an arrowhead, parting the strong current. Between the pillars are four symmetrical arches, elegant in their block construction. Over it, a steady flow of ox-drawn carts, donkeys, livestock. Dark-bearded men in brown cloaks and veil-covered figures draped in black push across the stone-paved surface in equal flow to the perpendicular current below them.

"How does the raised crossing not fall into the water?" Erol asks.

Bozkurt laughs. "Magic."

On each bank of the river, shepherds lead flocks of sheep and Angora goats, speckled in blacks and browns, down for a drink. Fishermen on small, reed-crafted vessels face upstream, trailing strings of chunked wood above their nets. Pole-built shelters, with grass thatched for shade, line the south shore, a market for the purchase of fish.

Bozkurt no longer looks down at the valley, but instead soaks in the expressions on the boys' faces, watching them with delight, as would a nomadic father after throwing his young son on the back of a pony for the first time. Some youth stand with their mouths still hanging open, others attempt to understand with crinkled brow, while most move their heads rapidly to take it all in, the whites of their eyes enlarged. The gray-bearded one chuckles to himself.

Most of the boys have never seen a city, much less lodgings made of anything but wood supports and felt. A few of the adolescents would have joined their parents on past ventures to small villages, trading their mutton and wool for grain and manufactured goods, like stirrups and pots. Duyal had once joined his uncle and brothers on such a journey to trade their fatty tails from the tower's Karakul sheep, the villagers using its tallow in their soap and candles. When leaving, Duyal remembered the remark from his father to uncle—"Why do we trade with these soft-handed people, when we can ride in with our fellows and take?"

Several boys exchange smiles with the old man. With no other elder to provide guidance, most have clung to Bozkurt as kin, their trust in him increasing each day. Duyal appreciates the gray-bearded Turk, as at this moment he truly is all they have in this foreign land. But Duyal feels a reservation, reminding himself that Bozkurt is not their new father, but rather a moneyman, earning silver at the boys' expense. Soon the supportive man will be rid of them. The gray beard seems to wish the boys well, but Duyal will not let himself lose sight that this trip is still about filling the old man's purse. Some of the Kipchaks have seen enough. These wander back to their carts. Perhaps they too recall that this is not a pleasure journey.

Duyal pauses to take a last look at the towers of cut stone reaching into the sky. He makes out the distant stations of tiny men in white, guarding the place from its heights.

"That is where we'll be living," Ox says, nudging Duyal's shoulder.

"We'll see," Duyal says, dreading the idea of being trapped behind walls so high, still wondering how so many stones could be placed to such heights. A pit forms in his stomach. Walls were meant to be fashioned from willow and felt, rolled up and moved when the group wished, not constructed of massive stones. How could men, especially those who once moved with their flocks, want to live in such structures?

The group climbs aboard their carts, and the drivers wind their way down the worn path into town. They cross the giant bridge, some Kipchaks burying their heads between their legs, until reaching the southern shore. They rattle past the earth-toned homes, where from squares cut in the mud the eyes of young women and old men move from cart to cart. Wooden doors hang crookedly on the entrances of some, while hand-cut stairs lead to others, their rock steps worn round in the centers.

The drivers push the animals uphill, past women with loads strapped to heads and fish held in hand, all stepping aside and looking away. The cart drivers refuse to rein in the oxen, even as kids occasionally bolt across their path and stumbling men dodge left and right, only feet from being hit.

"Dogs," their driver curses.

Some Kipchaks stand with clenched fists, prepared to defend themselves from the people, who move so closely to their carts. Bozkurt grabs the shoulder of the lead driver, tells him to halt. He walks down the line of carts, repeating the same words. "Easy. Nothing is going to happen. Easy."

They pass beneath the scrape of trowels, teeny pebbles bouncing into their wooden cart beds. At one building, workers stand on thin boards high in the air, spreading mud over coarse reed walls. Hearing the carts, they stop their work temporarily, so as not to drop their scrapings upon the travelers. Upon seeing the boys, they grimace, returning to their business of scuffing the wall.

Entering the gauntlet of stands, they are immediately bombarded by the chatter of foreign tongues and creaking carts. The air grows thick with breath. Men laugh and women gather. They bounce past endless rows of food and merchandise, the goods shaded by timbers extending into the rock, supporting roofs of stretched cloth. Neat piles of fruits and vegetables line the dirt streets, sorts unknown to him. And fresh fish, some stacked on tables, others skinned to the head, their pink flesh hanging in groups on thick hooks like fleshy flowers hung to dry.

In narrow stalls, vendors young and old sit half-hidden on wooden stools, amid bolts of cloth and shawls of every color. Blankets dangle from rusty clasps along the endless walls, as if to decorate the tedious white block. Every turn in the path, they pass pots large and small, some throwing steam and emitting odors thick with spice; others are suspended by long nails and hooks, or laid in the back of carts. Shiny metal trinkets, shells, and countless foreign items cover table after table.

Duyal recognizes the high boots of a Rus and the tunics of the peasant Turks, yet most dress strangely, many men wearing fine cloth wrapped about their heads and long shawls, which flow to their ankles. He wonders why they dress like women. Most are very clean. Many have faces dark and engraved with lines from the sun, yet they appear free from worry.

Standing across from one merchant is a man whose look is familiar. His tunic is homespun wool, topped with a long coat and thick belt, which holds the clothing tightly to his thin body. Under his crossed arms and circling each buttock are salted sweat rings from days spent in the saddle. His boots are roughly patched along the inside of his shins, due to the constant rub of his stirrup leathers; the rawhide tops are cracked apart, where his feet naturally bend while in stride. Although a young man, his neck is etched with deep wrinkles, dirt having settled in most of the crevasses. This nomad fixes his eyes hard on those of a fast-talking merchant, the well-being of his family this winter likely hanging in the balance of the deal he now strikes. Although he is not a man from his homeland, Duyal feels sympathy for this herder, the man out of place in the crowded city.

The carts roll through the competing smells of perfume, rotting fish, roasting meat, body odor, and urine. Duyal concentrates on one vendor, who twists his face, raises his nose, and begins to shake his head very quickly in response to another's offer. His turban moves with him, making his head appear long and odd. Three others draw their bargains calmly, while another two argue wildly, as if one had stolen from the other. None pay attention to the carts of human stock moving through the streets, concerned only with their transaction at hand.

Since entering the town, Duyal has seen more people cross his path than in his previous fifteen years of existence. He looks to Bozkurt and feels little comfort in the trader's easy smile, as the slave merchant watches his captives' heads pivot from side to side, the boys appearing unable to absorb the dizzying array of goods and the clamor of the street vendors. Ox strains his neck to view a stall filled with oriental jewels.

As they leave the bustle of the market, the carts clatter through a section of town where the buildings transition from humble dwellings to rock towers. On the path, a young boy with his mother points in the carts' direction. The black-haired child smiles and says, "Mamluk." His shrouded mother looks up momentarily with beautiful green eyes and thick lashes, but turns her head quickly away, pulling her son's hand down.

Further up the path, four kids just shy of the captives' age play alongside the path. They wear fine knit shawls and sandals made of sturdy leather. Each has an apple in hand, and laughs while kicking a gourd between one another. One stops to stare as the carts approach. He raises his lip in disgust and resumes the game. Duyal sneers at them, looking up to their stone house and the Turkish bread cooling on the sill as they pass.

The group closes on the fortress. Edging the path are giant beams, some stained with the dull brown of dried blood. He shudders. They continue, stopping in a short alley with high walls. Several boys stand to peer around the corner. An open square sprawls, covered in short grass, lined with great stone columns and arches of carved stone.

"We will wait here for a short while," Bozkurt says, walking beside the carts. With the words hardly out of his mouth, Bozkurt turns to the sound of clapping hooves. He grins. All in the carts turn toward the rear, following Bozkurt's eyes down the alley.

A rider sitting perfectly erect in his saddle cantors toward them on a large black mount.

Two more riders follow in trace, hidden by the first. The lead horse practically prances, his neck arching elegantly. Covering his back is a blanket of scarlet and gold; decorative silver stirrups hang just above the white on the stallion's ankles.

Upon hearing the hoofbeats, passers hug the alley edges, making way for the lead horse as if pushed aside by an invisible force. With eyes focused to the front, the horse ignores the pedestrians, seeming to know his prominent position on the path, cognizant that no harm will come to him if he chooses to stomp those inferior.

Butterflies fill Duyal's stomach. He is struck by the disparity between the man on the horse and those that line the streets: the town folk walk, the Mamluks ride; the vendors' bald heads are covered with cloth, while the lead rider has long blond hair, which flows freely beneath his yellow headpiece; the men in the markets have mustaches or long black beards, while the rider's facial hair is groomed blond; those in town wear drab cloaks of brown and gray, while this man wears a brilliant white coat and yellow trousers.

"Oh, look at them," the Ox says in awe.

Duyal is reminded of his younger years, when he and the other boys in the tower would run toward the gers when they heard the neighboring warriors thundering into camp to gather more riders for their raids to the west. He and the others would show off, shooting their bows and wrestling, all the while ogling the warriors' spears adorned with feathers and metal, their long blond hair tied back with leather straps, the heads of their anxious ponies dipping, fighting the reins, upset at their riders for breaking pace.

A hollowness seems to overcome him, maybe the final realization that any part of him that was still a boy has just vanished. These men arrive not to gather fellow warriors, but rather to separate boys on the verge of adulthood, dividing those who have the necessary skills to one day join their ranks from those who do not. His breathing becomes quickened, shallower. A stickiness forms in his armpits.

Look at them. How will a simple herder like himself ever measure up to the standard of these soldiers? What could they possibly see in him that would give them reason to put him on such a steed? Surely these amirs will be disappointed with the ragged bunch heaped in these carts. The Mamluks will reject them all.

CHAPTER

20

Ox
City square, Hisn Kayfa
August 7, 1236

A thin-legged Kipchak pries his fingers underneath the boulder, its rough surface worn smooth from the hands of previous aspirants. With bent back, he lifts with all his might, yet cannot budge the rock. Sloppy-clothed and wiry, the boy rises and walks around it, as if contemplating a better grip or lifting position.

Standing in line as instructed, with hands clasped in front of him, the Ox yawns. "Come now, little fella, it won't be any lighter from that side either."

Demir whispers from behind, "Get him out of here."

The boy flashes a look to the nearest Mamluk, who stands with tilted head, hands moving to his hips. Likely discerning that he cannot waste much more of the time of those who judge him, the boy squats down again, a look of determination now filling his face. Ox turns away, already knowing how this ends.

Sparrows dart between carved pillars of white stone. The smell of cut grass fills the courtyard. His eyes stop on the fourth and senior amir, who introduced himself earlier as Amir Safir. With no expression and black hands locked into the small of his back, Safir focuses on the skinny boy struggling with the rock.

Ox cannot take his eyes off the man's face. Black skin. The man has black skin. He had no idea there was such a thing. He stares at the shiny scalp, mostly hidden by a yellow and white cloth wrapped tightly about the head. He wonders if the black man is able to grow hair and if so, what it looks like? Would it be black too? He senses the firmness in the man's slender face and a steady confidence resonating in his dark eyes. He wonders if those in the citadel will also teach him such self-possession.

Unlike the three white-skinned juniors who accompany him, Safir's contrasting skin only adds to the impressiveness of his spotlessly white coat. Beneath the form-fitting garment, he wears a light shirt of chain metal armor, only visible at his neckline. His yellow trousers are stunning, highlighted with swirled ornamental designs, embroidered in orange. Only the richest of Kipchaks wore such colors.

His leather belt is studded with spheres of gold, tapering into tufted finials, a far call from the drab stiffeners worn by his old tower's warriors. While functional, these metal accessories also seem to serve in drawing the eye to the handsome sword that hangs at his side. This long blade is curved slightly near his knee, protected in a scabbard wrapped in engraved silver. The weapon terminates at his hip, exposing only its white-horned pommel and curled handguard of metal, its leaf and animal forms barely discernible from this distance. Ox imagines himself in the uniform and the impression he would make.

"Enough!" Safir says.

"Finally," Demir murmurs from the row of Kipchaks.

The boy falls to bony knees. He places his forehead on the rock, where his heaving pants transform into sobs. Bozkurt bows his leave from the amirs. He helps the boy to his feet, putting his arm across his shoulders. He speaks into the boy's ear, words probably meant to quell the bawls.

"Tell him how many dinars he just cost you, bearded one. That you should be the one crying," Ox says, just out of the amirs' earshot.

"Tell him his work bathing the amir's kids and wiping babies' asses will be less strenuous," Demir says.

The old man and boy reach the group of twelve, those who have already failed one of the first two stages of the amirs' screening process. Three in the group still cry, while the rest sit dejected, a distant look of worry in their swollen eyes, their only certainty in life being that they will not become Mamluks.

During the morning, dozens of other Kipchaks had entered the courtyard to join those who shared the long journey with Ox. While no judge of military efficiency, Ox has been impressed with the thoroughness and good organization of the amirs, having already finished a physical inspection of the group and archery test in less than half a day.

He and surely all of the other boys clearly understand what the amirs are doing. The men in white cull the weak, just as the wolves did to herds of deer and people of the steppe did with their flocks each fall. About the time when the women were adding a second layer of felt to the gers, Ox's tower moved through the whole flock, separating those sheep which had lost one too many incisors, had concerning discharge from the ears or eyes, or harbored unhealed wounds. Any sheep deemed unhealthy or not strong enough to make it through the winter was either sold to the Rus or killed for the fall festival. Just as the Kipchaks were not going to waste their precious winter hay on those animals who would likely die in the snow, neither were these Mamluks going to squander their time and silver on those boys who were not worthy of training in the stone house.

The sun sneaks over the high wall. Rocking his head back, Ox lets it warm his face, remembering many years ago his older cousin pulling open a ewe's mouth to expose for him the "spreaders," or narrow part of old teeth coming through the gumline of an old ewe marked for slaughter. "When you see the narrow nubs pushed up, the grass just slips between their teeth. That's when it's time for 'em to go," his cousin had said. He shakes his head, thinking of their own inspection this morning, dismissing the idea that these Mamluks will continue to view the boys as sheep once their real training begins.

Safir stepped before Ox, an odd fragrance in trail of the black amir. The tick of heel behind, as the archery instructor, Ekrem, followed to examine his backside. The man with the scroll slid to his place amid the line of Kipchaks.

"Bow your head." Safir's peach-colored thumbs parted his hair. "Head up." The amir pulled up Ox's eyelid, leaning in to inspect his eye. "Open your mouth." Ox spread his jaws half open. The amir stuck one finger in, pulled open his cheek, and checked his teeth. The same on the other side.

They grabbed his shoulders, squeezed his arms, moved every joint in each finger. They watched him bend at the knee repeatedly, then squatted at his feet, scrutinizing his toes. Ox ignored it all, head forward, his eyes set on the scroll, wishing no scratches to be made on its surface.

Safir went behind him. He whispered, "Loyalty." As instructed, Ox repeated the word, "Loyalty." His hearing test passed.

Back to his front, all three men. Safir looked down at the scroll and nodded. On to the next lad they went, a wave of relief surging through him as they stepped.

Ox smiles, trying to calculate in his head how much silver Bozkurt has lost on the thirteen who have been split off from the rest. He feels a nudge from the boy behind him.

"Will you spend the day dreaming, Ox?" Safir says with a scowl.

He is surprised the amir remembers his name. He walks to the rock and picks it up without a grunt. He places it atop one hip and walks the thirty feet to where an arrow sticks from the soil. He drops the rock in the dimpled turf, amid the whispers of the other Kipchaks and the half smiles of Safir's accompanying amirs.

He looks at Safir, hoping to read the amir's astonishment, yet the black leader merely loses his frown. Ox then squats and again picks up the rock, cradling it on his other hip as he lumbers back to the original location, where he dumps the stone with a thud.

Mumbles emanate from the courtyard.

"Silence," Safir says, pointing for Ox to join to the group of Kipchaks standing with their backs near the citadel's arched entrance.

Soon the Kipchak herd has been cut by nearly one third, those saddened chaps standing in the shadow of the wall and those so far successful standing under the great stone arch.

The four amirs huddle with Bozkurt.

"I told you we would have no problem with this soldiering. I bet our next stop is inside the big stone walls on the hill, where they will give us clothes as they wear," Ox says with a smile.

Duyal looks at him with doubt in his face. "Yeah, those walls. Built high and slick. Are they to keep enemy out, or Kipchaks boys in?"

"I don't see their use for walls. Who's going to win a fight against them? And what lad could sneak his way out of a fortress filled with these guys?" Demir asks, eying the amirs who now break their meeting.

With purposeful strides, the amirs move to separate corners of the courtyard, where they sit on wooden stools. Bozkurt meanders toward the archway with his eyes to his feet in thought.

Stroking his beard, he looks across the group. "What remains is a short interview with the amirs. Be respectful and just answer the questions. Sit cross-legged before them. Believe in yourself. Listen to what they ask. Listen, I say." He points his finger to his temple. "There is no need to be nervous," he says unconvincingly, looking at the forty-five faces that remain. Looking over his shoulder at the straight-backed amirs, Bozkurt sends the first four Kipchaks to the corners of the courtyard and then returns to pacing.

Duyal jogs over and sits cross-legged in front of Safir. Out of hearing range, all watch intently as the black man asks a question and then looks with piercing eyes as the youth responds. The amir sits forward on his stool, looking as if he is able to peer through Duyal's soul. The youth appears unfazed by the questions, palms squarely resting on his knees.

At times the amir's piercing eyes grow warm and he leans back against the rock wall, seemingly comfortable with the boy's answers. At one point the amir breaks his stoic bearing and smiles broadly, his beautiful teeth showing brightly against his dark chin.

In the adjacent corner, the man who led the archery test, Amir Ekrem, listens to a Kipchak who looks down as he talks, the boy giving his responses to the slippers on his feet. Ekrem crosses his arms and cocks his head to the side, his red hair hanging almost to his shoulders. Midanswer, the amir raises the boy's chin with his large thumb.

Something about this amir does not sit well with Ox. Too much interest in the physical part of their inspection.

Twice later on, during a lull in the process, he caught the crinkle-skinned man eying two of the fairest-looking boys. What did Ox know? The old man was here to find flaws, likely trained to pick up on debilities in the youth. Perhaps he was just doing his job.

In time, Ekrem points the shy Kipchak in the direction of the wall, already looking over the youth's head at the next boy in line.

"What? They're willing to dump a guy for not talking the way they want?" Demir asks.

"They can do whatever they like. Best not blurt out anything too stupid," Ox says.

"Look who's giving that advice," Demir says.

Ichami laughs. "Yeah, when in doubt, you might want to bite your tongue. But with confidence." He slaps Ox on the back.

The rebuffed Kipchak stands in disbelief in front of the seated amir, and then turns to Bozkurt with a look of confusion stamped upon his face. Bozkurt only shakes his head as the boy mopes over to join the other failures.

A creep of doubt enters Ox's mind. They will judge his words. He has never had to worry much about that before. He looks to the trio of leather targets in the center of the courtyard, riddled with arrow holes from their earlier test. Only eight Kipchaks had been unable to hit the target in three tries. Ox could understand why these boys were undeserving to begin training at the citadel, or how one not strong enough did not qualify, but how can the amirs destroy a boy's opportunity based on how he replies to a few questions?

"Ox, damn it!" Bozkurt snaps, pointing to the corner where Safir stares straight at him.

Ox feels his stomach rise into his throat. "Uhh, luck would have me drawing him." Has he already screwed it up without even uttering a word? He jumps up, sprints over to the amir, and drops down cross-legged in front of the man who will determine his future.

Safir looks at Ox as a shepherd would look at a bloated corpse, disturbed not by the sight of the stinking carcass before him, but more so as to how the pitiable sight at his feet came to be. "How long have you lived?"

"Fourteen years."

Safir nods. "Why should I allow you to serve my patron, al-Salih, in his regiment of Mamluks?"

Ox is thrown off by the man's accent and the way his black lips contort when rolling out the Turkish words fluently, but awkwardly. Inside the black man's mouth is not more black skin, but the same pink flesh of a white man. Ox wonders how many languages the man speaks.

He stares at him, then forces himself to focus on the question. "Because I am bigger and stronger than the others and able to shoot well with the bow, as you saw." Ox smiles, his nervousness subsiding slightly at the ease of the first question. He will be all right.

Safir turns his lip upward, leans forward on his stool.

Ox figures if his answer had been food entering the amir's mouth, the black man would have spit it out. He must do better with the next question.

"What if strength and marksmanship are not the requisites I find most essential?"

Ox wonders what else the amir would want to hear. His heart beats heavily, knocking against his sternum. He figured with soldiering, his size and strength would finally play to his advantage, just as it was mostly a curse back home, forcing him early into heavy tasks made for men.

His mind floats to the steppe. The dreaded tang of sheep and goats and smoke. The cramps and stabbing back pain from hours bent over the penned beasts. Blistered hands from clipping across the crotch and udder of countless ewes, prior to lambing. Sheep dung mashed into finger cuts; the pierce of hidden burrs. Toting overfilled baskets of "crotching" to the ice-cold river, where the smaller boys washed the shit, thorns, twigs from the foul spring fleece.

And at lambing time, while the other boys slept, Ox on night watch in the pen, alert for late-night births and lambs with labored breathing. Here again, being large and robust was his bane, as he was one of the few boys with arms long enough to manipulate the worst breeched lambs and the might and grip to swing a lamb around by its rear legs, dislodging excess mucous in the nose and lungs of some newborns. Surely his size and strength would not trouble him here.

"Then I would say that I also have a great desire to become a soldier. Ever since I heard my cousin speak of being a Mamluk, I have wanted the same. I wish to be like him, like you."

Safir looks only at Ox's eyes, the man seemingly trained to sniff out bullshit.

Ox swallows. The amir is not charmed by his compliment. The black man must be debating his destiny. The uncertainty he reads in the amir's brow makes Ox's hands start to shake. He crosses them.

"Ox, how many brothers and sisters do you have?" Safir asks.

"I, I have one younger brother." He questions what this has to do with becoming a Mamluk.

"Tell me your opinion of him."

Ox is confused, but he remembers Bozkurt's words— "Just answer the questions."

"Amir Safir, my brother was eight years younger than me. He was but a child when I left and we spent little time together, so I did not know him well."

Safir nods his head. "Where are your parents?"

"They remain on the steppe."

"And how do you feel about them allowing you to be sold?"

He pauses and then answers honestly. "I have no feelings on it. The decision came from our khan and was not mine to question. It is the way of our people."

Safir leans forward again, seemingly waiting for him to further elaborate.

"So... uhh... I'm not mad at my parents or our khan for dealing with the Mongols and selling me and the other boys. I'm now pleased for the chance it presents."

"And what opportunity do you see here?"

He shifts uncomfortably, his knees strained from sitting cross-legged. He feels a tackiness under his arms. "I see an opportunity to become a soldier, rather than a herder—a chance to gain position and wealth, as you and the other warriors have won."

Safir squints, sets his elbows on knees to inch even closer to the youth, as if hoping to crawl inside Ox's brain for ever greater perception. A furl forms in between the nonexistent eyebrows on the black man's face. He scowls.

Blood rushes to Ox's face. This was again not the answer the amir wanted. Is it possible for the black man to hate him in such a short time? He wonders if he will be forced to join the sick, the puny and those who cannot shoot. Will he be forced to watch a rich man's flock? This cannot be happening.

"So you wish to join our ranks to become wealthy?"

He clamps his hands together tighter to disguise their trembling, fluffing a waft of stench from his tunic. He senses a single bead of sweat running down his forehead. Safir's eyes follow the drip. Should he wipe it? He will not wipe it. Think. Think. He must answer this question correctly. But what is correctly?

"Amir Safir, I wish to join your ranks to become more than a common herder."

Safir leans back, appearing to let the answer sink into his mind. He pushes his hands on his thighs, straightening his back, all the while looking Ox over from toe to head, again stopping at the giant boy's small eyes.

Ox knows the amir makes his decision right now and that somehow he has made it difficult for him. He swallows hard and holds his breath, as his life's path is mulled by the black man. Sweat tickles its way over his ribs, soaking into the dam of his beltline. Unconsciously, he mimics the amir and slowly straightens his thick back, attempting to carry himself with dignity, as the amirs do. He must try to look like a Mamluk. He must become a Mamluk. Please let him become a Mamluk.

Safir points a pink-printed finger. "Join the others."

SECTION 2

Within
the Stone Walls

CHAPTER
21

Duyal
The citadel, Hisn Kayfa
August 8, 1236

They reach the gate. Gigantic planks held with thick bands of hammered steel. Duyal looks up the nearest tower. The hewed forms of a scorpion and snake leer at him from above a six-tiered arch. Fan-shaped rock carved in graduated depths. Midway up the pale wall, a strip of ornate symbols etched across the entire face. Squiggled lines and dots, the mysteriousness of their meaning as intimidating to him as the curled tail of the scorpion below it.

White walls span in every direction. Cream blocks connecting numerous towers, both rectangular and round. The outer towers are bigger than he had imagined, thousands of gigantic slabs stacked tightly upon one another, reaching far into the sky. Yet these are but half the height of the rounded inner turrets, which buttress the corners of the ramparts and palace.

He tries to envision how the stone was cut and then placed with such precision, such that every surface appears smooth, every corner meets perfectly. He imagines himself at the top of one inner tower. A tingle zips to his fingertips and toes.

Feeling watched, he looks up. Two guards in white tunics point their crossbows away at identical angles, looking down at the cluster of Kipchaks with dual expressions of coldness. Inside the distant towers and even behind the rampart, more guards, their black silhouettes thwarting the sun's rays from entering the cross-shaped shooting slits.

They pass through the doors, the smell of sun baking bitter wood. Up a gentle incline toward the inner walls, they follow the amirs. The passage narrows. Hearing the clattering of hooves on stone floor, they wait. A pair of yoked oxen begins their final turn out of the corridor. Surprised to see the group of forty-one, the beasts halt. The driver cusses his animals, snaps his thin stick to persuade them around the final corner. Navigating his empty wagon into the open, the man identifies the white tunics at the head of the group. "My apology, Amir." He fumbles with his reins, averting eye contact with the Mamluks by pulling down his brimmed hat as he passes.

"All in the city seem a bit timid around al-Salih's men," Duyal says to Ox, his soft voice echoing off the stone.

"One day they'll have reason to be scared of us too, my friend," Ox says with a smile.

The amirs lead the group through another gate, where two more guards with long-handled battle axes stand on station. Duyal meets eyes with the nearest guard, the Mamluk's face as sharp and stern as the wide blade alongside it. The tall-helmeted soldiers step aside, watching with contempt as fresh meat ambles its way through the opening and into a vaulted hallway, the boys trailing the amirs and their slave trader like puppies.

The air dampens, cools. He breathes the same scent of the caves he explored as a young boy. He looks up. How does the arched ceiling not collapse upon them? Again a tight passageway, the overhead lowers. Hardly enough light to see their way. A drip from above plops to his nose. A shine of natural light splays around a corner. The group dumps into a vast courtyard filled with many benches, neatly aligned on one end. On the first three benches, another lot of Kipchaks look over their shoulders, nomadic replicates who have also made the cut.

Duyal counts them. Thirty-three more. He thinks of varmints caught in the cylinder-shaped traps he fashioned from hardwood splints. Chipmunks, finding their way to the bait through the funneled end of the trap at night, yet unable to make their way back out the same small entrance to safety. Frantic animals, bouncing to every corner of the trap, probing the tight wooden mesh, with the hole to freedom just above their heads.

"Go sit behind the others," Bozkurt says to the group.

He sits next to Ox, looking about the spacious enclosure. More pillars and stone and high scribbles on the walls.

"Looks like our group just doubled in size," Ox says.

Duyal nods, scanning the backs of the boys to their front.

"On your feet!" Safir booms, upon hearing the pound of boot heel on rock echo in the corridor from his station at the entrance. Out of the darkness, a tall man bursts through the passage and into the light.

"My. Where do they find these guys?" Duyal whispers.

"The same places they found us," Ox says.

The amir strides with resolve, each step radiating an energy that practically illuminates every limestone rock he passes. His thick shoulders and V-shaped torso bulge, the muscles refusing to be hidden by his chain mail armor and coat. His belt draws attention to the slenderness of his waist and stoutness of his legs, while also holding the same white-handled sword and a jewel-studded purse. A plain pale turban hides the color of his hair, yet his white skin, blond beard, and facial features peg him as a fellow Kipchak.

His jaw looks similar to the white blocks, which mystically lock together the arch he walks under, tight and unyielding. Yet farther up his face are eyes somehow soft and a complexion perfectly clear. He seems to hold back a grin. An aura surrounds the man that Duyal cannot quite place. Moving behind the last bench, the muscle-bound man stops in front of his new recruits. As he does so, the reserved black amir smiles broadly at this man's arrival, the first time Safir has held a grin so long or wide.

"Be seated. My name is Amir Aqtay. I am an amir of Mamluks, in the service of al-Salih Ayyub, prince to the sultan, Governor of Hisn Kayfa. I'm the commander of this training regiment. The prince has purchased each of you and my sole mission here is to make you into his warriors."

He strolls in front of the benches, his darting eyes taking measure of every youth. "During your training, you'll be organized into a unit we call a 'tulb.' From this moment forward, you will be addressed as "novice," or *Mutaállim*, a Mamluk under training. Your instruction here will be no different than that at the best citadels in Cairo."

Duyal looks over to Ox, who raises his eyebrows, grinning.

"Your training here will be... most difficult. Some of you won't complete it." The faint smile disappears from his face for the first time. "But those of you who do graduate will become members of the prince's military household. The chosen ones—men picked like ripe fruit, by God himself, to not only protect our patron but also blessed to fight in defense of Islam and its lands."

The natural grin returns to his lips. A paternal look comes over him. "All who reside here once sat on a bench similar to where you sit now. Regardless of how you got here or why, your circumstances are little different from others who already wear the lion of al-Salih. Be not mistaken—it's a great privilege to be inside these walls."

He halts, faces them.

"In this place, raw iron extracted from the steppe is crafted into Allah's swords. This citadel is the cauldron, where we apply the fire and add the ingredients which forge *Mutaʿallim* into Mamluk steel. Here, the impurities of your previous existence will be melted away. Here, you will be pounded and sharpened into weapons of the highest purpose. God… the glorious weapons he has blessed us with… your patron, al-Salih… and your new brothers. These will be your only concerns for the next few years."

Duyal's mind spins. Years. Next few years? Behind these walls for years. His eye remains fixated on Aqtay.

"Until you graduate, you'll have absolutely no contact with those back on the steppe, nor with the wayward populace in town. You'll not eat from their tables, clean in their bathhouses, pray in their mosques, or contemplate plowing their daughters! You'll occupy only the west side of the citadel; troops of the prince's Royal Regiment fill the east side. They're already God's warriors—you'll have no business east of our training arena." The pleasantness again leaves his face.

Duyal shudders, frightened by the ease and speed with which the apparent two sides of this man swap.

"Here, you'll be blessed to learn the ways of God and his law. Your military and moral lessons will be taught in accordance with the *Furusiyya*, our cavalry principles. Aside from our martial doctrine and the Koran, no other text will fill your minds. For those fortunate enough to complete the training— the lance, bow, and sword in your hands will become lethal deliverers of God's will. You'll become more comfortable riding than you are walking with your own legs."

Duyal breathes a light sigh of relief, recalling countless deer and marmots dropped by bowshot. He remembers being tossed onto the back of his pony as soon as he could stand without wobbling. Surely this will give him and the others advantage.

Aqtay hesitates momentarily, as if checking that he has said all that he wanted. His eyes go over their heads momentarily. He raises his chin in communication to those behind the seated. "In closing, all will not earn the title of *al-Salihiyya* Mamluk, but those who follow the instruction and weather the storms of its challenges will win honor both in this life and the next." Aqtay solemnly scans the blank faces that sit before him. "*Mu'allim.*"

On this apparent cue, the courtyard explodes. Two Mamluks burst from the corridor like animals loosed from a cage, rushing up behind the novices. In rabid anticipation, they emerge in a flash of white and yellow, each Mamluk wielding a wooden staff, tall as their chins, its knobby grain worn smooth.

"Get up, worms! Move, move, move!" one screams, his baritone voice echoing off the high walls.

"Hur-ry yup! Hur-ry yup!" the other belts, as he grabs two slow-moving Kipchaks by the scruff of the tunic and tosses them side by side in line.

"Three ranks, three ranks!"

The Kipchaks scurry, quickly but clumsily learning what a "rank" is, so as not to become a target of the wrath and swinging staffs.

Fear fills his soul. Falling in line, Duyal notices a third Mamluk, a man circling the benches, silently watching all with dark eyes. Like the others who scream, his white tunic is bound with a black sash, highlighting a tight waist and wide shoulders, traits apparently common to them all.

His trousers are tucked into lion-crested gaiters, the yellow fabric billowing over his powerful thighs. His dark-complected face is lean, handsome, aside from the shaggy eyebrows and mass of bone on the bridge of his nose. Duyal recalls his cousin, who had a similar nose, and wonders if this short man, too, got his from never backing down from a fight.

The man's jaw muscles ripple below his ears as he paces. In one hand he holds his staff in a clenched fist, long forearm hair protruding from his crisp cuffs. In his other, he clutches a brilliant yellow flag on a staff with the number nine imprinted upon it. At least this man does not holler.

From behind them: "Silence!"

The quiet Mamluk walks up. The single thud of both staffs strike the rock floor in a sinister cadence. He pauses in front of the formation, eyeing them. He strides the ranks. Stopping at Ox, he looks him up and down. He pushes the flag staff into the boy's hands. "Go here." He points to the first spot in the front rank.

He turns to face them. "I am Cenk, your *Mu'allim*, or *Furusiyya* instructor. Raise your left arms out to your side, so your fingertips touch the shoulder of the man next to you." He leaves his arm outstretched in example.

They respond to the order, shuffling awkwardly to get their desired spacing.

Crack! A Mamluk from the rear smacks the arm of a Kipchak who holds his arm too low. Another uses his staff to ease down another arm.

"Fingers together!" A shout from behind.

Cenk nods. "This is how you will line up each time we assemble. There will be no speaking in formation. We'll now draw your gear. Go."

The tulb vacillates, the boys waiting for somebody to move. The two Mamluks step off at a quick pace toward the interior of the fortification. Ox follows, the yellow flag held across him. The recruits sprint to catch up, following them into the darkness. They make four turns through the long corridors. They suck in the odor of wet rock, half running to keep up with the tap of soles on stone. They exit into an exterior passage.

Three Mamluks approach from the other direction, the men steering away from the approaching novices. For some reason, Duyal homes in on a particular soldier's stride and inward pointing right foot. Duyal mumbles to himself, "It can't be."

As they near, Duyal stares. A clean chin and healed slash across the cheek of the Mamluk's face. He realizes that he is mistaken. Those hollowed cheeks and weathered skin are not part of the face he recognized. But when only six paces separate them, Duyal meets the Mamluk's green eyes. "Gozde!"

The Mamluk stops and turns. A wrinkled brow and raised lip.

Duyal holds back his tears. He remembers the December snow falling silently five years ago, the frozen tears upon his cheeks, certain he would never see his older brother again. "It's your brother, Duyal."

With this, the Mamluk smiles and takes a step toward the Kipchaks, but then stops, seeming to remember that to do so is forbidden.

"Whack!" He feels the bite of the staff across his shoulder, but ignores the pain. He continues to meet the eyes of his older brother, who now, apparently realizing he will cause his brother further suffering by coming any closer, turns to continue on his original course without looking back.

"Halt!" Clutching his staff in both hands, Cenk waits for the Mamluks to leave the space. He looks both ways, then pops Duyal in the forehead with the stout wood, snapping back his head.

He feels the blood race to a rising lump on his forehead, a throb of pain growing with each pulse of his heart. He tries to shake the stars. Putrid breath fills his nostrils, pouring in from the mouth of his instructor.

"You think you're special? That you can stop and speak out as you wish?!" Cenk yells.

He recognizes the fermented mare's milk on Cenk's breath. His heart sinks. Will this man be just another version of his drunken father? He must spend years with this man? A dizziness nearly takes him. He must not fall. Don't fall. He widens his stance, tries to remain motionless. His ears ring. A moist heat on his face. Spit. His hearing fades back in, yet he cannot comprehend the words. The grate of Cenk's teeth, those crushing jaws undulating across the taut dark skin.

"How sweet—brothers reunited. You think your brother can save you here? I own you. There is nowhere to go!" Cenk turns again to see if anyone of significance watches, then smashes his turbaned forehead into Duyal's. "You'll be the first to drop."

CHAPTER

22

Duyal
The citadel barracks
August 9, 1236

Duyal sits glassy-eyed among the novices. Ribbons of fire ripple along the block wall, flickering with a spastic glee before returning again yellow and upright. In the flames Duyal sees the forked tongues from headless snakes lapping at the drafts of air, mocking the weary boys who rest on their assigned mats. He counts the white blocks between flames. Thirty.

Two boys arrive with candle snuffers as long as the boys are tall. From either side of the hall, they begin smothering the line of candles with the arched, brass end—the signal for all to lie down for the night. From behind, the two novices are indistinguishable, their close-cropped hair suspended above the collar of the same baggy white tunics, exposing a streak of untanned skin on their necklines.

A dread settles in as the hall dims. It always did for him this time of day. As a child, this was when his father returned from his solitary labor. And as the sun would hide behind the undulating grassland, so would Duyal contemplate the night's hiding place for him and his brothers, as his father would be dipping into the hanging stomach bag of *koumis*.

If his father's drunken violence peaked at dark, the boys were adept at disappearing before the man began looking for them. Yet if the workday ended early and his intoxication crested at dusk ... this was not good for Duyal and his brothers. He learned to loathe the low light of the evening, which made them easier to spot. Twilight was a rope drawn taut to the breaking point, a breath held tight in hopeful anticipation of the black sky and the iron-fisted demon laid flat and snoring.

One by one, the quivering shadows are extinguished, those waving shapes cast long and ominous upon the high block walls, dancing across the strange writing elevated upon the smooth slabs. The pulses of light disappear, done paying their final homage to the words of the Mamluk God—the undecipherable phrases that guide these keepers of boy slaves.

The bell lowers upon the last candle. Darkness. Duyal tips over in relief. He shifts on the thin pad, attempting to avoid the raised edge of stone in the floor. He finds a tolerable position as the thin smoke arrives to his nose from across the barracks. Never has he slept in such close proximity to so many, while still feeling so alone. He closes his eyes, pretending the smoke entering his nostrils is from dung burning in his mother's ger. The thought calms him, slows his breathing.

He imagines that he does not lie on rock, but instead upon a sheepskin rug, covering a soft piece of meadow in his Volga country. That he does not go to sleep in this massive stone house, filled with serious men in white, but is instead surrounded by comforting felt overhead and above that, the open skies of the Kipchak steppe. He tops off his delusion, creating beside him not the breathing of young strangers miserable as he, but the familiar snores and rustlings of his mother and brothers. And in the gers on either side of him, he fabricates the muffled talk of blood relatives as they stoke their fires one last time before sleep.

A foreign voice pierces his ears, smashing placid thoughts. As on the night before, the infuriating song spills from atop the slender tower to the east. Its wretched whine and surging yowls bounce off the stone walls outside, seep into the corridors and down from the vaulted ceiling above him. Why must this man sing his sad tale every night? The odd language and eerie voice is like that of a lonesome ghost, reciting the same unworldly song just before sleep and again at dawn, so as to remind the youth that they could not be any farther from their homeland.

He wipes away the tears that well in his eyes, but refuses to sob. He digs the back of his head into the rock and covers his ears. He hates this place. How is it that he is actually here?

As the man ends his rolling hymn, Duyal slides his hand beneath his high collar and rubs his neck, chaffing from the heat and rough wool. Even at night they must wear the loose-fitting tunic and matching white trousers. They are thick, almost unbearable in the scorching temperatures of this land. He wipes the sweat from his face with a rough sleeve. In the vaulted ceiling, the last of the natural light turns the white stone to gray. He exhales, relieved to be out of the icy stare of his instructors, glad to be off his constant state of awareness, trying to avoid the rage of the *Mu'allim*.

His eyelids grow heavy.

"They want us to be miserable and to look sloppy, so as to not be or look like them. They want us to be like peasants, wearing bags of grain," Ox whispers.

Duyal sits up and turns to see the giant in the faint light, looking at him from one elbow. His hatred for this boy has subsided since arriving to the shared despair of the citadel.

"You didn't think we were going to show up and be handed ivory-handled swords and the reins to a fine horse, did you?" Duyal asks.

"No, I guess not."

The past two days have felt like two moons. Yesterday, their blond hair fell dead. Sun-faded locks, grown long on the free hills of the steppe, were grabbed in one fist and slain by silver-handled shears. In heaps of browns and reds and creams, their spiritual essence laid mixed on the ground, eventually swept by fellow novices into wicker baskets and taken away. With arms folded in approval, the leaders of the stone house observed it all, likely aiming to concurrently dispose of all the Kipchaks' memories associated with the hairs' undisciplined growth.

That afternoon, they were issued every complement of this new creature's gear. Made to strip off their clothes, they made their mark on canvas bags and crammed their Turkish garments within. Cenk then marched them to another room, lined with identical bags on wooden shelves, the sacks looking like rows of oversized caterpillars waiting patiently to hatch. To make room for their forbidden garb, Cenk ordered them to pull down sacks, also labeled with names but long covered in dust.

In this cramped space, the group unceremoniously slipped on the drab uniform of the novice. They filled the shelves with their crumpled bags, which held captive the last contents of their old lives, well secured with twine. At their feet lay the canvas bags of other fellows now graduated, young men who probably had little Kipchak left in them.

The novices carried the dust-covered bags to the north gate, where Bozkurt and his drivers were waiting for them. The old man watched as the boys placed the bags neatly into the same carts they rode in on. Abruptly, Bozkurt turned northward, banging and creaking his string of half-filled carts back down the curvy path toward the river.

Perhaps Bozkurt knew the Kipchaks were not allowed, or were too scared to offer any gesture of thanks to the dealer. Perhaps he did not care. What would Duyal thank him for anyhow—for delivering him to this stone prison, under the glare of these hollering men? Duyal just shrugged his shoulders, figuring the old man received his pay for delivering the prince his Kipchak flesh. He guesses that soon Bozkurt would return with the carts, likely filled with more boys to become slaves, wearing clothes pulled from those same sooty bags.

This morning, they were introduced to other instructors while standing in formation. Under the watchful eyes of Cenk, they did little more the rest of the day than sit cross-legged, listening to nearly nonstop orientations.

He listens for the quiet footsteps of the duty *Furusíyya* instructor. These men seem to walk on pillows. There would be no verbal warning if they were caught talking, only a strike from his staff, as he heard last night. He wonders if he should confide in the Ox.

"I . . . I fear that our instructor has already decided that he wants me removed from training. I shouldn't have called out to my brother yesterday. Fleeing might be my best course," Duyal whispers.

"Hush your mouth. You should have thought of that trick about three days ago. You saw the guards in the towers, those bows and axes. You think they won't use them?"

"It's hard to find a target in the dark."

"Shit." Ox looks around nervously. "And if you were lucky enough to get out and stumbled into a shelter of the locals, you think these people would grant you a cup of tea and a hot meal? This isn't the steppe, my friend. And if you escape—you think the amirs, the eunuchs would not question me as to your plans? Don't you think they would beat this conversation from my lips?"

"Maybe so," Duyal says.

"So shut your mouth about it. Listen, they've placed us here to be trained. Don't think so much. I'm sure enough of these boys will do enough dumb shit to give Cenk a reason to abuse them too. Don't worry, he'll spread around his anger."

"I'd see no reason to stop for help in this city. I'd just continue to the hills."

"I'm telling you, muzzle it." Ox shakes his large head.

"It could be done."

"And then you'd be done. Your white skin would blend in as well as a fire in the dark. You're not thinking. How long would you last as a thief, pinching the odd goat? Before you were worried about not seeing your family again. Shit, one of your brothers is also inside these walls. What do you want?"

Duyal puts his head in his hands, slumps to his back. He sighs. He would do anything to be back on the steppe with his family, to go back to the way things were. "Maybe you're right. When we finish, maybe they would allow me to serve beside Gozde," Duyal says.

"Uhh… there are hundreds of… I don't. Well, who knows? But that's a long ways away. What we both need to worry about is making it through the instruction."

"I've found one brother. Maybe I can also locate Baris here."

"Right." Ox rolls to his back. "Listen. When the sun comes up tomorrow, you might want to take a good look around, because those around you are what we have left. I wouldn't count on seeing much of your brothers. We're done chasing goats. Amir Aqtay wasn't spouting babble. Look left and right, my friend, these are your brothers. Your new brothers."

Duyal cringes. He feels the drip of tears across his temples and into his ears. He rubs the rough wool across his face, hoping that Ox does not notice.

"Things will get better. Or at least we'll get used to it," Ox says.

"Cenk has a target on my chest. I'll never survive years here. Never. I would've been better off dying beside my father and uncle, putting arrows into Tartars. At least I'd still be on Kipchak land."

"Yeah, well… that's the past and you're lying here now. Alive."

Ox sighs. "There's nothing left of our old lives and you'd best wake up to that in a hurry. Because if you don't, you may end up as a servant or stuck polishing the sword of one of these pricks for the rest of your days. What would your father want? Your uncle? For you to quit, to run? For you to become a servant to a rich city man, or to ride and fight with the best of us that remain?" He rolls over, putting his back to Duyal. His breathing slows.

Duyal thinks of his uncle. The man's laugh, his scorn for the people in the cities, and then the parting vision last month of his corpse stuck with Mongol arrows. He lies there, staring into the blackness, listening to the deep draws of sleep from the others.

Perhaps the Great Sky has placed him here. Perhaps the spirits have selected all these around him to be here at this very place, together. Even though the Ox speaks too much, Duyal realizes that he may well be right. There is no other option. He had best fight for a spot in this regiment. He had best help his fellow novices in their quest to become Mamluks. He had best prove to the prince, to Bozkurt, to Cenk, and to all those here that he is worthy of earning their title. He had best prove it to his family, who likely now watch his deeds from above.

CHAPTER
23

Singer
North of Hisn Kayfa
September 1, 1236

A bat dives toward his hat and circles on frantic wings. Another follows in trace, speeding, flapping in the murky night. Paper-thin wings hurtling through the air, finishing their hectic sweep, only to return again and again.

Singer looks over his shoulder. The fleck gleams through the fir tops. The North Star, confirming their southward direction. He gives thanks to the Great Sky for keeping the clouds at bay, for guiding them, for another new moon to mask their way.

Arriving at a cut in the rolling scrubland, he steers his mount into the bottom and frees his feet from the stirrups, his knee retaliating. He ignores his pain, focusing instead on the mare beneath him. She has limped for two days and now froths heavily from the mouth. She no longer eats. She cannot go much farther.

Hidden in the draw, he slips down her side onto his own shaky legs, landing gingerly on toes still numb with frost nip. He caresses her drenched neck. Looking into her eye, he believes he sees a tear forming. He buries his head into her cheek, saddened that he tortures her. He takes in her scent of salty sweat and dirt.

He sighs. Getting three remounts was critical, and it didn't happen last moon.

He and Ferdi watched from below. Ilker lowered his Mongol watchmen to the ground, their friend pushing forward the pony-tailed head to silence the gurgle from the warrior's slashed throat. Moving to the ponies, Ilker removed the hobbles and stumbled down the opposite slope, yet fell, losing his grip on the second bridle. The stallion bolted back to his brothers over the hill, dragging the lead.

Ilker ran several steps after him, but caught himself, seeming to know that capturing the pony was unlikely and returning to steal another was suicide.

Singer yawns. For the first seven nights, the three riders stayed a course south and west through the entire lower Volga country, alternating between the five ponies as the beasts fatigued, staying just in front of the pursuing Mongols. During the days, they hid in ravines or under the low branches of conifers, their stolen ponies agreeable to rest beside them.

On the eighth night, a pony died. To avoid detection, they butchered him in the river, anchoring the stripped carcass in a deep hole. Midriver they sat upon the rocks, encircled by flesh, gorging in silence on the best raw cuts, covered in blood up to their elbows, eating until on the verge of puking.

More than a week ago, with the towering Caucasus Mountains upon the horizon, they had decided against making east for easy passage in the foothills of the adjacent Dagistan Mountains, as the locals confirmed that the Mongols were not only up and down the Khazar Sea coast, but also stationed in the thirty north-looking watchtowers that lined the Derbent Pass narrows. So the boys moved west, choosing an offshoot from the Darial Pass, merely a goat trail away from the traffic, gatekeepers, and crooks found on the main route.

They convinced a young Georgian herder to guide them to the trailhead, just east of the glaring white tooth of Mount Kazbek, which seemed to snarl them a warning of cold hardship to come. In payment, they killed a second pony gone lame, giving part of the meat to the boy's family and again stuffing themselves, before packing the remaining meat among their three ponies. Weaving through the high ferns and thick-stemmed groundsels, their guide led the way. But upon waking the second morning, the boy was gone.

They continued without him, past the ramparts of Gog and Magog, where they gathered mulberries and walnuts at dusk and slept huddled in a ball behind a rock, the wind gushing around them. Daylight brought bend after bend of sheer limestone, the endless gray broken only by drifts of snow, contorted in wind-swept curls, some hanging precariously above their pathway. Everywhere waves of icy crust swallowed the trunks of pines and massive stones, surrendering only down low, where clumps of gravel and grass and wildflower still predominated. Dissecting the bottom was a braided flow, chalky-blue and bitter cold.

Farther up and four days through the gorge, they picked along the narrow path, shut in by the high white faces on one side and the thrashing tributary of the Terek on the other, regularly blocked by great slides of chipped stone littered with the skeletons of both man and beast. There, they cut and peeled away a fur cloak and wool wrap from two stiffs found off the path, wrapping the scraps about their heads, feet, and hands. They rested little, knowing to stop for long meant a death by frost.

They arrived auspiciously to bubbling thermals, which drained putrid and yellow across the rock. Here the boys washed and warmed their feet, while the wind howled. And then mercifully across grass-covered glens, tablelands trimmed in monkshood and bellflowers, the blue and purple drooping and spilling over fields mixed with yellow primrose. There, hospitable herdsmen, not accustomed to travelers and showing pity on the ragged boys, welcomed them around their fire. Their women pushed forward bowls of boiled lamb and waved them along their way with bellies full. And then back down the south side through the pines and eventually past the shiny-leafed plants and giant ferns down lower, they stopped for a full day to let the exhausted ponies feed in the lush valley of grass.

Rested, it was not long into their southward journey when they come upon the Karasu and Taurus, more of the high mountain country to be traversed, where game was scarce. Only now do they drop down to more hospitable climes and terrain.

"I'm sorry, girl," Singer whispers to the mare. He remembers dawn-till-dusk rides as a lad on his favorite pony, but never had he covered such distances, day after day. That they had made it this far unmolested, clear down into the Anatolian hills, is unbelievable to him. He rubs her forehead and hums a herding tune in her ear. She had embraced her fate with dignity, surely knowing the riders were fleeing for their lives. Duty-bound, she plowed forward.

Ilker leans against his pony, cradling a leg to pick stones from his mount's hoof with a dagger. "His damn toes are wore off down to the white."

Ferdi eases down from his saddle and collapses into the dew-covered grass, arms out and grinning at the stars. "Pricks never did catch up with us."

The sweat on Ferdi's face catches the starlight, casting him swollen and ghoulish. Chunks of peeling skin flake from his cheeks like bark off a pine. His sliced long coat is bound shut, crusty-black, while outward from this center, the dust in rusts and browns has attached to the moisture, making his torso appear like the cross-section of some ancient tree.

They come to his side.

Singer scans the high ground for any sign of trailing enemy, and then back at Ferdi. "Your dressing, it's time to change it again." He stoops to place his water skin to Ferdi's lips.

Ilker moves to his mount, pulling his blade to cut off another piece of wool from his pony's blanket.

"Don't bother, Ilker," Ferdi says. "This is where I will speak my final words to the Great Sky."

Ilker drops his knife to his side and stares into the multitude of stars that encircle them, keeping his back to his mates. He turns. "Bullshit. We didn't drag your gimped ass this far for you to give up now. You'll be better after a little rest. Lift up your shirt there, goat sticker, so I can dress that scratch."

"I'm serious. Even if I do survive the rest of the ride, how well will a carved-up lad present to the Mamluks? I won't taint the chances of you both being brought into their ranks. We didn't come this far for me to bugger it."

"Hush," Singer says. "We'll finish this ride together. This won't be the first time they saw a dagger wound. If these soldiers are supplied as you say, they'll be able to properly treat your wound."

Ferdi unbuckles his deel and fights his way up to a seated position. He lifts up his tunic, unwraps the binding, and pulls the matted piece of blanket from his wound, the long, rolled dressing splotched in patches of dark and light. He flings the soggy tube from him as if it were a dead snake. With mouth open sideways, he stares wearily at his ribcage.

"Damn it, leave that thing alone. I got it," Ilker says.

They push Ferdi to his back and drop to one knee. They each sniff the wound and inspect it, their eyes but inches away from the pair of gashes that span from armpit to pelvis. They feel the swollen edges, a dribble of pus rolling to his waistline. From the sweet smell, Singer surmises the red perimeter skin has now turned to gray. He winces. The ruggedness of the ride has caused their stitches to break open again; the deep slashes refuse to seal.

Ferdi goes to one elbow and then drops to his back. "Fuck it, I'm done. Think I can't smell the rot? The fever comes stronger. I've won my last race."

Singer looks away, unable to meet his friend's eyes.

"You know it's true—no sense in me going on," Ferdi says.

Singer has not the heart to argue. He looks up to the stars, wondering why the Great Sky had chosen this path for them. He and Ferdi were no more than castoffs from their towers, joined by fate, only to again be spurned, this time by the Mongols.

Ilker. Just another bartered good, shoved by his tower to the invaders in hopes of escaping the Black Tartar's rage. Together, the three were exiles, again exiled by the spirits, their greatest hope now being the burden of military slavery.

"At least you two are free from the Mongol brand. Time for us all to be back among our blood," Ferdi says.

"Yes. Back to our blood, my friend," Ilker says somberly.

Ferdi nods and smiles, wrinkles and bags about his eyes. "Remember when I spoke of my brother? What he did a few years back?"

"Yeah," Singer says.

Ferdi struggles back up to one elbow. "If he was able to convince the traders to take him on, you should be able to do the same. I was even thinking… as close as we must be to Hisn Kayfa, you could go straight to the citadel. Skip the moneymen. Surely their khans, err, their amirs would prefer to pay nothing for good troops."

Singer and Ilker look up from their friend, their eyes meeting blankly.

Singer pretends to wipe the dust from his brow and eyes. He wonders if the gods curse him. First his parents, then his siblings, now his comrade. Every life he touches turns to early death. He regains his composure, reminding himself that it was not just his plan, but their plan, the gods' plan. They had a new moon; the Mongols had made it clear that they were no longer welcome.

> *Singer felt the snap of his man's neck, followed by the crumpling dead weight. Then to his right, the rip of wool as the larger guard slashed to free himself of Ferdi's reins, which cinched tighter and tighter across the Mongol's windpipe.*
>
> *Singer arrived in time to hear the crackle of breaking cartilage, his friend refusing to believe the watchman dead. He pulled free Ferdi's hands and pushed him downhill toward the ponies, his friend murmuring, "He's nicked me, he's nicked me."*

"My brother would send messages home," Ferdi says, a flicker beaming in his eyes. "His silver coins from Cairo fed us over the winter more than once. Their amirs, they allotted him a small plot with crops on them. The damnedest thing. A slave collecting coin from a farm that he hardly visited, where he not once shed a drop of sweat." He chuckles softly. "That could be you two one day."

"Don't worry about us," Singer says. Tears again well in his eyes. This time Ferdi sees them.

"Ahh, don't worry about me. The ravens must eat too. Sun will be up soon. Keep south. And take my bow, it's of no use to me. Just leave the dagger," Ferdi says with a half smile.

Singer and Ilker pick up Ferdi and move him to the north side of a scraggly cedar. They kick out the lower branches and nestle him under the twisted sprawl on a spongy bed of spent needles. Ilker ties off Ferdi's pony to a branch.

Ferdi shakes his head. "No, no. She'll do me no good. Singer's pony is nearly buggered."

Ilker looks to Singer with lips pursed. He shrugs his shoulders, dips his head. Singer removes the saddlebag and places it under Ferdi's head. He slips the sheathed dagger under his friend's thigh. Ilker leaves, returning with two filled water flasks, and lays the last of the dried meat at Ferdi's side.

"Git. For all we know, the Mongols could be just downstream. I will see you on the other side, my friends," Ferdi says.

"On the other side, Ferdi," Ilker says.

Singer grabs Ferdi's forearm and clenches it tightly. Ilker does the same. They release, tears streaming down their cheeks.

Singer mounts Ferdi's mare. He gives her his calves. She takes one step forward and stops. Her ears go back and she nickers softly. He pulls her head south and they depart, trailing the lame mare. Singer wipes a sleeve across his eyes and tries to clear the tightness in his throat.

As his mother would have had done, he will pay honor not with the bawl of a broken soul, but with vocals, strong and clear. He chants the death song in time with the drag and thump of the pony's hooves. His notes reverberate against the dusty slope, pure and true. He can only remember two verses, so he repeats them, until well out of his friend's hearing.

The pair wind their way southwest through the lower drainages of rounded hills, staying to the fingers, avoiding draws choked with crème-spiked hare's beard, where butterflies flutter joyously between blooms, unsympathetic to the heavy hearts of the passers.

Down the hills and through the drainages, the endless gray and brown of burnt grass interrupted occasionally by gangly patches of pink thistle. And on, stomping through fields of catchfly, where stem-suspended bladders, ribbed in scarlet stripes, clutch the necks of spent flowers, looking like patches of little pregnant bellies.

They clomp into the blinding sun, dust filling their nostrils. Hill after hill they pass without seeing a living creature, only the vultures watching them from currents on high. The grass thins; tan rock begins to overtake the landscape.

They stop for the night, where scarcely a word is muttered, a small fire between them bouncing heat against the slanted rock face at their backs. As the sky darkens, the last flicker of flame also retires, leaving a mound of throbbing coals at their feet. A star shoots across the sky.

"Ferdi's spirit?" Ilker asks.

"Maybe."

For two days more they ride, the country only becoming grayer, more arid. Where they see the rounded imprint of sheep or the black tents of people, they steer clear.

Riding south, with pink clouds over their shoulders, Singer wonders of these men they call Mamluks and what lies ahead for him and Ilker. Will these men of his own stock accept him and Ilker, or will they again be scorned? He ponders them while the sky shifts from magenta to rose, from ruby to vermilion. Ultimately, with the horizon cast in a bloody crimson, he decides it best to think of other things.

The next morning they come upon a trading route, the grass beaten down by hoof and wheel. They follow it.

"You smell that smoke?" Ilker asks.

"Yeah."

They nock an arrow, place their bows on thigh. They follow the tapered path, which straddles a rock-strewn hill. Suddenly, they face a graying man on foot. The ponies spook. Seeing the animals, the man takes two steps downhill and stares at his uphill sandal, its leather heel strap burred from dragging. Fear falls on the man's brown face as he spots their bows.

Singer puts both palms out and moves forward slowly. "We move in peace. Where do you go, friend?"

"To find trade beyond the hills," the man says, shifting the weight of the bundle upon his back.

"Are we near the Mamluk Citadel?" Singer asks.

The man looks up slowly and raises eyebrows long and peppered, the question shifting his eyes even farther from their faces. "Yes. You are near the headwaters of the Tigris, just follow the river downstream north of town. You cannot miss the fortress on the opposite bluff. You... you are Mamluks?" he says, almost apologetically, looking confusedly at their pony's thick legs and their ragged attire.

"Ah, no, no," Singer says.

The man stands straighter, looks them up and down. "They don't like visitors from common folk up there, especially those bold enough to show up armed, or on horseback." Then his jaw drops and his eyes enlarge, as if the man just now grasps some large mistake. An instant of clarity. "If you are emissaries, please forgive me. I will move along and very much hope my words are helpful for you in reaching that place safely."

Singer and Ilker look at each other as the old man gives a polite nod and steps off, making a wide arc around the ponies. They turn in the saddle to watch him shuffle away.

"What was that?" Singer asks.

"Tss, I don't know, but I don't have a good feeling about this."

"Yeah."

They continue on the path, its course switching up and down the bluffs along the river. They pass others, none speaking a word to them. They make a turn. Across the river is the white stone of the citadel, glowing gold in the morning sun.

"Whoa," Ilker says.

Their trail broadens to a road. They cross an arched bridge, the clap of hoof on stone quieting the idle conservation of the men they pass and silencing the laughter of container-carrying women, some wrapped in vibrant colors. Others scowl, while looking the other way; most look straight ahead, losing the previous expression on their faces.

They weave through the streets, Singer ignoring the endless merchandise and bustle of the place. He heads for the white tower, thinking only of the big-stoned building and their chances of joining the Kipchaks there. Short of the gate he stops.

"Think we should lead them the rest of the way?" Singer asks.

"Yeah, probably."

They dismount, stow their bows. Walking beside their ponies, they place their hands out, palms facing the two guards manning the large wooden gate from above. Scared as he ever has been, Singer walks beside his friend. Before them: white block walls. Square towers, with two men standing in each, crossbows trained on them. He takes a deep breath.

"If you have some sway with the spirits, this would be a good time to call on them," Ilker says.

"Yeah."

Two guards exit the fortress, one tall, one taller. They push closed the heavy doors behind them. The pair stands in form-fitted coats, white as river foam, gray mail exposed about their necks. Around their waists are broad leather belts, stiffened with rectangular adornments of silver. Inscribed on the leather is the wavy script of some foreign language and the tiny shape of swords neatly burnt. A metal lion is their belt buckle.

Dangling on suspension hooks are cream handles, with sheathed blades hanging ominously. Their trousers are bright yellow, as if smeared with the petals of the brightest flowers. Their boots are the best Singer has ever seen, covered atop with decorative gaiters.

Clenched across their bodies are long-handled axes, the same lion etched across the thick head of the blade. Their stance suggests anticipation, possibly a yearning that the coming interaction will be a chance to employ their recently -whetted steel. Their look is not one of arrogance or even over-confidence, but just that of two men itching to put their weapons to use.

"What do you want?" the taller guards asks.

"We come with only good intent—with hopes to join your force," Singer responds, keeping his hands in plain view.

The taller guard looks inquisitively at their torn deels, then at the birch-covered bows strapped to their mounts. "And w is to trust Kipchaks who serve the Mongols?" he asks.

"We were forced into service," Ilker says.

The tall one cracks an unbelieving smile, his eyes squinting beneath the brim of a bright enameled helmet, red as blood.

"Turn around. Walk two hundred paces away, mount your ponies and leave," the taller one says.

Singer clears his throat anxiously. "We have traveled far and only wish to serve you and your prince. Could we please talk to..."

"Listen, all I have to do is raise my left arm and you both will have bolts sticking out of your ears. I suggest you go now," the taller guard says.

Singer looks to the wall of the fortress. A second pair of guards stand behind the short wall, crossbows loaded, bodies erect and oriented for a quick shot.

Singer begins to worry. "We have nowhere to go. We only wish to prove that…"

"There's nothing to prove. You're both too old. The amirs will not have you."

"But…"

"Go."

The doors swing open, both guards seeming to assume their comrades inside will assist them in ending the conversation. The men turn to walk back in, taking an angled approach, allowing them to keep an eye on the boys.

The guards stop. A man walks out, the doors swinging partially closed behind him. The guards raise the axes across their bodies and face the Kipchaks, their dual scowls no longer inviting a scrap, but promising swift death for any mishap.

Singer feels a tingle in his fingers, his intuition telling him to be gone quickly. He freezes.

The advancing man looks out of place, wearing a yellow cap, a simple tunic and only a sword at his side. His hair is black, matched by skin that is tanned to near the same.

As the man approaches, Singer is surprised to see the taller guard face him smartly, click his boot heels together and bring his hand across the shaft of his axe. "Good morning, my father."

"Good morning, my sons," the man says kindly.

Singer crinkles his brow. How is this blond, light-skinned guard a son of that dark man?

The guard drops his salute smartly and resumes the more nervous disposition of the fellow at his side, lowering his axe toward the unwanted guests and tightening his lips. Their stance dares the Kipchaks to move.

"Who do we have here?" the man says with a strange accent that matches the old rider's earlier in the morning.

"Wanderers. They were just leaving, my father," the taller guard replies.

The man looks over both Singer and Ilker with interest, looking closely at their thick leather boots and long coats and then to their faces, dusted and cracked from their travel. "Are you Kipchaks?"

"Yes," Singer says.

"Where have you come from?"

"From the Volga Country. We left the Mongols to serve the prince of this citadel and join the other Kipchaks," Singer says.

The man smiles, but then tightens his thin lips and wrinkles his forehead as he again inspects their faces. He addresses Ilker. "You crossed the Caucasus to escape Mongol impressment. And then over the Taurus, through Seljukid lands... to come specifically here?"

"Yes. A friend of ours who died en route knew of this citadel and of a prince who wished to have more Kipchaks in his service," Ilker says.

The man's grin now spreads across his face, revealing beautiful teeth, straight and white.

He tilts his head sideways. "Is that so?" He stands and stares at them for a long while, as one would look at a badly wounded varmint refusing to die.

The guards move up to each elbow of the man.

The man then squints his eyes and runs his fingers through his groomed beard. "By Allah," he says, resting his palm upon the hilt of his sword. He nods to the conclusion he makes in his head. "My sons, come in. You will stay the night and be rested, fed. I wish to interview you myself tomorrow."

Since the man arrived, a third and fourth shooter have joined the others. Unlike the first two crossbowmen, who remain protected by the thick-blocked wall, these shooters stand exposed, each leaning their weapons on the top block on the tower, fingers on the trigger, weapons aimed at Singer and Ilker. In the opposite tower, a fifth shooter settles in.

"My father, I beg that you allow us to carry out our duty," the taller guard says to the man.

"Of course, of course," he replies, turning to leave with his head down in thought, hands folded in the small of his back.

With this, the taller guard raises his right arm out to his side and then down to his thigh slowly twice. He looks up to the towers and then to the gate, where two identically armored men emerge from the doors.

"Slowly take off your coat and boots and stand with your legs apart," the taller guard says.

As Singer drops his deel on the ground, the new guards swoop in and begin patting down both him and Ilker. Anxiety swells in him again. "Our ponies and gear, will we…?"

Checking to see if the man's back remains to them, the frisking guard moves his open hand into a fist that lodges upward into Singer's groin. Singer grunts, the wind leaving his lungs.

The guard bends to Singer's ear. "Shut up. You will not speak again until asked a question. Make a sudden move and you're both dead."

CHAPTER
24

Cenk
The citadel hippodrome, Hisn Kayfa
September 9, 1236

The pair slowly approach each other, moving sideways like water snakes across a lake, looking for an opening to strike. One tries to snatch a leg, the other sprawls, releases. They circle.

"Will you girls dance or fight?" Cenk asks from his perch. He scans the hippodrome's empty seats and then looks up to the blue sky. Allah has given him a fine day to train his recruits and these two in his pit prefer to frolic and feign attack, rather than scrap. He pulls the fresh air into his lungs. God willing, he will make them warriors.

The thick-armed recruit grabs Singer by the shoulder, sweeps a leg, and throws the newcomer to the ground, riding him to the packed dirt with a "thud."

"Ichami, Ichami." Cenk repeats the fighter's name to himself, driving yet another of their names harder into his memory. The boy is way too pleasant, too polite. No matter, he will beat this softness from him, from them all. But this Ichami appears not only strong, but also clever in the fight. This is good.

With the wind knocked from his lungs, Singer arches his back to avoid getting pinned, his *qayah*, or white skull cap peeling back along his head. Ichami cinches an arm and drives his shoulder into Singer's chest, pinning his opponent to the ground.

"Done!" Cenk says, rubbing his aching head.

Ichami shoots a smirk to Singer, as if to reassure his friend that it was nothing personal. He extends a hand to pull Singer to his feet.

"Lose that smile. Retract your hand! He's the defeated!" Cenk says.

Singer pulls himself back to his feet, snatches his cap and quickly places the dusty cover back upon his head. He locks his body in preparation for Cenk's launch into another verbal assault.

"We can only hope that our new novice from the Mongols represents the brute force of the infidels he served. Get out of my hole!"

Cenk only wishes his words were true. As the pair scrambles over the chest-high wall, Cenk slips back to 1235, to that huge valley near Sinjar where he put eyes on the Mongol horde for the first time. Creeping over that hill with six of the advance party from al-Kamil's army, he saw thousands, their black-armored bodies crawling about like beetles on a carcass. About them was a huge herd of war ponies, tripling the number of warriors.

He had been in awe, crawling backward and then returning to report, trying hard to not show his worry. Al-Kamil, the sultan, cared not for a look himself. In only minutes, the main body of Ayyubids retreated back across the Euphrates to fight another day.

Cenk eyes his novices lining the depression's circumference, spectators awaiting their call to grapple. He sighs. All of them—just raw *Muta'allim*, clumsily clad in their white uniforms. He shakes his head in disgust. Militarily, they are hardly better than when they arrived more than a moon ago.

The eunuchs had already removed twelve of his boys from training, those novices who had contracted the fever. Cenk has lost nearly a fifth of his troops and they have hardly started training. Quarantined from the others, these boys are as good as dead, of this Cenk is certain. Rarely were those fresh from the steppe able to fight off the sickness so foreign to their systems. He recalls his own training, when eighteen died within their first three weeks in Cairo. Dreaded morning inspections, with instructors passing through the ranks, pulling any boy who showed the signs of fever.

He grimaces. So far, he has found this new duty frustrating. For weeks he has busied himself in preparation work, studying the cavalry doctrine he already knows by heart and coordinating logistics with Safir and the weapons instructors for the upcoming training evolutions. He was told by the older instructors to be patient. "You know the progression—we create Muslims first, warriors second," they said.

But Cenk has barely trained a single troop since his recruits arrived, and it was driving him mad. To cope, he has attacked his required administrative tasks early each morning, giving him most of the day to spar with any willing instructor. For weeks he has regularly roamed the arenas, propositioning instructors between training revolutions for a match with sword or lance. The instructors, with few gaps in their schedule, now avoid him, just as the pious men in Cairo avoid the back alleys, where loose women make their vile offers.

He trains for war each day. If the current curriculum will not allow him to improve his novices' weapons skills, then he will at least maintain his own. He refuses to lose his edge. But despite the discipline of his routine, he feels an unsteadiness in his life. He knows his problem has less to do with being apart from his novices and more to do with what happens when the last candle has been blown out each night. This is when his troubles begin. The nightmares. Always they are of the clash with the Khwarazmians, but he is bewildered as to why.

He was certainly no amateur when it came to living through the horrors of battle. He had served Amir Turkmani for eight years, three campaigns alone throughout the Jazira and Anatolia. He saw comrades killed in the relatively blood-less campaign at Amid and endured the butchery in prying this very fortress from al-Masud's obstinate garrison, here in Hisn Kayfa nearly four years past.

Worse yet, he experienced full-scale carnage in the summer of 1234, when al-Kamil convinced sixteen Ayyubid princes to travel up the Euphrates to extract territory from the defending Seljuks. Countless attacks against barricades of stone and wood resulted in the needless death of several friends and many of his training mates, his *Khushdashiya*.

"Fool," Cenk says under his breath, thinking of the sultan and his senseless escapade.

But somehow that ambush along the trade route to the south is what repeatedly torments him. Perhaps it was the trauma of losing his patron, Turkmani—a greater role model than any relative from his native Bashkir forests. In the familiar nightmare, instead of surviving the battle he often awakens gasping for air, his throat slashed by sword or his hands trying to pull an oversized arrow from the chest of his patron.

He now fears sleep. In the evenings, he frequently finds himself in Hisn Kayfa's back markets, overpaying the Turcoman traders for skins of *koumis* in hopes that their fermented mare's milk will smother the memories and put him into an inebriated slumber. Although the mind-altering drink from his homeland does little to ease his angst, this reality has not stopped him from drinking. He rationalizes. Once this moon is gone, the Turk's mares will produce less milk and his supply will dry up. He hopes he will not move on to wine.

His novices wait in silence, their hands locked in the smalls of backs. He looks around the circle, searching for his next pair of victims, looking each boy up and down. Staring back at him is an unblinking third eye from the trouser crotch of each novice. Sixty-two pale red dots, signifying acceptance of their new religion, their stains born from the eunuchs' daggers, foreskins removed to make these converts closer to their prophet. All endured this ceremony without a whimper, as to do otherwise would be considered a sign of feebleness before their God.

He spots Duyal and smiles. For weeks this novice has been lying low, attempting to miss the eyes of his instructors. The boy is not stupid. He would have done the same himself.

"Duyal, did you think I had forgotten about you? Come down into the center, so your fellow worms can witness your destruction," Cenk mocks in a gentle tone.

Duyal hops into the pit self-assuredly, faces his instructor, and rests the back of his hands atop his buttocks.

Cenk scans, his eyes only stopping on the meanest, quickest boys in the tulb. There. Yes. Demir, meaning "Iron" in the dialect of the Kipchaks. This recruit carries the dashing fair looks of a Mamluk, plus arms and shoulders nearly twice the size of most boys in the tulb. Cenk chuckles, mumbles to himself, "We'll see how the amir's baby brother does against this beast. Demir!"

Demir and the giant, Ox, look to have emerged at the top of the tulb, as their faces remain clean. Nearly all the others are smattered with bruises and cuts upon their cheeks, foreheads, and necks, as his young dogs tussle at night to find their place in the pack. Without prompting, such happens in every class. It is necessary. Today, each novice has already fought at least twice. This is good—the more that is settled here, under his supervision, the better.

He smiles. Always the biggest and strongest start off earning the respect of their peers. This will change in the coming moons, as brawn remains important but dwindles in magnitude, the novices coming to realize that the reputation of a cavalry warrior comes primarily from his possession of courage and weapon skills upon horseback.

Demir hops into the pit and struts straight toward Duyal. He stops to face his instructor. The boys wait for permission.

"Go!"

Demir charges, grabbing at his opponent's tunic, yet the wiry Duyal fights him off. Demir slows his approach only when Duyal shifts laterally; otherwise he moves in, always forward, like the badger.

During his younger days, Cenk was always wary of this animal. As a hunter inched closer with spear in hand, a found badger would hiss and snap his jaws in warning. Demir reminds him of this solitary beast, one who prefers to be left alone, mindlessly digging for grubs and ground squirrels. Until confronted, when the lumbering creature looks up with beady eyes and broad shoulders and surprises nearly every foe with his strength and agility.

"By Allah, fight!" Cenk says.

Demir snatches a leg and slams Duyal onto his back. Their peers let out a collective groan. Quickly, Duyal manages to flip onto his front, but not before Demir secures an arm.

Cenk is surprised at Duyal's quickness, though perhaps he shouldn't be. After all, whether he likes it or not, Duyal is the younger brother of Gozde, the amir who earned one of the three ribbons of valor when taking this very citadel. Cenk spits. Gozde is good, but he was just another Mamluk who did his job that day. He just happened to do it under the eye of al-Salih, while Cenk's own comrades faced the worst of the defender's arrows on the north side.

Demir attempts to turn the boy over, all the while grinding Duyal's face into the ground with his massive fore-arm. Sand and small pebbles grind into Duyal's forehead, blood quickly staining his blouse and neck. Duyal struggles to push himself up and free.

Cenk jumps into the pit. "How dare you bleed in my pit, disgracing this sacred ground! You allow your uniform, graciously provided by our prince, to be soiled with your own useless blood!"

His own blood thumps through the veins in his tem-ples, intensifying the pain in his head, spurring the rage. His fury notches up one heartbeat at a time. "And Demir, you can't thrash this weak-hearted louse without drawing blood. Pathetic!"

Cenk squats, lurches his head toward Duyal, the strained tendons in his neck sprawled and exposed like the base of a swamp cedar. "Time to quit. No blood need be shed, while serving in the cook's crew. Come on Duyal, three meals a day... life in the rear guard. Let the other fellows do the fighting. I can arrange these things."

At the comment, Duyal manages to slide his head from Demir's lethal hold. Cenk rises and paces, disappointed that his words seem to motivate the lad. "Demir, you can't even pin this measly bread baker? Maybe your clumsy dick skinners would be better suited stirring molten naft." Not impressed with either fighter's skill, Cenk turns his back and shakes his head. Let the tulb know he demands excellence. He sighs, crosses his arms, and grunts.

Demir regains control again and turns Duyal on his back, only to have Duyal spin out of the hold.

Knowing the match will not last long, Cenk returns to the pair, squats, and whispers loud enough for Duyal and only the closest novices to hear. "Duyal, I'm not teasing. I'll personally guarantee the new assignment." He then stands to look across the packed dirt and around the empty benches. "Or are you waiting for your favorite amir to save you from the pain? But… but… there's no amirs around here." Cenk's eyes circle the pit's perimeter, checking if his comment baits a novice into smiling. But all have learned such tricks and stand with locked lips.

Cenk remembers his vow to Turkmani—eliminate the weak. It brings him potency. "Quit! You don't have what it takes!" Hunched like a primate, he orbits them, kicking dirt upon their backs and heads.

The wrestlers ignore him, each struggling for control. Although thoroughly outmatched, Duyal refuses to yield. Demir digs in harder, pulls in an arm with bone-breaking strength and finally pins Duyal's shoulders to the ground.

"Done!"

Demir rises from his victory and begins to imitate the flight of a hawk, a learned response from hundreds of matches won on the steppe.

Cenk rushes over and boots Demir in the ass. "Enough! You stupid dog! Where do you think you are?

Demir looks down.

"Guidon, get all of them away from my pit. In formation!" The novices scurry in response. Cenk turns to Demir. "You stay. You insult the sanctity of the arena. You insult your God. Dig. Until I say stop."

Demir places his palms on the ground and begins running in place, bringing each thigh up to his armpit, while his alternate leg extends straight out during each stroke, as instructed prior.

Cenk looks heavenward remorsefully. "Oh, Allah. How will I make these into warriors of the faith? Cooks. These could be. Please deliver me a fresh lot of fighters, so that I may send these to go cook for those befitted to serve you. I need those who will fight."

Fight. Little it does to help Cenk. Despite the daily exhaustion from his own sparring over the past weeks, he cannot seem to shake the anger he feels inside. He knows not from where it stems exactly, only that storm clouds come often and follow him from the citadel to his home. He regrets his conduct over the last few moons. He recalls how hopeful he was last moon. He being a new instructor. A new wife on the way.

> *"That must be them... has to be," the man next to Cenk said, cupping his hand over eyes to better view the line of approaching carts.*
>
> *Cenk rested his elbows on the stone ledge of the north rampart. He took in the evening air, content with his surroundings. He turned and smiled at the Mamluk. Soon the carts of girls rambled their way up toward the citadel, beds full of blonde heads; bodies still draped in the rags of the Kipchak.*
>
> *When their young faces came into view, there was chatter and smiles and backs patted along the line of bachelors. Cenk eyed several of the prettiest, his loins hungry.*
>
> *"I'll take that one," his comrade joked, pointing to a sweet lass whose breasts jiggled with each bump in the road.*
>
> *"Yeah," Cenk said with a grin, but knew those decisions would be made by their prince.*

All were grateful for al-Salih's benevolence, their master having purchased forty-nine girls, one for each of the older bachelors in his regiment. While all knew their prince mainly shouldered this great expense to keep his men away from the available women in Hisn Kayfa, this did not dampen their enthusiasm. Most preferred their own kind, rather than the dark-skinned Turks with scheming fathers and backgrounds so foreign to their own.

The group marriage was a grand celebration: a feast of sheep and goat; a line of apprehensive girls in long dresses. Brides, receiving that day not only new husbands, but also a new religion. Each seemed too scared to refuse either, their bright headscarves hiding their appearance, but not the expression in their eyes.

The grooms were ever impressive in summer dress coats of white, the cloth taut across knotty muscle. Their prince was every bit the proud father of ninety-eight. He gave a solemn speech, followed by intimate well wishes and embraces, passed in sincerity to each new couple. They were his children in every sense of the term, and he acted as a father, his eyes constantly blinking out tears of joy and thankfulness to Allah.

Cenk was happy to take the girl chosen for him, Fidan, a fourteen-year-old from the upper Don River country. That day her high pink cheeks, peach-sized breasts, and soft voice seemed heaven sent. She was gorgeous and well-mannered, yet even the *hijab* she wore poorly camouflaged her sadness in being separated from her family on the steppe. He could not fully make out if the melancholy in her behavior was just a product of her homesickness or trepidation in accepting him. He had tried to be patient with her.

Perhaps part of her sadness lay in losing her gods, the abrupt changes required by her conversion to Islam, Fidan and the other women had become Muslims only days before the wedding. Their prince had taken care of this indoctrination, of course. Yet the women were educated very little on the traditions of the life of Muhammad, or *hadith,* the requirements guiding both men and women in dressing and behaving modestly in public.

He had broken her of the habit of meeting his gaze, and she now seems more willing to wear the veil in public. In fact, she seems to prefer to wear it at all times, almost using the veil as a means to hide herself from him. Hopefully she will adjust.

In the mornings now, he often awakens to find Fidan having snuck away in the night, choosing to sleep on the fire-side mat. Usually he will not remember what happened to warrant her action. Only the bruises up her arms and swelling about her eyes the next day rekindle fragments of his isolated memory, his mind at nights so often numbed with drink. Like a dog too often beaten, she now cowers when bringing him the fish, yogurt, and poultry—those dishes taught to her by the older Mamluk wives. In the bedroom, the flicker of intimacy that burned the first few nights has been extinguished.

He knows that he has already stressed his marriage. He wishes he could start over, but figures he would probably mess it up even with a new wife. What did he know about women?

Deep down, he is dismayed by his behavior and the incongruity of his life, especially as compared with those he trains today. This morning, his recruits were in the cleric's class, reviewing the Six Pillars of Islam: testifying that there is no God, but God; the five daily prayers; helping the needy; fasting and reflecting at Ramadan; making the pilgrimage to Mecca; the path of Jihad.

Yet for days, while his troops embraced these tenets and learned the ethics of their new religion, Cenk, their own *Furusiyya* instructor, broke them—missing prayers and even drinking during the past holy month of Ramadan before their arrival. What kind of example is he?

He is remorseful and knows one day he will be judged for his shortcomings. But he has faith that when his own book of deeds is placed on the scales in front of Allah, his diligence to the Sixth Pillar alone will ensure his entrance into paradise—his dedication to Jihad, the Holy War. In honor of God, he has fought honorably for almost a decade.

He pictures those Muslims down the hill, the townsfolk in the mosque, some of their foreheads flat from years of pressing head to stone in attentive prayer. He spits, cursing the pious, those who cling only to the dreamy concept of the *Umma*, or community of believers, ignoring the realities of politics and war across the lands of Islam. Sheep. These cowards only pray and judge others, but refuse to shed blood and risk their sacred lives for God and their prince.

He spits again. Action, righteous performance on the battlefield has to be more pleasing to Allah. It must be the surest pathway to heaven. A pilgrimage to Mecca? It would be the right thing to do, but only if his prince were going, ideally to occupy the place for the glory of God.

He scratches his left tricep, feeling the rope of scar tissue beneath his tunic. If his past combat proves lacking in God's eyes, then he is confident that his coming performance at the citadel should tip the scales in his favor. He can hardly think of anything but improving the skills of and toughening the novices in his care. He will overcome his failings in virtue by properly training his recruits for Jihad, all for the glory of Allah and al-Salih.

He sighs. And if even the next years of instructing prove inadequate, he knows in the back of his mind that martyrdom remains a likely prospect. It is only a matter of time before he is back into a combat unit. How long can he really avoid catching that killing blow, or dodging that arrow with his name on it? He grins, letting glimpses of those near misses float to the front of his memory—arrows passing under his armpits, banging into his breastplate, slicing open his trousers. Almost too many to count.

He recalls one battle at dawn after no sleep, ducking his head for no reason as a blade from behind hissed overhead. Back thrusting into the infidel's gut, he twisted the blade on the way out and spurred off with intestine still dangling from his hilt. Surely God has given this sixth sense to him for use in executing the Sixth Pillar. Allah has spared him this long for a reason.

But one day a blow will take him. And that day, amid the dust and stench of battle, he hopes God will allow for his transgressions and turn a holy eye away from those times when his loyal subject snuck a few sips of *koumis* and missed the odd prayer. Hopefully, his occasional disobedience will not overshadow his nobility, his willingness to die on the battlefield, only to further Allah's plan.

For now, he must exercise what patience he has, while his novices spend a majority of their day receiving religious training. He acknowledges the importance of the clerics' and eunuchs' work in ensuring that the recruits win what many call the "Great Jihad," that triumph of the heart over one's "lower nature." They cannot become Mamluks until they cast off their pagan gods. He supposes he feels some gratitude that years ago he never had to confront this issue, arriving to his initial training in Cairo as a Muslim, his people converted by the Bulgars decades ago.

It matters not. He knows the "Great Jihad" is the easy part. For him and most Mamluks, the Sixth Pillar is the core of Islam: "Jihad of the Sword," the military struggle on behalf of God. This is the pillar that separates those who talk and preach from those who will draw their swords and bend their bows to protect Islam. And this Sixth Pillar is why Allah placed him in the world.

CHAPTER
25

Duyal
The citadel hippodrome, Hisn Kayfa
September 19, 1236

Another tulb approaches from the opposite direction, a rectangle of tight white and harmonized boot heels hugging the right side of the wide corridor. While the instructors seem to go to great lengths to keep the training units sequestered, such encounters are inevitable, maybe even planned by the *Mu'allim*.

Duyal is intrigued by the other units, curious what many moons behind these walls makes one into. He has seen this unit before, figuring the other tulb is a couple of years or so into training. Only thirty-eight of them march, their numbers likely halved from when they first arrived at the citadel. Like antelope that suffered through a long winter on the steppe, only the fittest and mentally strong now comprise their ranks.

In step with his fellow novices, Duyal centers himself on the boy to his front. He shifts his eyes right, ensuring that he is also properly aligned on the recruit beside him. He times the move to buy himself a few seconds of inattention, a moment of reprieve from Cenk's critical eye. As the two units close, Duyal keeps his head straight so as not to be noticed, but shifts his gaze left, as far as his eyes will allow.

A tall novice carries their guidon smartly, the stitched number five fluttering upon their yellow cloth. Bronzed, hardened forms march smartly by, not one moving an eye or head to see who passes. Any roundness in their faces has been chiseled away by constant training; any gentleness in their demeanor long wiped clean by their instructors' sternness.

Their *Muàllim* nods to Cenk, paying little attention to those in his charge, as cover, alignment, and general discipline are now old lessons mastered by his novices. As they pass, a draft of seasoned wool trails them. The confident stomp from broken-in leather passes by in threes.

Duyal wishes that he was among them, that he acted like them, smelled like them, unsure if those in his own tulb will ever rise to be like these. If all novices had arrived as crude oak saplings, these recruits were now ready lance shafts, their rough bark and lighter sapwood having been whittled away over the years by their instructors, leaving only honed dark wood in its place. All that remained was for their blunt ends to be fitted with heads of Mamluk steel, during the last few moons of training.

Swop! "Keep your filthy head forward," Cenk says.

As Tulb Five passes, Duyal envies their clean, form-fitting garb, not only tidy-looking but obviously designed for swift movement. So unlike the stained, baggy outfits his tulb wears, the same ones tossed to them on their arrival, the trousers especially burdensome, always slipping down, the drawstring always needing retying. These awkward moments during training always gave Cenk and the other instructors a chance to whack or kick a novice.

He figures the uniform issue is just another part of the greater Mamluk design—anything received here will bear a dear cost. Only after a year and a half can the worthy of his fellow "worms" shed their tunics and ugly trousers for the superior uniforms of these "horsemen."

He ponders the strangeness of it—the oddness of their circumstances. On the steppe, the word "slave" put fear in his people's bones. At best, slavery meant being absorbed by another tower. Most often, it meant the end of nomadic life for a lad, that roving self-determining existence endured, yet cherished by his ancestors. Just two moons ago, with the extinction of his tower, Duyal saw for himself a dreaded future of endless menial labor.

Yet he is learning that slavery in this place is altogether different from his preconceptions. Here, bondage, servitude to al-Salih is not considered a curse, but a blessing. A privilege. While he did not come to this great stone lodge by his own choosing, he is beginning to understand the pride of being within it. Those who have already earned the title walk its halls with purpose in their steps, stand straighter and taller than the novices. More often he finds himself looking forward to achievement on his only viable path forward: becoming a slave soldier in the service of al-Salih.

They pass into the wide expanse of the hippodrome. Despite having entered several times before, the sight of it takes his breath. He feels a sense of importance in just being there. Both the lower benches of wood and the higher stone seating rise up to the sun in perfect trajectory from the groomed training surface. Duyal reckons if the place were full of spectators, not one would have his view obscured by another. The seating alone leaves little doubt as to what the inhabitants' focus is here—brilliance on the field.

In the far quarter, three novices pull wide rakes across dirt upset by horses' hooves. In another, a group watches the example of their long-haired instructor as he parries a lance blow from a novice. Adjacent to them, archers release arrows into wooden-legged targets, while black-belted instructors stride with hands clasped behind their backs in identical fashion.

Located in the center of the citadel, the hippodrome is architecturally the gigantic divider between the training tulbs on the west side and the barracks of the prince's regiment on the east side. Common sense says the prince built the novice barracks and training chambers on the west side to keep his youngest sons as far as possible from both the ungodly influence of the city and the hands of his regular troops. But while the hippodrome serves as the novices' eastward boundary in the citadel, as going any farther would certainly warrant a beating, Duyal senses its true function is far from being a barrier.

Each dawn, tulbs stand in the darkness, waiting in the hippodrome's bowels for Amir Aqtay's determination that sufficient light is present for training. Even then, early morning instruction is typically given under the crackle of torches lining the gray stone walls. At "candles out" for the novice barracks, Duyal regularly hears the distant clank of Mamluk swords ringing from the arena, the din continuing well after blackness obscures the interior barrack walls.

Duyal feels this place is the heart of the citadel—its pulse pounding and reverberating continuously. Logically partitioned into sections, each training area is customized by the citadel's four groups of weapons instructors, those specializing in lance, bow, sword, and horsemanship. And just as the human heart's chambers receive purple blood and pump back to the body's extremities blood nourished with oxygen, so do the arena's quarters collect the prince's human treasure from every corner of the stone house, and—through the instructors' collective wisdom—churn out lethal Mamluk scarlet, refortified with the collective verve of the place.

The tulb heads to the four rows of mock horse mounts and their neatly staged armor. Demir—their gear guard— awaits them, standing front and center with his hands overlapped in the small of his back. His face is slick with sweat; his silk cap so wet it has turned transparent, showing through it his dusty-brown hair. All realize guarding the kit within the citadel walls is unnecessary, yet Cenk and the other instructors require it, pounding home security and accountability for every piece of equipment at all times.

Cenk halts the tulb. He faces them left. Duyal locates his gear, eying it as he would a dangerous adversary. He runs through Cenk's words this morning, recalling the proper order, the speediest methods. He wonders how anyone could fight while wearing it all. He remembers his uncle's saying, "Travel light, freeze at night." This will not be the Mamluk way.

Concentrate. "Be efficient, be efficient," Duyal tells himself.

"Gear up!" Cenk says.

Fifty-nine novices hustle for their makeshift mounts and identical stacks in a controlled panic. Reaching his pile, Duyal fumbles with his chain mail shirt, or *kazaghand*, its tight iron mesh covered in a pinkish wool layer, the brilliant red scorched by years in the sun. He tries to calm himself with the words from their manual, "Always, left before right." He jams his left arm into the sleeve, then his right. Grabbing the bottom edges, he brings the heap above his head and wriggles the heavy shirt over himself. The mail smells of river clay, but the wool padding reeks—sweat and dirt from countless novices worse than the stink when shearing muddy sheep.

He drops his left shoe. His right. He stoops to align their heels before pulling on his thick-soled riding boots, the only gear properly sized for the individual recruit. With shaking fingers he cinches the cord on his boots and buckles on leather gaiters over them, round scabs of bare hide dotting these covers.

A grunt next to him. Air driven from the lungs of another. His mates are already fighting on their leather chest pieces. His heart races. Securing the last strap, he snags his cuirass, or *jawshan*, and raises it above his head. He recalls his instruction, "Make thin like a lance." He pulls together his elbows and sucks in his breath, causing the armor of hardened leather hoops to slide down his torso, coming to a rest on thick shoulder straps. He twists it into place, straightening the hoops, bound together by leather bits of varying thicknesses and lengths, the armor looking as if cobbled together by a dozen hands.

He completes his transition by slamming the aged helmet wobbly upon his head—its leather inlays so stretched that the shell sits flush upon the crown of his head; its hardened shells bearing layers of red and black paint, chipped and cracked. Like all of their equipment, the helmets provided in the initial issue are deemed "serviceable," but are not the generation of modern armor worn by the Mamluks.

As with their gaiters, the lion emblem has been purposely scraped from the helmet's surface, as none wearing them have earned the honor to bear the prince's symbol. Personal inscriptions and designs, once stitched into the fabric or etched into the flat pieces of armor, are now but obvious vacancies. Tiny holes from cut thread and scuffed sections of discolored leather serve as reminders of what these boys are not yet.

Duyal locks his body next to his saddled structure, relieved that he is not the last of them dressed. Eyes fixed forward, he stares at the backs of the boys before him. A glob of huffing pink in crooked helmets, standing beside the burdensome contraptions. Several still struggle with their *jawsans*, their movements becoming reckless, more desperate, as these novices sense most of their mates finishing.

To his front a novice stands perfectly erect, his helmet straight, his gear lying naturally upon his body, as if he were meant to wear it. Singer. Duyal is increasingly impressed with the newest member of their tulb. Short, but with over-sized thighs and calves from his time spent combing the mountain country, Singer hides easily among them. Only two weeks into the routine, Singer already knows more and out-performs nearly the entire outfit, providing little reason for Cenk's attention.

He found it odd that the eunuchs placed Singer's sleep-ing mat next to his. Once hearing that Singer had served with the Mongols, Duyal refused to exchange a word with him for days. Yet recently, Duyal has found comfort in their late-eve-ning conversations, respecting Singer's escape and sensing that the young man had not picked up on all ways Mongol. A couple of years older than most of them, Singer possesses a quiet peace that is welcome in this place.

"Hayri, you're slower than two camels fucking!" Cenk bellows, slowly wading through the ranks until he stands in front of the one who is last to plop the lamellar bucket upon his head and tighten his body to the position of attention like the rest.

"Did you fall from your pony as a boy? Land on your stinking head?"

"No *Mu'allim,* this novice has no excuse," the slight-built Hayri replies, pushing up the brim of his helmet.

Duyal winces. Some are indeed slow to learn.

"Did I say you could move? And no, there is no ex-cuse. And no excuse for sounding off with the voice of a girl. I'm about ready to reach down and check for a slit between your legs."

Two in the tulb chuckle. The rest stand expressionless, a smile the furthest thing from their lips. Incredibly, Cenk lets the pair's infraction go unpunished, perhaps amused with himself, or choosing to instead focus his energy on Hayri, the novice they call "Smiley."

"Useless." Cenk waves a hand and looks away. "You're not worth my breath. In no time you'll be gone. To the river, washing uniforms with the other girls!" Cenk pops his brim into Hayri's forehead, knocking the helmet from the novice's head.

Cenk turns to the formation's front. "We don't have time for this."

Their *Mu'allim* paces, then stops. He pulls his coat taut under the black belt. Using his thumbs, he flattens the material from front to back, perhaps trying to recall where he left off.

Earlier in the day, their instructor revealed the basic skills of the "*Furusiyya*," or the Mamluks' cavalry principles. As there were six Pillars of Islam, there were six skills of the *faris*: mounting the horse, employing the lance, use of the sword, holding the shield, shooting the bow, and the game of polo. Cenk explained the *Muta'allim* will progress through many work-up sessions in all training areas, following their instruction with competency tests at various levels. This morning they started on the first skill, mounting and dismounting the structure, over and over.

Duyal found the exercise ridiculous. Every Kipchak had grown up on the back of a pony. Do the amirs worry that some of the boys will have trouble adapting to the taller Arabians? He wonders if they will start the instruction of every skill at such a basic level. He supposes it does not matter, as having a say in any subject in the great stone house is one concern he need not worry about.

Beside Duyal stands his mock horse, its cross-beamed frame supported by rough-sawn timbers, its wooden legs beaten black from the endless scuff of boot soles. In place of hooves, thick metal spikes secure the creature to the deck.

A barrel-shaped structure sits atop the frame, composed of slatted timbers, replicating the torso of the great Arabians. Strapped to this is a high-backed saddle, its identical pommel and cantle constructed of wood; its seat of buffed leather. Reins nailed to the front of the barrel rest upon the horn. The reproduction stands at sixteen hands, the average height of the Arabians or Cyrenaicans ridden by the Mamluks, three to four hands higher than the steppe ponies from his past.

While marching past the high portals a few days ago, Duyal had caught glimpses of the authentic animals, elegantly grazing in the prince's fields, with brilliant coats of chestnut, gray, and bay. While he occasionally still contemplated scaling the stone walls at night and making away on the back of an Arabian, these thoughts were few and kept to himself, as speaking such would now only be a signal of frailty to his training mates.

His stomach gurgles. A surge of nausea rumbles through his guts, the sun adding intensity to the growl. Beads of sweat trickle down his forehead and neck. He prays that he has not caught the fever, which has already killed seven recruits in his tulb. As before, he must hide his symptoms, or risk Cenk escorting him to join those pushed into the quarantined area. And this would be a death sentence. For within that chamber, if not already infected, he would certainly catch the fever from those dying. He pushes these thoughts from his mind. The food. It has to be the food.

Although Safir had directed the Turkish cooks to slowly transition the recruits away from their simple steppe diet, often olive oil, cumin, pepper, and paprika found their way into the recruits' meals, the cooks often feeding Cenk's tulb the identical food prepared for the Mamluks on the other side of the citadel.

Accustomed to yogurt, goat, and lamb, and able to make the adjustment to the Turkish sardines, some of the boys had trouble with meals containing chickpeas, apricots, and the abundant wheat. And a novice had no choice but to eat what was put in front of him, as leaving even a morsel on his plate was labeled an unthinkable offense to their master. Maybe it is the oil causing his symptoms, or the vegetable they called "eggplant," which had just come into season.

Perspiration soaks through his skullcap, pouring into the corner of his eyes. He blinks repeatedly, a vain attempt to keep the burn from his eyes, knowing better than to raise his arm and wipe his face, as even when turned his instructor somehow sees all. He tenses his ass to keep from shitting himself. He forces some deep breaths, tries to will away the queasiness. He must not draw attention. He cannot get caught wasting food or dishonoring the training ground.

"A review of mounting the horse, just as we did this morning," Cenk says in an uncharacteristically patient tone. He stands on the left side of the saddled mount, with his whip and reins in his left hand. "I have seen some who claimed to be good horsemen, before they had gained a firm seat on the Arab horse. These are the men often on their backs at the end of a jousting match, or in battle, lying about with their guts in the dirt."

With his right hand, Cenk grabs the pommel and places his left foot into the stirrup. "I make sure my left foot does not hit what? Singer?"

"The horse's elbow, *Mu'allim,*" Singer says.

"Of course," Cenk says. He then springs effortlessly into the saddle, landing centered between the horn and cantle. With his shoulders and back straight, his feet centered in the stirrups, heels down, his palms facing toward heaven, he sits in the saddle naturally, somehow managing to appear distinguished even on the back of the crudely built replica. "Remember, good horsemanship—*libaqa*—begins with a firm seat, an upright body. Solid feet and the reins held properly.

God Most High created his Mamluks absolutely straight. This is the way he wishes them to be always in the saddle."

God Most High—Allah. Duyal feels a warmth in his heart that briefly cuts the stab in his turning stomach. The revolving band of clerics and eunuchs, who for weeks taught the recruits from the Koran, brought not only a profound sense of understanding of God, but also the only sense of calm available to Duyal's soul amid the regimented mayhem of the citadel. The contrast was incredible: inside the clerics' chambers flowed the soothing words of the text; everywhere else poured the shouted abuses from their *Mu'allim*.

The holy men made it very clear that the Great Sky, Father Mountain, Mother River, and all the spiritual guides, figures, and invisible forces contacted by the Kipchak Saman, were actually the work of one God. And it was this one God who saw promise in them and plucked the boys from their diminished towers to be his selected warriors.

Duyal could not help but admire the man they called the Messenger of God. Mohammad, the Prophet. While unworthy to warrant comparison to the Prophet, Duyal and the others feel a connection, as Mohammad was also an orphan, a warrior, a man who rose to prominence despite a path full of obstacles. Duyal feels a fire inside. A craving to be more like Mohammad.

Last week, in ceremony, each in the tulb pronounced their faith to one God, fulfilling the First Pillar of Islam. Three in the tulb, one the son of a Saman, refused and were forced from the citadel that evening. But the remaining novices now heartily embrace their new religion and the place they will one day hold in it—as God's instruments, who wage Jihad against all infidels.

The afternoon sun transforms the hard leather on his head into a cooking pot, slowly simmering his brain. The pressure builds in his bowel. Cenk jumps from his saddle to the ground and bends to adjust the stirrups on his mount. Sensing an opportunity, Duyal pulls the seat of his trousers to the side and releases a gush down his leg, while his instructor's head is down. Two novices near him also see their chance, stooping to heave in silence, at once bringing sleeves to their mouths and scuffing dirt over the evidence.

In two swipes from his boot, Duyal covers the mess at his feet and resumes his position. The smell of shit emanates. Residual fluid dribbles down his hamstring to his calf. Into his boot.

"Rea-dy... mount!"

Duyal lands with a slosh. He frets. Cenk will see the stain in his trousers, smell his stench. Duyal glances down at the wet spot beside his mount and then at his trousers. He thanks God that his excretion is mostly clear. He wishes for the air to clear, before his instructor arrives.

Cenk smiles. "By Allah, could it be that we all got it right this time?" The instructor strolls the ranks, stooping to push feet forward in the stirrups, pulling heads back, straightening backs, twisting wrists ever so slightly to the proper position.

"Warriors. We will make you into warriors," Cenks grunts.

CHAPTER
26

Duyal
The citadel, Hisn Kayfa
September 24, 1236

Duyal takes a lemon half, dips it in his bowl of salt, and rubs the fruit across a section of the already-shining basin. With a cloth pressed to the heel of his other hand, he buffs the treated brass, lost in the metallic array of figures across its surface. Inlaid with both silver and gold, the scenes depict riders and throned figures, men dressed according to their rank.

Servants, bowmen, polo masters—all bearing gifts for their ruler. Unicorns, leopards, griffins, lions, elephants, sphinxes, camels. The man in the center of the bowl must be al-Salih, has to be al-Salih.

A thump of boots coming up the stairs. Stay to your task and no man will bother you. He redips his lemon in the salt and works the green parts under the bowl's rim. The footsteps turn his way down the corridor. They close on him. Duyal turns. "Good evening, amir."

He smiles, chucks the lemon and cloth, and hugs Gozde. His brother's scent fills Duyal's nostrils, flooding him with memories of Saiga hunts and siblings huddled in the shivering cold and games played underneath the warm felt of their ger.

Duyal glows. "Great to see you. Thanks for tracking me."

His brother grabs him by the shoulders, nods, looking him in the eyes. "It's not easy and not without its risks for both of us. I can't stay long. How are things?"

"About as well as can be expected. Cenk—we're pretty sure the bastard is crazy."

Gozde nods. "Remember that most of it's a game. Grasp the rules quickly and then just follow them. But learn every battle skill, because, by Allah, you'll need them." He shrugs. "Many have made it through before you."

Duyal smiles, still amazed at the crow's feet around his brother's eyes and chiseled lines about his forehead. His brother is a man. A man. "Are you still leaving?"

Both their heads snap toward the hallway. Bootsteps echo in the distance.

Gozde waits until satisfied that they move away from them. "Yeah. I'll be gone far to the north for several moons, so we won't be able to talk for a while."

A melancholy fills him.

Gozde seems to read his brother's face. "It's all right, I'll be in good company. And so will you. I'll be back. Remember, on your side of the house—it's all just a gut check." He wraps his arms tightly about his younger brother. He releases, cuffing Duyal in the head.

Walking away, he looks back to Duyal and grins.

CHAPTER
27

Ox
The citadel hippodrome, Hisn Kayfa
January 21, 1237

Sitting cross-legged, Ox looks up. Freshly chiseled stone overhead. A line of tidy Arabic slashes and punctures and curved blades making up the Koranic words. While he cannot read the text, he knows the verse by heart: "We gave out iron with its great power and use to the people in order that Allah might know those who would support Him and His Messengers. For God is indeed Powerful and Mighty."

He closes his eyes and lays the flat of the sword blade to his nose, drawing in a deep breath. The tinny smell of piss fills his nostrils. This clears his mind, temporarily blocking out the dull clunk of metal striking felt and the mundane tone of instructors counting strokes.

He nods to himself in satisfaction, their instructor's words many weeks ago ringing true. "If the blade of your sword has a smell resembling cow urine or a frog, or the smell of clay, or the smell of a dog, then the sword is good. If it smells like a tortoise or the smell of blood, then those are the worst of swords. Refuse to go into battle with such a blade."

He opens his eyes, a smile parts his lips. The smell of a good blade is the smell of silver, the scent of victory, the perfume of God. If smell is akin to taste, then he can almost taste his future. Once proving his worth through victories won, he pictures himself in a jewel-studded belt, the overlord of a large fief, bringing in a steady stream of wealth. He can hardly wait.

Then women, beautiful women, will accompany him down the streets of Hisn Kayfa, or maybe even Cairo one day. Perhaps he will settle with a rich merchant's daughter. At the thought, a tingle of joy radiates to his fingertips and toes, followed by a shudder as the winter wind pours down the empty hippodrome seating.

He thinks back to the warriors of his tower. The nimble and fur-clad, who protected the people and raided for winter goods. How many times had he and the young boys on the steppe reenacted their victories, rushing over hills aback frothing ponies, charging through valley with bow and blunt-headed arrow, screaming wildly with crudely carved pine swords raised overhead? Those swords, no more than whittled clubs, ripping down through the air upon the heads of faux enemies once quivers ran empty. While their bows had shot both predator and game, their swords were as bogus as the invisible rival the young boys chased.

But hell, not even the most seasoned of their childhood heroes carried the real ones. "They're heavier than a sheep leg and a hundred times more dear," a warrior once told him. Typically in the Dnieper River country, only the khan and his kinsmen had long blades hanging from their belts, and those were mostly stolen from the Rus and carried for show. And upon the backs of the tower's finest ponies, just these men could afford to lug the extra weight, as they would be taking a share of the booty from every man on a raid, not burdening their own mounts with stolen goods.

He figures most Kipchak warriors would not have carried one if they could have afforded it. Sword, bloody steel: the dreaded symbol of letting the enemy get too close. For on the steppe, whenever mounted archers heard the unmistakable scrape of blade on sheath, this often meant they had made a mistake.

Ox struggles to conjure up tales of post-raid glory told about the evening fire, those forays won solely by the sword. He recalls none. Kipchaks seemed always on the wrong end of the blade. He pictures his uncle's cousin, drenched in blood, galloping to his wife's ger, knotted hemp tied about his stub, for some reason still holding his own detached arm across his thighs. And twelve years ago, in the early spring, when the Rus poured through their camp undetected, slaughtering the young, inflicting wounds so deep the Saman refused to treat them. Being just a nipper, he watched the attack from the flap of his ger, until fear overtook him. He then hid behind the stacked gut bags stowed under the cot, quietly sobbing, waiting for it to be done.

He shrugs, pulling the tunic farther up around his neck to keep out the chill. Those days are gone. How remarkable that just six moons prior, every novice in the tulb probably associated the sword with defeat, yet since being indoctrinated by the men in red, these warrior-boys-in-training now connect the weapon only with victory for God.

He grins. It is good to be on the right side of the blade. And so it is with him today. With steel in hand, he is already more talented with it than any in his tower had been, and his sword training has barely started.

"You will disgrace the uniform provided by your prince, before my very eyes!?" an instructor screams.

The novice ignores the man, refusing to become flustered, instead remaining fixated on the task before him. The blemish from the novice's sin is obvious: four streaks of crimson decorating the right sleeve of his white tunic, like bloody chevrons. With a stout chest and gangly limbs, the boy is a natural at using the leverage of his body type to chink away at the felt with no apparent effort.

Ox nods. Ichami. Since day one, this novice has been special among them. His Turkish name translates as "Inspiration," and he has been just that to his brothers since their first day here. Always the lad had a smile plastered to his lips, regardless of the shared hardship. Ox figures the boy would still be grinning if his hair were set afire. Strong also in archery and with the lance, the novice is so free of worry that he is able to focus upon improving the performance of the others. What a strange creation this boy is. What a fine Mamluk he will be.

Being undisturbed by the pace of the citadel and seemingly immune to the tirades of its black-sashed inhabitants, Ichami is quick with a laugh, his hoot the most earnest when the gag is on him. After playing a series of tricks on his mates, involving eggs stolen from the citadel's coops, he once stuck a foot into his own boot lined with them. He struggled to remove his drenched sock, rolling on the ground in hysterics until the howling assemblage was cut short by the click of instructor boots.

Ox grunts. If they were all like Ichami, life behind these walls might approach being bearable. Such thoughts are unrealistic, of course. But to their credit, many of his fellow novices are finally learning, the instructors often forcing them into making uncomfortable decisions. Presently, Ichami will take the verbal abuse all day for degrading his uniform in return for not losing his grip upon the hilt of his weapon. For if the steel slips from his bleeding fingers, he fails. And failure in graded events is what places a novice one step closer to being on the wrong side of the gate.

Thirty of his mates whack at the felt-covered clay, lumped upon sturdy tables. Cream chunks spit from their blades, bouncing off the chests and legs of their instructors. The mist from their breath engulfs each platform, as if the felt they hack was instead a slaughtered beast with entrails exposed to the cold. His ears ring with the clamor of blades on block, loud as if every butcher in Hisn Kayfa were cleaving every goat led in from their grassy hills.

The flailing blades catch the sun, rippling flashes to his eyes, as once did the rapids on the mighty Dnieper in late afternoon. He dips his head and averts his eyes, closing them tightly. With bright specks shimmering behind his eyelids, he covers his mouth to chuckle in earnest. This training. He feels grateful for the ease at which he has moved through it, yet is less so with the boredom of its pace.

It had begun at an elementary level. A joke. Twenty-five strokes per hand with the two-pound sword into the soft clay beds, the hilt only allowed to be held with the thumb and forefinger. Any novice caught allowing his other fingers to touch the cracked wooden hilts wore ripped skin from the whip or bruises from the staff, which soon corrected such behavior.

Each day, twenty-five additional sword strokes were added to their regimen. Gradually, blades of additional weight and varying styles were introduced, until at the end of stage one each in the tulb had earned their "proof of attainment" on the five-pound swords at one thousand strokes per hand. Once into the second stage, the instructors added two to three layers of heavy felt daily atop the clay humps.

The amirs' program has been beneficial to most. Many of the boys who arrived at the citadel with thin arms and slight shoulders now have tunics that do not fit so loosely.

Those whose left hands were nearly a burden to them only a few moons ago, now have a second appendage with power to match their favored arms. Most have developed a grip with both hands that rivals osprey talons.

But it is not just the training that has bulked up his mates. Since arriving at the citadel, all have eaten three times the meat they did on the steppe. Fresh fruits and vegetables rolled in continuously during the summer and fall. These were devoured. This consumption, combined with the drill, has stacked quick mass to the novices' frames, much like gaunt winter sheep gorging on the first spring grass.

Yet he also has grown to realize that the sword is not all about muscle and force. The instructors preached that on occasion the recruits must be able to apply not just a killing blow, but also a wounding blow. Further, the sword master sermonized that at some point in a novice's career, he would face overwhelming numbers of enemy. At these times, his life and usefulness to God would be at stake, and he must employ the most efficient blows, expending just enough energy to disable the enemy, but not so much as to fatigue himself. To meet this end, upon the thick-legged tables the instructors placed reams of scroll atop pillows. Here, the novices were required with one stroke to cut only through the paper, leaving the pillow unscathed. Often it was this blow that gave the novices the most grief.

So far, five novices have not passed the almost continuous testing. Some events warranted retesting, yet these instances were few. Often after failure, these recruits vanished. Their mats, their gear, every item issued to them—gone. These discharged boys are now ghosts, their fading memories floating through the endless corridors, lingering about the training fields like spirits not yet settled. Scarcely a novice will bring up their names, as if even mentioning the departed might bring the former lad's bad luck upon those conversing.

Ox cares little what may have become of those ejected. They were not up to the challenge. The prince had paid serious dinars to bring these boys into service; surely he was going to get at least some utility from them. Al-Salih certainly was not going to allow the washouts to jump aboard Bozkurt's empty carts and head back north to their families on the steppe. Plus, who would welcome them back anyhow?

It does not matter. It cannot matter. The focus within the citadel walls is and should be on training novices, not on worry for those who are pushed out through the heavy wooden doors, some leaving gladly, some clawing, screaming to get back in.

Shouts from the guards below. Ox dropped his rag, soiled from the tarnished brass, strolled to the rampart.

Below, two slave traders stood outside the gates with hands on hips, looking up at their escapee, the sure-footed reject scaling the smooth-faced wall.

The guards laughed, signaled for others in their detachment to watch, for his task was pure folly with a known end. But when the Kipchak's effort took him from ten feet, to thirty feet, to forty feet, they no longer smiled.

The guards first threw insults and threats, raising their bows and long axes in warning, but the long-limbed boy concentrated only on his finger and toe holds, keeping his butt out for stability, scanning upward for his best line, where the masons left him even a tiny crevice to ply.

The first arrows were only warning shots, blunts purposely shot to ricochet off the wall and raise fear. But these had no effect. When a broadhead took the felt hat off the boy's head about fifty feet up, the youth said, "I'll take no offense. Won't be needing that nohow. At this hour, I reckon my brothers are on the lance field... believe we're in helmets this day."

With this, the guards let the novice continue his climb un-
molested, even grasped his forearm to pull him over the parapet
at sixty feet. The eunuch, Safir, was also at the top when the
youth swung his leg over, summoned aloft by the commotion.
The eunuch said nothing, but escorted the climber back down
the stairs to his chamber.

It is said the boy got himself a retest and remains in his tulb.

"Crazy damn goat," Ox murmurs to himself.

Fifty-four novices—his entire tulb—test today on six-ty-four layers of felt. By the end of the second training stage, they must cut through one hundred layers in less than the same numbers of strokes, per arm. Only then will they have earned the privilege to enter stage three, the technical train-ing, where the instructors teach use of the blade against an enemy, even how to fight with two swords at once.

"Through!" "Through!" "Through!" the instructors call, as one-by-one novices sever the last of the sixty-four layers in less than one hundred strokes per arm. Some have hacked through the required felt sections in as few as fifty strokes, while some reached the clay beneath in as many as ninety.

Demir catches his eye and nods his head in satisfaction. Ichami holds back a broad smile. For all who finish, anxiety appears to release through their bodies, same as the sweat that dots their pores. These wait for the others, standing be-hind their small tables with sword tips extended just off the deck, their other hands held smartly behind their backs.

Only two recruits remain swinging, the din of hol-low thumps now reduced to the identifiable smacks of two blades striking sturdy felt. These two sense that all eyes are upon them. The nearest, Bulut, clenches his teeth in exer-tion, knowing his future hangs solely on his ability to slice through the packed sheep fiber on the table. Ox heaves a sigh, as the slight-armed Kipchak hacks with all his power. To this novice, the mud-covered table must be as lethal as a startled bear, hunch-backed and bloody-jawed, raising a bristled head from a carcass and charging him, the repercussion in failing to slay either generating the identical result: The End.

"Through," his instructor calls on the lad's ninety-eighth stroke. Bulut smartly drops the sword to his side, his chest heaving, his left arm barely able to keep the tip of the blade off the ground. He looks skyward, likely thanking his new God for answering prayers of assistance.

Ox again covers his face to let loose a giggle. "Useless, scrawny fuck," he mumbles.

Cenk orbits the remaining novice, Hayri, with hands on hips, his thick back flared wide. The whack from the neophyte's blade grows slower and weaker with each stroke, his edge having cut only halfway through the stacked felt layers. Cenk quietly calls out the cadence along with the lad's instructor, "Eighty-eight, eighty-nine, ninety..."

Ox is not surprised where his instructor waits. At test time, Cenk made a habit of hovering over the likely training casualties. Like a vulture spending many days circling his victims from above, Cenk's elevated vantage allowed him to pinpoint flaws in each novice. From close up, yet afar, he identified that prey within the beige walls who was nearest to death. He knew exactly where to swoop in for a meal.

Now, as if with sharp beak snapping in hungry anticipation, Cenk moves closer, his small black eyes concentrating only on the ever-slowing rise and fall of a furred torso. His *Mu'allim* waits patiently for the inevitable. "Ninety-five, ninety-six..."

Clang! The novice loses his grip, his sword smacking the table and then flipping to an awkward rest on the stone-laid deck.

Heads turn, expecting to witness a swift blow from the boy's instructor, as blades hitting the ground were as gross a violation as missing noon prayer. Instead, just as a screeching vulture hops about his corpse on forked feet and spreads his giant wings to ward off other foragers, so does Cenk.

He laughs with head thrown back, the vulture flapping his wings excitedly, squawking with delight as the heartbeat of his wounded prey ceases to pound, signaling flesh ready for the tearing. Hayri's instructor, the counter in red, knows the protocol. This Mamluk walks behind the table and crosses his hands across his belt buckle. Cenk's signal being very clear to all—his appetite for carnage knew no end. He would always be the first to feed on the dead or dying.

Hayri drops to both knees, his head sinking to chest. His back convulses rapidly, like the death shake of a wounded antelope. He sobs, reaching for the weapon, but Cenk steps on the boy's hand.

"Keep your filthy hands off my sword! Peasants don't touch Mamluk steel!" Cenk says, grinding the novice's hand into the stone with his full weight. He picks up the weapon to inspect its edge, eventually wiping the blade and hilt under his arm, as if to remove all evidence of the one who had been unfit to touch it.

The vulture returns his attention to the corpse beneath him, leering sideways with head cocked. He squats beside the dejected novice, his boot still on the boy's hand, a sympathetic expression falling over his face. He places his hand on Hayri's shoulder. "Come on, there's no shame in digging moats. You'll still serve our prince and never have a sore ass from riding an Arabian," Cenk says softly.

He stands, circles the novice. "Git! To the barracks! Pack your kit for restore! Get out of my hippodrome!" He points a thick finger to the arched exit.

Koray, the sword master, cuts the performance short. "Prepare the tables," he says. Like Aqtay and the eunuch Safir, Koray is another in al-Salih's "first generation" of Mamluks, one of the first thousand purchased in 1228, when the prince's father was away from Cairo on campaign. While the instructor says nothing of his combat experience, Koray is the stuff of legend at the citadel. Trained in Egypt, he subsequently fought every imaginable foe—Frederick's crusaders prior to the treaty, the Mamluks of two other Ayyubid Princes, and of course the Seljuks during the entire Anatolian Campaign. His left ear was sliced clean off, removed during an interrogation by King Frederick's demons, where Koray evidently gave the infidels nothing but saliva to wipe from their faces.

Half his other ear is also missing, a result of close fighting against the Seljukids at the deadly stone walls of Gok Su. His gray-flecked beard covers his face in thin, absent patches, like a wolf suffering from mange, the thick scar tissue about his chin and neck no longer allowing the tender hair follicles to bloom. He makes every attempt to avoid being seen in short-sleeved tunics, his attempt at humility.

But Ox once saw him roll up his tunic sleeves, just past his elbow. On the inside of Koray's massive biceps was the expected, a long scar along the base of each bicep, those unexplained lacerations shared by every Mamluk in the citadel. Yet also upon his forearms alone were countless slash wounds, the purple crevasses and raised mounds of flesh crisscrossed with ancient impressions of expedient battle stitching. All serve as seldom-revealed badges of honor, more respected by the Mamluks than any silken ribbon pinned upon red coat.

Ox can sense the corps' admiration of Koray in the way the other instructors greet and look at the old man. The novices are drawn to him as well, while Koray seems captivated only by his God and weapon of choice. Ox knows that one day he will also be admired in the same way. Minus the wounds, he hopes.

Ox and the others rise and step forward as the finishing novices rush to peel the mangled felt sections from the packed mud. Flopping the mess over their shoulders, they dump them in a pile and move to the fresh stack of precounted pieces.

Down the line of thirty tables are the stone cold faces of his peers, who like himself will be tested next. Most stand confident in their ability. One gnaws at his lower lip in a scraping motion; another blows air through pursed lips in swift bursts. Ox feels nothing. He is more worried about losing count than not being able to get through the packed layers in one hundred strokes.

Beside him, Singer conceals a yawn, relaxed as if he were ready to hit the mat for sleep. Ox ponders if this comrade has any flaws. While only a year or two older than most of the novices, Singer has the swagger of a man ten years their senior. All knew Singer grew up without the support of a tower, and his experience in self-preservation now serves him well.

Ox stares forward at the mud on the scarred table and shakes his head. Even mud must meet the standard here—carefully measured and cut by slaves from the banks of the Tigris, cleaned by novice working parties of "mud wenches" and then stowed between layers of stiff horsehide in the cellars.

"Instructors, check 'em," Koray says over the ruckus of fresh felt being plopped atop the clay slabs.

"Rea-dy!" Koray twists his entire torso to view the raised thumbs of his instructors, the sword master unable to fully turn his neck, likely a lingering reminder of a stab wound collected in some foreign land. Each recruit stands in the identical position, with the sword in his right hand, elevated only to the level of his cheek, his left leg forward and right leg back. A final thumb is raised by an instructor at the end of the line, signaling "All ready."

"Begin!"

Ox swings down, his first blow ripping through three layers. He chops heartily at wide angles, his rhythmic slices sending wedge-shaped chunks of felt flying away like spent wood chips from a sharp axe. Each strike brings forth a waft of earthen odor, taking him back to barefoot days in the Dnieper country, of swimming races across the wide river.

"Forty-six, forty-seven, forty-eight. Through!" his instructor says. Ox takes a step left, switches the position of his legs and sword and begins to hack with equal vengeance with his left arm upon the other side of the felt. Blood begins to pump his triceps full. To avoid the onset of fatigue, he remembers his instruction, concentrating instead on creating power from his chest and back.

"Forty-nine, fifty, fifty-one. Through!"

He avoids eye contact with the thick-necked instructor. Do not act cocky. Hardly fatigued, he takes a step back behind the table, lowers the blade and puts his right hand behind his back. He is the first done.

His eyes focus past the training area and into the seating, where a sole figure watches. He recognizes the gray beard and nervous hands of Bozkurt. As promised, the old man comes back to check on them. Beside him is a large sack, possibly scrolls written by another tulb. Maybe some of the slave trader's words were true—that after a year or so he and his mates would be taught to write. Bozkurt would return to the steppe with scrolls and read them aloud to their kin back home.

The other novices finish. All twenty-four in this round have passed.

Novices heap strips of felt onto carts, others collect bits from the floor. Boys hand their swords to one novice at each rack, who wipes each blade with a pair of rags before placing the weapons back into their racks.

"Eyes!" Cenk says.

Every recruit freezes, turns his head directly to their *Mu'allim*. Silence.

Hayri has reentered the arena and stands with his hands behind his back, next to Cenk. The boy looks down, wearing the Turkish tunic that was given to him by Bozkurt nearly six moons past. The colored neckline now seems gaudy, out of place.

Cenk looks over his shoulder, seeming to check that the hippodrome is free of senior amirs and other dubious ears. He also sees Bozkurt, likely taking into account the man's presence. He places his hand on Hayri's head. "Gone is your fellow worm, Hayri, his arms too weak to wield the Mamluk sword."

Cenk pushes Hayri's head toward the main passage. The boy walks, eyes still lowered.

"Worms. I'm sure some of you wish you could join such a nice lad to do more... civilized work," Cenk says matter-of-factly, his tone holding a hint of believability. "I welcome any and all to fall out now. I will not say a bad word of it."

Cenk turns to the slimy tables. "Now, there must be someone who yearns for a softer life than this," he says, with his outstretched palm open to a clay slab mauled beyond recognition. "Just go. Follow your friend out the corridor, out the gate to a better place."

Adam, a decent performer, turns and tramps toward the archway, where Hayri stands.

"I'll be damned," Ox mumbles.

Cenk's eyes light up. "I see Adam knows better than to stay in this rathole, where the only thing to look forward to at manumission is an endless string of battlefields... a life of little sleep, dodging arrows and eating slop. What smart boy would want it?"

"Sorry, I can't live another day behind these walls," Adam says, looking down.

"Oh... oh, he is right, my friends. It's terrible, and the gray blocks only seem to get higher by the day," Cenk says.

He looks about for more takers on his offer. None move for several moments.

Seeming to sense that nothing more will be gained from his latest tactic, or simply unable to carry on his pleasant character any further, Cenk switches back to himself. He rushes to Adam, who stands at the arch. "Go on, piss off! I won't let them look at you." He kicks, but misses. "Go with your sweet girlfriend. The guards wait for you both at the gate!"

CHAPTER
28

Duyal
The hills, south of Hisn Kayfa
January 26, 1237

In twin columns they tread mutedly on either side of the dusty path. The jingle of gaiter buckles. The slosh of feet in soaked wool joins the monotonous thump of soles on frozen dirt. Down a draw, they enter where the trail is choked with scrub oak and thick-trunked sage, taller than the biggest among them. They duck their heads and plow through it, only the screech of branches on hardened leather giving warning of the obstacle's locale. Some grumble obscenities and snap branches as they exit, the sweet sage oil lingering on their tunics.

Duyal rakes a hand across the back of his clammy neck, pulling a handful of tiny dried leaves and broken branches out of his neckline. He pushes the brim of his helmet up. Cold air funnels across wet hair. Mist rolls from the sweat-soaked tunic in front of him. He extends his arm, ensuring he remains an arm's reach away. To the east, the horizon smolders in a seared orange, the abyss above giving way its star-specked black to a deep navy.

They curve their way past shadowed outcroppings, through high rolling hills covered with scraps of winter-crushed grass and patches of juniper and misshapen pine. Reaching a hilltop, the parallel columns in front appear as a pair of armored centipedes, leaking steam through their segmented bodies, the twin creatures shuffling in unison over undulating terrain on sore bellies.

Dropping back down, they follow the drainage silently, along a path of water-swept sand. The smash of pocket ice, boots quickly pulverizing the thin crust into dust. The stench of ripe armpits and dried apricot farts feathers in and out of the ranks, the nauseating odor encasing the columns, only lifting its cloud when a northern gust blows across them.

This training march, or "drudge" as the Mamluks call it, had been spontaneous. Its birth seemed to come only moments after the candles were blown out, Duyal then pleased to be curled on his mat for the night. He awoke to movement, rising blurry-eyed to the flicker of candlelight and the scurry of novices grabbing their gear, wine fumes tracing the path where Cenk had been. Knowing that he must not awaken the eunuchs, the *Mu'allim* curtailed his usual banter, instead smacking heads and kicking blanketed lumps, whispering the same slurred words to his worms, "Full kit, outside now."

Some novices stood in formation half-dressed, pulling on tunics and trousers as their instructor appeared from the darkness with the last of them. Accustomed to such formations and aware of the penalties for tardiness, many novices slipped boots onto bare feet, as taking the time to pull on their woolen socks meant potentially becoming a target for his madness. None thought they would be going anywhere—it was surely just another gear inspection. Both guards at the back gate chuckled as they watched the tulb stumble into the cold dark, away from the river and south into the endless hills.

Duyal skips in place to get back in step with the novice in front of him and then resumes placing his boot in this boy's print.

"Stay in step!" a novice hollers from the rear, the rippled accordion effect having reached the end of the stretched-out column.

His lower body throbs. His stomach churns. He tries to ignore his feet, the repeated sucking sound in his boots taking him back a world away into shin-deep marshes in the far north, where he, Gozde, and Baris were occasionally forced to track wounded deer. He pictures the liquid now in his boots, pus from broken blisters mixed with blood from the continual rubbing.

He mutters under his breathe, "Fuck it." He must carry on. Those with no socks are surely worse off than he. The novice to his front stumbles on a rock. Duyal grabs a fistful of armor and lifts the lad to keep him from falling. He pushes him forward to keep the formation tight.

"At times the terrain will force the *faris* to lead his mount, not ride it. This doesn't mean the Mamluk will arrive to his objective late. He'll just walk into the night, before meeting the enemy," Cenk says, standing between the columns so he can face them as they pass. He then runs back to the front of the formation, swinging his staff.

The march seems to have sobered him up. The squatty Bashkir hardly sweats, his stride as fresh as when they stepped off. Duyal is convinced the man is not human. He wonders how far they have trudged. He has no idea; he doesn't really care. What does it matter? They will stop when they stop. He hopes Cenk knows where he is going.

The cold and dark suspends time and place, shrinking their world to the bouncing back of armor to their front and the throb in their legs. The columns are just a brainless mass, pounding forward on momentum and grit alone. Blank minds with heads set down, young men simply grinding over the rocky trail.

"Not a grunt in all of Egypt throws barbs at the *al-Sali-hiyya*, knowing each Mamluk on the back of an Arabian could outmarch the best infantryman in their own ranks. This is the way it must be," Cenks says, again centered with arms crossed, columns slinking by him.

Ching! Whack! Seeing a gap in the left rank, Cenk delivers a crack to a helmet, followed by a backstroke to the calves as the culpable novice passes. "Gaps in the ranks make for strung-out formations and dead Mamluks. But you care little of this, worried only about a little fatigue in your own legs. Allah help us."

They round a bend in the dirt road. The citadel rises above them, basking in the yellow rays of morning. The pace quickens, slouched backs straighten. None wish to be seen beaten. They come to the intersection in the dirt road.

"Stay right," Cenk says, guiding the tulb away from the fortress's thick wooden doors.

Not a peep of complaint is heard from them. They slog the steep path encircling the high walls. Guards watch them from above unsympathetically. Coming again upon the same junction, Cenk gives the same order.

On the sixth lap, Cenk relents, seeming to realize that he will not get a single moan from them. "Left... halt."

The guards push open the thick-planked doors, casting glares over their shoulders as the novices limp to a halt in the wide courtyard. Cenk looks up and down the ranks with squinted eyes, likely assessing the disposition of each. He looks for a target.

"Stow your gear in the barracks, then to your morning stations. Go!" he says.

They scurry to the stairwell.

As Tulb Nine is no longer the most junior at the cita-del, Safir has spread the auxiliary duties owned by a recently graduated tulb among Cenk's recruits. Duyal and the others embrace the morning and evening tasks—sweeping the long corridors, bagging grain, burning excrement, preparing clay, shining brass, and doing an assortment of other odd jobs.

This week, Duyal and Singer were assigned to the stalls. He considers the duty a good one, the amirs unlikely to bestow the privilege of being near the Arabians upon the undeserving. Having staged their gear, the pair plod through the maze of corridors on tender legs, Duyal's spirits rising ev-ery step away from Cenk's torment and the eyes of the other instructors.

"How're your feet?" Singer asks.

"Not looking forward to taking off these boots."

"Yeah, me neither."

"I guess this is why the Mongols make sure they each have three ponies, eh?"

Singer chuckles. "And why they give Mamluks a camel and donkey, plus the horse."

They chuckle, the clunk of their heels echoing as they enter a narrow passage. A smell akin to mushrooms pervades as they drop down a set of stairs. Along the passage, Duyal reaches out, his fingertips gliding along the bulges and dim-ples, becoming slimy from the oozing rocks.

"Do you worry of being ousted?" Duyal asks, his words resounding, deeper than his actual tone.

"It doesn't worry me. We can't let it happen. I think only of the next test, what we must do to be ready. And if I can spot something, do something to get the others through. In between, it's just trying to get from chow to the hippo-drome without Cenk in my face."

"I suppose that's it."

"I think that's it."

Duyal shakes his head. His friend has a way of sticking to the meat of things, an efficiency about him that he admires. Singer seems to approach all things with the same sense, possessing a knack to embrace and then adjust to any new surroundings, to any strange technique, to different people. Maybe it has something to do with the fact that his friend is a little older than most of the others, that he was so long without elders in his life, he had nobody else to count on.

Regardless, no matter what is put in front of him, Singer has a way of seamlessly changing his tack and excelling. Proof of this is on Safir's scrolls, which bear the name and deeds of every recruit. Only beside Singer's name are there no entries for misconduct or training failures. Duyal wonders why Singer befriends him, as he certainly does not measure up to his friend's ability.

"At first, I could only think of how to get out of these walls. More and more, I fear for what I would do if expelled from them," Duyal says.

"Don't worry. You won't be. We'll make sure of it. We're the kind our prince wants to keep."

Duyal smiles. His friend brings a sense of confidence, free from the stench of conceit. It is refreshing.

They exit into a great hay field, stubby frozen stems collecting sunlight on their coats of morning frost. Duyal looks forward to spring, when both the prince's horses and those of the amirs will openly graze this field, as well as the adjacent fields of clover and lucerne.

"Ah, you know... I've been meaning to ask—and you don't have to talk about it—you told me how you and Ilker joined the Mongols, but you never really said why you left them," Duyal says.

Singer nods. "It started out fine, but eventually there was no trust, and it was just a matter of time before they took us out. We had to go. Each day was getting worse. They weren't going to let us leave alive."

"I will get my revenge on them one day. I hated you—and Ilker too—early on for riding with them. I couldn't understand it."

"I wouldn't expect you to. I'll make no excuse for riding with the enemy. But you must remember, we had no tower, no ally. Few choices. A man alone has mainly enemies."

"Right."

They veer right. Before them is the L-shaped stable, an overbuilt fortress of fat oak beams and endless arches of stacked rock, which divide the horse stalls. A tightly thatched roof keeps the rain off the backs of the regiment's prizes. Termed the "Royal Stables," the building holds nearly four hundred stalls, most with a polished brass plate attached to the gate identifying the stall number, the name of the Arabian and its owner.

Duyal pulls open the hatch. The comforting smell of dried grass and burning oil hangs in the air. Heading toward their assigned numbers, they walk beneath the wide arches—heavy rectangular blocks fitted perfectly in place. They peer left and right into empty stalls, where straw lies evenly spread by fork into every corner.

Along the walls and in adjacent storage wings, tack of every variety is staged in precise order. Hand-tooled saddles gleam with fresh polish, set upon rounded beams, the decorative silk on cantles showing every imaginable color. Spare stirrups, their side bars and foot plates intricately engraved with dark-etched flower patterns and winding vines, hang neatly by their attachment loops on angled metal rods. Fine leather halters with bronze pendants dangle by the dozens. Each is hung from its crownpiece on a wooden peg, worn shiny smooth. Horse armor drapes over taut hemp like fine curtains in a castle, blankets of thin buff leather secured by stitch to scarlet and gold cloth, adorned in exquisite patterns. Leather headpieces, worn by the Arabians in battle, are stacked within each other's hard lamellar shells, suspended by dowels run through their eyeholes.

Reaching stall number twenty-four, Singer pulls two forks from the wall mount. Duyal pushes a cart into the space. They begin scooping up the manure and plopping it into the wooden cart.

"I wonder if they let us work here to give us some hope," Duyal says.

"Hope?"

"You know, let us work near the animals, giving us a peek at what it might look like if we make it through. One day not being the ones shoveling dung, but being Mamluks checking on our own mounts."

"That could be," Singer says with a smirk, flinging a forkful over his shoulder without looking up. "But I think they also just need this dung cleaned up."

They laugh. Duyal grabs the cart handles and backs his way out. They move past an occupied stall. He peers over the gate. Inside stands a bay, upon its thigh the brand of al-Salih, the same long-tailed lion that occupies the regiment's pennant.

"So different than the short-legged stock back home. It's like Allah made them for desert war. Slight of build to not sink in the sand, big eyes to see the battlefield, large nostrils to take in take more air on the charge, a high arching neck to spread fear," Duyal says.

"They would have scared a few warriors back home. They looked so strange at first, eh? Not so much now."

They move into the next stall and begin their work.

"Yeah, I can't wait to be on one's back. What do you make of that bulge between their eyes—I wonder what use Allah had in mind for that?" Duyal asks.

A bony hand pulls the gate wide with a slow creak. "That would be what my people call the '*jibbah*'—the sinus cavity helps the Arabian breathe in the dry desert air," a haggard voice whistles with the accent of an Arab. An old man smiles, exposing toothless gaps and varying shades of brown and gray on the chipped stubs that remain in his mouth. His grin deepens wrinkles already well entrenched about his eyes and mouth. The turbaned Bedouin pulls his tattered shawl tighter over his hunched body, his thin robe in the design of those from the south and west, hardly adequate for winters in the Jazira.

"Ishak," Duyal and Singer say together, smiling.

His name means "The Prophet." Known throughout the citadel as the most jovial of the Bedouin grooms, he is also the eldest among them, kept on staff less for his physical ability to break and train the young Arabians that continually filter in from the Bedouin camps, but more so because of his detailed knowledge of the pedigrees. Gifted with a mind that does not forget, once Ishak hears a Bedouin recite the verbal history of a subject horse, he is able to fit the new piece into the puzzle of bloodlines he has memorized previously. This makes him invaluable in determining fair prices and occasionally catching some of the Bedouin traders in lies.

"Good morning, my friend," Singer says.

"How are the unfortunate ones from Cenk's throng today?" the old man asks, his standard greeting passed in his usual solemn tone. He clasps both boys by their shoulders, still grinning.

"One day closer to manumission," Duyal replies, turning slightly to avoid the reek emitting from the man's mouth.

Ishak's smile widens, the sparkle in his left eye drawing attention away from the dull gray clouding his right. "Yes, yes, another step closer to graduation day."

"Has the prince been by this week?" Singer asks.

"Of course, he never misses a visit, never misses a detail," Ishak says.

"Will you be breeding the mares soon?" Duyal asks.

"Well… more and more al-Salih prefers the horses brought in from the Bedouin camps—that's the ideal place for breeding Arabians. No different than he insists on his Mamluks being born on the Kipchak steppe." The old man chuckles. "Though we'll soon be breeding Aqtay's stallion, Hursit. Get some of that al-Bahrayn stock into the herd."

"That's eastern Arabia?" Duyal asks.

"Yes, yes. Have I told you the story of where they come from?" Ishak asks.

"The Bahrayn?" Duyal asks.

"No. Well, yes. I mean all of them. Every one of them forever."

"They're from Syria and upper Egypt, right?" Singer asks.

"Sort of. I mean, have I shared how the first breeding stock was chosen?" Ishak asks, squinting.

Duyal looks to his friend vacantly. "I don't think so."

"Well then," the old man says with a single knuckle to his chin. "The Bedouins say that when Muhammad was on a long journey through the desert, he decided to test the loyalty and courage in his herd of mares. Seeing an oasis in the distance, he set the Arabians loose to see which would reach the water first. Just before the lead horses reached the waterhole, Muhammad blew his war horn, commanding the animals to return to him." His eyes open wide; his bony fingers go to his mouth, curled in the shape of the described horn.

"Only five mares came back, while the others continued to the oasis to find shade and quench their thirst. These returning five became Muhammad's favorites, that day forward being called *al khamsa*, or 'the five.' These faithful mares became the founders of the five strains of the Arabian."

"Were those Arabians…"

A flash of red appears, a large man occupying nearly the entire entrance to the stables. At his waist, the dreaded black belt. The novices instinctively lock their bodies at attention.

"You worms want me to warm up some tea for this gathering?" the *Muallim* asks.

Upon seeing Ishak, the instructor's face lightens. He nods and unsuccessfully hides a wink to the old man. He turns to the novices. "When the good master has finished with you, I'll expect to hear nothing from this stall except the thud of shit on wood."

He stomps off, grumbling, "Useless sheep stickers."

"Ahh… here I am, keeping the worthy novices from their work. Putting my young friends in bad standing with the *Muallim*."

"No, no, my friend. We thank you for your words," Duyal whispers. "We're used to being in trouble around here."

Ishak cracks his toothless grin and shuffles out through the straw. "Yes, yes. It is the nature of things on your side of this house."

CHAPTER
29

Singer
Citadel archery yard, Hisn Kayfa
March 16, 1237

The tulb moves in tight formation, passing through the vaulted corridors, down one echoing stairwell and up another. Angling through a dark hallway, Singer hums to himself, loud enough to enjoy the notes bouncing off the blocked walls, yet still indiscernible to Cenk at the formation's rear. In his mind, the tune changes the flat stones under his feet to soft dirt, the pocked walls to a canopy of hardwoods in his home country.

> He ran on short legs to keep up with the long stride of his father. The lean man slowed, not for his son to catch up, but to view a stand of young chokecherry trees.
>
> His father circled each tree, until staring at length at one, his eyes flashing at times to his panting son. He then pulled a small hatchet from his belt and hacked down the straightest of them, discarding all save a five-foot section of the trunk.

Once at the ger, his father removed the bark and then rolled away small shavings of the tree with his knife, before switching to a more delicate blade for the finish work.

"A new bow, father?" Singer asked.

The man gave only a short smile, raising his eyebrows playfully.

That first bow from his father's hand would always be his favorite. The ends gradually tapered, the darker heartwood on the inside belly able to withstand the bow's compression point, while the lighter sapwood on the back was positioned to best handle the tension when pulled. Twisted horsehide was looped to one end and wrapped tight upon the other, its wood surface coated originally with the fat from an old porcupine.

From that day forward, he carried the weapon with him everywhere. Within a week, he killed his first animal with a headless arrow, a rat, proudly adding the plump animal to the family's pot. Later in the summer, he stuck a marmot, then a deer, until eventually he provided a majority of the game for his family.

He started sleeping on his back, his arm through the string, the curved limbs lying on his chest. When he wasn't hunting, he was wandering shaded strands of willow and maple, where the shoots grew tall and true. At home, he chipped stone heads, bent heated arrow shafts over his knee and fletched arrows.

At seven years, when stalking a group of does far from the gers, he came upon a thief, crawling his way through the alders toward the tower's sheep. He circled and closed on the man, putting a broadhead into the back of that Kangit, one whose people routinely raided the herd. He waited long enough for the crook to bleed out, about the duration his father had taught him for deer. He then moved slowly toward him, eventually prodding the man's shoulder with the tip of his bow, before turning over the heavy body. Upon seeing the man's tongue hanging long and his big eyes fixed open and wild, he ran, not stopping until reaching his mother's ger.

The tulb breaks into the open air, a stiff wind blowing across their faces. A novice giggles.

Cenk stomps forward. "Halt. Who's the fool that laughed?" He walks along the formation of straight-faced novices. "The worm who thinks this next training evolution a joke best step up, or I'll have the whole lot of you digging 'til you spew."

Singer holds his breath. A reluctant novice steps forward with head down. Umit. Singer is surprised the bandy-armed troublemaker confesses.

"Come to the fore, worm! Dig," Cenk says.

The guilty one drops to all fours and begins running in place with his hands flat on the citadel rock. The remaining fifty-one watch as Umit thumps the ancient stone in solitude, the rock tinted black with the old blood of Artukid warriors, who had defended this original part of the fortress from al-Kamil's Ayyubid invaders only four years prior.

Singer wonders how this recruit has remained so long in the citadel. The flippant lad does not deserve the opportunity he has been given. He closes his eyes and quietly hums another tune to vanish from the place, attempting to mimic the stringed music from his cousin's *kemence*.

> *He watched from the rise, wondering if they would spot it before it spotted them. He stepped behind a boulder. To signal would spook the animal.*
>
> *His siblings emerged from the woods, only the points of their hats indicating their crouched route through the waist-high grass. Then appeared the head of his younger sister, Nergis, with spear raised at the ready. At her shoulder, the younger brother's eyes elevated just above the browning stalks of grass. He came abreast.*

Their heads conveyed a whispered count, followed by the re-
lease of spears in unison. Nergis' weapon plunged clear through
the back of a marmot, which stood peering cautiously from its hole.
Singer smiled. She squealed with joy and popped Baki in the
shoulder in jest for his errant toss. Both sprinted toward the flop-
ping varmint, the creature inhaling in raspy pants.

The marmot's labored gasps morph into the wheezes from the digging novice. Singer opens his eyes, saddened at the thought of his family. Squinting, he turns his head from the intensity of the sun's glare upon the great ashen walls.

Two small puddles of perspiration form beneath Umit. The boy rounds his bony back and pushes his butt in the air, his pace slowing. Cenk turns to the parapets, where a guard watches the event with half-interest. Their *Muallim* nods to the guard. The watchman, understanding the cue, looks away, his eyes back toward the white-cliffed river and slant-roofed shacks of Hisn Kayfa beneath him. One does not lie to the eunuch's questions, if one sees no wrong.

Cenk kicks Umit in the ribs and lands another grazing shot to the chest. The blows propel the exhausted boy to his back. He curls into a ball, lowering his arms to protect the bruised ribcage. He prepares for the next flurry.

"Did I say to stop? Dig, worm! Is it all so amusing now?" Cenk asks.

The tall recruit crawls back to the feet of Cenk, regains his stance and returns to churning the stone. Yet upon the wind rides the familiar chant, the call to afternoon prayer.

"Allah saves him this time," a novice whispers to a friend.

Cenk puts his heel under Umit's armpit and sends him tumbling. "You're the joke, but I can't bring myself to laugh. Back in formation!"

They continue to the courtyard, where basins fed by carved horse heads discharge steady streams of cold water.

They clean their foreheads, mouth, and ears. They then move into a single file, entering the archery yard with their right foot first, just as required when entering the citadel's mosque. Waiting for them is their instructor, Ekrem, his name meaning "Magnanimous."

Singer gazes at his arrow-shooting idol, the only man in the citadel who refuses to carry any other weapons into battle, save his bow. Fittingly, the man looks no different than the birch shafts he so expertly shoots, his frame lean, his posture straight. Even his auburn beard, which reaches clear to his collarbone, is groomed to a tapered point. He faces away from the sun with hands clasped behind his back, his upper arms casting a shadow that appears like the blades on an arrowhead, right down to the bony barbs of his elbows.

Among the Mamluks, Ekrem is considered ancient, timeless. While wrinkled in the face, incredibly, not a speck of gray dots his beard or locks. He had been the property of an amir at the start of his career, serving ultimately under al-Kamil, fighting the Franks at Damietta in the summer of 1221. In subsequent years, he accompanied his master in exacting bloody policy upon the forces of the other Ayyubid princes.

He was even on the escort in 1229, when the sultan inked what all in the citadel saw as the "ruinous agreement," which surrendered Jerusalem and a stretch of coastal land that still serves as the Frank's lifeline. Rumor is that asking Ekrem any question about his trip to the holy city is perhaps the only way to upset the instructor's composed demeanor. While he will say nothing to disrespect the sultan, Singer once saw red blotches form on Ekrem's neck when the man spoke of Cairo's ruler.

Singer takes a reed mat from the stack and gets back into formation. On their knees they face Mecca. As one, they raise their hands with palms facing outward and deliver the *Takbir*: "God is the Greater."

Moving their hands to their sides, in unison they recite the *Fatiha*:

> *In the name of God, the Compassionate the Caring.*
> *Praise is to God, the sustaining Lord of*
> *all worlds. The Compassionate, the*
> *Caring,*
> *Master of the day of Judgment.*
> *You do we worship and You we ask*
> *for help. Guide us on the straight*
> *road.*
> *The road of those whom You have given on them*
> *Not those with anger on them, nor those who have gone astray.*

All forty-nine novices then quietly deliver a Koranic verse of their choice, the low tones hardly above a whisper, mixing into an indecipherable mash of hisses.

"And fight in the way of Allah, and know that Allah is hearing, knowing," Singer says with head lowered.

They work their way through the remainder of the *Rak'a*, or prayer cycle, and then begin another. Regardless if the training evolution falls on one of the five required prayer times, Ekrem demands two prayer cycles before every archery session. Singer respects this in the calm man, his instructor's methods setting always the proper tone.

Honor to their God. Reverence for the bow and the unremitting quest for perfection in its employment. In the archery yard, these dual subjects were woven together like two twisting vines climbing heavenward, until the thickened stalks pressed together, melding into one solid core. By Mamluk design, the archery yard was a holy place to honor the most lethal implement in Allah's arsenal. And here, prayer meshed and crisscrossed into archery technique, like the artful figure-eight pattern of a wolf pair hunting in an open field.

With both his forehead and hands flat on the mat, Singer finishes the final *Rak'a* and returns to the sitting position, with his left leg folded under him and his right leg straight back. They rise without instruction and filter toward the bow stands, where the weapons are arranged by weight and length.

Just as the instructors had with the sword, they had begun bow training slowly and at a rudimentary level. Yet where the sword master progressed methodically forward, like a builder spending much time on the foundation and then moving steadily upward in setting row after row of stone blocks, the bow training had been very different. Here, archery instructors were first forced, in many cases, to knock down entire walls and roll aside many poorly laid blocks, before they could start with a more solid foundation of skills.

Six moons ago, the novices began with two varieties of flexible bow, the *kabad,* similar to those Kipchak kids toted on the steppe. But before nocking a single arrow, the recruits were forced to relearn the weapon, which already seemed an extension of their arms. The required changes were all-encompassing, involving stance, alignment, draw, and release. For days, the novices "dry shot" the simple bows, drawing and shooting with no missile. Thousands of times they applied the proper technique, until their thumbs blistered, bled, and finally callused.

When Ekrem finally introduced the featherless arrow, the instructors drifted between the novices like honeybees from blossom to blossom, patiently adjusting stances, aligning hips, and repositioning fingers, elbows, and arms. To the novices, the instructors were, *are,* God-like. With bows in hand, the staff sniffed out problems in draw and release and provided quick examples, which invariably resulted in an arrow stuck into center black.

The novices shot with a progression of four bows, until they advanced to the fifth and heaviest bow—the *qaws*—the same recurves used by Mamluks in battle. Since the bowstring on the heavy bow was strong enough to rip apart a shooter's thumb, the instructors trained them to pull the string back with notched thumb rings made of leather, bone, jade, copper, and horn, similar to those used by some of their fathers on the steppe.

The archery instructors are an oddity—the only men since the religious teachers to speak without a roar to the novices. And their message is clear: the sword was a slashing weapon for close quarters, whereas the bow is delicate, re-quiring endless patience and precision to be effective. Both weapons suit Singer, yet for him, the archery yard has become a sanctuary like no other training ground in the citadel. It is a place of peace, where imams of marksmanship focus solely on the craft of steadfast repetition.

He moves past the light bows and pulls from the stand the same recurve he has used the past few weeks. It is exactly the length of his arm. He grabs the bow and smiles, the grip fitting his hand perfectly. Beside him, Demir searches for his favorite, the novice's right cheek looking as if he had done battle with a mountain lion. Singer returns a smirk to Ilker, whose right ear looks like cauliflower, capped with a thick scab. Singer has remained free of such marks, adapting his former crude style to fit the instructors' wishes.

In sword training, slow learners identified themselves by the scar tissue traversing their backs, the instructors not hesitating to whip proper performance into their pupils. Yet those novices deficient in archery skills wore marks even more humbling, and certainly more revealing—that being wounds gained through self-infliction. Each blemish in a recruit's technique also disclosed itself often on the shooter's body: raw skin on the inside of forearms, chins, ears, and cheeks scraped clean from contact with the hide strings upon release. The bow itself was both the identifier and corrector of poor shooting, a vigilant guard dog that chose bite over bark. In the archery yard, the bow made certain that poor shooting would be associated with soreness, until the poor form was remedied, or the novice failed training.

Alone, extracting a bow from an isolated stand which holds the longest weapons, Ox lets out a deep sigh. Duyal takes a detour from his route to his shooting station and pats Ox's heavy shoulder, turning only briefly to flash a grin of encouragement as he continues on. Ox just nods to his friend with no expression.

Ox turns back to the gear. His right ear is mangled—tissue burning red, exposed cartilage beaming white, like the petals of some painful bloom. Dried pus hangs yellow and crusted on his earlobe, the same substance leaving a muted tinge on the shoulder of his tunic. The novice's left sleeve is stained maroon, the youth's evening washes unable to remove the recurring stain from his garment.

On the steppe, archers wore thin leather shields, or bracers, on the inside of their bow arms to protect them from string contact. Yet the Mamluks forbid these devices, the thin leather dulling the sensation on the inner arm and thus preventing the shooter from a learning experience. For the powerful string only hits the inner arm when a student breaks a fundamental rule in twisting the u-shaped clutch of the bow hand, what the Mamluks called the "falcon's talon."

Singer walks up to the giant. "Today, my brother, nothing but black."

Ox raises his eyebrows. "Easy for you to say. You haven't been more than a hand away from the bull's-eye since you got here."

Singer looks over him to the turret. "You'll be there in short time. Think through each step of the method. You'll get them in there today."

"Let's hope so."

Singer worries about this brother. Never short on words, the Ox seems to say less and less in the archery yard as each moon passes, as the target distance increases. He struggled hitting the black at sixty paces last week. Yet to meet Ekrem's requisites for graduation from the archery yard, each novice must consistently hit the three-foot black section of the target at one hundred paces. He is not sure his friend has it in him.

Ox moves toward his station, his shoulders slouched. Demir intercepts him, grabbing his tunic, moving close to Ox's face to make his point. Ox raises his chin and nods. Demir shares more words with scrunched brow, points to the targets and raps Ox twice on the back. He pushes Ox away in what would appear as outright anger, but is in fact the primary way this novice shows love. Singer smiles.

From pegged racks, the novices grab leather quivers and continue toward small barrels, containing arrows organized by length. Singer grabs an arrow from the eighth barrel and holds the nock to his chest. He extends his arms to double-check its length. He looks down the shaft to verify its straightness.

Repeating this sequence, he fills his quiver with target arrows the instructors call "blunts," for their rounded points and barbless blades, which prevent the entire arrow from going clean through their targets and thus ease their removal. He secures the quiver belt loosely about his waist. He walks to the shooting line and takes his place next to Ox, nodding at the man-sized novice standing among adolescents.

He sits, places both shins against each limb of the bow, and peels back the c-shaped weapon, while Ox places the string loops on both grooved ends. He catches the reek of nerves emitting from Ox's pits. He assists his friend in stringing his bow and then withdraws to his stand.

He takes a deep breath. And releases. Another. He rolls up his tunic sleeves, three folds on each arm, ensuring the folds are of equal width and void of bunched-up material. He steps up to the shooting line, looks the one hundred paces down range at the sixty *al-buttíyya* targets, perfectly aligned and standing chest-high on four wooden legs. He focuses on the black mark in the middle of the leather, which denotes a "killing shot," the only shot acceptable to the Mamluks. He tries to push away the tingle in his stomach, shake off his surprise at the size of the shrunken black dot at this distance. He must rise to the task.

Atop the tower, the red-lioned pennant of al-Salih snaps in the wind, its sharp point blowing proudly across the forming line of shooters. The yellow flag then slinks down the pole like a snake retreating into its hole, only to rise up again to its original flutter. He closes his eyes and turns his body, until his face is directly in the wind. He blocks out the smell of new grass blown in from the fields, envisioning only the invisible push on his arrow shaft. Cursed wind.

He recalls his arrow sailing past the tail of a huge buck in the mountain country and the stare of his young brother, silently accepting that their bellies would be empty for another night. Not here. He must overcome it today. He opens his eyes to see Ox, grimacing.

As the last of them sit cross-legged across from their targets, Ekrem approaches the shooters, with his hands still locked into the small of his back. "My sons, it's a good day to shoot, for Allah won't stop the breeze when the infidels storm over the horizon. Remember well your lessons in working with it. Even the oak tree must bend with the wind, not fight it."

As Ekrem turns, his archery instructors leave his side and disperse along the line.

With the bow across his thighs, Singer relaxes his shoulders and begins to rock. He quietly chants Ekrem's poem, long memorized by each recruit to reinforce proper technique.

... My feet are my base with most weight toward my toes; feet lined up with target center, so my arrow goes. My body held upright, as if pulled up by my head; bow arm straight with forward pressure will shoot enemy dead.

Bow hand relaxed, as falcon talons gone to perch; yet no bend left or right, like the tall growing birch.

My drawing forearm is a chain, with just my elbow I draw; using only back muscle to power, as when working a saw ...

He ignores the jumbled voices of those on either side of him, visualizing each body motion, every step in the shooting sequence. Swaying his head in a half trance, he runs through all forty lines and then begins again. Upon finishing the final verse, he envisions himself at the shooting line taking three shots at actual speed—all hitting the center black.

How difficult it had been to break his old behaviors. How awkward it was to use his thumb in drawing back the heavy bow, instead of the three-finger method taught by his father. How unnatural it first felt to pull the bowstring back past his ear, instead of to his brow. But he had accepted the Mamluk ways, and his arrow groups were tight most days. For this alone he is grateful. He begins to feel that this corps is his new tower, filled with skilled warriors to learn from and brothers always by his sides, all wishing for the same thing: for each of them to be more lethal with the weapons than they already are.

Enough mental chatter. He breathes in deeply through his nose to clear his head. "Make each shot count," he tells himself.

"Next moon you will qualify at one hundred paces. Shoot like it's test day," an instructor says, strolling behind them.

Singer stands, takes another deep breath and steals another look at the waving pennant. He continues his ritual. He runs his finger along the inside of rolled sleeves to smooth out more material. He then pulls all the excess cloth away from his chest, tucking it neatly back and down into the thin quiver belt with his thumbs. He tightens the belt two notches. He pushes his shoulders forward and stretches his hands over his head to ensure no constriction of movement.

Nearby, Ekrem stands behind Ichami, his left hand atop the novice's own on the grip, his right thumb covering Ichami's upon the drawn string. Rarely would another instructor take a stance so intimate, yet such is Ekrem's desire to teach. Singer feels the archery master breaks protocol only to increase novice proficiency. And fortunate for Ichami that Ekrem has so often taken such great interest in improving what are already the fine archery skills shown by the boy. Ichami nods his head to the words spoken into his ear.

Singer grasps the bow grip and reaches into his pocket, pulling out his leather finger sling. He cinches the device down on the thumb and forefinger of his bow hand, leaving the proper slack hanging in front of the bow grip. From his opposite pocket, he slips the wooden ring onto his right thumb and rotates it into place. He looks down at the wool-filled target. The twang of bowstrings, the zip and flutter of arrows fill the air. Another deep breath to push all distractions from his mind.

He no longer hears the distant "thuds" of metal puncturing leather from adjacent shooters. He assures himself there is no rush, only his target matters. Assuming the proper feet and body alignment, he pulls an arrow from his quiver and places it in the raised leather nocking point on his string. He raises his bow arm, until it is parallel with the ground. He breathes in and draws the string back, his curled thumb methodically touching his inner arm, his cheek and then ear, en route to its destination past his ear. He releases his breath, putting the small reed sight on the left edge of the center black, taking into account the now-steady wind across his front. He slowly releases the thumb ring's grip.

His arrow slams into the right edge of the black on his target. He frowns. He must move his aiming point even farther left on the next shot.

The click of Cenk's boots behind him. Ignore him. He is not there. He is not there. His *Mu'allim* walks past and stops behind Ox. Singer pictures Cenk staring at Ox's *al-buttiyya* target, the leather already littered with loose groups of arrows. Ox shoots an arrow into the right edge of the target and softly curses.

"Concentrate. You still pull with your arm, instead of your back. You move your right index finger too quickly off your thumb—this ruins your release," Cenk says. Perhaps realizing his voice is too loud for the archery yard, Cenk backs away.

Ox releases another shot. His arrow skips twice off the ground, leaving a plume of dust well beneath the target. Half the shooters snap a peek at the one responsible. Singer keeps his eyes forward.

"Ehh. You drop your arm too quickly. Follow through. What's your hurry in viewing another shot out of the black?" Cenk asks.

Singer fires another arrow. Center black. He peeks out of the corner of his eye.

Cenk kneels near the giant. Ox strokes the fletching with stubby fingers and nocks another arrow.

"Your bow hand shakes. Stressed? Stress is three hundred Franj with long lance and broadsword, bearing down on you and your brothers, wanting nothing more than to lop your head and steal our lands," Cenk says. He looks for Ekrem. "They won't have any problem finding your oversized melon. Will they? Will you be able to drop them from their mounts before they raise their nasty cleavers? No, I doubt it." He rises and begins pacing behind the line, muttering to himself.

Singer thinks only of the black dot and his consistency with each step of the shot. He releases. His arrow crashes through the fletching of two others, which are stuck firm in the black. Cenk's head turn toward him, but he pretends to inspect the next arrow he withdraws.

With all one hundred and fifty of his arrows shot and recorded, he joins the others in returning their gear in silence. Placing his arrows back in the barrel, he thinks only of the shots outside the black and the mistakes that caused each to miss its mark. The novices stay away from Ox, afraid his poor form may somehow rub off on them.

He walks up to the large one. "Keep your confidence, my friend. We have plenty of time before the next test."

"Shit," Ox says.

Ekrem approaches them. "Singer, next session I want you again in position next to Ox. You'll shoot none of your arrows until you have watched Ox and talked him through the flaws you see in his first thirty shots. Perhaps the calmness of a peer will assist."

"Yes, my Amir," Singer replies.

Ekrem turns to Ox. "You just need to settle down. Relax. Let your training take over."

"Yes, my Amir," Ox replies.

The two step off to join their mates, who make their way to the courtyard.

"One other thing," Ekrem says. "Has the command questioned either of you on my teaching methods, my conduct?" His eyes narrow.

Singer hesitates. "No. No, my Amir."

"And your mates as well?" Ekrem turns toward Ox.

"No, my Amir. Not that I know of," Ox says.

"Very well. Carry on."

The two step off quickly, knowing that even time spent answering instructor questions will not save them from the attention of Cenk. Ekrem places his bony hands behind his back and slowly returns to where his fellow instructors gather in conversation.

A safe distance away, Ox looks back to Ekem and then turns to Singer. "Fuck him. You know why he never married? Because he likes the younger boys. He gives me the crawlies."

"No way. He's married all right—to Allah and the bow. Those are his two loves."

Again Ox glances back. "Horseshit. I talked to a novice from Tulb Ten on evening duty one night. He said Ekrem lured a mate of theirs past the east boundary and took the boy against his will. The novice warned me to not get caught in a passage alone with Ekrem."

Singer scrunches his brow. "I don't believe it."

"Believe it. He's a wolf in the sheep pen."

"And why wouldn't these novices have told Safir of this misdeed?" Singer asks.

"Tsst. The same reason you wouldn't—fear. And you'll shut your mouth on this."

Wary of being heard, Singer holds his words as they near the formation, where Cenk walks in tight circles in the yard. They fall in with the others.

"Guide on, dress down the pennant. I wish for none to identify my colors with this pathetic gaggle," Cenk says.

Accustomed to the command, the guide pulls two pieces of twine from his pocket and carefully rolls the silken number nine, until the entirety is wrapped about the standard. He ties it off with the cord.

"You embarrass me. Your shooting is the worst of any unit here. I fear for the Mamluks who will be forced to serve with you one day," he says, sneering up and down the ranks. His eyes are glossed, nearly blood red, as if he had been holding his breath while waiting for them.

He walks straight to his first squad leader. "I see now why your fellow worms call you Ox—you couldn't hit an ox-sized target from twenty paces. Or is it because they know after your removal from the ranks, you'll be yoked to a cart, hauling arrows and ger poles?" He storms away on thick legs, as if physically unable to stomach looking at Ox.

He returns, madder than normal, seeming to hold back tears. "You don't listen. Your skills are a disgrace. You'll get comrades killed!" He stops pacing, his face going blank as he concentrates on the giant.

Ox's lips quiver in anger.

Cenk's eyes brighten. "Is this uncomfortable? Wait until your saddle is soaked with your own urine, as the enemy bears down… your thick shoulders and bull legs of no use. Only your bow will be able to reach the enemy." He stops one pace from Ox's face. "You'll soon fail the archery test and be done. Perhaps duties of the sea will suit you. You long for the sea, eh?"

Ox takes a step forward and looks down at Cenk, staring into his eyes.

Cenk seems unable to hide his delight. He smiles, begins to gently flick his fingernail on the top of his scabbard. "You know I'm right. In just days, only days, you'll be out. A blessing from Allah. You step up because you think you can take me?" he asks.

Ox takes a step back into formation, likely realizing his move was insanity, composing himself enough to perhaps recall that he will be removed from the citadel if he hits Cenk even once.

Cenk steps closer, possibly unwilling to lose his opportunity. He scowls and looks up at Ox. "Clench up that dick skinner and throw a punch at me. You've got me. I will say nothing. I promise. Do it."

Ninety-eight eyes, which were locked forward, now strain to the sides to see what their mate will do. A tense moment drifts by.

Singer wonders if there will be a repeat of last month's ordeal. It had taken all of his strength to detach only two of Cenk's fingers, wrapped about Demir's neck. It took four novices to pry back the remaining meaty appendages, his fingers much like tamarack roots at the river's edge. He does not think Cenk recalls any of it; not a word of the instance was ever uttered. One simply did not know why or when their leader's rage would snap from instruction to destruction.

"You're nothing but a soft-handed, cattle-eating pussy from easy Dnieper country. The instructors know it. Your fellow worms know it. Nobody needs your clumsy ass around," Cenk says with complete sincerity.

He waits, repeatedly lifting his sword out of its scabbard a few inches by its ivory pommel and then letting gravity seat the blade home with a click. "The eunuchs allow a novice to defend himself, if an instructor threatens the novice's life. By Allah, my hand is upon my sword, giant one. Your fellow worms see it, will be able to answer such when questioned... and surely... this old man could not possibly get his sword out in time to defend himself against a fighter as strong and quick as you."

Ox stares straight ahead, not biting on the offer.

Cenk looks both ways, disappointment on his face. "That's what I thought." He looks over his shoulder and then rams his knee into Ox's groin, stepping aside as would an axe-man who just heard the final fibers of a massive tree give way.

Ox crumbles, falling forward to his knees, both hands cupping his jewels.

Duyal drops down, ducking his head under Ox's arm. He strains to hoist him back to his feet and into formation. Demir comes to the other side, dips under the other armpit.

Together they struggle to raise him.

"Leave him. You! Leave him be!"

CHAPTER
30

Cenk
The citadel, Aqtay's chamber, Hisn Kayfa
May 4, 1237

Cenk clamors up the rough gray stairs, gritting his teeth.
He stops to lean on the cold wall, burying his head in
the bend of his elbow. Why has the commander of the citadel
called upon him? Easing his fingers through his hair, he makes
a fist of his locks and tugs in anger.

His tulb has thus far graded out in the middle of the
pack. While disappointing, surely they would not relieve him
for poor performance. By Allah, he cannot shoot arrows and
cut felt for his worms.

Was it Fidan? Did one of the other wives inform the
command that it was her intention to leave him? Not that
he cares. She has become a burden. He could live in the barracks, was tired of her whining and staying to the corners of
the room. Would Amir Aqtay be taking him aside to counsel
him on how to manage a wife? Please ... his only real concern
on Fidan was in insulting al-Salih. His prince had provided

him a gift that he neither appreciated, nor properly nurtured. For that he is sorry.

Was it his drinking? Could one of the other instructors have known and ratted on him? Maybe a guard? He cups his hands and breathes into them, attempting to detect any lingering vapors from the wine he drank in the early morning hours. They would dismiss him if found out, might be justified in lopping his tongue. He could almost hear the most righteous of them: "Now he'll be able to pour it down with no obstacle in the way."

He cannot bear the thought of disappointing his prince. A stickiness builds up in the pits of his tunic. He opens the first two buttons of his coat; flops the front of his tunic, allowing the air to fan the subtle reek. Putting his uniform back together and checking the alignment of his belt buckle, he regains his confidence.

Up the winding passage. He will not be caught. Nobody knows. The bastards waste his time. His novices are on horseback today, and he should be on hand to observe their instruction. He runs through their faces in his mind. Could one of the little pricks have spoken to a eunuch after prayer, or in the barracks some evening? Would they have smelled it on him? Maybe.

Arriving at the command hallway, Cenk halts. He takes a deep breath, collects himself. Three knocks on the amir's planked door.

"Enter."

He pushes open the door, takes one step in, and stands at attention. He stares over the seated amir's head to the lioned pennant on the wall behind. A musty fragrance hangs in the air, mixed with the smell of lingering smoke from a candle just blown out.

"My Amir, reporting as you wished."

"Cenk, have a seat," Aqtay says.

A chair sits directly in front of the commander's desk, its finish rubbed raw only on the front of the seat. More moisture in his armpits. He sits, placing his callused hands on each thigh, giving the illusion they prop up his erect body.

Scrolls on the large desk. A pen box given to him by the prince. A shadowboxed sword on the opposite wall, a plaque from his first command.

"How's your training going, Cenk?"

"Very well, my Amir. My novices gain skills daily. With some luck they'll become Mamluks."

Aqtay nods, a thoughtful look on his face. "You'll be glad to know that al-Salih has much faith in you. He feels you're as dedicated as any. Steady... devout in your faith."

Cenk feels the compression in his chest lighten. He silently thanks Allah.

Aqtay pushes away the scrolls in front of him. "And it needs to be so. No duty in the realm is more important than yours. Our prince is not short of enemies of the sultanate here in the north, eh? One day your young men will be needed."

"Yes Amir, I know my duty is vital. We must keep our prince's ranks strong."

Cenk stares at the flag behind Aqtay—the red lion, its curled tail, its sharp claws. His novices could be called upon very soon, and every moment he is not in the hippodrome advancing his tulb's skills is another moment he does a disservice to al-Salih. And right now their prince is silently writhing in the trap set by the Syrian princes to the south. He curses the sultan, al-Kamil. Another calamity caused by al-Salih's father. Not only had the sultan's two-year war in Anatolia killed Cenk's best friends, the political conniving behind the sultan's military adventure in the north had allied the Syrian princes against Cairo and, more importantly, endangered al-Salih and his territories in the Jazira.

He looks at Aqtay somewhat impatiently, yet respectfully, waiting for the amir to arrive at the meat of their discussion.

Aqtay leans back in his chair and laces his hands behind his head. His arms, the size of some men's legs, strain the stitches of his white wool coat. "You're fortunate. You could be stuck in a burrow like mine, counting coins and signing scrolls," he says with a smile, his hand waving to the walls about him.

Cenk looks him in the eye with no expression.

Aqtay squints, accentuating the premature wrinkles along his brow. He pauses, as if to carefully choose his words. "Cenk, you've seen the peasants in the south working their fields?"

The question catches him off guard. "Yes, my Amir."

"The best of these work dung into their soil plots each fall, repair their irrigation ditches—blister their hands and those of their children in pulling out the invading weeds. These efforts give their lords the best crops. Right?" Aqtay looks into Cenk's eyes to see if his analogy takes hold.

Cenk hates the obvious, unnecessary comparison the amir is feeding him. The crops are his novices and somehow the commander feels he is falling short. Get the lecture over with. He wishes to tell Aqtay that these useless peasants he speaks of would find purpose in the dung that spills from his commander's mouth. He feels a heat rising from the center of his gut.

He nods respectfully. "Yes, my Amir, all of my energy is spent on my novices. And weeding out the weak is a task I do not shy from." He shifts in his seat, wishing the amir would be straight with him. He reasons that Aqtay has spent too much time with the eunuch, Safir. The deballed black man, with his soft voice and gentle ways, is beginning to cloud the commander's mind. Allah help us.

Memories of his time in Cairo flood his mind—the eunuchs who oversaw his own training at *Bok Deligi*, "the shithole." The pale-faced Byzantine, the castrated prick always smirking with each swing of his switch. And the fine meals prepared for these special ones, quickly whisked away by servants to comfortable chambers, while the remainder of the staff and novices ate slop elbow to elbow.

Aqtay tightens his eyebrows and speaks in an almost fatherly tone. "We must remember that most of the prince's *Muta'allim* already have the raw skills needed to become Mamluks. Our novices are like seedlings that have risen from the soil, needing only the farmer's tending. Am I being clear?"

"Yes, my Amir."

Aqtay leans forward in his chair and rests his bowed forearms on the desktop, hunched over like a curious bear. "You remember, Cenk, it wasn't that long ago when you and I both were tending flocks and hunting antelope on opposite ends of the great steppe ourselves. Were we really any different than the boys you received into your care ten moons ago?"

Cenk reasons his amir spends too much time in his chamber. Perhaps he would know the difference, if he spent more time in the hippodrome observing the training. No. Aqtay should stay away from him, remain in his quarters, where he can do no harm. He tilts his head, politely urging the amir to his point.

Aqtay leans back in his chair. "Look, as they grow into men here, we need only convert their hunting skills into battle dexterity and transition their thinking away from the ill-disciplined acts of the individual warrior, toward the orderly conduct of Mamluks in formation. That's the mission. Cenk, your novices only need to be cultivated, molded... like clay."

"My Amir, I only follow the *Furusiyya*. My recruits haven't missed a session. I know their performance is not where it needs to be, but I'm fixing this. In all due respect..."

Cenk stops himself short. He must not be defensive, must maintain his bearing. He is speaking to the commander. Nothing can be gained in argument here. He compels his breathing to slow. Breathe deeply. Breathe deeply.

"Cenk, nobody questions your effort or adherence to the cavalry principles…" Aqtay stops and closes his eyes and then smiles, seeming to regain his own composure, or perhaps deciding on a different tack. "You've been selected from many to be the dragon, yet you're also tasked as the primary artisan, the one who'll shape the prince's raw clay into fine pottery. You mustn't be only the slave driver to these novices, but also their older brother. We must build up and train this regiment, not decimate its training ranks."

Cenk listens, knowing that his time to speak is finished.

Aqtay balls his fingers into a tight fist. He raises his top lip. "Our prince has too many dinars, too much planned for these novices, to have them all become moat fillers. At your unit's current failure rate, you will have no novices to train in two years. Do you understand me, *Mu'allim?*"

Cenks fumes, struggling to hide his disgust. He imposes a calm upon himself. Should he really act like no more than a fluffy-minded potter with his novices? Is this the type of leadership required to expand the prince's regiment? He wishes Allah to strike Aqtay dead right here. Of course the eunuch Safir is behind all of this. The ball-less one would have him bring the feeble and poorly skilled into their ranks. Cenk works to control his breathing, folds his hands to keep them from trembling, as if evenly reflecting on the amir's words.

He clicks back to his boyhood, recalling a dominant sire in his tower's herd, one that covered the other stallions with bite marks and bruises from his kicks. He had admired this animal's spirit, spent much time just watching him among the others. Yet when eventually gelded, the pony thereafter stayed to himself, never again to prance when the mares came into heat or fight for his place among the males.

It is Safir. He causes this trouble. As the story goes, al-Salih purchased Safir in Cairo for nearly double the dinars of the other Mamluks in the citadel, Safir having had his penis and balls taken in his teens at the cutting block of some greedy African trader. As he typically did with new eunuchs, al-Salih placed him into the rotation guarding the prince's harem, where Safir soon became one of the prince's favorites, winning him positions of increasing importance and eventually placing him ahead of the other eunuchs.

In time, al-Salih sent Safir to the best educators and eventually assigned him to one of his most entrusted amirs, Husam al-Din. Under this amir, Safir even assisted in the early education of the prince's youngest son, Turanshah. Yet this closeness to the prince came at a cost. Safir became an outcast, holing up in his chamber when not with the prince, Husam al-Din, or Aqtay. The more the regiment pushed him away, the more al-Salih protected and elevated him. And the more diligently Safir executed his duties.

Cenk feels his pulse course across his temples. Eunuchs. Curried favor by every prince in the Islamic world, they are no better than the guard dogs of his childhood, their balls lopped off to keep them among the gers, not fighting or prowling at night for rodents or bitches in heat. He figures most Mamluks simply despise the preferred treatment the princes grants their eunuchs: the best education, choice command slots, fiefs that bring sometimes seven thousand dinars in revenue per year, ten times the typical amir's.

But in Hisn Kayfa, Cenk sees the common slave soldier envious of those two things most precious in the realm—the high trust and vast amounts of time al-Salih spends with his ball-less cadre. For ultimately, the *Salihiyya* are no different than children in a disjointed family, maneuvering constantly for their father's fondness and attention. And naturally, the father's most beloved become the most loathed by the rest. As his mother often said, "Jealousy is the mother of hate."

"Cenk, do you understand?" Aqtay repeats, annoyed at the silence.

Cenk nods his head, pretending to have seen the light, the error in his prior ways. "Yes, my Amir, I understand."

"That is all," Aqtay says.

Cenk rises from his seat and snaps to attention. "Good afternoon, my Amir." He takes a step back, faces about, and closes the door behind him.

He grumbles, moving quickly down the stairs. He cannot get far enough away from the command chamber. Midway down the stairs, he sits, putting a shoulder against the damp wall. He needs a flask. He closes his eyes.

"Zulu! Zulu!" Amir Turkmani commanded over the thundering hooves, his former patron waving his sword arm in distress, giving the order to shoot and evade. The foe was sizable, likely hundreds. And these Khwarazmians appeared from nowhere, like ants emerging from the ground on all sides. Their shell-backed colony shook with anger, crawling, fighting over themselves to taste Mamluk blood.

Leaving their booty-laden camels behind, the enemy outmaneuvered the Mamluks, circling Cenk's comrades and showering long, heavy arrows upon his brothers. Too many of them, quickly closing every avenue of escape. More men falling. Screams. Turkmani lost control, incapable of punching his small unit through the quivering death perimeter.

Miraculously, Allah provided bands of sleet near dusk—cover the Mamluks used to flee. But still the enemy arrows came. Cenk looked over his shoulder to watch three from his squad dropped from their Arabians. His commander, fighting with four arrows sticking from his legs and chest, eventually fell.

Cenk and two others rushed in, slashing with sword and dagger at the Khwarazmian ants, who snapped their hideous jaws upon his patron.

He cups his head in his hands and sobs, just as he did when they placed Turkmani into his mausoleum. Turkmani would not have listened to Aqtay's babble. Yet his old master would also be disgusted to see him now, just as he would be to witness Cenk's frequent drunken visits to his mentor's tomb in the late evenings.

Aqtay spoke of nurturing seedlings. Seedlings. Turkmani's amirate, Cenk's *Khushdash*, were also seeds. Seeds blown from the protection of their pod, only to land on barren rock.

His remaining brothers scattered about the realm, unable to support each other, relegated to strangers in their new units. Of course it had to be done. Al-Salih had to dispel the bad curse that had befallen them.

He pounds his head into his knees. "Enough." What if an amir sees him? He rises, clenching his forehead in one hand. In with a deep breath; tears wiped with clenched knuckles. His oath to Turkmani's lifeless form bleeds into the front of his mind—keep those of weak mind and short skill out of the ranks.

He shakes his head, as if to clear the cobwebs, as if to push out the femininity that had entered his ears. He quickens his pace, opening his eyes wide, allowing the air to circulate and reduce the swell in his eyes. Loyalty to al-Salih remains a must, but never must he forget that pledge made to his original father.

"Forgive me for this frailty, dear Allah. And forgive me, forgive me, Turkmani."

CHAPTER
31

Duyal
The citadel barracks, Hisn Kayfa
July 31, 1237

The air hangs stale and oppressive. A bead of sweat detaches from Duyal's hairline and rides the slick surface of his skin to the corner of his mouth. He sucks the wet salt from his lips. He stands locked at the position of attention, his eyes fixed over the face opposite him, focusing in and out on the intersecting seams between the stacked blocks that confine him and his mates. With Cenk's back to him, he slightly bends his knees, ineffectively working the stiffness from them.

Twin files stretch the length of the barracks, opposing tanned faces contrasted against their chopped blond hair and muted garb. The welts of their boots kiss the beige edge of aligned blankets, the burred surface of the horse covers mounded with the gear of the *faris*. Arranged in an identical manner are: one pair of slippers, one pair of gaiters, two pair of wool socks, two drinking flasks, a pair of trousers, a tunic, a chain mail *kazaghand*, a piece of *jawshan* chest armor, a leather lamellar helmet, and hat.

His stomach grumbles boisterously. A twinge of adrenaline runs through him. Surely his *Muallim* heard it. He braces for a verbal attack. It does not come.

It has been only six days since the sighting of the moon's crescent, signifying the start to Ramadan, a time of fasting for Muslims. During this period, the gates of heaven are opened, the gates of hell are closed, and Satan is put into chains. At its core, Ramadan means no food or drink from dawn until sunset. No alcohol. For both the soldiers and the citizens of Hisn Kayfa, the days during the holy month begin with a main meal in the evening, just after the sun dips, and another in the predawn hours of morning.

For the average city dweller, the holy month is little more than a blessed inconvenience in their lives, a touch of discomfort to remind them of the Prophet's sacrifices and the painful realities experienced by the poor. The civilian's fast is made tolerable, as their pace of life is purposely slowed during the month and two large meals often take the place of their regular three. Yet for the Mamluks, the bare actuality of Ramadan bites a little deeper. The vigorous training tempo does not slow to accommodate heaven's gates swinging open for thirty days. Allah's work still needs to be done in far-off places and young warriors must be made competent for Jihad.

In town, the holy month is less about deprivation and more about the moral and spiritual level. Civilians try to avoid sin, such as slander and anger. They strive to cut the distraction from their lives during the fast, to better experience Allah as the only true reality. On windless nights, words from the Koran bounce through the small alleys of the city, reaching up to the guard towers and through the fortress portals.

While many of Hisn Kayfa's inhabitants will reread the entire Koran during the holy month, Mamluks spend their evenings reciting only the most essential text, receiving encouragement from al-Salih and the eunuchs to focus their holy reflection on the Sixth Pillar of Islam, their personal obligation to Jihad.

The training tulbs simply mirror the fasting schedule of al-Salih's regulars during Ramadan. However, Cenk has predictably used the holy month as another means to challenge his novices. Instead of backing off on the training sessions, he has increased their number. The only thing he has scaled back is the quantity of chow found in the evening meal. Further, it has become standard for him to cut short the morning meal, purposely running the mealtime very close to their first training evolution of the day, requiring the novices to scarf down their rations.

Duyal has dreamt of lamb and goat and yogurt each of the last five nights. Once he rose in a panic, thinking he had broken the fast. The ping in his gut convinced him otherwise. Maybe the evening breeze carrying the aroma of evening feasts from the town people into the barracks brought forth the dreams, or perhaps it was just a test set by Allah.

No matter. Enduring a lack of food was nothing new for them, as this condition on the steppe was not unusual. But the absence of water during the hottest of summer days has punished them. "The purification of the fast will only clarify your understanding of God and the *Furusiyya*, our cavalry principles," Safir said at the start of the month.

A double clunk of bone on stone breaks the quiet. On the far side of the column, white-clad forms break their ranks. They stoop over the subject, whispering. A tunic is placed under the downed boy's head.

"Who said move? Back in formation!" Cenk says. "Now! Let him lie. If he's dumb enough to lock his knees, he's where he deserves to be."

A scurry of activity, as novices snap back to their rigid stance. A line of sunken faces and dried lips. Duyal does not remember pissing today. He does not recall any in the tulb pissing yet today.

His instructor crouches to grab a flask from among Ichami's full kit. He rises and holds the flask upside down in front of the handsome novice. "I guess the talented one will ride into battle with no stopper in his flask." Cenk moves closer. "Will you fight the infidels with your thumb stuck in its spout? Or when realizing yours empty, will you then borrow drink from your brother and let him shrivel in the desert with you?"

He hurls the hardened vessel across the barracks, the flask skipping across the stone floor, terminating with a crash against the gray wall. Ichami remains firm, a stern expression on his face, his eyes set over Cenk's head.

Another three paces echo across the stone. Cenk stops at the next blanket. He takes a knee, looking closely for holes in Erol's socks, rips in his trousers, any item missing. The constrained air whistling through his thick-boned nose, he pulls a tunic inside out and looks for untrimmed seam threads.

Duyal tries to lose himself in the Arabic scribbles etched high into the walls above them, passages from the Koran, only decipherable by the eunuchs and a handful of instructors. His eyes pass over them as they would a crowd of unrecognizable faces, looking for the collection of symbols that represents his favorite verse. He tries to sort out the past year, the fingers of eunuchs pointing to the lettering on the various blocks and the holy men from town reciting the words, making the novices repeat them, the verses shaming the novices to correct their shortfalls.

There it is. The best of the wall squiggles from their God. The one that had returned faith to his heart when his motivation was lagging so many times: "And be not weak-hearted in the pursuit of the enemy; if you suffer pain, then surely they too suffer pain as you suffer pain, and you hope from Allah what they do not hope; Allah is knowing and wise."

"Erol, what is the definition of unselfishness?" Cenk asks, tossing the tunic at the novice's chest.

Erol remains at attention as the tunic bounces off him and falls to his feet. "*Muʿallim*, unselfishness is the avoidance of providing for one's own comfort and personal advancement at the expense of others."

Duyal smiles inside. Erol. He stands a full head shorter than the rest of them, with arms the size of twigs, his voice nearly as slight as his build. The boy seemed doomed from the start.

Erol was pointed to the group of rejects.

"Let me shoot," he blurted. "I bet my life that I can outshoot any among you."

The amirs froze. They stopped their physical inspections, looking over their shoulders at each other for a shared chuckle. Silence.

Safir pulled a strung bow from the rack, handed it to Erol. "You have eight arrows and the attention of the entire room. You waste them and I may take you up on your bet."

Erol nocked an arrow and shot, pushing the first arrow just outside the black. The boy put his eye to the string groove and looked down the length of the limbs. He nodded, flipped the weapon, catching it at the grip.

His next arrow hit center black. The following shattered the arrow already stuck in the black. Yet another slammed in beside it.

"Look at that little shit," Ox said.

> *Erol's fifth shot split the fletching of both arrows.*
> *Safir scowled and waved him off, halting the spectacle.*
> *He pointed the boy in the direction of those Kipchaks already accepted.*

"Oh, very good. Why is it you know the definition of this holy trait, but ignore it in practice?" Cenk asks.

A pause. A confused look falls upon Erol's face. "*Mu'allim,* this novice does not understand your question."

"Unselfishness. How is it that your kit is in fine shape, while those of your mates are a disaster?" He moves into Erol's face for further clarification. "It's clear to all that you care only for yourself."

"No, *Mu'allim.*"

"Bullshit!"

Duyal hopes Erol sees through Cenk's game. For the past week, the training had started an hour earlier and was not finished until sunset, leaving no time before "candles out" for the novices to clean and mend gear. Erol had been the exception. Forced by the eunuchs to nurse an injured arm the past three days, he was able to prepare for this inspection, yet was given no access to his brothers' gear.

Cenk centers himself on Ilker. He takes a step back, turns his nose away from the novice. "When was the last time you bathed?"

"*Mu'allim,* this novice bathed three days ago."

"Three moons ago?"

Using his staff, he flips Ilker's helmet up into his hand and inspects the felt inlays. They droop, coated in a waxy brown. The leather pieces suspending the leather crown hang thin and frayed. Cenk puts his nose into the bowl and then turns away, a sickened expression upon his face. "Ilker, the foul pig. Do you shit in this helmet at night?"

"No, my *Mu'allim.*"

"But you let the rest of the tulb shit in this helmet?"

"No, my *Mu'allim.*"

Cenk heaves it across the barracks, the ticking from its lamellar shell resonating across the cavern. "Hold out your hands." He looks down at Ilker's filthy fingers. "Worms are built to slither through the mud, not claw at it. You're a disgrace."

Cenk picks up Ilker's spare trousers. A brown stain mars the crotch. "By Allah, sheep have less shit attached to their ass. Ughh." His look of repulsion switches to one of rage. "How does the *faris* define bearing?"

"*Mu'allim*, bearing is creating a favorable impression in carriage, appearance, and personal conduct at all times."

"Is that right? Is that what you do, create a favorable impression?" Cenk asks.

"Yes, my *Mu'allim.*"

Cenk clenches his lips and nods his head slowly. He snags Ilker's *kazaghand* from the blanket and crinkles his face at the mud pressed into the recesses of the armor's weave. He drops the chain mail on Ilker's feet with a thud.

He snatches a leather gaiter and flicks at the broken metal buckle on the shin protector with a thick fingernail. He strikes Ilker across the chest with it, knocking the recruit back.

"You think this gear will protect your leg when riding?"

"No, *Mu'allim*," he says, stepping forward and returning to the position of attention, his heels revisiting the blanket's fringe.

"Was this gear in such condition when you drew it from supply?"

"No, *Mu'allim.*"

"No, of course not. Ilker, you're the scoundrel that gets Mamluks killed. Too lazy to repair a buckle on campaign, your shin will go raw from the stirrup leather. Being spineless and ill-disciplined, your focus will be on the scrape and away from the enemy when he strikes. When you take an arrow and your nasty body falls from the mount, there the enemy will exploit the gap in our formation."

Cenk walks away. He returns, his face now reddened. "And once in close quarters, the infidel slays not you, but your brother—the better man—the one relying on your worthless ass to cover his flank!" On this last word, Cenk raises the leather guard, feigns another strike at Ilker, but instead swings around with both staff and gaiter, striking Duyal across the jaw.

Not expecting the blow, Duyal is knocked to the floor. He rises to his elbows and knees.

The barracks spin. He wobbles, then finds his feet. He runs his tongue across a split lip, tastes the iron. He swallows it. He pushes his tongue through a broken tooth and finds another sloppy in its socket.

He looks on the floor for any sign of blood. Satisfied that he does not desecrate the grounds, he finds the busted tooth in his mouth and slowly tucks it away with his tongue. He resumes his station and locks his body.

Cenks turns, slowly striding along the blanket-lined path. He spins his staff about the wrist strap, catching it every third revolution.

Whoosh, whoosh, whoosh. Snap! Whoosh, whoosh, whoosh. Snap!

"Ilker, already your neglect makes the blood of your brother flow," Cenk says. He turns and stops in front of Duyal, tilting his head as if to examine some unusual object.

Duyal concentrates on the top of his instructor's turban. He holds his breath, the wild mint leaves tucked into Cenk's cheek hardly covering the stench of sour *koumis* emitting from the man. Bloods drips from Duyal's chin to his baggy tunic, his uniform already stained brown about his knees, yellow bands ringing his armpits. A cherry trickle courses over his throat and into his neckline. He wishes he could stop the flow, keep away the blood that will only feed Cenk's frenzy.

"You ungrateful rat. You ruin the tunic provided by our prince. Why would al-Salih provide this herd with new uniforms, when you abuse the gear you have? None of you are worthy."

His comments achieve the unintended. These words only motivate Duyal, and likely his mates as well. Cenk had timed the inspection so that all would fail, yet the eunuchs will not let the results prevent the forty-five novices in the *tulb* from receiving the new kit. Everyone knows this.

They have paid their price to wear the lighter-weight trouser, white sash, and leather belt.

They will soon begin to look more like Mamluks. And in only six more moons, they will also be blessed to wear the form-fitted tunic. Further, instead of novice working parties washing the *tulb*'s uniforms along the muddy banks of the river, the recruits will be allowed to use the citadel's laundry quarters and the clean ground water from the cisterns.

"What is endurance?"

Duyal forces the words slowly through his mangled lips. "*Mu'allim*, endurance is the mental and physical stamina, measured by the ability to withstand pain, fatigue, stress, and hardship." He keeps his eyes on the turban, the silk wraps distorting, fading into a blotch of blurred mustard. The blotch departs, leaving him to again watch the gray stone wall.

Cenk sighs. "Obviously none here have enough respect for their prince or themselves to keep their kit in proper condition," he says, his face twisting in disgust. "This inspection has concluded! *Kazaghand* in left hand, *jawshan* in your right… move!"

On the command, all scramble to grasp the gear from their displays, returning to their previous positions.

"I see we also have no urgency. Again. Back."

They rush to place the gear back on the blankets and then return to the position of attention.

"Sloppy and slow is not the way of the *Salihiyya*. We can do this all night. Move!"

Swiftly they grab the heavy chain mail armor in left hands and the lamellar leather cuirass in their right. With chests pumping, they wait for the command.

"Up!"

The novices raise fists of armor to their sides, until their outstretched arms are parallel to the stone floor.

"All the way up, worms."

Short breaths and concealed groans beside him. A burn sets into his shoulders. He swallows another mouthful of blood and then departs the place.

The sun dipped as they reached the top. A vivid burgundy permeated the landscape. He and his brother stood for only a moment to catch their breath.

About them, patches of top-heavy fronds and bronze stems rolled and licked the opposite hillside like raging flames, amid the endless green of the steppe. Below, the wind drove rising smoke sideways from the open flap atop his mother's ger.

And there, leaning against the entrance with crossed forearms, their father had already spotted them. Surely he saw their high loads and the antler points radiating atop Gozde's head.

Weary legs and the dig of the animals' spines prodded them onward. They moved downhill under their carcass backpacks, deer leg straps formed by pushing front hooves through slits cut in the tendons of rear legs.

A throb in both legs, as if both kneecaps could burst. The bath of blood, which had covered their backsides from head to boots, had now dried into a tight layer of new skin on their necks and calves. It stretched and cracked at each step.

As they reached the bottom, the old man nodded in approval. Then, most unnaturally, his scarred face broke into a smile, the occurrence seeming to embarrass their father, forcing him to duck back into the ger.

"Erol, you have to be the weakest bastard I ever laid eyes on. How will you trade blows with the crusaders, when you can't even hold up your own armor?"

Soon others succumb to fried shoulders and arms, the gear falling to the novices' sides in a steady chain of thumps.

"Pitiful, rabbit chasers. Pitiful! Drop 'em and prepare to dig."

With arms mostly numb, Duyal drops his gear and falls to the deck, his belly heaving against the stone.

"Up!"

The tulb push themselves up, popping their left knees to their chests, their right legs remaining straight out.

Ahh. He was slow to respond. He grimaces, hoping his instructor was looking the other way.

"Duyal wants to take his sweet time! We'll now dig twice as long. Well, except for Duyal. He's lost a little blood and isn't feeling well."

Cenk kicks a stool into the walkway. "Please, please, Duyal. Sit. We can't have the amir's brother engaged in this sort of drudgery... not when in such a dreadful condition."

Duyal remains in position, hoping his instructor did not mean what he said. He waits, trying to will the exercise to begin. Let him take part in the punishment he helped cause. He will dig hard to make up for his dawdling.

He waits for the next command to commence the exercise. The sound of heel on rock. Closer. Louder. He has made another mistake.

The heels stop at his face. "I'm sorry, did the novice not hear his instructor?" Cenk asks.

"Yes, *Mu'allim*."

Wham, wham! Duyal takes two kicks to the rump and thigh. He spins to his buttocks and sits perfectly straight, with his hands flat on his thighs, eyes forward.

"On the stool, you stupid sheep sticker. Face them."

Duyal runs to the stool and sits. With a screech, he rotates it a quarter turn.

"Dig!"

CHAPTER
32

Duyal
The citadel hippodrome, Hisn Kayfa
September 6, 1237

With a slight tug on his right rein and calf applied to right flank, Aslan rotates his chestnut Arabian in a tight circle. Spotting the final cone lying on the hippodrome dirt, he dips the head of his lance and drops his hands, guiding his mount forward. He snatches it with the lance tip, as if the staff and iron head were as one with Aslan's own appendage. The twenty-foot weapon raises with the tip of the cone married to the lance point, until the shaft is perpendicular to the ground.

Turning his horse toward the line of viewing recruits, he flips the cone up in the air and catches it on his left fist and stows in with the others in a bag strapped to his saddle. His horse returns at a lope to the mounted recruits.

"Whoa," Duyal says, looking at Singer with a grin.

"I guess that's why we address him as lance master," Singer whispers, as their instructor nears.

Aslan's chestnut, not too proud to boast in front of even the humblest of audiences, prances laterally toward the group with head high, hooves kicking up clumps of brown. At his mount's behavior, their instructor shoots a contagious smirk, his long blond hair bouncing upon thick shoulders, in perfect time with that of his manicured stallion's mane.

He halts. "Right. That of course was the old Khorasan style. Now what did I do wrong?"

Twelve novices stare at the grinning Mamluk. His name means "Lion," and while he is the youngest of the masters in the citadel, at twenty-four, he is also the most decorated by al-Salih.

"Come now. By Allah, you won't hurt my feelings. We don't have all day," Aslan says, looking across the hippodrome at the other twenty-nine novices who train under his subordinate instructors.

Erol raises his hand. "Speak," the man says.

"My Amir, your hand was higher than four fingers' width up the butt of the lance," he says.

"Hah! Good, good—you see past my intentional flash to the substance. If I grip too high on the butt, the lance may end up in my sleeve and the cursed Franj may have their way with me," he replies. "What else?"

Aslan's horse shakes his head with the impatience of his owner, flipping sandy hair out of his eyes to reveal a white patch, wider at the forelock and tapering to a lance-shaped tip on the muzzle. He scratches the beast behind the ears.

Duyal works up the courage and raises his hand. Aslan points at him.

"My Amir, on the fifth cone, your right elbow was away from your side. The lance was not pressed against your belt," Duyal says.

"Good. Detail. Improper technique eventually spells death. But you neglect the obvious, *Mutaallim*," he says with a grin.

Duyal remains tight-lipped, but feels a warmness inside. He wishes to be like Aslan one day, confident as a rutting buck, yet void of any conduct that smacks of arrogance. He admires his instructor's sole mission: conveying all in his tactical brain to those of his pupils. And that he has done. Concentrating on one exercise per week for eleven moons, the recruits have progressed two thirds of their way through the seventy-two exercises which make up the *Bunud*, or lance exercises of the *Furusiyya*.

For those that remain, Aslan begins to treat the novices like little brothers, like the young Mamluks they are changing into. In fact, in small bits, many of the instructors have started to allow the recruits to feel at least a little like Mamluks. Similar to the old man who tosses the odd crumb to keep the pigeons cooing near his ger, the instructors provide just enough reward to prevent the novices from losing heart.

Only two days prior, the tulb earned the privilege to wear the lighter trousers and leather belts to hold them up. Protocol had the recruits drawing the new gear one year from their arrival date, but of course Cenk would have none of it. "Please, my worms do not deserve it," Cenk had complained to the eunuchs with his novices listening in formation.

The eunuchs acquiesced, delaying the new issue until the thirteenth moon from the day of their arrival. And with the new trousers, Duyal and the others feel a surge of confidence. In exercise on foot, they feel more coordinated; on horseback, they feel more like the *faris*. No longer are they constantly fighting to keep the heavy material from slipping below their waists. With one less distraction, all perform the drills more efficiently.

Duyal senses the forty-one novices still in his tulb are not just committed to the training; they are devoted to a life of soldiering. He feels they can see nothing else. His fellows now focus on what the Mamluks call *yetenek*, meaning not just competence or the ability to physically accomplish the exercises, but to do so with flair. The magic formula in reaching this level of performance? There is none, save repetition of proper technique, the right attitude, and hard work.

Again Aslan looks over their shoulders at his instructors across the arena. A yip, as one of his assistants races two novices through the cone course.

"Come now. What does the *Furusiyya* say about a good lance? Is this one a good choice for me? Ox?" Aslan asks, snapping his head toward his pupils, holding the lance out to his side with fist tight.

"Yes, my Amir, the lance is of medium thickness. It fits your hand well," Ox says.

Aslan tosses the weapon to him. "So it's good then?" he asks with a broad smile.

The Ox follows their inspection procedure, pushing the bamboo through his large hands, while twisting it. With his eyes only inches from the shaft, he checks the wood for cracks, worm holes or decay at the joints. Satisfied, he grabs the weapon midshaft and shakes it, paying attention to its flex.

"Yes, my Amir, the weapon is light and does not vibrate too much," he says, handing it back to Aslan.

"So if someone hands you this lance, with the Franj bearing down, you would fight with it?"

"Yes, my Amir."

"Yes, yes. Its tint is even pretty to look at, eh?" Aslan says.

Ox smiles broadly, as do several others. Aslan then jabs the weapon into the ground and pushes, stressing the middle of the shaft. It shatters. He heaves the butt section at Demir, who catches the frizzled end of the cane with one hand, just before it strikes his face.

Aslan scowls at the group. "Remember this—beauty means nothing. It's hollow as an empty cistern. Decoration, a fine finish, shine on a weapon. These mean nothing. Nothing."

He meets the eye of each. "Beware of the gorgeous woman, who lures you in with long hair and flirting eyes—you'd best check her for soul and backbone too, eh? Be smart."

Aslan nods. "Don't be blinded. Even flawless lance skill will fail with an unsound weapon in hand. The *Furusiyya*! Does our text not state we should avoid a yellow or white lance, as this indicates bamboo grown on low ground? Too little sunshine causes defects, correct?"

Ox blushes, shakes his head in self-disappointment. "Yes, my Amir."

Aslan steers his mount backward, so all can see him clearly. "The battlefield has compressed. All arrow shafts are expended. A ghulam tosses Ox a faulty lance. It breaks easily. With no choice, our brother pulls his sword. A pair of scraggy Franj keep their distance from our big friend and skewer him with their own lances. The end . . . "

He grabs his gut for effect. "I've seen it, my brothers. I wish it not on you. So we'll only accept lances of brown-colored bamboo—that grown on high ground, nourished with abundant rain and sunshine to give it strength. Right? Right?"

"Err," they respond.

"Enough talk. Let's begin." Aslan nods at the squad leader.

Ichami spurs away from the group and places another six cones on the course, scattering them widely across their section of the arena, the mouths of the cones oriented in various directions.

"For this exercise, I will assign each rider to pick up the cones with his lance, using only the tilting style I choose—Sagr, Damascus, or Khorasan. You'll perform a transfer of the lance on every cone. Singer, let's start with the Khorasan style. Speed and accuracy. In two days we test, eh? No failures here."

With the reins in his left hand and pinned to his horse's shoulder blade, Singer presses his calves to flank, guiding his horse to the first cone on his right. As the horse closes, Singer extends his right arm, keeping the head of the lance close to the left cheek of the horse. He leans on his left stirrup, without moving his buttocks off the saddle, ensuring that his right shoulder, the left ear of the horse and the head of the lance are all in one line. He dips the steel point and scoops up the cone, using his left wrist to help bear the lance's weight.

Duyal watches with pride. The rigid steps of the tilting methods, which were bungled by all early in training, are no longer individual movements needing thought, but rather are now a series of motions joined together seamlessly, almost intuitively. His friend moves like water over rocks, with a fluidity that comes only to those granted a gift from God himself. Regardless of the weapon, Singer seems able to watch the instructor and immediately absorb the smallest shreds of detail, adding them all to his own personal repertoire.

He raises the lance and heads for the barrel. He dumps the cone, circles and orients on another. He switches the lance butt to his left hand, hoisting the bamboo over his horse's head, executing the transfer perfectly.

Duyal follows Aslan's eyes. From the viewing stands, al-Salih raises his eyebrows and nods the approval of a pleased father. Now wearing the same uniform as his amirs, he makes an effort to visit their tulb at least twice per moon, always addressing the novices in formation.

The prince's words are invariably positive, usually tailored to where the unit stands in the training process. It is said that he knows the name and history of not just his nine hundred thirteen Mamluks, but also the four hundred twenty-four novices sequestered in the training ranks. Yet Duyal has not once heard the prince speak the individual name of any in the tulb. He wonders if to the prince, they are all just Tulb Number Nine.

But there is no doubt that al-Salih is the patriarch for all who reside in the citadel. When not in the sister city of

Amid or in meetings, he bounces between training arenas and even roams the ramparts at night to speak with those Mamluks on watch. All within the walls crave his notice; all strive to be recognized, probably no different than the concubines in his harem.

The eunuch Safir arrives and sits next to his prince. Safir talks with his hands for a short time. The prince locks his lips and runs his hands through his hair in despair, dropping his head. He then turns to glare at Duyal.

Duyal looks back to Singer, his heart beating fast. Do not stare at the prince, fool. Concentrate on the training. He slowly turns his mount, so that his back is to the seating.

Singer snags the remaining cone, dumping it in the barrel before rejoining his fellows.

"Very well, Singer. Demir, you're next. Sagr style."

Demir begins his exercise.

A pat on Duyal's boot. Duyal looks down. Al-Salih. Startled, Duyal dismounts and faces his patron at attention, reins wrapped about his hand, his thumbs tucked in trouser seams.

"Forgive me, Father, this novice did not see you approach," Duyal says.

"Please come with me," al-Salih says, catching the attention of Aslan with a quick nod, before strolling away with head down.

Duyal tosses his reins to Singer, who snags the leather with wide eyes. He runs to catch the prince at the edge of the arena. The prince turns to face him.

"Duyal, your brother, Gozde, was sent to conduct a reconnaissance in the lands to the north. He is missing and … presumed dead. There was a skirmish that killed several Mamluks. We think only two men in his patrol made it out to safety. I can say little more, except that I am very sorry, my son."

Duyal feels a lump form in his throat. He wills away the tears that flood to his eyes, clenching his teeth. His patron must not see him cry. He recalls his brother, Baris, forced to ride off with the Mongols and then his father's white face, the Mongol arrows stuck in his body. He now sees Gozde's face on that body. Not again. A hollowness fills him, as it sinks in that he is likely the last of kin left.

"We will know more in the coming days, when the two survivors return to the citadel," al-Salih says, grasping Duyal's shoulder.

CHAPTER
33

Ox
The citadel barracks, Hisn Kayfa
September 12, 1237

Ox plods eastward through passages unfamiliar, his socked feet pounding the hard stone, while those of the novice behind him remain silent. Up the snaking stairs and through corridors forbidden sneak the lads in white. Stopping to catch his breath, he looks both ways down the corridor, before shooting across to the vacant parapet. His head peeks over the blocked edge.

The river shines blue. Distant foot-travelers go about their business, pushing carts, carrying loads. His eyes travel up the rolling path that leads to the fortress gate, past the rogue hanging on the cross. Farther and farther up the road, where he might catch a glimpse of his friend.

A wrenching in his gut pulls his eyes back to the cross. It is him there. Oh, dear Allah.

The naked man tacked upon the oak is nearly un-recognizable to him, yet he slowly makes out the form of his friend. Ichami's biceps bear his weight, the novice's long arms wrapped over the top of the rough timber, bound by hemp straps. His head is cocked back against the wood; his mouth hangs open, hinged on twisted jaw. His eyes are swollen shut. A deep cut on his head oozes blood, which runs down his neck and chest; his blond hair lies matted, flat and maroon.

Ichami. The boy his parents named "Inspiration," one of few in this world able to live up to the title he bore. Was there any among them who so effortlessly excelled in every facet of soldiering? He had been a swallow, gliding through air busy with obstacles and foes, supping on the easy insects of life that floated about him.

How could they do this? Not Ichami. Ox crumples to his buttocks, his tunic bunching about his neck as he slithers down the coarse wall. He presses massive palms over his ears to muffle the groans from the damned below. Tears fill his eyes. He rises for another look, only to confirm once more that the mangled boy is his mate.

He slinks back down, his heart pounding in his ears. Do not be a fool. If seen by the guards, he will pay dearly, possibly with his own life. He remembers Ilker at the corridor intersection.

His accomplice's head moves alternately between the two approaches. Why did he ask Ilker to join him, his mate's vision in the distance being so limited? Ilker seems to sense that all is clear. He sprints to Ox's side.

"Is he there? Did you see him?" Ilker asks, panting, with his back against the rock wall.

Ox nods.

"Is he alive?"

"He won't be for long."

Ilker sneaks a look and then eases his way down. "The fuckers pinned him to the rood? Don't they know they've got the wrong bastard?"

"Quiet."

Ichami's moans escalate, becoming a howl of anguish that bounces against the walls.

The novices exchange a hopeless glance. They look anxiously down opposite directions of the hallway. Ox's chest heaves, his breathing gone shallow and fast. Facing away from Ilker, he wipes the moisture from his eyes.

He cannot believe it. The eunuchs had been brief with their explanation that morning at formation: "Ichami has proven himself unworthy to serve the prince and will be removed from training; his punishment will be in accordance with our laws, matching his offense to al-Salih and God."

Earlier, Demir had told him and Ilker that during his evening watch, he had heard a slapping of skin in a side corridor last night in the forbidden spaces of the regiment's east quarters. He told Ox in private that he might have recognized Ekrem's voice, yet Demir had not been sure who it was.

What they were sure of is what Ilker saw after his own watch later in the night—the blood stains on Ichami's trousers, the shame in his face as he was being led away by the guards, the despondency in his gait as he disappeared from the flickering light of the corridor toward Safir's chamber, mumbling, pleading his argument of being coerced into the deed, threatened with removal by an instructor.

This morning, Demir told only Ox what he had heard, hesitating to notify Safir or any other. Demir was not certain who the culprit was, had no authority to cross the east wall. Plus, alleging any Mamluk of a career-ruining offense was not something a novice contemplated—one whose influence was minuscule, one who was far more expendable than those already wearing scarlet and gold.

This was especially true when the only evidence on hand was incidental and scant, maybe nonexistent, and certainly easily deniable by any suspect. And, whether guilty or innocent in the eyes of the command, any blamed Mamluk had the law on his side. He would not be executed himself. More importantly, the wrongdoer would not forget the snitch. One day the accusing novice would have to face not only the accused, but each in this man's *Khushdash*. Nobody wanted to go through the hell of earning their place in the regiment, only to be a target once free of the west walls.

Ox does not blame Demir for his decision. He rises slowly and peeps again.

Ichami rears back his head and roars. He shakes and squirms to free himself, as would a rabbit caught in a snare. He kicks his legs in a vain attempt to free the spike, which runs through both feet. He screams, not a shriek of pain or desperation—but a yowl seeming to originate from the base of his soul, his vocal cords resonating the agony of one who not only acknowledges his own miserable end, yet also the injustice in it.

The convicted then goes quiet. Ichami slowly begins to rock, as if trying to calm himself. At first, the thick-timbered cross ignores the lurch of his neck and shoulders, yet as the novice adds vigor to his task, the mass of strapped wood begins to sway in cooperation, the creak of metal peg in wood in time with the expulsion from his lungs.

Ox becomes engrossed in the scene. The fear of white coats and blades finally sobers him, ducking him again behind the wall.

"What's he doing?" Ilker whispers.

Ox shakes his head, closes his eyes to somehow comprehend it and then peers again.

The sway of his cross has become wide now and its base in the loose sand has turned slack. The crucifix makes its final swing, tips, and eases downward, pushing up the sand like a windblown pine. The crosspiece hits first, before it and rider tip to rest with a thud. Ichami faces heavenward and cackles like one who has lost his mind. He flails every limb to work himself free.

Three guards push open the tall gate and walk with long battleaxes in hand to the downed cross. Ichami yells garbled insults at them, giggling all the while. One guard looks at the other two. He strikes twice with the butt of his axe handle across Ichami's head. Their friend goes silent.

The trio plunge their axe butts into the ground and lock weapon heads. They squat either side of the crosspiece and struggle to erect the monstrosity. Once muscling the timbers upright, they stomp the soil about it until firm. They roll a rock either side of the post to be sure.

From atop the minaret, the muezzin begins his eerie chant. The call to prayer reverberates off the gray walls, slicing through the cloudless sky. Is this what God wishes? Could God just let this happen? What of the book, the Prophet? The holy men said Allah was a just God. His law would allow this?

"Ekrem has done this. He's the one who violated Ichami," Ox says, his lips quivering.

Ilker's eyes widen. "How do you know?"

"Because I heard the prick did it to another novice from a different tulb. And we've all seen him eyeing up Ichami."

Ilker nods his head. "Maybe. But you don't know. We should've made Demir talk to the eunuch. This all might not have happened."

"It's him, Ekrem," Ox says, collecting himself. "We must keep this quiet. You'll keep this quiet," he says, pointing a stubby finger at his friend's chest.

Ilker meets Ox's stare. His eyes go narrow.

A guilt flows through Ox, yet is purged quickly by the futility he sees in the situation. He scowls. "We won't get Demir in the middle of this so that we not only lose one friend, but two."

Ilker looks up to the sky and shakes his head. "We can't come in late to noon prayer—let's get out of here."

With tears braiding their cheeks, they scamper westward, back across the narrow passages, down the winding stairs. They reach the barracks out of breath, dropping to their butts to pull on boots with a fuming haste.

"Was he there?" Duyal asks, his eyes alternating between Ox and Ilker as he stuffs Ichami's gear into a wide-mouthed bag.

Ox looks down and shakes his head, tears returning to his eyes. "He… uh…"

"On your feet!" a novice shouts.

All drop the gear in their hands, cease their chores, and snap to attention. Safir wades through the silence with a long face. Gone is the usual bounce in his step.

Ox feels no sympathy for him. One of the eunuch's primary duties was protecting the youth from the predation of the Mamluks, who lived in the citadel's east side. While Safir could not be expected to watch every novice during all hours of the night, he was paid well to ensure their safety and had the power to voice his objection to rules, to Islamic Law, unfairly applied.

Yet apparently for Safir, common sense and decency played no role in the application of justice. It would have taken only one word from the shiny-skinned man and Ichami would have been spared, yet the eunuch conceded, blindly followed the book. The bastard not only let their friend suffer the humiliating transgression, but followed this by ordering the worst possible punishment.

His blood boils. He will not forget. He glares at the man who literally has no balls; his cowardice has caused the death of their friend.

"As you were. We'll pray. Arrange your mats," Safir says.

Ox sulks, pulling his mat with the others behind the eunuch and orienting to the south wall, facing Mecca. Safir leads the recruits through four prayer cycles, the foreign words rattling empty in the barracks. Ox stays silent for it all. For him, the prayers remain merely a string of strange sounds. Empty, foreign words—most always uttered with no thought or emotion, forced into the novices' heads many moons ago by holy men encouraging rote memorization through the bite of their staffs and snap of their switches.

He still does not get it completely. All in the citadel are vehemently respectful to Islam and its traditions, yet few have a good word for the Arabs. And yet the Koran stays written in the language of the Arabs. Further, only a minority of the Mamluks actually speak the language—those pressed to learn Arabic doing so only because of the necessity of the regiment's business dealings.

Safir begins an individual prayer:

> *"Thanks be to God, who granted the Muslims supremacy over the infidels and despots, who raised their value and their standard over that of the rebels and those who are indecent, by blessing them with various kinds of horses and saddle-animals and who taught them the art of using arms. Thanks and gratitude be to God."*

Tears again form in Ox's eyes. He mumbles the words to himself, "...raised their value and their standard over those who are indecent." Right. And "gratitude be to God." Not today, not for allowing their brother to be slain.

Safir rises from his prostration and sits upon a gear locker. The novices stow their mats and gather around him. Ox sits cross-legged with his palms on knees. He wonders which will be more agonizing, listening to the eunuch or having to keep his legs awkwardly folded for yet another class. With his knees and hips already rebelling, he stares at the amir's dark face. His brothers fill orderly rows beside and behind him.

"Today is not a good day... a fellow novice of yours has been removed from training. Our prince has lost a prized son," Safir says, looking over them at the stone wall, likely trying to find strength from an engraved verse high behind them. He lowers his eyes, scanning the faces, probably trying to sense their disposition before proceeding. "But Ichami's dismissal brings life to today's discussion. *Muta'allim*, we'll continue covering our corps traits, as begun by Amir Aqtay last week."

Speaking his mentor's name brings a look of resolve back to the eunuch's face. Always, Safir can be found by the side of Aqtay, the eunuch's loyalty to the man only exceeded by his devotion to al-Salih.

"Demir, which was the first corps trait covered by our commander?" Safir asks.

"Amir Aqtay covered *yücelik*—magnanimity," Demir says.

"Good. And how do you define it?"

"Magnanimity is the quality of being noble in mind, high-souled, and dutiful to our God."

"And from last week's discussion, Erol, why is this corps trait so important?" Safir asks.

"Amir, because a *Salihiyya* Mamluk must be able to not only slay the enemies of Islam, but also embrace the Third Pillar of Islam in helping the needy," Erol says.

Ox shifts his legs to regain circulation. He thinks of his friend on the cross. He wonders if the ravens have begun to peck at his brother's eyes. Was executing an innocent brother and ignoring another's crime against God part of the "noble-mindedness" of the regiment?

"Very good. Now Ox, would you please identify the second corps trait?" Safir asks, leaning forward on his elbows in keen interest.

Ox feels a ping in his stomach. Had the eunuch read his mind, or perhaps his thoughts were transparent upon his face? He takes a breath and focuses on Safir's yellow turban, unwilling to meet the eunuch's eyes.

He relaxes, knows he can play this game. He envisions the long-necked birds in the lower Volga country, which hunted along the wetlands. He will regurgitate the answer from memory and feed it to the eunuch, just as the mother heron spews minced fish pieces into the narrow beaks of her babes. In come the words. Up comes the soggy gray mass of tails and bones and flesh—the exact scripts the eunuch wishes to hear.

"Amir, the corps trait of courage, *cesaret*, is the mental quality that recognizes fear of danger or criticism, but enables a man to proceed in the face of it with calmness and firmness," he says.

"And why must the prince's Mamluks possess courage?"

"Because al-Salih relies on his Mamluks to face the infidels and enemies of the sultan in *all* instances, especially when his other forces will not."

Safir looks thoughtfully, nods and raises his eyebrows. "Ah yes, and Ox's response leads well into our topic for today, our final corps trait… which is what, Duyal?"

"Amir, the third corps trait is *sadakât*—loyalty, the quality of faithfulness to Allah, Egypt and the corps," Duyal says.

The eunuch grabs his chin, tugging it in bobbing confirmation. "Yes. Yes."

Safir stands, takes one step and stops. "Eventually al-Salih will lead us back to Egypt. And once there, you'll one day travel just south of Cairo on the River Nile, through the Giza Plateau. And here you'll see a series of structures of such magnitude that my words could never properly describe them. Ancient monuments so high, they reach heaven's height." Safir raises his hands.

He walks a few steps to his side, where a blanket covers a pile. "Their shape, unlike any you know," he says. "The building blocks of limestone so tall, some would reach your necks. The most amazing of these creations are called pyramids. One of exceptional beauty is called the Pyramid of Khafra. When you see this one, I ask that you reach back to our talk today, for I believe this pyramid's color, shape, and construction embody Mamluk loyalty."

He pulls the horse blanket from five triangular pieces of rock laid on the stone floor, two large sections, polished whitish-gold on their outer edges, the smaller three buffed a dazzling green. Lost in thought, he walks around each tapered part. He crouches to feel their rounded edges, chipped from years of use by amirs, men making the same speech to hundreds of novices prior.

"This piece," Safir says, running his hands over the smooth surface of the largest stone. "It is the bottom section of the structure. For the *Salihiyya*, this piece represents loyalty to whom?"

The room remains silent. The eunuch smiles. "What's our foundation? Who provides a stable base, upon which our corps exists?"

Silence.

"Come now, as you did with Amir Aqtay last week, speak freely today, my sons. I have no cane in my hand."

The eunuch nods to someone behind Ox.

"Amir, our God, Allah, supplies our foundation," a novice says from the back.

Safir smiles. "Absolutely! Is not every action in arms on behalf of our God? For Islam? The call to Jihad? Upholding the holy laws? This piece forms the base of our loyalty structure, not because it symbolizes the lowest form of our devotion, but because without it, the remaining structure above cannot stand." He studies the faces of his novices.

Bending, he again rubs the bottom layer of rock. "Faithfulness, loyalty to our God," he says, pointing his open fingers to heaven. "Now, the second tier… it signifies loyalty to what or whom, Ilker?"

"Amir, to our patron, al-Salih," Ilker says.

"No, but close. How about our prince's homeland?"

"Egypt, my Amir."

"Yes. Egypt is the pivot point for all of Islam. Her location connects the African continent to the holy places—Mecca and Medina—and to the Caliph in Baghdad. Adjacent to Palestine and the seven Syrian provinces, she is Allah's jewel and the mother of our corps," Safir says.

He picks the second largest piece off the deck and sets the white limestone on the bottom pale triangle, adjusting it until the three sides align perfectly. "Now Duyal told us that Mamluk loyalty was faithfulness to Allah, Egypt, and our corps. Yet I have three pieces left. How can this be?" the eunuch asks with raised brow, looking down at the three green rock slices.

He ignores a hand raised in the front, the lad oblivious to the amir's rhetoric.

"I mentioned earlier that of all the pyramids at Giza, the Pyramid of Khafra embodies Mamluk loyalty. You see, Khafra was a pharaoh many hundreds of years ago. The pyramid built for him was unique in that the outer facing of its base was constructed of limestone," Safir says, pointing to the half-built model on the deck.

He stoops to touch the slabs. "Yet the top third was built of a brilliant green stone, buffed to a sheen… so these last three pieces together, the tip of the pyramid, represent loyalty to our corps."

He rises, faces them. "Now this form of loyalty is nothing new for you. Yes? On the steppe, was there any force more dominant than allegiance to your own towers, sisters, and brothers of blood?"

He paces with his hands behind his back. "But with Mongol hordes pushing the Kipchaks north and west into the scheming hands of foreigners, your flocks were scattered and slaughtered, your towers, your families broken up. That old life is gone, forever changed… but among this misfortune, you were plucked from the fire and placed into God's hands. While your people were slain, you were saved. And now, after thirteen moons within these walls, where is your tower? Who are they now?" Safir asks, searching the novices' eyes.

"Our tower is our corps, Amir," Singer says, after receiving a nod from Safir.

"By Allah! The *Salíhiyya*. The *Salíhí*. Our corps—its amirs, its ghulams, its sappers, its line of slobbering camels and oxen, bearing both sustenance and implements of victory—all of it, all of us. Can a campaign, God's work, be carried without each element of the force?"

They shake their heads in the negative.

"No. As a whole, we are the gleaming gem near the pyramid's top," he says, rubbing the biggest green piece in his hands.

He sets it atop the white edifice. "Are you not obligated to honor it… to be dependable in preserving it? As you have been taught, faithfulness to our corps—the prince's regiment—and the *Furusíyya,* is the base of the green rock."

His pace quickens, seemingly excited by the topic. "Yet what two pieces finish off the top of the pyramid, my sons—your commitment to which segments of our corps?"

Safir strolls, shows his white teeth. "Look around, at those who arrived to Hisn Kayfa with you. Broken boys, those frail of limb, some recently out of chains, all with sorrow in their hearts. When training is complete, who else could be your family? When you have met the regiment's standards, proven your mettle, will not all from this tulb be bound to your *Khushdash,* obligated to defend your brothers with both words and weapons until your dying day?"

Safir places another emerald chunk onto the stack. He stares at it, his smile widening, seeming to admire the beauty of it.

Ox looks to Ilker beside him with a raised lip, and then back to the eunuch.

"Duyal, you look as if you have a question," Safir says.

Duyal takes a deep breath. "Yes, my Amir."

Duyal looks up from the stone floor and square at the eunuch. "Respectfully, my Amir, but has not this whole tulb already failed in faithfulness to our *Khushdash,* as Ichami, a brother of our unit, is being pushed from the citadel for being only the sufferer of a misdeed, while the unknown man who inflicted the wrong goes unpunished?"

Safir remains calm, nodding his head, as if anticipating the question. "You're obligated to honor those of your brothers who have earned the title, *Salíhiyya* Mamluk. Those who've met your prince's requirements. Only these are worthy of your protection and fidelity. Has any here completed their training, graduated, been manumitted by our patron? Does any here wear the lioned emblem of al-Salih?"

Safir's placid eyes then go hard. "Ichami not only hadn't finished his training, he proved himself unclean, he broke the Sharia. The penalty for his offense was very clear. He was undeserving of the honor to wear our scarlet and gold." His gaze burrows deep into Duyal's.

The eunuch's words hang like a stink in the air.

Ox fumes. Horse shit. All knew that Ichami would graduate. All knew Ichami was one of their best with the weapons of the *faris.* And here, as they sit and talk of loyalty, Ichami hangs on the cross like some criminal.

Ekrem. Ekrem had forced himself upon Ichami and Safir had allowed it. Ekrem had humiliated and bloodied their friend, just as he had done moons ago with another novice in Tulb Ten, and in response, Safir executed Ichami instead of the rapist.

"Bloodied... blood," Ox mutters under his breath.

For a long moment Duyal takes the eunuch's reply with a stern face, refusing to avert his eyes. Ox nods. Duyal's balls hang low like those of the alpha bull.

Safir diverts. "There'll be no more talk of it. This ties into our last piece, the apex of the pyramid." Safir walks to where the tip of the pyramid sits.

As the man turns, Ox sneers.

Safir pivots back toward them. "When the *Muta'allim,* the Mamluks under training, accomplish all the requirements set before them, they then have proven themselves worthy. Worthy to whom? Who's deserving of your most unwavering loyalty?" He crouches to pick up the small green point of the model on his outstretched palm.

Ox knows that all could speak the answer, yet none wish to utter his name.

"Who's the man responsible for removing the chains that once bound your legs? Who selected you, half-starved and covered in wool and tattered skins, to train in his beautiful citadel, where we hone your battle skills upon horseback, mastering technique with lance, sword, and bow? Who snatched you from deadly winters, from a life of steering sheep and eating mice, placing you instead in quarters fitting the rich, with future opportunity to fill offices once held only by royalty?" Safir's sneer slowly spreads to a forced grin.

"My Amir, he's our prince, al-Salih," a voice rings sober from those seated.

At his name, the recruits lower their eyes away from Safir, so as not to convey any gesture that might be interpreted as belligerent.

Ox fixes his eyes upon the *saulaq* purse that hangs from the eunuch's sword belt, identifying that his grade warrants leading forty horsemen in battle. The prince. Yes, the prince. He must not lose sight of his goal, his focus. Only by gaining al-Salih's trust and confidence has Safir risen. Such will not be the case with each of those seated here. To gain the prestige and wealth he feels is his destiny, he must make sure that he is also among the trusted.

"By Allah. And this you mustn't forget my sons," Safir says, glaring at Duyal. "These are difficult times for the Ayyubids. For four centuries, caliphs, sultans, and princes have employed Mamluks to bear their states' harshest burdens. When the words of diplomacy fall on deaf ears, our prince will turn toward this regiment to execute his will. We must be willing and able to answer."

A tranquil disposition again settles upon the amir's face and body. He walks circles about the pyramid. "If you can pass what remains of your training and thus satisfy our patron's physical, mental, and *spiritual* requirements, you will have fulfilled your fate in becoming one of the chosen. Chosen by Allah, chosen by our corps, chosen by al-Salih to exercise God's will—to serve under the red-lioned pennant. At these times of worry for our prince, only then will you have the privilege to repay him for his kindness to you… to demonstrate your loyalty."

CHAPTER
34

Duyal
South of Hisn Kayfa
September 29, 1237

Duyal watches them from the darkness, listens from the periphery as the two speak, the faint light of the torch highlighting the wrinkled skin of an old man and the tight skin of a teenager.

Amir Ekrem smiles at Erol. "No, I think the weather will cooperate today. The wind will stay down for us."

"My Amir, where would've been the windiest place you were forced to engage an enemy?" Erol asks the archery master with the fascinated gaze of a child.

Again the old man smiles, nudges his horse closer to Erol's. "I ... would have to think a bit on that one."

Most of the novices have lost interest in the idle conversation long ago, Ekrem directing his answers only to the slightly built novice. The Ox slowly backs his horse, turns his head from the chat. The giant eyes Demir, who has already done the same, a grimace fixed on the youth's face.

A guard approaches the instructor and salutes. "Amir Ekrem, I believe we now have enough light."

Ekrem looks to the sky and then down toward the horizon. "Yes, yes. I think there's enough to keep us both out of trouble." He grins, looking over his shoulder to the novices, who already begin to fall in behind him. "Six," he says, reaching into his pocket to hand a piece of parchment to the lead guard.

The square-faced man eyes the string of novices, the youth now sitting straight in their saddles, white uniforms glimmering in the dark. He leans near his torch and jabs a stubby finger at their names; he verifies the wax seal pressed at the bottom of the page. He leaves to scribble in his logbook and returns to hand the parchment back to Ekrem. The other guards lift the massive latch and muscle open each steel-banded door.

"Good day, Amir."

Ekrem returns their salute. "Good day."

Duyal squeezes his calves. The stallion ignores him. More pressure and some heel and soon he is following his instructor and the others out the south gate. He takes in the wide sky, the stars now dulling to the east.

They clomp down the winding road at a trot, its rutted surface flushed with the iridescent blue of dawn. Blanket-wrapped stragglers walking the path move to the side in deference upon hearing the pound of hooves.

The riders meander along the alleyway, just short of the shuttered shop district. Their hoof thumps bounce between mud walls and sheer stone faces, where inhabitants living in holes emerge by the dozen with sleepy eyes. Ill-hung doors are cracked and quickly closed upon view of the red cloak at the formation's front. The riders push through the aroma of smoldering fires, steeping black tea, and baking *pide,* the locals' crusted white bread.

They head toward the prince's supplemental training grounds, opposite the city center, just past the lesser-populated southern reaches of Hisn Kayfa. Though their prince designed his sprawling fortress to be self-supporting, its walls built high to keep his novices from viewing the ways of the populace, on rare occasions he did let them out—primarily to execute their variety of chores, or to train, in the odd circumstances when the hippodrome hummed beyond full capacity. Duyal often wondered if such trips were just another test, or a way to gradually acclimate the novices to life outside the gate. But whether by design or necessity, Duyal has been outside the gate but three times in the last fourteen moons.

Ekrem leans back in his saddle, slows his horse to a walk, driving pedestrians to the edge of the thin path like a shepherd parting his flock. Duyal holds his breath, in a ridiculous effort to avoid sucking in the same air as the townspeople.

Three more from his tulb awoke this week soaked in sweat and shivering. The eunuchs burned these novices' uniforms and sleeping mats, segregating the unfortunate youths to the cramped misery of the medical wing. There, good novices will die. Since the day they arrived in Hisn Kayfa, the illness has picked away at their tulb, like the mountain lion revisiting his cache, the fever returning again each day, each week to tear at the tulb's flesh. He hopes the disease will not strip his unit clean, or any others. The eunuchs say the source of the novices' illness lies outside the citadel walls, just another reason to steer clear of the locals.

Back to the trot, they pass merchants organizing their wares, raising canvas refuges and spreading leather goods, vegetables, and silken scarves upon their tables. A fisherman gimps toward a covered stand. Strapped across his shoulders is a wicker basket half filled with fish, a dark line of dripping water tracing his path from the river. His trousers are cut away on one leg to accommodate an infected foot and calf, swollen into one grotesque form. Two blocks farther, men pull color-ful rugs from a cart, several sneaking a glance at the horsemen from under the cover of their sagging rolls.

Clear of the population, they resume the pleasant three-beat gait of the canter, making for several rolling fields, which butt up to foothills covered in both rock and grass. They break into the valley, pointing the heads of their beasts at the sliver of sun, soon to creep over the purple ridgeline. Ekrem flashes his palms, allowing his students to break for-mation and come on line, yet the novices stay a full horse length behind him.

Duyal's horse uses the opportunity to bite at the Arabian beside him. He pulls him away. "Enough!" He circles the horse twice and then once settled, gives him the heels to catch up with the others.

A year ago, such action would have been closely su-pervised by a detachment of guards to their rear. Yet this precaution was deemed unnecessary by the eunuchs last moon, when a novice from another tulb was shot full of ar-rows while making a break for freedom, the boy shot dead not by the accompanying guards, but instead ridden down and slain by his own brothers in training.

Ekrem slows them back to a trot as they come within view of the training paddock. Tall targets form a curious out-line on the treeless vista. The edifices loom large, like wooden shrines erected by a lost people in honor of gods long forgot-ten. With as much superstition as if this were so, the populace in Hisn Kayfa avoid this area. Fearful of those who visit this place of warrior pilgrimage, the locals steer clear. Even the worn road heading north toward the city makes a wide arc around the field, not by governor mandate, but by the travel-ers' chosen path.

Reaching the training ground, they rein in among the tight rows of sand-filled baskets, ground targets the Mamluks call *al quiqaj*. Despite their value to the masses in Hisn Kayfa—each basket could carry ten eggplants, or twice as many fish—and the ease with which they could be stolen, the baskets remain untouched, as forbidden as religious relics.

The same holds true for the *qabaq*, literally meaning "gourd" and used by the Mamluks as an elevated target. The heavy wooden planks of the *qabaq*, reaching the height of four men, are dug into place and adorned with a metal-framed circle at its top, a border for the felt target behind. The oak timbers, precious because of the shortage of planks in such lengths, would make perfect support beams in any shelter. But the locals shudder at the thought of the musclebound men in scarlet and gold finding this lumber in their homes. And perhaps there is some self-regulation in place, those town folk with some foresight realizing such training devices help produce the Mamluks, who ultimately protect them and the city.

Ekrem sits with palms braced against his pommel, scanning the ridgeline above and then the training area. Duyal looks down at the hawk wing insignia on his tunic, the emblem reminding him that it is he for whom Ekrem waits.

Every two weeks since early August, Cenk has rotated four different "Novice Amirs of Ten" and a single "Novice Amir of Fifty" to assist him in coordinating logistics and moving the tulb between training evolutions. While Cenk needs no assistance, the posts force the recruits to lead, rather than always being led. Duyal and the others see no honor in the appointments, as they could only wear targets on their chests to better attract Cenk's rage.

Nevertheless, the citadel staff keeps a careful eye on those novices in the leadership slots, seeking *muta'allim* with the ability to command and taking note of those who stumble when placed in charge. To avoid any confusion with the resident Mamluks, who hold the rank in earnest, the recruits' insignia is backed with scarlet felt, designating the recruits' rank as but training positions. Yet such a safeguard is more symbolic than vital, as none could confuse the novices' whiskerless faces and stained garments with those of the prince's actual amirs.

Ekrem turns to him impatiently.

As the acting "Novice Amir of Ten," Duyal recalls Amir Ekrem's plan for the day and the arrangement of targets for the test. "Two men per basket target, first three targets on the right, last two on left up to the gourd... seven paces between all," he says. His order is mere formality, as all know exactly what must be done. Yet the five in his squad snap to work, as if the directive were critical and coming from the mouth of an amir.

Duyal nods. He feels fortunate, for not all in the tulb receive instantaneous cooperation from their brothers. And perceptive instructors, such as Ekrem, know that the degree of promptness and thoroughness with which a novice's peers execute a billet leader's task is typically in direct correlation to how well the leader executed similar duties when not in charge himself.

In case the instructors miss such subtle nuances, Safir requires each novice to rate his squad members via monthly "Peer Evaluations," nicknamed "spears" by the recruits. Duyal feels these are brilliant, as some in the tulb are keen to be good novices, but only when under the command's eye. The criteria for the "spears?" The very leadership traits which have been beaten into their heads since day one: dependability, bearing, courage, decisiveness, endurance, enthusiasm, initiative, integrity, judgment, magnanimity, knowledge, tact, unselfishness, and loyalty.

Ox walks with his arms encircling a basket, his chunky legs pounding the ground. Duyal moves his mount closer to the work, pretending to closely inspect pairs of his friends dragging baskets and pacing out the course. It is nonsense, as they need no supervision, but he must play the part, illustrating to the instructor his ability to give orders and supervise the task without being drawn into the work himself.

Duyal's mind moves to today's work and how they came to this juncture. Early in bow training, he thought the starting point was basic to the point of being mad, its pace like that of a crawling turtle. On the steppe, he and his mates saw bowshot as an instinct employed to kill prey, a form made lethal from repetition no doubt, yet more so a knack inherited from ancestors. Nearly all Kipchaks could shoot, but the skill was a gift from The Great Sky, nothing more. Putting arrow on target was but a single action, a process that flowed naturally, like the rise of the moon. As an antelope need not learn its speed to avoid predators, nor a bear be taught to apply teeth and claw to defend territory, so the Kipchak largely felt his marksmanship innate to his being.

Here, he would eventually see the error in his philosophy. While initially annoyed at his instructors' approach to the weapon, in due course he embraced their methods. For the Mamluks expected a level of competence that made the average Kipchak warrior's skills look second-rate. To get there would involve a change in thinking.

Contrary to Kipchak ways, poised instructors broke down archery into its minute subactions, peeling back each novice's marksmanship as a cook would shed layers from an onion. If the Mamluks discovered a rotten segment in a shooter's form, this layer was removed, then grown anew, so as not to decay the whole. If too large a portion were spoiled, the archery master would discard the entire root ball and begin growing the shooter's form from seed. Those novices whose root would not take in the citadel's soil were destined to shrivel and die.

He eyes his mates. Gone are the abrasions and open sores from substandard marksmanship. At the bend of their right thumbs, where the thumb rings rest, blisters have formed into calluses. In the webbing of left thumbs, bow grips set in shooters' "falcon's talons," like rock cradles. Scabbed ears have healed, or those permanently scarred have grown thick with skin and cartilage. On the inside of forearms there is no fresh blood, only faded brown stains on left tunic sleeves, now patches of proficiency worn by his brothers, born in sweat and pain.

Technique on the ground was followed by the more difficult skill of employing the new shooting style from horseback. Starting with weak bows and atop loping horses, they shot at only two consecutive basket targets, merely thirty paces apart. Yet over the last seven moons, their instructors added targets, decreased the distance between them, added tempo and even staggered the targets on both the right and left sides of the shooter. Similar to their ground training with the four-legged *al-buttíyya* targets, the recruits accomplished their requirements while working through a succession of three bows on horseback, until reaching the stiffest bow, the *qaws*.

The archery master stressed "rate of fire" and overwhelming the enemy with "arrows on enemy." Through a tactic the Mamluks called "shower shooting," a tulb of well-trained men could put thousands of arrows into enemy ranks in seconds, causing most foes to flee before a true engagement ever ensued. "While a *Salíhi* is not shy to splatter enemy blood on his uniform, his favorite battles are those where his quiver is empty, his lance head unsoiled and his sword still stowed," an archery instructor once said.

To meet this effect and hence to graduate from the citadel, Ekrem required a novice to deliver three arrows in one and a half seconds. This could only be accomplished by using a technique the Mamluks nicknamed "finger dancing." This method required Mamluks to shoot consecutive arrows from shafts staged in both their bow and draw hands, rather than pulling a single arrow from the quiver each shot, as did many warriors from the steppe.

The focus was, of course, not only on shooting speed, but also accuracy. Despite the time investment made on the novices who now remain, those who could not make shots, both fast and true, were removed from training. On horseback, the standards were even more demanding than those from the ground. The end requirement: the riders must complete a course of ten staggered basket targets at a gallop, spaced the same as those today, only seven paces apart.

Duyal jumps off and tosses his reins to Singer. He walks down the line of baskets, verifying the distance between them. It is test day. A twinge of nervousness pulses through his fingertips. No practice allowed. They must engage the course on test day, as they would engage an enemy—cold. He thinks of his brother, Gozde. He does not want to let him down, even if his childhood idol is with Allah now.

The single *qabaq* target anchors the end of the course, looming like a one-eyed beast. Duyal stares it down and then points to the sky, as has become habit—in honor of his fallen brother.

Ekrem rakes his red beard with hand, seemingly pleased to watch the novices work; content the course has been set up to standard. The wrinkled man smirks. The sage seems a man at peace, executing his passion in life, serving his God by creating the best archers in the land. And for the past eight years, he has done only this. Resembling a loving mother pulling her baby from its crib, he now pulls his bow from the leather case, his smile broadening as the full length of his weapon is exposed.

On this action, the novices mount their horses and surround him. Despite his growing reputation as a predator, a man rumored to bait unsuspecting novices into the citadel's dark places, Ekrem still holds the tulb's esteem due to his technical skills and combat experience only. Duyal feels that in spite of their distaste for the wrongs he has likely committed, the novices remain wise in listening to Ekrem's expert instruction, would be fools to not glean the lessons learned from the old man's battles.

Ekrem secures his case, its brown leather turned black from repeated exposure to blood, rain and oil. Its surface speaks to Ekrem's experience: a deep scrape from his action in Damietta; a diagonal slash from fighting too close in Edessa; a flap worn thin from an Anatolian campaign waged too long.

"Don't let the speed of the course remove you from your center," Ekrem says, cradling his bow in both hands. "Those who excel forget the pace and stay true to both their horsemanship and marksmanship fundamentals. Remember, this weapon isn't an extension of your arm, as some would say. It is your arm. As your arm is bone, flesh, blood, and arteries, so is your recurved bow—wood to bone, horn to flesh, glue to blood, and sinews to arteries. Only God knows better."

Unprovoked, Duyal's stallion kicks sideways at Ilker's horse. Duyal pulls left on his reins with both hands and turns the beast away. "My forgiveness, Amir." He circles his horse away from the others. He halts the animal and leans down to the horse's ear. "Don't start this shit."

The Bedouins named this stallion "Desert Splendor," as the animal is of top nick and unparalleled bloodline. His striking coat, gray with unusually large spots, forms the perfect natural camouflage in his homeland, the deserts of Arabia, giving further impetus to the animal's title. Yet hardheaded, competitive with the other stallions and widely known among the novices as one of the most uncooperative mounts in the training herd, this Arabian has earned a more apt nickname—"Exodus." More than once, Duyal heard the horse's name uttered between tears behind a eunuch's door, once even shouted from outside the gate, as guards escorted an unwilling novice out of the complex forever.

And while nasty, Exodus was certainly not the only odd-behaving horse in the line of training mounts. The instructors insisted the novices ride only stallions, and only those handpicked by the prince's grooms to be of the rowdiest temperaments. Further, never were the *Muta'allim* allowed to learn the mischievous nature of a single mount, as the command constantly rotated the rebel horses through the training tulbs. Geldings were of course forbidden, the instructors having no use for an animal whose demeanor resembled anything approaching calm and manageable.

Like throwing water on an oil fire, whenever possible, the instructors rode mares in heat. During practice runs on both the lance and bow courses, instructors were often seen circling the recruits' stallions, attempting to unsettle the mounts and drive reproductive conflict between them. When the stallions began to pound hooves, shake froth about their heads and bite the flanks of their stable mates, the staff would then begin the exercises.

While they worked closely with stable hands in selecting these batches of rogue horses, the instructors allowed novices the "privilege" of assigning stallion to rider. This veiled act of benevolence was clearly the opposite, just another trial. On a typical test day, once entering the hippodrome with their string of mounts, the instructors gave the recruits only one passing of sand through the smaller hourglass to make their decisions.

Most often, the adolescents designated the best riders to the most difficult horses, in an attempt to improve the odds for all to pass. Instructors routinely eavesdropped upon the recruits' delegation—taking note of each pupil's judgment, observing which novice would let his ego enter the discussion and simply monitoring how well the group made decisions.

But on test days, the staff was especially watchful for evidence of unselfishness, or a lack thereof. For there was little better indicator of this corps trait than a novice willing to put himself at risk for his brothers, placing at stake not just his personal safety, but also his place in the prince's regiment.

On this day alone, many moons of training and a career of wealth and status could be erased by a single training failure, or serious injury. And once the test began, the instructors gave no latitude for those who rode the more demanding mounts. On test day, all that mattered was whether each novice met the requisites set in the *Furusiyya*.

In this morning's dark, when Ekrem and his ghulams arrived with the mounts, the novices' eyes shifted to only one horse. Exodus. Duyal broke the silence among them. "I'll take that prick," he said. The others could not mask their relief, assigning the remaining horses with half the sand still in the top bulb of the hourglass.

Duyal pretends not to fret. He pats Exodus on the thick shoulder, hoping the stallion will sense no fear, yet more than likely, the brute already perceives Duyal's trepidation. If only the horse will behave long enough to complete the test. He worries about the consequence if he fails. He imagines his gear being cleared from the barracks; being forced to live in town, away from his comrades. He pushes these thoughts away. He will prevail. He must.

Ekrem looks to Duyal, raising his orange eyebrows. Duyal turns his mount to face his fellow recruits. "I'll go first—break this course in."

Singer nods him good luck. Ox clenches his fist and pumps it slowly, the usual smirk gone from his face.

Duyal turns his reluctant horse away from the others. He digs his heels and puts the animal to the gallop, stopping at the far side of the course. He returns with the horse agitated at the bit in his mouth. He recalls an archery instructor's words. "Sit deep in the saddle… you and horse together become just another wave on the sea… flow… shoot when you and horse reach the stable crest of the wave."

Exodus snorts through enlarged nostrils in anticipation of the event, shaking his head against the reins in defiance. Duyal pulls the strung bow from its case and lays it across his thighs. He turns from the others and closes his eyes. Just execute the routine.

Timing. He digs in his breast pocket and slips on his thumb ring. He twists it into place. He uses his tunic to dry the sweat between his fingers on his left hand. He pushes his right palm across his chest twice and in returning his arm back to his side, wipes the moisture from his last three fingers on his sleeve. Focus. Focus.

He reaches into his quiver, pulling out a fistful of thin-shafted arrows. He counts nine, placing two with damaged fletching back into the quiver. He nocks an arrow into his bow and takes a deep breath. Fletching end down, he places three arrows firmly into the U-shape of his bow hand. He slides each, until the fletching touches the bottom of his hand. He twists the nocks, until all are parallel with his fingers.

Leaving an appropriate slack in the reins, he clamps down on them between his middle and ring fingers. He raises his bow to check their length, slipping a little leather through fingers, ensuring he can still control his mount. Again wiping the moisture from his hand, he places another three arrows across his right palm, aligning the fletching with the flesh of his thumb. He closes the last three fingers of his draw hand and rotates the nocks, until all are in the identical position.

He squeezes the sides of his horse, moving the Arabian forward, stopping him short of the course. He relaxes his breathing and slips the string onto the notch of his thumb ring. He leans to the horse's ear. "Just work with me."

He gives Exodus his heels and pushes his hands forward, putting him into a full gallop. Standing in the stirrups, he leans forward, squeezing his right knee inward to move the horse a touch left. Closing on the first target and feeling the rhythm of hoof beats, he twists to the right, draws, waits a half second, releases and sticks his blunt headed arrow in the first sand basket.

Without thought, Duyal executes the "finger dance." The product of endless practice, he slides the top shaft up with the middle finger of his draw hand and pushes down with his index finger, until the shaft rests on top of his thumb ring, the notch sitting lazily in the bowstring. The meat of his thumb on the bow hand raises the arrow and nocks it home. He draws. Again feeling the point when all four hooves are off the ground—the crest of the wave—he releases.

Whisk, thud. Another arrow slams home.

Remaining at the gallop and repeating the sequence in less than two seconds, Duyal scores on the third basket. Twisting left, he snags the first arrow from his left hand and shoots the first basket on his left. He is in his groove.

"Execute, execute," he tells himself.

Once more with his horse's hooves suspended in the air, he snaps off his fifth shot at the last ground target. His arrow hits home, yet the horse jerks his head aggressively in response. He worries the arrow passed too close to the fussy stallion's ear.

"Just one more, you prick, just one more," he says.

Putting the elevated target on his right, Duyal tries to steer the horse farther that direction, yet Exodus ignores the leg command. The horse seems to swell beneath him. Duyal knows what is coming. Remaining calm, Duyal pulls right on the reins, just as the animal starts bucking. He hurries his release.

The arrow pings off the metal ring. Turning backward to fire his last arrow as the horse bucks, Duyal misses the target. His horse is off the course; his shot would not have counted, even if accurate.

He pulls the reins hard left, until the horse's nose touches the top of his boot. Exodus stops bucking and moves into a tight circle. With the reins taunt, Duyal waits, feeling the animal settle beneath him. He then pulls the reins in the same manner to the right side and waits. Cinching down on the reins to keep the horse's head up, he leans into the stallion's ear, chatting calmly and patting his neck.

He returns to the group dumbfounded. He has failed the test. Tears already stream down the face of Ilker. Singer buries his face in the mane of his stallion. Ox makes fists with his reins.

"My Amir, may this novice speak?" Singer asks.

"Go ahead."

"We've been trained to take responsibility and not place blame on others. Yet at some point, that horse needs to be eaten. Too many good novices have failed on his back, not from lack of skill, but because of the steed's make-up."

Ekrem remains expressionless, yet disappointment carries on his voice. "I don't disagree with you, yet plenty of novices have passed events on him. There're rules that must be followed. Next rider," he says.

"But Amir Ekrem, please, please," Ox says.

"Next rider," he says firmly.

Duyal leans over and pukes. He remains hunched over the saddle, chin buried into the pommel. He is gone.

CHAPTER
35

Duyal
Amir's corridor, citadel, Hisn Kayfa
October 18, 1237

Duyal shoves the wood-slatted bucket with his heel, easing it backward, so as not to spill any water on the smooth floors of the corridor. He dips his swab, sloshes it around and stoops to wring the clouded water from the fibers. The smell of mold and stone. Resuming the tedium of dragging mop over deck, he mulls his situation.

Two weeks ago, Safir pulled Exodus from the training string, declaring the stallion "an agent of Satan." The eunuch's action had little to do with the number of novices who had failed upon the horse's back, as within hours of Duyal's failure on the basket targets, the stallion threw an instructor in the hippodrome, breaking the Mamluk's shoulder. Duyal realized this circumstance was a stroke of luck. Or more likely—the will of Allah. Regardless, in two days Duyal will retest, Safir permitting any novice who failed on the back of the horse and who still remains in the citadel to be retested on "mounts more obliging to our God."

Cenk did not share the eunuch's view.

Through swollen eyes, Duyal took a last glance at his gear, neatly piled on the storeroom counter.

"Well, that looks like all of it," the clerk said, a hint of sorrow in his voice.

Cenk barged in, shoved a bag in his face. "Put it back in the bag. Apparently the eunuchs pity you. Must be nice for an incompetent to survive on Amir Gozde's reputation alone."

Cenk turned before leaving the cramped space. "But, I worry little. You cracked under pressure once, your bungling fingers will mishandle again in the retest. In the end, it's the novice who must shoot true and fast, not the horse. Not your dead brother!"

For a petty offense a few days later, Cenk placed him on solitary evening chores after training. Kitchen duty—just an excuse to separate him from the encouragement of his brothers; a means to isolate his prey. And so it has been for nineteen days. At first, Duyal felt exposed, like a wounded deer on the steppe. If he fails the retest, he will be ejected from the citadel without further consideration. This is as it should be.

Yet as each day passes, he feels more convinced Cenk's strategy will fail. The *Mu'allim* misjudges how his quarry uses this time, how his victim turns negative to constructive. For even a doe with fawn, deficient in fang and brawn and split from her herd, can muster the will to pound her hooves upon the head of a predator when her blood's treasure is threatened. And Duyal feels much the mother doe. Under his arm, he guards his infant career as a *Salihiyya* Mamluk and a life with the brothers he has joined.

These days of seclusion have become his ally. And this new companion only furthers his resolve, enhances his concentration. Whether cleaning floors or cutting eggplant, Duyal separates his mind from mundane task, using the time to rehearse every movement necessary on the course, memorizing each adaptation he will make for every contingency brought on by the next erratic horse.

One night in the empty kitchen, he whittled off the sharp edges of wooden switches, used by cooks to light fires, turning them into hasty arrow shafts. Having hidden them behind the pots, he pushes through chores each night, looking forward to the precious moments when he can practice his drill, simulating the "finger dance" of arrows in his hands.

Rearing back on imaginary bow and twisting to shoot black pots and cutting boards from the corner of the butcher's bench, the pings of wood drop on stone at his feet conjuring the strike of arrowheads in his mind. He has not missed a night of the practice since his isolation. In his mind, he has not missed a target. When it counts, he will not falter.

"So you're saying you want to cut eight moons from their training," a deep voice sounds through a closed door near him.

Duyal leans on the mop handle.

"Our prince needs Mamluks in the field now, not in fourteen moons. If al-Asharaf hadn't died, the enemy's forces would be resting in our cots this very evening. Al-Salih doesn't wish to tempt fate again."

He recognizes the voice of Safir.

"The senior tulb has only progressed through weapons training—they've barely started tactical formations," the deep voice pleas.

One of his riding instructors?

"They'll have to pick up these skills from their units in the field," Safir says. A collective grumble in the room.

"There was a reason we spent four years at *Qal'at al-Jabal*. Four years," a man says.

"Of course. You think I want this? It's of necessity," Safir says.

Stools groan under the shifting weight of edgy amirs. He hears the bleat of a single stool being pushed away from the table and the heels of a large man pacing near the door.

Duyal puts his head down and flips the mop back into action. When the sound of heels makes its way deeper into the chamber, Duyal moves back near the door, propping the mop handle back under his armpit.

"What's the alternative? The prince still believes he's done well in pulling the Khwarazmians into his flock. These heathen auxiliaries exceed five thousand. Do we wish to be even more underrepresented?"

"Khwarazmians? So the chatter was true," Duyal mumbles to himself.

For the most part, the prince had successfully insulated his novices from the complicated world outside the citadel. But for moons, the recruits had picked up enough stray conversation to know that the world below their old Volga country only became messier the farther one traveled south and west. A third civil war between the sultan and his relation was brewing.

From two Turks whispering, while working ladles in the chow line: "The other Ayyubid princes of Syria conspire against the Sultan of Egypt... the sultan's own brother, al-Asharaf, leads the coalition." Last moon, from the grooms feeding out Arabians: "I hear with al-Asharaf's death, the brother, Isma'il, succeeds in Damascus." From a vendor delivering fruit: "To join the enemy alliance, the Seljuks have been offered our own Hisn Kayfa. Allah help us!"

To keep up on the drama, much less follow the cast of changing characters, was a challenge. But whether accurate or not, the novices were onto these clips of gossip. When passing in the chow hall, the adolescents spread the rumors to other training tulbs. In late evenings, recruits on watch traded word on the competing princes' exploits. All wished to know where their brothers would fight and how their prince was responding to the crisis. If a line of chitchat was heard twice, it was considered truth and strung together with the other bits into an overall picture of the situation.

Duyal looks in both directions down the passageway, continuing to swab past the door. He twists the mop in his hands so the draining water falls quietly along the tapered side of the bucket.

"Underrepresented—this is the issue more grave, brothers, not the length of novice training," the voice of Amir Aqtay rings for the first time. "One recruit in fifteen has passed from the fever, and our prince's treasure runs thin. Bozkurt is two weeks late in bringing down more Kipchaks. We're not growing the regiment at the pace required by al-Salih."

A thick arm wraps around his throat. A knee is jammed into his thigh. The jolt of pain crumbles him. Falling back, Duyal hears a hiss and feels a wisp of warm breath across his face. A sour scent finds his nose. Cumin, onions, and a bite of fermented mare's milk.

"Oh dear Allah," Duyal says to himself.

The chokehold is tightened around his neck. Duyal pulls against the forearm, struggling to breathe. He considers fighting off his attacker, but knows better. He must simply take the abuse and wait out his fate.

He releases his grip on the mounded bicep and straightens his arms in submission. He backpedals to lessen the pressure on his neck. Yet with this docile gesture, his assailant only drops his shoulder to deepen his winged clutch. Duyal resorts to grasping the tight material about the beefy forearm and hanging on, while being dragged by his heels to an adjacent corridor. He is flung to his back, a boot pressed to his throat.

"Promoted to senior amir, I see. Compelled to join the meeting?" Cenk whispers, snapping his eyes toward the hallway corner before they settle back to his victim.

Duyal works his watering eyes up the towering figure. A wide chest of scarlet. A thick tunnel of hair inside flaring nostrils. Dark eyes open wide.

"Amir Aqtay would not take kindly to a spy in his training ranks. Around here, they lop the heads from moles caught in the act," Cenk says with a sneer.

Duyal again places his hands out submissively. He nods in agreement. In short gasps, he labors to pull air through a windpipe half closed. He wishes Cenk would just end it. Just kill him now. His *Furusiyya* instructor must see in him the pathetic death stare of an antelope. The indifferent, blurry-eyed gape of a creature sapped of strength, drained of blood and awaiting the deathblow.

The uniformed figure looming over him becomes fuzzier. He blinks some clarity into his vision.

Cenk grinds his teeth, his thick jaw muscles rolling under skin drawn tight. But then the monster's face seems to melt. His jawline muscles relax. His chin drops down, parting lips that expose white teeth. His eyes rise from his captive and stare thoughtfully down the dark passage, as if Mohammad himself approaches.

With this Duyal gains hope. Perhaps his instructor just now realizes that Duyal will make a loyal Mamluk... that he has paid his dues and will perform to standard... that he meant no harm in listening...

Cenk's mouth closes into a smirk, which then creeps into a full smile. He releases some of the pressure from his boot.

Duyal gasps for air, his chest heaving. His eyes remain fixed on Cenk's dark face, trying to read the clues that will decide his fate. The smile. A fear swells in Duyal's stomach, as if all the evil in the world were being pulled in through the expanded opening in his windpipe—an unwanted brew of iniquity and dread pouring down his raw throat. He does not want to hear Cenk's words.

Cenk peers again down the hallway and then takes a knee, looking down at him with raised lip. He squints his black eyes, beady like those of a snake. "You'll provide a service to me, and in return will have your status here preserved."

Ignoring every fiber in his body, denying every scrap of intuition, Duyal nods his head. More darkness cascades into his gut, filling, filling. And as if the iniquity were now overflowing, spewing from his mouth, he coughs on the rancid tang.

"Shut up," Cenk says with pointed finger.

Duyal swallows, trying to hold down the devil lodged in the pit of his gut.

"The two weakest in the tulb—Umit and Bulut. They need... persuasion from within the ranks to improve their conduct. You understand?"

Duyal looks blankly at Cenk.

His instructor shakes his head, rolls his eyes. "They neglect their duty, betray our prince. Even the best instructors have failed to improve their skills. The pair needs a beating from their peers to correct their conduct. Tonight at candles out you'll gather your worms and get this job done. Understand?"

Duyal's head swirls. He recalls shivering in formation with his mates, with only their tunics to keep them warm—group punishment for Umit caught sleeping on watch. And "digging" for hours in the high sun, after Bulut failed his third uniform inspection. He reckons no other pair in the tulb has created more suffering for the whole of them. Both novices do only enough to meet the bare minimum. He despises them both. But he could not beat on two of his own, much less ask for help in doing so. Plus, what if they were caught by the eunuchs?

Cenk turns his head, then reapplies the pressure to his boot. "I won't wait all day for your answer. You're in no position to bargain. I won't have those two goat stickers dragging down my tulb's standing."

Cenk belches under his breath, puffing the putrid smell of wine milk. "Do this, or by morning you'll be tacked to a crucifix. You know well as I that the eunuchs would see yours as an integrity violation."

Duyal can only gape at the man.

"And their beating will not be just a pat or two on the head. You understand? I want these two bloodied, so as to... develop the proper motivation. Do this work half-assed and I will treat it as if you refused the mission."

A twitch agitates beneath Cenk's right eye. Duyal wonders if Cenk now realizes that he could also be the *faris* removed from training if caught forcing this deal. Another slave fixed to the cross.

"Do you understand?" Cenk repeats.

"Yes," Duyal groans.

He removes his foot from Duyal's throat with a kick from heel to neck and walks away.

He stops in a shadow. "Put away your cleaning gear. Go now."

CHAPTER
36

Singer
The citadel hippodrome, Hisn Kayfa
October 31, 1237

Whoosh. The last stub of arrow spins in the air, its fletching twirling the cut shaft to a soft landing on the raked dirt. Demir turns his mount, already nodding, smiling. Noticing the scroll pressed to Koray's face, Demir flips the flat of his blade to rest against his bent forearm. He raises his arm, making the sword appear an extension of his elbow. Pushing forward his mount while pulling him up, he causes his horse to prance through the conquered bits of wood.

He bobs his head with mouth open, his tongue reaching midway down his chin. Reaching his comrades, he clanks the steel twice against his leather helmet. Singer sits his horse with no reaction to the boasting, while some grin or shake their heads at his conceited jest. Yet most respond to his performance on the hippodrome's packed dirt with the customary compliment of guttural barks. "Errr!"

These cause Amir Koray, their sword master, to look up, crumpling the scroll into his pocket. "Good, Demir. Good," he says. He then opens his other hand to stare at the hexagonal grip and the dragon-tailed quillons in his palm; tilts his wrist, allowing the dull sky to illuminate the mottled bands snaking about the blade. He runs his fingers through his dappled beard, leaving the course hair bristled, like an angry cat's. The man loses his smirk, his eyes now hypnotic on the weapon.

Singer doubts the scroll contained anything but words regarding logistics or a change in his busy schedule. He reckons their instructor's mental wandering not a rudderless daydream, but something spawned from the design engrained in the blade, that handsome byproduct begotten from the hand of some Syrian bladesmith, invoking his fire magic upon the wootz steel. The wispy pattern, formed by the smith folding, twisting, and pounding the red-hot metals, likely takes their leader back to some God-forsaken desertscape of his past.

He follows his instructor's eyes down the flowing waves of his Damascus steel, perhaps its contours reminiscent of land sculpted from windblown sand. Although his lips remain pursed, Koray's eyes and forehead partner to express alternating emotions of sadness, then anger, then delight. He imagines Koray's grief is of comrades lost, his fury toward enemies loathed, and his pleasure in victories won. He doubts any present here will ever know the old man's thoughts. But the emotions sweep across the warrior's face, as if the desert squall in his mind was like blowing sand, covering up one satisfaction only to uncover another suffering. Watching a wave of sorrow again cross Koray's face, Singer is reminded of his own anguish. He wonders what has become of his friend. Is Duyal still alive?

The tulb assumes the worst. They have seen it too many times. Good friends, competent novices—gone in a blink of an eye. For two weeks his mates have dreaded the appearance of a new crucifix erected outside the gates, but none has been raised. Vegetable dealers told novice unloaders this week that no young bodies hang from the other oak posts, which line the paths into Hisn Kayfa. The Mamluk command has gone silent on the topic altogether. He wishes his comrade would be allowed to return, yet each passing day makes that more unlikely.

His friend was solid. How many times had Duyal come to the assistance of the others? How many others possessed that unique sense of knowing when a comrade was down, instinctively using the right approach, harsh or soft, to bring the boy back into the fold? He thinks of their talks over chores, his friend's willing ear. The first to jump on any task, the last to whine when things went awry. He never had a friend like Duyal. He shakes his head. The pain sets in again. His eyes flood. The amirs are fools.

Duyal's tactical proficiency alone was reason for the command to have kept him. On the lance, he was without peer in the tulb. What a waste. He remembers their mantra, blurted so often in joke: "Singer with bow, Duyal on lance, side by side in battle, the enemy stands little chance."

He wipes a tear from the corner of his eye. He rebukes himself for thinking of his friend as if he were already dead. Yet already few in the tulb speak of him, as if this were already so. Losing tulbmates this far along in training always hurt, but not like this one. He feels a stab in his stomach, the same felt when finding his younger siblings so many moons ago, their skulls crushed by Mongol club. The same endured when riding away from Ferdi.

Duyal should have refused Cenk's order. The tulb should not have been so willing to help. Duyal could have told Safir the truth. If he had, there was a chance his buddy could be with them right now.

He rocks, humming in time with the soft squeak of his

saddle. His mother called the song "Return to the River," one that gave her peace when the men were out on a hunt or raid. He wonders if he should have disregarded Duyal's promise to protect the rest of them. Maybe he should have also confessed to Safir, joined his friend wherever he may be, whatever his fate now held.

Three raps on a gear box echoed across the stone walls. To the mats of Umit and Bulut the four snuck. Socks pulled across the mouths of their prey; struggling arms restrained by blankets smothered over them. Spare candlesticks, stuffed inside cheese sacks employed in place of fists, to keep knuckles clean of incriminating cuts.

He held down Bulut while they thumped him. Over his shoulder, two others had joined Ox in pounding the arms and head of the other slacker. Like a pack of wild dogs, two, three, four more jumped in without thought, once realizing the target was the pair who were of no use to the group and were instead better suited as a meal.

So they pummeled, maybe forty seconds of frenzy, finally stopped by Duyal. "Enough, enough. None of you know shit. It was all my doing. They will pull not a single name through my lips. By Allah, I promise."

Umit never regained consciousness. Bulut lay curled in a ball, sobbing for several minutes, then silence. At sunrise, only Duyal confessed.

Safir scowled when forcing Singer to recount the events. The same story again. The same lie; the eunuch knowing the beatings were not the work of one.

With the tulb's training at such an advanced stage and with the fever still cutting at the ranks of all units, the inquiry ended abruptly. Possessing a sole culprit's admission, the staff turned their heads back toward bigger issues.

Koray snaps from his trance, wiping a smudge from his blade with a sleeve. "You'll see one day... that of all weapons that'll soon adorn your body and saddle, the sword will be your favorite brother," he says. His horse snorts and stomps a hoof, as if in exclamation. Several novices in the back push closer to the sword master until they surround him, none wishing to miss his words.

Singer looks down. The training weapon at his side could hardly be considered a favorite, the locket on his scabbard peeling away, the chape at the holder's tip bent enough to keep the sword inside from fully seating. Exposed and unprotected is a half foot of over-sharpened edge, burred with scratches and deep chips. Above that, a wooden handle sullied black from a thousand novices' hands and a rounded pommel with splits radiating outward like the bottom of a dry creek bed.

Koray allows them to gather, then continues. "When the enemy flees to narrow places, you may first reach for your tall brother, the lance. In these instances this weapon will be willing, but unable to come to your assistance. If you stay with this friend only, you'll fight not just the enemy, but the lance as well, this gangly sibling of the sword. If wise, you'll drop this lanky one in the dirt and reach for the blade at your hip."

Koray looks up to the sky, as if waiting for Allah to confirm his words. He leans slightly, gives his horse just a touch of calf, causing the Arabian to slowly turn. He surveys those about him. "And on the sea, when waves batter the planking and wind fills hungry sails, our bowmen from atop the rigging will be rendered useless, their arrows fluttering with no effect into the ocean. They'll be forced into spectatorship, watching below, where grapple hooks are thrown and swords drawn for the wet work to begin."

Away again Koray goes, maybe this time to a deck made slippery from blood and splashing saltwater, where canvas overhead claps in adulation at the carnage playing below its span. "For when we beat armies, our senior amirs will recount that we conquered them by the sword. This is no statement of generality. Often in the climax of battle, the distance between jihadis and infidels is shrunk. And then, so close to the Franj that you can smell wine through the heathens' pores, your training with brother sword will be put to test. And at these moments, when Mamluk and horse and foe breathe the same rotten air, the battle will be won or lost with the fired steel in your hands."

Koray looks beyond the novices and whistles to a young ghulam, who stands with his hands locked behind his back. "But of course battles aren't won with talk. The blade isn't mastered by moving our lips, now is it?"

"Errr!" the novices respond.

On Koray's command, the barefooted ghulam sprints to a short barrel. With a bundle of arrow shafts in each hand, he stoops at eight-pace intervals to snug the projectiles into bamboo shoots, predug into the hippodrome's surface. Deemed unserviceable by the instructors, some of these arrows have lost their fletching, most are warped, cracked. The ghulam presses each into its submerged tube one hand-width deep, as marked on the arrow. He tests each for a tight fit before moving on to the next, stopping when ten arrows are dispersed about the course.

Singer looks over the horses about him. Beneath him is "Fire Bum," a brilliantly colored chestnut, with scars across both shoulders and a divot missing from his nose, none being wounds from splendid battles, but instead residual damage from the unproven swords of novices.

Ilker is aback "Snow King," an eight-year-old, named for his roan coat and an anecdote of carrying a frozen Mamluk home during a snowstorm, over the Zagros Mountains in Persia. His vigor now extinguished, the poor stallion serves out his remaining days in the hippodrome. The tip of his right ear is missing and he is known to stop in his tracks when the flash of a shiny object riles his unpredictable dislike.

"Daydream," a dopey bay with tan scars and chunks missing from his legs, wears depression in his eyes. While not much over seventeen years, this Arabian is in a bad way. With a swayed back and graying hair about his drooping lower lip, he holds the look of a horse on his way out. Sooner than the others, he will be quartered and hung from meat hooks, collecting flies at some stall in Hisn Kayfa's market, or slopped onto the novice's wooden plates. Despite his hard years of service, none give the mount much sympathy, evidenced by the fact that today he must bear the weight of Ox.

Erol moves away from the group to face the course. He twists the reins in his hands, winding the leather into a tight coil and when unable to wind any farther, changes direction. All the while, he picks at the thick cuticles covering the corners of his pea-sized thumbnails, unaware that blood begins to dribble from one.

Singer pushes his horse over to Erol's. "One arrow at a time. Save your arm. Think only of the basics—sword just as high as your shoulder, lock in your outside knee first. You got this. Unforced motion—just like a river, just like the bow, my brother."

Erol gives a quick smile and nods.

Since his first day at the citadel, Erol never relinquished his position as the bow-shooting envy of the tulb. Regardless of distance or course, Erol's accuracy was unwavering. Whenever waiting his turn on the archery line, Singer forced himself to pick apart Erol's form, as a flock of chickadees would pick clean the flesh from each bone on a carcass.

There are no flaws in the slight boy's motions. He would not be surprised if Erol were the best shot of all the citadel's novices. But the same slender limbs and stringy muscles, which compelled him to near-perfect form on the bow, were a detriment on both the lance and heavy sword.

And it was not that Erol did not dedicate himself to adding beef to his physique. Scarcely did one hear a word come from Erol's mouth when the novice sat to eat. Instead, the thin boy wolfed down veal, fish, chicken, grapes, apples, dates, until his belly rounded. Even his *Furusiyya* instructor showed concern in this regard. In one of Cenk's few acts of regular compassion, he often pointed Erol back toward the platters for a second round, if the lad attempted to sneak by with one serving. If the training schedule dictated an abbreviated meal break, Cenk sent Erol to the front of the line.

Singer could tell Erol hated the chow hall, surely the boy associating the long benches and endless chorus of metal scraping wood with cramps, gas, and stomach aches. And for all the aggravation, Erol seemed to only grow ganglier. Like an oven that could only burn red hot, Erol's internal fire torched every morsel of food that hit his gullet before the nutrients could add bulk to his limbs.

"This time, I want only four hands' width left on each arrow. Four hands. Let's go," Koray says.

"Yes, my Amir," Erol says.

The youth vaults toward the first arrow on his right. At the gallop, he stands deep in his stirrups, leans right and swings the heavy sword, taking two hands off the arrow, as required.

His mates shout encouragement. "Err!"

With ease, he raises and lowers the sharp edge four more times, on each occasion tumbling the sections of fletching and arrow shaft upon the hardpack. Turning his mount, he exchanges the reins and sword into alternate hands and digs in, guiding his horse to the last five arrows on his left side. He buries his right knee into the saddle, leans left and strikes. A clean cut. He raises it and brings it down again, yet the tip of his sword bites into ground, a clank of steel on rock, reverberating through the hippodrome seating. When the blade finally makes contact with the arrow, the sword's momentum is lost, breaking the arrow midshaft. His timing askew, he rears back the heavy blade in preparation for the next arrow. With a lurching underhand motion, Erol misses the arrow long, yet connects with the outer sole of his boot.

He yelps, looking down to see that only the dangling sole of his boot keeps this chunk of foot from falling to the ground. His face goes instantly white. He continues, seemingly keen to finish the course, yet likely grasping his situation, reins in and returns to the cluster of novices.

Erol grits his teeth. Blood streams from his boot, leaving a splattered trail upon the dirt. His horse turns his head to the rear with nostrils flaring. Two novices catch his mount and another removes Erol's feet from the stirrups. They pull their slender friend down. Koray backs his horse, using the opportunity to watch how the novices respond to a wounded brother.

Recalling his prior instruction, Singer unbuckles Erol's sword belt and cinches the device below Erol's calf to restrict blood flow. He rises and steps away, as two more move in to comfort him.

Ilker already heads across the arena to where a basket of dressing and binding rope hangs from the rail. He jumps from his mount and jams the supplies into his tunic. Then he hesitates.

Turning to confirm his instructor's eyes remain on Erol and that no other instructor watches, Ilker snatches a small dagger from an adjacent rack and slips it into his sleeve. Reaching the group, Ilker pushes his way to Erol, lifting his arm not just to pass by his mates, but to allow the blade's grip to ease into his armpit. Once in place, he clamps down with lowered arm.

His mates lay Erol upon his back, remove their

wounded brother's helmet and cram a tunic under his head. Ilker lays the bandages and cord upon the boy's horse blanket, blood soaking into the yellow fabric, obscuring the worn, split-leaf design. He then backs away, his eyes bouncing from novice to novice to instructor and then eventually up into the stands. Anticipating Ilker's eyes coming upon him, Singer looks down to the quivering lips of the boy.

"Let me bleed out. Damned if I will be a cripple," Erol cries, now kicking at the novices who assist him. They pin down his flailing limbs.

Singer jumps back in, pulling the belt tighter around his calf. He grabs Erol by the hair and speaks calmly, "Stop it. This wound will heal up."

"I'll need a foot to run. They'll be done with me," Erol says, a pathetic look on his face.

"Make a hole!" Singer is shoved aside as Cenk bulls his way in. The Bashkir stands over the wounded boy with hands on hips.

"What is Dependability?" Cenk asks in monotone.

The ill-timed test causes the novices to slowly move back, the boys knowing their instructor has more to come.

Erol looks up in disbelief, beads of sweat dotting his forehead. "Uh...uh...the certainty of proper performance of duty," he says between short breaths.

"Duty for a Mamluk means the able employment of all weapons—not just the bow. How will you perform all duties for our prince, when you chose to lop off your own limbs, rather than those of the enemy?" Cenk asks. He walks away and then returns, shaking his head, his mouth contorted into a pile of revulsion.

Singer knows that this is all the love the gruff man can show for the loss of his most lethal bowman. This surely tears their instructor up.

It becomes too much for the man to watch. He shoves

his way through them and paces behind the gaggle with clenched fists. A madman seeking clarity. He returns. "Will you all stand and watch, while this worm lays here desecrating the prince's hippodrome? Finish wrapping him up and get him out!"

CHAPTER
37

Duyal
Citadel prison, Hisn Kayfa
November 6, 1237

The familiar voice of the muezzin surges through the small window. The sharp rise and fall of his calls ricochet about the hard floor and gray walls, both rock surfaces worn smooth from the greasy backs of prior occupants. Duyal opens one eye, then closes it.

"God is the greater. Rise up for prayer. Rise up for salvation," the muezzin beckons in that foreign tongue.

Salvation. He does not believe it will come to him; he is not sure he deserves it. Yet he will honor his God.

A waft of ripened air pulls under the door, across his face and out the barred window. The smell of shit on wood and rancid urine, soaked deep into stone. With a groan, Duyal rolls off his mat, its wool stuffing mostly depleted, its damp covering glazed in a waxy brown from years of collecting oil and filth.

He attempts to shift the rug so that it points southward toward Mecca, yet the moisture leeching from the stone has bonded the fabric to the floor. He pulls it. The suction releases with a wet kiss. He shivers, his tunic saturated from the clamminess of the place. From his knees, he sighs, shooting a plume of frosty breath against the wall.

He assumes the prostrate gingerly, taking care to keep the raw flesh on his hamstrings from touching his calves. Down the hallway, he hears the jumbled words of others, who have already begun their prayers in solitude. Duyal lowers his head and works through the *Rak'a*, and then the same personal prayer he has repeated five times per day since arriving here. He thinks it is day eighteen or nineteen.

"Praise be to my Lord most high. Oh, He who pardons. Please forgive me for the killing of my brother, Umit. I accept whatever punishment you have in store for me, yet ask that you preserve this warrior. In your gracious name, I ask that despite my shortcomings, you allow this humble servant to go forth and use the skills that you have bestowed upon him, gained only through sweat and your blessings. I ask this only for the further glory and good of your name. God is the Greater."

Duyal elevates his forehead from the moist stone and rests on his knees. He hopes God understands the sincerity of his request. The killing of a fellow Muslim was a sin against Allah, and for this he feels deep sorrow. Further, he feels shame for falling short of God's expectations and an equal disgrace for taking the lead in killing one in his *Khushdash,* his tulb of brothers.

Although deep down, he knows he has helped his mates by eliminating their weakest novice. Perhaps Cenk was right all along, he did not deserve to be a Mamluk. Maybe the only thing he deserves is to be executed. He sighs.

The rising sun sends a beam through the window, casting a trapezoidal form with three vertical dividers to the opposite wall. He stares at the patch of sunlight on the blocks, lost in thought. A hunched figure, with pointed shadow ears, creeps into the trapezoid. Duyal slowly raises his head up toward the window. A dark-coated rat, facing away, nibbles a morsel found on the thin ledge.

Duyal launches himself at the animal, grabs its tail, and pulls the creature into his cell. Using the momentum of his grasp, he swings the hefty rodent above his head. The rat claws at the air, squealing in distress. Gaining sufficient momentum, he smacks its head on the wall once, twice. He slams it to the floor.

On the rock slab, the rodent quivers, its cries now subdued. Blood leaks from its peach-colored ears. Duyal drops to his knees and snaps the stunned rodent's neck between his thumb and forefinger. He stops, listens for the screech of stool legs, the cadence of hard leather on rock.

Several moments pass. Nothing.

He looks down at the mound of fur before him. He cries silently, his head convulsing in a manner that surprises him. His lungs pull hard for air, creating a sucking sound that is heard through the corridor. He coughs twice to disguise his sob from the guards.

Weakling. This is no time to cry. Could it be that Allah has heard his prayer? Does God wish to nourish him? A surge of thankfulness streams through his body. Could Allah actually find him worthy of saving? Perhaps he is justified to sob.

Again aware that a guard could arrive to investigate the commotion, he hides the rat under his mat, his stomach grumbling its protest. After waiting several moments, he snatches the plump body and goes to the bucket in the corner. Inside it, his feces have begun to lose their frosty coat from last evening. Three flies fight off the morning chill, buzzing the thawing section of stool in a cold-induced intoxication.

Even in this, Duyal is grateful. For if there were no flies, the bucket would be empty of shit; if there were no shit, then they would not have been feeding him. While his meals have consisted mainly of scraps, he knows it could be worse. He rationalizes they would not go to the trouble of feeding him twice per day, if they intended on him rotting in this cell for the long term, or sticking him on a cross.

He forces a grin. Actual meat in his hands. Chow is morale. He takes the rat and runs the base of its tail across the sharp edge of overlapping steel on the bucket's middle band, using his fingers to loosen the skin above it. On the broad side of the band, he saws through the spine, leaving the tail skin intact.

He pauses. Again satisfied that his work is undetected, he steps on the on the tail, places three fingers under the back skin and pulls the rat's fur over its head in one tug. Grabbing its head, he does the same with the remaining fur on its lower legs, pulling it cleanly off the pink-fingered feet. He stuffs the skin under his mat.

Looking down at the dark red meat, more tears cloud his eyes. He drops to both knees and gives thanks to Allah. He returns to the bucket and makes a cut down the fat animal's belly. Blood flows into his hands. The smack of lips on rosy skin; the slurps of precious crimson from the varmint's chest and belly. He licks his fingers and then the blend of tears and blood from his matted beard.

Discipline. The hunger must not erode his willpower. Think. Be prepared if the guard arrives. He wipes a drip of blood from the bucket, then moves to the opposite corner of the cell, where the opening door would swing toward him, buying him a second or two to hide his meal. He brings over his mat and bucket and sits with his back against the wall. He pulls free the rat's entrails. He runs the intestines through his thumb and forefinger, emptying the thin strip of twisting sludge atop his own shit.

> Atop that plateau, overlooking their gers, his father and uncle sat about the fire, squeezing lamb innards through their fists into the hissing coals. An eruption of laughter beside him, as two men tied the ends of emptied intestine.
>
> With great care, they then poured the animals' blood back into the casings. Around them, more chuckles and smiles that always preceded a big meal. More men arrived, some sprawling on their sides with hands supporting weary heads, watching them.
>
> The chatter of anticipation increased as the steam rose from the blackened pot. When their coiled creations slithered into the water, the chatter lessened, the men eventually sitting silently, savoring the scent of those bloody sweet vapors.

He shoves a heap of guts in his mouth like some ravenous swine, barely taking the time to chew. Licks to his fingers and knuckles. The tang of iron and salt. Using the bucket to cut around the rear legs, he carefully wipes the blood and hair from the cutting edge with his grimy sleeve. He twists the rear legs from the carcass, hiding them under his mat for later. Again more licks to clean himself, to hide the evidence.

He then rips into the flesh, savoring every fiber of meat and tissue. Gnawing on a front leg bone, he nods to himself. No real regrets last moon from the interrogation in Safir's chamber.

> "Did your Furusiyya instructor design the attack?" Safir asked, looking down at him.
>
> "No, my Amir," Duyal said.
>
> "Who else helped?"
>
> "None, my Amir. I beat them both."
>
> A frown on the shiny black face. "You know that murder is punishable by death?"

"Yes, my Amir."

Pushed next door into the small room, he placed his palms upon the blocks and received the alternating blows: to his back, to his hamstrings, to his back, to his hamstrings.

While he took each strike from the slender bamboo with equal silence, he felt no pain upon his back, his father's drunken handywork having already dulled this flesh with scar tissue years ago. But this condition did not keep that skin from turning to flapping pink strips. Same on the back of his legs.

Then back to Safir, where he took those questions seated with his hands flat upon blood-drenched trouser legs, looking through Safir's scrutinizing gaze.

"Did your Furusiyya instructor design the attack?"

"No, my Amir."

"Who else helped?"

"None, my Amir. I beat them both."

"You know that murder is punishable by death?"

"Yes, my Amir."

By day six, the limestone in the small room was decorated with a chin-high collage of Duyal's palm prints, as if children had dipped their hands in maroon paint and decorated the eunuch's interrogation chamber with crude art. The stool where he sat was covered with dark-ribboned imprints from his mutilated trousers and flesh, like winding impressions left by snakes just emerged from their blood-filled swamp.

Junior recruits, most only several weeks into their training and serving punishments of their own, manned the switch. One bawled as he struck him, such was the gore.

"You mustn't cry," Duyal said. "Tisn't suitable of the *faris* you'll one day be."

When the sessions were over, Duyal turned to again see those who did the whipping. Sad eyes and baggy-white uniforms, splattered bright red like a butcher's apron at day's end.

With his uniform in tatters, one day a guard threw him a dusty bag. On the bag was his mark from the first day. Inside it—the Turkish garments given to him by Bozkurt. It was only then that he too cried.

And then it ended. For thirteen days since, he had nothing but silence, interrupted only twice per day, when the door creaked open and a wooden plate slid across the floor. Often on it: chicken bones, apple cores, and (if he was lucky) a hunk of lamb grizzle, other scraps brushed from the plates of novices.

He thinks of his victim, Umit—his greasy hair, his pimpled face, his flippant way. The lazy one did not deserve to be at the citadel, but he did not deserve to die either. Duyal doubts it was his own blows that killed the novice; so many had jumped in to reap their own justice for the misery he had caused the tulb.

It does not matter now. Even if the command chooses to put him to death, at least he has kept his promise to his mates, those in his *Khushdash* who deserved to be in the ranks. Allah must see some honor in this.

He does not know why he protected Cenk. Despite their mutual hatred for one another, he feels bound by a strange devotion to the man. Perhaps somewhere deep in his soul, he knows that his *Mu'allim's* methods will serve a greater purpose down the road, that somehow Cenk actually means well. If nothing else, his *Furusiyya* instructor's insanity forced his mates to connect. Somehow, Cenk was the bizarre glue that united them. Even if Duyal will never be able to join them again, the knot that binds them is tighter because of their *Mu'allim.*

His tulb. Tears return to his eyes. He loves them, even the worst of them. Ilker, Ox, Erol, Singer—what he would do just to be back on the field with them. He had nobody to blame but himself—had no reason to listen to the amirs' meeting. If he had just stuck to mopping the floor, he would be training with his brothers right now.

He figures the command is too busy to fuss with him. Half the citadel is squeezing a year's worth of training into six moons, the other half is preparing to deploy to Diyar Rabia, as instructed by the sultan. He may literally rot here.

The rat is now but a pile of rumpled hair. He feels energized. Again he puts his knees to the rock in thanksgiving. Hoisting himself up to the window, he heaves the bundle of fur, never hearing it land. He licks his palms and inserts each filthy finger into his mouth, so as to not waste a speck of sustenance. Using his incisors, he cleans the red and black from under his nails. An echo off the walls as he spits into his hands. A hard rub to his beard and then back to licking his palms, as would a round-bellied cat.

He is still alive. He still has a patron, whom he adores. He still has a God. He still has brothers in training. He will continue to drill—out of obligation to them all. He must not fall behind. If on the odd chance he is released, he must be ready to ride and fight with the others.

He drops to his belly and begins the push-up exercise. On each raise of his body, he pushes the air forcefully from his lungs. Any bad thoughts, any sin is exhaled along with the spent air—all of it extinguished across the stone. Finishing his last repetition, he rests on his knees, his hands on hips.

Two cells down, he hears the grunts from another lad. And then a snort from the cell farther down the corridor. A grin spreads across his face. His activity has become contagious. The other boys, perhaps even a Mamluk, follow his lead. Even the bars and thick walls cannot prevent them from fusing.

Those scrawls in Arabic. That verse high on the wall. It comes to him now:

"And be not weak-hearted in the pursuit of the enemy. If you suffer pain, then surely they too suffer pain as you suffer pain. And you hope from Allah what they do not hope; Allah is knowing and wise."

He leaps to the window, pulling himself up by the vertical bars, his forearms lodged against the window ledge. Scabs near his elbows tear open—abrasions formed from past sessions. He lowers himself until his arms are straight and then powers himself up again. For seconds at a time, the slice of land and sky between the white-blocked towers offers its solace, his only view of the outside world.

Sky… wall… sky… wall… sky… wall. Thirteen, fourteen, fifteen… He embraces the familiar two-pitched resonance of his boots as they scrape up and down the blocks. Do not think, warrior of Allah, just train. Just train.

CHAPTER
38

Cenk
Citadel hippodrome, Hisn Kayfa
November 10, 1237

As they pass in mounted formation across the hippodrome seating, Cenk uses his nose as if it were a quill, drawing an imaginary line straight down from the ear, shoulder, hip, and heel of each rider as they pass. To a casual observer, he appears pleased, nodding his head repeatedly, as if in agreement with what he sees.

Cloaked in hooded chain mail, his novices materialize as faceless deliverers of death, emerging from the depths of the hippodrome in line. Dark eyes beneath enameled helmets, torsos cloaked in sun-parched red. Upon their hips, feared Damascene steel. In their hands, lances of rigid bamboo. Frosty breath curls from metallic faces, like smoke billowing from lungs of the devil's own horde.

He cannot recall even half the number of bloodless battles he has witnessed. When the manifestation of Mamluks en masse, appearing over a dune or around a hill, caused shit to coil into the trousers of enemy infantry, or the steeds ridden by the foe's cavalry to shake nervous heads after absorbing a tremble from their riders' legs. Just the sight of their red-lioned pennants, nipping at the breeze, and the earned reputation of those who rode beneath them, were enough to send most armies fleeing.

But a glance to the maces secured on each rider's saddle extinguishes his reminiscences of martial superiority, dispels his memories of intimidated enemy. The felt-wrapped heads on the onerous weapons rest in their metal rings, the burred shafts patting the horses' flanks in concord. He chuckles to himself, pleased that he was able to acquire the bludgeoning devices, long ditched by the Ayyubid cavalry, satisfied that each in the tulb has the burden of lugging them as punishment for the unit's shortfalls.

"Rabbit chasers," he says to himself.

He cracks his knuckles and snorts, reprimanding himself for any smugness just felt. So far, he has failed. Failed al-Salih, failed his God. He has not yet made these young men into the Mamluks they need to be. It eats at him. At this stage of training, below him should be horsemen, just polishing their skills for battle. Instead, on the field are half-trained, untested novices. The familiar prick of worry sets back into his gut.

Is it only he who sees beneath the outward flash in their appearance? Hidden behind the woven steel of the riders' aventails are beards of peach fuzz and the soft features of faces still boyish. Beneath the armor, which droops in silvery ripples over their necks, are shoulders, few of which have ever raised a bow to drop enemy from their mounts, nor hoisted a blade to sever a single infidel's head in revenge. His novices are themselves like pretty swords, recently plucked from the metalsmith's coals, gleaming and scuff-free, yet still a mystery as to whether their steel will break when metal clashes.

The sun breaks from a cloud, warming his red coat. The pleasant thump of hoof on dirt. He yawns. The mental fog from another sleepless night sends him momentarily into a daydream, yet one boy below pulls back his attention. The novice rides slightly slumped forward, throwing off the desired equine linkage from head to heels. At this rider, Cenk stops his methodical line drawing and groans. He need not see the face of the offender, recognizing at once the thick back of the goon, Demir.

"Hopeless," he grunts. He will correct him later.

Two instructors lead each column, cantering their Arabians eastward in parallel rows through the largest sector of the hippodrome. The novices hold lances in their right hands, their weapons in the "heads up" position, their horses aligned with the recruit in front of each.

"Dispersion, keep your dispersion!" another instructor bellows, trotting opposite the formation at a distance.

As they again cross his position, Cenk looks for bamboo between their fingers, indicating an improper grip, his eyes flitting up and down the long spears. None. He leans back to better view any shaft slanted in error left or right, front or back.

"They begin to move like a unit, *Mu'allim*," a deep voice sounds from behind him.

Cenk spins, surprised someone has approached without him hearing. "Yes." His eyes snap back to his troops.

"May I sit?" his fellow *Furusiyya* instructor asks.

"Of course, of course," Cenk says.

The instructor they call "Heavy," for both the immensity of his build and weight of his chosen blade, sits down, leaving enough space between them to fit two more men.

Already forgetting he has company, Cenk keeps his eyes fixed on the formation below.

With a horse-length interval separating riders, the novices follow the instructors, turning their mounts to their respective outside, peeling each line formation outboard in two delicate arcs. All sit deep in the saddle, as if the leather and wood frame were itself the base of their buttocks. Only their hips move to absorb the rock of their canter.

The pound of hooves drops to that of a muted patter as the horses slow, flinging freshly raked dirt in their wakes. The sweet smell of turned soil. He belches a rancid mouthful of *koumis* and then cups his mouth, blowing away from his visitor the incriminating scent of mare's milk turned wine. He tries to squeeze the pain from his temples, pretending to shield the glare from his eyes.

In perfect synchronization, the novices begin their wide turn on the same spot, all the while managing to maintain their proper spacing. They continue the semicircle, until doubling back on their original direction of travel. From the high seating above, the dual columns look like a spraying fountain, the chain of riders suggesting the gurgling rise and cascade of pulsating water.

"They have *libaqa*... they will serve well," Heavy says, referring to the Mamluk quality of superb horsemanship.

Cenk turns. "Don't you still have a tulb of your own to look after? Surely you didn't come here to sprinkle compliments upon my lowly outfit, now did you, *Mu'allim?*" He smirks, flashing his narrow, bloodshot eyes to affirm the intended bite of his statement.

Heavy, with his elbows resting on sturdy knees, drops his head and grins. "No, my brother. Just wanted to tell you that as our tulbs near their finish, it was you at my heels that kept me pushing these past moons. It's competition between units like ours that makes the regiment stronger." Heavy reaches out his hand.

Cenk looks into the man's eyes, detecting some sincerity. He grasps Heavy's hand. His own is immediately swallowed, like a child's mitt in that of his father's. He quickly releases.

Pleasantries between competitors. He could do without it. What he could use more of is the attainment of more battle skills by his tulb. The proof: posted on the scroll outside Safir's chamber yesterday, were the combined scores on all inspections and weapon tests. Of the five training tulbs, Cenk's was ranked second, while Heavy's tulb was ranked first. More disturbing, Cenk's unit was third in weapons proficiency. This turns his stomach. His worms underperform; he knows their mediocrity is owned by him alone. If he had excelled, they would have excelled.

His prince will also see it this way. As a *Sayfiya*, a Mamluk purchased after the death of his initial patron, Cenk knows he remains a pariah in al-Salih's regiment. His situation will forever be more precarious than his peers, and is soon likely to become more so. Entrenched in the training regiment and not allowed to join the anticipated deployment with the bulk of the regulars, he will be stuck behind the walls, while his peers gain status and honor on the battlefield. Out of the prince's view, Cenk cannot afford to have his novices finish in the middle of the pack.

He mulls the situation in Damascus, the city viewed by the empire as second in importance behind only Cairo. The prince there, al-Ashraf, died last August and succession fell to the brother, al-Isma'il. Attempting to reconfirm the coalition of princes, al-Isma'il had already lost the support of al-Muzaffar in Hama. The Syrian alliance, their ploy to stand up to the sultan, was falling apart. Without the strength of their combined armies, Damascus, Homs, and Aleppo were all in peril. Traitors.

The Sultan al-Kamil surely smells opportunity; a gap in the alliance to exploit. He will try to make the princes pay for

their disloyalty. Runners report that the sultan and his nephew, al-Nasir Da'ud, have already moved their armies out of
Cairo, north through Palestine. It was only a matter of time
before they laid siege to Damascus. Cenk heard nothing of
the role their own prince would play in the coming engagement, but surely al-Kamil would task al-Salih with a mission,
if for no other reason than to verify his son's allegiance.

And where would Cenk be when the combat started?
Still training novices. But what more could he do? This was
his assignment, and these were the novices thrown into his
lap. From the seventy-four he started with over a year prior,
he now has thirty-two novices in training, two being treated
for injury and one in the dungeon. He watched his personnel
drop in droves the past four moons alone—training failures
and casualties of the fever. He actually lamented the departure of several.

But he is grateful that the weakest of them are gone. He
smiles, certain that Allah assisted in purging the stench from
his ranks. While he did not witness his novice jump from the
rampart last week, he did identify him afterward.

> *The guards turned over the crumpled body, the novice's skull
> spilling mashed gray matter upon the sand-colored stone. The
> exposed face was mush, but he recognized the front teeth and
> wavy hair of the youth.*
>
> *Looking over the body, Cenk felt as if he had just killed a
> sick sheep, one which had been spreading disease among his flock.*
>
> *He tightened his lips to hold back a smile, feeling Safir's eyes
> upon him.*
>
> *Shaking his head in bogus pity, he looked up from the stiff
> and said to the eunuch, "It is he, the novice, Bulut."*

Cenk had actually gained a little respect for the dead recruit
that day. The boy had to have known he was not up to the

task of soldiering, but for many moons was too selfish to quit. The life of a servant or laborer not suiting him, jumping was a logical way out of his dilemma. Maybe Bulut finally recognized that after Umit's death, he had become the tulb's most pathetic. And perhaps knowing that a brother better than he was in the dungeon because of his own poor performance had finally gotten to him.

Who cares? It is better the boy had flung himself to his own death now, rather than blundering in battle later and causing the death of many good Mamluks beside him. In hindsight, the assigned beatings of both novices worked to perfection, as both incompetents no longer poison the others with their presence, nor drag down his scores. While he did not intend to have the weaklings killed, he feels no grief for how it turned out. He again belches a mouthful of acidic *koumis*, swallowing hard to limit its burn, while chewing on the mint leaves stored in his cheek.

Although given the choice, he would have rather not lost Duyal in the process. Despite his deficiencies, the youth had grown talented with the lance. While Cenk would never say so publicly, he figured Duyal had the potential to match the skill of his late brother, Gozde. Nearly unbeatable in the jousting matches, Duyal would have served his fellows well.

He wets his parched lips and sighs. Hopefully Allah would approve of him sacrificing one decent novice, in order to remove two weaklings. He pictures the squinting eyes of his former patron, Turkmani. He too would have agreed that the ends justified the means in this case.

He wonders if his own involvement will be discovered. Doubtful. Duyal is too hardheaded to rat out his instructor; the boy is faithful to a fault. And compared with most of his peers, the novice is a pain merchant. Even if Duyal does squeal during one of his beatings, Cenk will deny any accusation of participating. It would be his word against the novice's, and he would convince the command of his innocence, if need be. It likely will not come to this. Within days, he guesses the eunuchs will execute the youth.

He turns, forgetting that he had company. Heavy mirrors his own smile, his fellow instructor incorrectly sensing a lightening in his rival's demeanor. Cenk recounts their topic at hand. "Our competition is not yet finished. I only wish that we had another year to continue it, so I could bury you."

Heavy shakes his head, his smile widening briefly. "I'm sure Allah will still shine down on you for finishing behind me." His face goes somber, as his eyes flip back to the riders. "This campaign draws near… I don't wish to field our *Muta'allim* even as reserves, when they only own skills of the individual warrior. What's more dangerous in combat than those with little understanding of formations and unit cohesion?"

Cenk's throat clenches. Maybe Heavy is sent by the eunuch, Safir, to dig up slander, to solidify a case against him. Of course their novices are not ready to augment the regiment's Mamluks. No instructor agreed with the decision to cut the novices' training short, but that was only one of the regiment's problems. Possibly the eunuchs want Heavy to pull him into a conversation about the Khwarazmians.

Al-Salih had gathered them all a few days back, announced that Khwarazmian auxiliaries would likely fill the bulk of al-Salih's striking force in any coming mission. Some twelve thousand of them had been in the service of the Seljuks in eastern Anatolia for nearly six years. Yet when Ghiyath al-Din came to power last year, he arrested several of their khans and the bulk of the Khwarazmians fled to the Jazira.

Rather than have these warriors of the north join their rogue fellows in picking away at the caravans, his prince wished to put these men to work. Al-Salih described the alliance as necessary: a way to keep Hisn Kayfa's merchants happy, keep the subsequent tax revenue flowing, and a solution to bulk up the forces he would need to win in battle. "While I'd put my regiment up against any in the empire, we'll need sheer numbers to beat a sizable force," his prince had said.

For weeks the topic has spurred much controversy in the ranks, yet even the sultan had blessed al-Salih's request to enroll these fighters into the prince's service. Cenk understands that with enemies to both their north and south, his master is desperate for troops, but to welcome these thugs into adjacent ranks? He understands these men likely come cheaply, but Cenk half-expects the Khwarazmians to attack al-Salih's Mamluks if the two ever meet with arms. He pushes away his visions of those dirty-faced thieves he faced in 1235. Allah help us.

Cenk deflects, avoiding being drawn into a statement that might call his loyalty to the prince into question. "I suppose we don't control the length of the training, nor how our novices will one day be used. We can only direct how we use the time the command gives us," Cenk says, pleased with his tactful answer.

Heavy raises an eyebrow and nods in agreement.

Cenk's comment pulls his own attention back to his troops below. The two ranks of novices form an inner and outer circle, the inboard rank trotting left to right, while the outboard rank moves in the opposite direction. As the swirling formation spins before him, the brass bosses on the riders' small leather shields send strobes of reflected light into his dry eyes.

He cups his hand and focuses only on the left arm of each rider. He traces a line from the elbow, through the lower arm, down the rein to its termination in the bit. Scanning their hands, his eyes drill down on pinky fingers tucked under leather reins and thumbs facing up, technique pounded into the novices' heads. Finally, most have shed their undisciplined riding habits learned on the steppe.

Breaking out of their respective circles, the riders apply their heels, pushing the Arabians into an effortless gallop. As they pass, Cenk switches his concentration to the loins of each horse, looking for any blood, signaling the opening of scar tissue from aggressive spurring. He sees none, grunting his approval.

Mounted novices now stretch across each length of the hippodrome. Upon the instructor's command, two novices flip their pennants up, halting the columns. The opposing number nines emblazoned upon each yellow banner wave in the breeze. Another command follows, and the novices turn their mounts ninety degrees in place to face the opposite line.

Several horses snort. Another taps a front leg on the dirt. Others bow their elegant necks and sway in the way of the Arabian. Waiting for the verbal commands, which will commence the joust, each novice eyes his opponent directly across from him. Several agitate their horses in an attempt to intimidate their challenger. Two horses rear. Other novices make final adjustments to armor and kit.

"Read-dy!" The preparatory command reverberates across the ancient limestone walls.

At the termination of the second syllable, thirty-two callused hands respond on smooth-wooded shafts with a single "Pop!" the riders snapping their lances down in unison to a position parallel with the ground.

An instructor wheels his horse to check all are in the proper sparring position. He gives the Arabians a chance to catch their breath, using the break to inspect the mouth of every horse for the slightest sign of inflammation. He stops at no rider.

"Remember, my young brothers, cumbersome ash in the ham-fisted grip of the Franj is no match for Mamluk cane employed with vigor!" the instructor blares.

"Errr!" the novices respond.

Cenk shakes his head. The Franj. Why continue to feed this convenient illusion? All in the citadel know the first enemy rank faced by these novices will not be manned by infidels, but instead filled with fellow Muslims from another Ayyubid's army, a result of blood-tainted squabbling from within the empire. He only hopes that he has trained his young men better than the opposing princes have trained theirs.

"Engage!"

The thud of hooves and clank of tack bounce off the empty hippodrome seating, echoing in Cenk's ears.

The enemy. In the end, does it matter who he is or what God he worships? No. As if any Mamluk would hesitate to fight any foe designated by al-Salih. His eyes haze and his mind floats south to that cold day in the cliff country, north of Aleppo. He doesn't want to see it, but the dwindling effects of the *koumis* have just enough punch left to pull him there again.

Hooves on hard ground. They must hurry. How could there be so many? No, it was just their own horses' resonance off the stone. The enemy would not follow. Riders spotted through the dust. Have the damn Khwarazmians encircled them, pushed them against the cliffs? Uh, his fellows have moved too slowly.

Distant arrows sprinkled in, like the first heavy drops before a downpour. Metal tips dinged off rocks, shattering wood shafts; other heads drove into the surrounding sand with harmless "whiffs."

An Arabian caught the first projectile, the mare's shriek amplified by the sheer rock wall to their front. A shudder crept down his spine. An identical squeal in echo. Another horse joined the wailing. Cenk's own mount, now unnerved, lurched his black-maned neck both left and right.

A man yelped as a long arrow plunged through the thin armor atop his back. The half-moon arrowhead sliced through leather, bone and meat, its progress not stopping until it joined rider to horse—the three-feathered fletching resting upon his brother's shoulders like some gruesome epaulette.

Trapped by the bluffs and their own indecision, the tulb tried to regroup, the smell of horse, clay, and blood filling Cenk's nostrils. He sensed fear in his brothers' faces, as the sounds of dying men, injured horses and deep-voiced orders were amplified by the steep rock about them.

The lofting, distant shots ceased as gradually as they began. Finally the storm passed? No. The Khwarazmians closed. Leather flaps on enemy quivers, half-filled with light arrows, flipped shut. Looking over his shoulder, he saw the anxious hands of the enemy dig into adjacent quivers. They pulled heavier arrows, half the length of their bows, adorned with tight fletching of four right-winged vulture feathers. And once again the air sung, the lazy buzz of arching projectiles replaced by the flat zip of hefty ones.

Heavy rises to leave. "I'll see you tonight at the dinner." He stops and stares at his fellow instructor. He walks away, looking back solemnly only once, his rival's glassy eyes remaining riveted to the arena's center.

"Disengage! Disengage!" the mounted instructor blares, ending the few fights that linger.

Cenk's eyes refocus. He gawks at his troops below, wondering if they have already sparred, or if the instructor has given the wrong command. He looks at the bench beside him. How odd for the always genial Heavy to leave without bidding him a word of farewell.

CHAPTER
39

Duyal
Citadel prison, Hisn Kayfa
November 24, 1237

Boot steps scuff to a halt at his door. A key clanks in the sloppy metal lock. A click. The hinges mutter their same rusted moan. The scrape of his wooden plate across the stone floor. The door whines shut in a pitch two notes higher, punctuated by the ominous clank of detention.

Duyal does not bother to look down at the slop, knowing his dinner will be scraps of lamb bone and fat and if he is lucky, a rotten apple, maybe some discarded figs. He is ravenous, yet has not the motivation to eat.

He stares at the block wall in front of him, the rounded pocks in the stone bringing him back to his Volga country—he, Baris, and Gozde frolicking in the ponds, spacious bowls scraped clean and deep by God. Laughter. Early spring dips in the ice-cold water, followed by the wide-eyed, furious paddle to shore. The year-plus since he last saw either brother feels like ten. The old sting of their absence has long been replaced by a dull ache down deeper. He will never see them again.

The splashing water in his mind is silenced by a man's whistle. He tries to envision the source of the sounds, which now pour through his window from the courtyard below. The clang of metal and stomp of boots mixes with the clatter of hooves and groan of wheel on axle. Faint voices pierce the fading light, but he cannot make out the words or speakers. The regiment must be staging gear in support of the sultan's greater campaign in Damascus. Finally al-Salih's father has ordered his son against the prince's uncle, Ismail, the rebel.

He raises a buttock off the floor and arches his back to relieve the numbness in his legs, but it does not help. A spider above him rides his web down from the dripping stone. If only he could slide down a rope unseen and deploy with the others.

He had hoped the regiment would one day face the same Mongols who had crushed his tower. This would not happen, at least not yet. He is learning that the community of Muslims, the unity of the Ayyubids, was not quite as tidy as the clerics had described nearly eighteen moons past. He knew power corrupted, had seen it on the steppe, yet never dreamed the *Salihiyya* would turn their bows and lances on fellow Muslims, especially the prince's own blood. But this the regiment would do willingly for their patron. As would he.

He bows his head. While this moral dilemma will likely be encountered by his mates, Duyal doubts he will have to cope with this challenge, as his likely enemy will be the fever that creeps its way through the chambers, cell by cell.

He wonders if his brothers in training were pulled early from the citadel to join the coming movement. Could they be among those staging below? He cannot bear the thought of them leaving for battle without him, regardless of who they fight.

The scent of cumin interrupts his thoughts. He looks down at the plate. Steam curls from thick chunks of meat and a mound of rice, covered in a thick yogurt. Hot food? Dates and grapes heap over the plate's lip. He crawls over and plucks a piece of meat from the sauce. His eyes grow wide—goat. Wonderful goat.

From his knees, he scoops a handful, grunting in satisfaction, pushing air through his mouth in short bursts to keep from burning his tongue. Hunched over the plate, he wolfs down rice like a rib-baring dog. He chokes, an errant kernel finding its way into his airway. He coughs a moist clump in his hand and once clearing his windpipe, plops the wad back in his mouth, licking his hand clean.

He stops chewing. Would they be poisoning him? He has not had a meal anywhere near this quality in almost two moons. Why now? He shrugs. If this is the way the Mamluks wish for him to die, then so be it. He gorges. Pulling a grape from its stem, he plops it in his mouth, savoring the juice that squirts between his teeth.

Two sets of footsteps approach. Nearer. Duyal snags the clump of grapes and places them behind the small of his back, knowing the guards waste no time in removing the plate and waste bucket from the cells. Yet instead of cracking the door as usual, the guard swings the large wooden hatch open, throwing rays of light into his musty cell. He shields his eyes with one hand, irritated, waiting for the door to slam shut.

A cane pokes him on the shoulder. "Get up. Come with us," a guard grunts.

Duyal hears only the rich sound emitting from the man's throat, the first words uttered to him in nearly a week. Then the meaning of the words, the impatience in the man's tone sinks in. Move quickly, or the next strike will be violent. Still chewing, Duyal leans his shoulder into the wall and attempts to rise, but his legs remain asleep.

He pulls a tingling leg up to his chest with his hand and reaches up the wall with his other, digging his fingernails into a gap between blocks. He grimaces, knowing how pathetic his struggle must appear. The cold from the cell and duration of his seated position feel as if they have partnered to shrink the joint sockets around his bones and turn his muscles stiff as oak.

From the corner of his eye, the cane appears—incentive to speed him to his feet. Duyal flinches, anticipating impact, yet the second guard lightly grabs the swinger's elbow before the downward stroke. This man looks vacantly into Duyal's face.

As the cane is lowered to the guard's side, so does Duyal's heart drop. Why would they show mercy now? A profound dread is birthed within him, easing its way through Duyal's limbs, like a slow spreading fog. As the frightful mist reaches his throat, he fights off a whimper, pulling himself to his feet with a grimace. The day has come. The second guard sighs and points his thumb into the corridor. "Walk."

Duyal steps through the doorway with needles of fresh circulation pricking his feet. Up the winding stairs, the air becoming drier as they pass the guard station. The smell of strong tea and the same goat dish. A prod of cane in his back. The icy scrape of steel on sheath behind him, as if he needed a reminder of who was in charge.

"Left."

Duyal stumbles down the dark corridor with the guards in tow, his tingling, half-numb leg stomping its progress through the fortress. His breathing quickens. Will they kill him now? Of course they will. The good meal—it was not poisoned, it was his last. He works the stray rice kernels from his cheeks, knowing these to be the last morsels that will ever enter his stomach. He sees the faces of his uncle, his mother; the features of his father and brothers. He must put them in the front of his mind. And his brothers, his *Khushdashiya*, his comrades in training. They too were his family, and he must think of them now.

So close he came to finishing. Tulb Nine. He recounts their appearance, sees them in the hippodrome, in the barracks. Singer releasing a confident arrow. A scowl on Ilker's homely mug. The sideways glance from Demir and wholehearted laugh from the Ox. He tries to bring up the faces of his entire tulb in rapid succession, so that they will be easy to recall when he reaches heaven—or hell, if that is what is in store.

"Here."

Duyal stops and faces the steel-banded wood planking, behind which hangs his fate. While he has never walked this passage, nor seen behind this door, he knows well where he is. Often the eunuchs had warned of the place the Mamluks call "the chop room," where thieves lose hands and harem raiders part with their penises. On the east side of the citadel, it was said the speech of close to a dozen Mamluks had been reduced to grunts and hand signals, the result of losing their tongues in this very room for speaking poorly of their patron or elders.

Reaching over Duyal's shoulder, the guard raps twice with his cane. The clink of latch lifting from within. The door swings open.

Inside, two thick-necked guards stand expressionless with axes in hand. Duyal's legs go unsteady. He cannot move. A push from behind. In passing, he examines one of the well-sharpened blades, becomes captivated by the etched lion on the steel face. He imagines the lion enjoying the taste of his blood. He is halted by the block of wood at his knees, the timber hacked and maroon. The smell of musk and cloves fills the room, bewildering him.

"Kneel before your prince," the guard says.

Duyal turns.

Al-Salih takes a step forward from the shadow of a wall, stands with crossed arms, wearing not the yellow turban of the Mamluk, but the black linen of Jihad. Surprised to see his master, Duyal faces the man and drops to one knee, the posture of a peasant. He lowers his head. Al-Salih's attendance confirms that today is his last.

He eyes the open door. Although he would be sliced in the process, he might stand a chance in slipping past the four guards and making a run for it. But even if he could reach the stairs, how far would he really get before the axes and swords hacked him apart?

No. He will not die in flight. His tower was killed while he ran and hid. Not today. Such will not be the parting memory his prince has of him. Still crouched in a bow, he clasps his calf to hide the shaking.

"Rise. Stand before me, my son," al-Salih says in a somber tone.

His head swims at just hearing the voice of his prince, the great one addressing only him. Al-Salih had only spoken to him one other time in the past fifteen moons. He figures most novices in his tulb had yet to hold a conversation with their master. But this was not abnormal. Surely al-Salih was a busy man, with many vying for his time, but it was not a shortage of time or excessive duties which kept their prince distanced from all novices in the training command. Nor was it that he simply did not care for them, as all knew the novices were unquestionably his most prized possessions. While his interest in them was genuine, it was understood that he stayed aloof because at this stage, his primary concern was for the whole of them, not the individual—at least until the *Mutaʿallim* earned the title of Mamluk.

The only exception: when a novice was to be executed. In these instances, the prince would not only gather the facts and judgment from Safir or Aqtay, but he would also question the novice personally. If the verdict was agreeable, al-Salih would be on hand for the death sentence.

Further, it was well known that al-Salih would routinely time his visits to the sister fortress in Amid so that he could finalize any executions at that fortress, or witness any Mamluk being borne up on the crucifixes or hanging posts, which ornamented the winding switchbacks out of town. Whether he did so out of obligation for having blessed the decision to end the man's life, or to monitor the intensity and duration of the condemned's punishment, is unknown.

Duyal is saddened that his only conversations with al-Salih in this world will both revolve around death: his brother's, his own.

"Why did you kill your fellow novice, my son?" al-Salih asks.

Without thought, the words pour out frankly. "Father, this novice did not intend to kill him, only to beat him into improved performance—so he would better serve you."

Silence. A drip of water plops into a puddle on the rock floor. A guard shuffles his feet.

He hopes his response did not sound contrived. He looks up to the smooth, dark skin on al-Salih's face and then straight into the prince's warm eyes. Even in this quandary, he is awestruck being in his master's presence.

"Are you aware that several moons ago the other novice from your tulb who was beaten—Bulut—threw himself from the ramparts? So two were lost because of your actions." The prince looks at Duyal with eyes both thoughtful and distressed.

Duyal looks back to the floor. He did not kill Bulut, and feels little sorrow for the novice's self-slaughter. "No, my Father. This novice was not aware."

Al-Salih looks to the lead guard, checking the honesty in Duyal's answer. The bull-necked man nods once in reply.

The prince opens his mouth to speak, but then holds back as if catching the wrong words before they were released. He rubs the thick hair on his chin in thought. "As a result of your conduct, the assembly of amirs has decided upon your execution. I approve their judgment."

Duyal is unaffected. His family long dead or missing, his surviving people scattered to the west and now separated from his brothers in arms, he sees no real reason to live. He thinks back to his training and before that to his capture, and then drifts to the rolling hills of his homeland, to thick-legged ponies and thin smoke coiling from the top of his mother's ger. He is no longer afraid. A strange calm seems to cloak him.

"Have you anything to say?" the prince asks.

He hesitates on what will be his last words. He will not wallow before his prince; he will not beg for his life. Again, the truth flows from his lips, the words seeming to sit so far atop his heart that they push upon the cartilage in his throat, leaking out.

"This novice is only sorry he has failed you, my Father."

Inside of him his words ring shallow. His prince will never understand the depth of his regret, how sad he is that he will never be put to use in realizing his master's aims and spreading the will of Allah. There is nothing to be done now. He hopes in heaven there is plenty of grass and only fast ponies. Or even Arabians. Yes, Arabians…

As if these thoughts were a signal to begin, two guards grab his shoulders and swing him around to again face the block. They push his head forward onto the splintered slab, the crisscrossed axe marks scraping across his throat. He breathes in the putrid smell of oak soaked in aged blood. Where his head will land—two stained rocks, and some dried dribbles scuffed about the perimeter.

The guards step back from the block. Duyal places his hands upon his thighs. He sucks the damp air evenly through his nose, so as to leave the wood tight to his throat. Give them a clean cut. Don't breathe so hard. Don't move. Make it a clean cut. His breathing accelerates.

"Proceed," the prince says.

An axeman steps forward.

He loses all sense of time. He tries to think again of his family, his friends, but his mind goes blank, his ears waiting intently for that ominous thud.

He no longer feels the cold in the room. The pain in his knees subsides; his shivering stops. His mind drifts to where the wind blows stubborn grass in far-off meadows. Undulating brown tufts rolling waves across the valley like the surge and fall of the ocean. He smells freshly cut hay on the breeze, and the dusty comfort of stick-pounded felt. He will be there soon. Allah will take him there. The thought of his native soil and his God steady the trembling in his arms.

Finally, the guard moves a leg back to better swing his axe. Duyal closes his eyes. Behind his lids, he sees the bright sky of the steppe and the flight of a solitary hawk tilting its wings, leaning a lazy turn toward him. Will it be the hawk that takes him to God?

A whoosh of air across his face, followed by the clomp of blade into wood. A hum in his ears.

Yet he feels no burn of cutting edge upon his neck, his head does not mash into the rock floor. He opens his eyes.

The lion's ass end and curled tail. The entire edge of the blade, buried in the block. He breathes in the sharp smell of steel. His mind spins; blood pulses through his temples in quick bursts. He does not understand what has happened. To miss was impossible.

He is pulled up from the block by the scruff of his neck and turned to face the prince, kept down on his knees by the press of hands on his shoulders. The door creaks open. Gozde steps in from the shadow. He wonders if he now dreams in death.

The room whirls, a haze takes over his head. Tears stream down his face. His eyes bounce between his brother and his prince.

Al-Salih takes a step forward. "Your brother. He convinced me you were the purest among my sons… that your integrity, your loyalty could never be in question. As you now see, I insisted on a final test."

Gozde stands tight-lipped, his hands now in the small of his back. His eyes not on the younger brother he just saved, but upon his master, his commander.

"This coming campaign to Diya Rabi'a. You're aware of it?" the prince asks.

"Yes, yes my Father," Duyal says, trying to regain his bearing.

"If you're even half what your brother is, I need you in my ranks, not buried under the ground."

Al-Salih raises his chin to the senior axeman. Both men lock their heels and depart. He turns to the remaining pair of guards. "Please give us a moment."

A pale fear shows on the face of the younger. He is frozen, likely fighting every instinct, countering every shred of training he received that tells him to stay with his prince. Duyal does not blame them. Why would they trust the novice murderer, who was only an axe blade's width from a justified execution?

Al-Salih smiles. "It's fine. We'll only talk for a moment. I'm in no danger here."

"Yes, my Prince. May we stand midcorridor?" the senior guard asks.

"Of course." The prince turns to Duyal. "Take your feet."

Duyal rises on wobbly legs, gathering now that he has wet himself. His hands shake uncontrollably.

"I handpick Mamluks to serve in my vanguard unit. They operate forward of our main body and collect necessary information, often out of uniform. They're mostly junior amirs, but I sprinkle in fresh Mamluks among them. Your brother, Gozde, is a member. As you know, this past fall, we lost several men on this team—one being our best lanceman," al-Salih says, his face straining. "Gozde mentioned you'd be of great value, once graduating. Said you were made for only the most challenging assignments. I wanted to see your interest in joining this team... to go with the forward element into Diya Rabi'a."

Duyal only stares at the man, overwhelmed. Nearly beheaded seconds ago and now being assigned to a prestigious position, his brother's outfit no less. Standing before his living brother and his prince in urine-drenched trousers, how could al-Salih possibly have such faith in him?

"My Prince, I thank you for the confidence, for the honor. I'd like nothing better than to serve you in the company of my brother. I'll of course do whatever you wish. But I... I ask for no special treatment. We, I... have also made an obligation to my brothers in training. I'm duty bound not to abandon them. I wish for nothing more than to serve my master alongside them."

Gozde looks down, smirks at his brother's response.

Al-Salih wrinkles his brow in disgust. "Do you understand the status that comes with this assignment? Men in this regiment would..." He stops himself. His lips tighten.

Duyal wonders if al-Salih will bring back the axemen. He cannot believe that he has just rejected his prince's most gracious offer. Or was it an order? He hopes both men understand there was no arrogance in his response, no conceit in his heart.

The left side of al-Salih's mouth rises into a snicker, and he puffs out a half-hearted chuckle. He turns to look at Gozde, who is just now losing his grin. His prince leans his head back with closed eyes, smiling, seemingly both pleased and upset at the same time.

CHAPTER
40

Duyal
The citadel courtyard
December 13, 1237

Standing at rest, giant clumps of snow plop on to the formation of novices, creating a short-lived armor of crystal points upon their shoulders and caps. A swirling wind kicks up, whipping through the courtyard, depositing tickling flakes onto Duyal's eyebrows. One lands atop his eyelid. With Cenk not on hand, he could get away with wiping his hand across his face, but he maintains his discipline in respect for the novice out front. He squints his left eye, slowly thawing the frigid mass into a hefty tear, which eventually frees itself, winding down the curve of his nostril to his lip. The artificial teardrop seems to prime his emotions. He holds back a real one.

His previous tears had been one moon past, when Safir entered the chop room and informed him that he would be returning to his tulb. He would resume training. With head buried between his knees, tears ran down his cheeks, converging at the tip of his sparse beard and dripping to the wet stone. Tears in place of his blood, puddling atop the rock. And much like the numerous branches of the Volga, such were his thoughts, which fed that river rolling down his face.

He was joyful in the miracle of his release, yet shameful in knowing that Gozde's performance and words with the prince had saved him. He was blissful when hearing he would rejoin his mates, yet distressed that he had missed nearly two moons of training. The subtle tips on weapon employment and new tactical maneuvers covered would be lost to him, instruction that would have made him more useful to both his mates and God. He was worried—that somehow he might still be separated from his tulb upon graduation and assigned to another unit.

When his face dried, he was alone. Just him, his puffy eyes and the wooden chop block. It was then that he prayed vigorously to Allah with more passion than ever before. With no prayer mat, he welcomed the ache of bone on rock, hoping the throb in his kneecaps would bear proof to God of his thankfulness; that through the dull pain, Allah might know the grace in sparing him would not be for naught. It was this day that he became a true believer.

The snow coats his shoulders and tunic sleeves. With a loose grip, he holds the shaft of his mace, its ornate head wrapped in felt and secured with twine. Prohibited from allowing it to touch the ground, he rests the heavy weapon on his boot, as do his peers. Since Erol lopped off part of his foot by sword two moons past, they have shit, pissed, slept, and eaten with their maces. Upon rejoining his tulb, Duyal was issued his own bludgeoning device, even before receiving a new uniform.

Singer filled him in on the why of it. Because of Cenk's dissatisfaction with the unit's performance on horseback with the weapons of the *faris*, their *Furusiyya* instructor claimed he had convinced the senior amirs to transition the tulb into an

infantry unit. Cenk had even stowed their riding boots, is-
suing them the thick leathers of the infantry. They would be
relegated to ground-pounding duty, yet would not have the
honor of carrying the sword and spear of Egypt's infantry, instead only the mace and shield.

"That's right. For this tulb, the regiment will bring back
the 'infidel pestle.' Soon your only training will be in padded
qarqals. We'll have you rabbit chasers hitting each other with
lame ass crusader cocks all day long," Cenk said.

Although the weapon had been removed from the
Mamluk saddle a decade ago, Cenk declared the spiked ball
on shank was about the only one his troops could master
without maiming themselves. They were issued two-footers,
not the longer devices carried with pride by a previous line
of Mamluks, long dead. The tulb would be allowed to finish
their cavalry training, but their days on horseback were said
to be drawing to an end.

For several moons now, at the end of each training
day, Cenk personally alternated a laborious "mace drill" with
forced marches. In the dim light of the setting sun, they could
be seen cresting hills in dusty columns, toting veiled weapons
over shoulder, or heard past candles out, the hollow gong of
club on bronze clanging through the sand-colored walls. Cenk
insisted this work be done at night, not only because of the
shorter winter days, but also due to his supposed embarrass-
ment. He would covertly train his new grunts and then quietly
push the disgraced away from the corps, like a mother pushing
an unwanted child from her ger in silence, the bloody bundle
passed to a waiting horseman from a neighboring tower.

Unable to round up thirty-four maces with identical
heads, Cenk had equipped his boys with whatever weapons he could dig up. It was said some arrived from as far as
Damascus, even a few captured from crusader stocks, long
ago crated. Theirs is an odd lot: shafts of steel and hardwood,

iron and bronze heads of every design. Of course Cenk insisted that coverings remain on their weapons, triple knotted so only a sharp blade could free their wrappings. He could not stomach the individualism promoted by each novice carrying a different style in public. And surely no semblance of dignity would be granted to those novices who, by chance only, possessed a mace topped with a rendering of the prince's heraldry, the lion's head.

Through the wool, Duyal made out his mace design to be the flared head of a cobra, or possibly a dragon. His fellow novices clandestinely carry maces garnished with the heads of scorpions, serpents, traditional spiked balls and fluted spheres of steel.

But these are only temporary. Cenk asserts the metal smiths are busy fabricating their true unit heads now. They will be ready for graduation. He says repeatedly that Syrian artisans labor, day and night, forging the appropriate symbol to place atop the tulb's weapons—rabbit heads.

So for moons, the entire west side of the citadel has stared at their wool-swathed clubs of indignity. Some snicker. How could a unit so close to graduation, already wearing the tapered tunic and white sash of seniority, still be humiliated by their *Mu'allim*? And though most doubt Cenk's assertion of unit conversion, the intensity of their mace exercises and bruises sported from their sparring have made all in the tulb speculate from time to time as to the possibility of some truth in it.

Duyal could not care less if Cenk's fabrication is genuine. He was born to be a *faris*, but is content to be back with his tulb, in whatever form their unit takes, wherever they shall go. His fellows, nearly immune to both physical and psychological abuse, also seem to embrace their situation. Regardless of the tulb's future direction, they will soon finish. Together. They will soon serve their patron.

In false anticipation of receiving their new weapons, his brothers have taken to calling themselves "bunny thumpers." Turning humiliation on its pathetic rabbit head and shaking it into a twisted pride, the tulb coined a battle cry. This exclamation is too often blared against the west walls of the citadel, most always followed by a disguised chuckle or two.

Spontaneously shouted from the back of formation on night marches, prior to jousting, or after completing a well-placed shot upon the elevated gourd targets, the most vocal of the novices blast their bogus motivational grunt—"Thumpers!" The instructors are on to it, but are uncharacteristically sympathetic, doing nothing to halt this senior tulb's mild protest. Strangely, even Cenk ignores the outbursts.

Two turbaned men in matching coffee-colored shawls stroll into the blustery corridor with delicate step. "We're prepared for you," the older Egyptian says to the lead novice in a thick accent, the man's face etched with deep wrinkles.

The tulb leader faces about, brings the unit to attention and instructs the novices to file into the chamber. They brush the snow from their tunics and stage their maces against benches, posting a sentry, in case Cenk sneaks in to snatch one. Inside, two more of the prince's tailors, or what the Turks call *terzi*, stand with their hands folded across the front of their identical shawls, in cordial deference. These are the prince's best, men chosen by al-Salih's "Master of the Robe" to leave Cairo years ago and accompany the prince to Hisn Kayfa. They are conscientious in appearance, with neatly trimmed beards and turbans of bright white cloth wrapped about their cleanly shaven scalps. They stand beside tables that balance on a single leg, anchored by a thick piece of wood with tiny horses and riders carved into its four faces.

About them, hanging on rows of long pine rods, are the winter uniforms of the Mamluk: red coats of every size, bisected with thick silver buttons; gold-shaded trousers, arranged by girth and length, embroidered with subtle red patterns of concentric circles, stripes and crisscrossed lines. Thick belts, splayed with gold stiffeners, line three-tiered racks, like orderly strips of lamb drying in the autumn wind of the steppe.

Duyal catches himself not breathing, in awe of the sight. The spectacle brings a sudden hush to the room. He had tried to envision the day when they would no longer be novices, but *Salihiyya* Mamluks, when the training and nonstop drills and ceaseless instructor tirades would end, bearing fruit in the form of valiant conduct on the field of battle. Many times he dreamed of riding faithfully behind their prince, their guidon with the number nine replaced with al-Salih's red-lioned pennant. Here and now, amid this vast assortment of scarlet and gold, the goal feels near and real.

"Ah, if divide in three groups, we start," the wrinkled man says in broken Turkish, a single palm outstretched, the other hand politely laid across his chest. He turns to his associates and rattles gruff commands in his native Arabic. Each *terzi* places a silk tape over his forearm and takes station at his chest-high table, opening a large, leather-bound book, careful not to spill the flanking inkwell.

Duyal shuffles behind Ilker, where the closest column takes form. Their tailor fashions a nervous smile and nods to the first man. Ox steps forward. Some novices grin, while others wait with a look of intensity, as if they were in line to meet Allah himself. Yet all hold postures erect, their faces tanned and clear. In his weeks away, more of the thin-armed and scrawny have taken on the flared-back shape of their mentors. The training, ample chow, and puberty have pulled in unison to make young men of lads.

He feels a warm confidence in not just their physical potency and battle skills, but in their character. Scanning across their faces, he recounts defining moments, when quitting was the plausible option for each. But none would have it.

Not one in the remaining thirty-four fell for Cenk's promise of softer professions outside the block walls. None present would disappoint their brothers. When the time comes, Duyal knows he will willingly fight alongside them.

And they may soon get their chance. Word was rampant of al-Kamil's siege of Damascus. The sultan had already diverted the River Barada and all other streams feeding the city. Mangonels were in place to bombard the walls. For all they knew, the city had already fallen. Surely the sultan would send al-Salih to bash another of the radical princes elsewhere. Maybe it would be in Homs, or the conniving grandmother in Aleppo.

As the experienced hands of the tailors pull measuring tapes down arms and in-seams, Duyal realizes the brilliance behind what the Mamluks have done within the citadel's confines, possibly the weeks of silent reflection in the cell turning him more pensive. While physically extracting sweat from the boys for moons, the staff also inexplicably withdrew every drop of Kipchak blood from the novices' bodies. While none have forgotten their roots, rarely does one hear longings for the steppe. In its place, the Mamluk leadership injected the common fluid of jihadi brotherhood into the tulb's veins. Now in their vascular systems, where the blood of competing khans and ancient towers once ran, is the fresh red flow of the Mamluk, pushed by the single beating heart of the *Khushdash*.

In just over three moons, al-Salih will preside over their manumission ceremony. On this day, the novices become *Salihiyya* Mamluks—*Salihi*—members of al-Salih's military household. But they will also become free men. He wonders if any of his brothers have thoughts of leaving the stone walls after the ceremony. He doubts it. While the bindings of slavery will be formally released, their ties of indebtedness to al-Salih will not end.

How could they leave him, after such treasure and time has been spent to feed, clothe, and train them? Their collective futures are tied to him alone. Chains of obligation, opportunity, and duty will soon supersede the physical shackles that once held them.

As if these compulsions were not enough to keep them put, the invisible fetter of the *Khushdash* provides an additional restraint. They will not, they cannot leave their brothers. Ironically, with the ceremony, this symbolic severing of slavery's chains, they will only be bound tighter, through bonds indiscernible to the general populace of Hisn Kayfa.

Pulling his thin tape around the large head of Ox, the *terzi* raises his dark-tufted eyebrows, expanding the white around his hazel eyes. He feeds more silk through his hands. Those waiting in line chuckle.

"Never has this man seen a grape the size of yours, my friend," Demir says from the adjacent line.

Ilker digs in. "Sad... two families will have to sacrifice their winter oxen, just to make a helmet that will squeezes over Ox's noggin." Several novices chuckle.

Ox, clad in a tent-sized red coat, with sleeves extending past his first knuckle, nods in fake acceptance of the well-slung shot. "Yeah, Ilker, fortunately the *terzi* do not measure the length of our scepters, as they likely don't have a tick on their tapes short enough to measure that pus-dripping worm of yours."

With this the room erupts into a roar of deep-gutted laughter. Ilker sneers, raises a lip. This response only prolongs the hilarity. While understanding only the gist of the mostly unfamiliar words spoken, the *terzi* is initially confused, but then pulled into the merriment, his head rolling back with mouth open, yet uttering no sound. His shoulders bounce about and do the laughing for him. Looking over to the unaffected face of his wrinkled boss, the tailor stops the giggle in his shoulders, squats down to make a chalk mark on the red cloth at Ox's wrist. With a lingering smile on his lips, he records the measurement into his book as the glee subsides.

This will be only the first fitting. In another moon, the novices will be back for the second. The time and effort to custom-fit the garment, plus the superiority of its materials, place the jacket's cost at around four hundred dinars, a fortune to most in the city. And the dress uniform is but one sign of their master's generosity, as the tailors will distribute the entered measurements to a wide array of smiths and craftsman for use in producing the remainder of their uniform and kit.

Watching the *terzi* neatly print the squiggles on thick pages, Duyal figures the amirs would not allow the measurements of an undeserving novice to make their way into a book as important-looking as this. They would not tolerate a second-rate novice even placing his arms through the sleeves of a Mamluk uniform, unless it had been decided that the recruit was one of the chosen. Duyal reckons these before him will likely graduate.

The *terzi* looks Duyal's body up and down for several seconds. He ponders, reaching under his turban to rub the rough stubble on the back of his head. Nodding in agreement with his mental self-chat, he decides on Duyal's size, turning to grab both trousers and jacket from the poles. With trousers neatly hung across his forearm, he holds the red jacket open for Duyal.

Duyal slips it on. At once he feels undeserving to be wearing the uniform.

Standing with one foot in Baris' locked fingers, he reached to pull free his father's metal helmet from the support beam—that forbidden armor that had hung out of reach for years. Placing the sloppy iron piece upon his head for several seconds, he looked at his brother. Panic spread across Baris' face.

Not sure if the look was from Duyal's appearance, or the possibility of their father walking in to catch them, Duyal squirmed inside, thinking of the Rus who died in it and the near-death condition of his father when his uncle snatched it off the soldier's head.

Picturing gray skin and a tongue hanging from the mouth of its owner, Duyal jammed the helmet back on its peg, afraid the ghost justified in wearing such armor might haunt him.

He looks down the sleeves, admiring the quality of the cloth and the crafted buttons, their silver swirled into delicate patterns. Again that tinge of shame eases into him—for his training missed while dawdling in the cell. He feels the eyes upon him.

Three lines of novices stare at him, beaming satisfaction. He catches the smile of Singer. From nowhere, moisture comes to his eyes. He fights it off, looking down. They want him in the scarlet and gold. With no words, they let him know he is worthy. With the press of the *terzi's* chalk across his shoulder and back seam, Duyal pushes out the guilt, permitting a quietness to settle over him. This may be the most satisfying day of his life.

With a pat on the shoulder, he is finished. He joins the gathering of others who have been measured, content in listening to the barbs tossed at the last of the novices being fitted, these jests thrown over the low drone of conversation and soft chuckles shared between them.

Cenk busts through the arched entrance. "What do we have going on, ladies—a celebration? One would think you've already earned the cloth on these racks... that battle streamers already hang in glory from your lances." Veins in Cenk's neck fill with blood, pushing up the white scar tissue from an old wound.

With this, the novices retrieve their maces and fall into formation. Only Cenk's bootsteps and the soft-spoken commands of the *terzi* can now be heard, as the last two novices are fitted.

"Let's not rejoice too early, my *Muta'allim*, as our training time together isn't over yet. Just because you're measured for Mamluk scarlet doesn't mean that you'll ever wear it. You're still merely sheep dung, stomped thick on the bottom of my pen floor."

He circles the formation. "Surely one of the mouse eaters on your teams will cause the whole to fail," he says, referring to the final team event drawing near, where all members of the four-man team must finish together. "Mark my words, a team or two will get lost in the dark, then I will be the one who makes merry. Yes... remember that feel of *Salihi* wool, as for some it'll be your last. There's rabbit thumpers here who'll be wearing the grubby turban of a camel tender for a living instead."

CHAPTER
41

Singer
North of Hisn Kayfa
March 10, 1238

A faint batter of wings breaks the early morning silence. Lying on his side, Singer opens his eyes, listens. The grunts of a pigeon in distress. He tosses aside his horse blanket and runs barefooted down to the pebbled wash, buckthorn branches slapping his face awake. Cursing under his breath, he hops over rocks, covering the frost-covered gravel in bounds.

Reaching his snare line, he approaches the struggling bird from behind, snatching its feet and neck in one motion. Clinching the pigeon's head, he loosens the horsehair noose and carefully removes the tangled feet with his free hand. He spins the bird by its neck, smiling.

Setting it down, he takes a knee and unties each of his five snares from their drag sticks, carefully winding each section of twisted hair into a compact circle before placing them in his pocket. He picks up his seeds that remain on the ground, dropping them under the flap of a half-filled pouch, which hangs from his other hip. He looks up, giving thanks to Allah for the bird and his God's grace in permitting the contraband for his trap.

Thank God for the snares. They had gathered and stowed the material for the traps with great calculation, as to be caught with anything but their horse blankets, uniform, and shared goatskin during the exercise preinspection would have meant a minimum of fifty lashings on the back. For those with a prior offense, the penalty would have been worse, possibly dismissal from the citadel. Yet they did it anyhow. So when alone on stall duty weeks before the event, Singer had cut strands of horsehair from deep in the tails of three Arabians, later sewing the fibers into the hem of his tunic. Duyal had done the same with cord from the grain sacks at the stables.

While the instructors would not say as much, Singer doubted they cared if the boys cheated. He gathered they expected, maybe even hoped the novices were clever enough to find a way to break the rules. And at least several novices were, Singer overhearing in the barracks two boys whispering of their food caches dug into the cold ground by locals far from the citadel walls, these lads already pledging a yet-to-be-earned chunk of their first pay, their *Jamakiya*, so confident they have earned a spot in the regiment.

He carries the pigeon by its scaled legs, walking gingerly on blistered feet. Rarely had he experienced such maladies on the steppe, or even in the mountain country, often going barefoot in the summer and resorting to fur-lined boots only when he could no longer bear the cold. Back then, his soles were a mass of hardened skin. His time in the slippers and leather boots of the Mamluks had actually softened his feet, probably part of the Mamluk plan in increasing the misery for this evolution.

His stomach grumbles. They had eaten little in two days, a situation bearable, if they had not been covering such great distances. None would mention his hunger, but the cheeks of his friends have hollowed since last moon and his own belt is secured two notches tighter than normal.

Thirteen days prior, Allah had smiled upon them, a small fallow deer having stumbled into their tree snare. They quickly cut the meat into thin strips and tied them atop their bedrolls, the flesh dangling, drying as they covered the barren country, its rocky landscape blanketed in crawling goat's thorn and milk vetch. This meat was now just a memory, all that remained of the beast being the rawhide bands taken from the hide and the pouches on their belts. Since then, their meals had been the chance rodent or bird, the occasional batch of dried fruit or bird eggs snatched from high in the mountain firs.

He returns to the pine canopy of their bivouac site to find Duyal and a tall novice, Galip, rolling up his blanket, their own gear already staged to move. Duyal snaps a glance to his hand, gives him a nod and a wink. Singer lays down the bird and wipes his feet on the instep of his trousers. He pulls a thorn from his heel, before slipping on his filthy socks. He picks up the goatskin, the vessel smothered with camel grease in the way of the locals, and takes a small sip from it.

The lanky Galip has stopped his task, unable to take his eyes from the bird. A full head taller than his mates, the youth is known for his insatiable appetite. While possessing a near-perfect record on weapon tests, his infractions at the citadel have all been food-related—fruit hidden under a blanket in the barracks, an extra mouthful taken when the order to cease feeding had been given at the tables, figs found stuffed into the bottom of his pack on a field exercise.

Singer knew Galip's placement on their team had been more than mere coincidence, Cenk having grouped all the trios with hopeful conflict in mind. Evidence abounded. From within their tulb, two of the fastest were joined with a heavy-footed novice; a couple of brutes were matched with the scrawniest lad. Those of hardheaded disposition were forced into a threesome, as were those known to be less competent at trapping, fishing, and snaring.

On this exercise, hunger, fatigue, dehydration, and sleeplessness would only accentuate the differences among them, or speed the consequences resulting from their common weaknesses. Unlike his fellow *Mu'allim*, who prepped their novices for the event and grouped them according to their complementary skills, Cenk's goal was to give all his novices their best shot at failing the last major event. The novices would have expected no different from him.

Duyal pulls the feathers from the bird in handfuls and then removes the sharpest cutting stone from his pocket. He cuts the flesh into equal portions and lays the bloody heaps upon a flat rock. Seeming to sense Galip's hungry eyes, Duyal pushes another morsel from his pile into Galip's.

For the last six days, Galip has received more than his share of the available food and water. Initially their teammate objected, yet he no longer does so. Singer does not begrudge him, realizing his friend's body needs more to sustain itself. If a few extra mouthfuls for Galip help the team finish together and on time, then so be it.

Duyal snags a leg from his mound, sticks it in his mouth and detaches the thigh meat with several pulls across his clenched teeth. He chews with the orange-scaled foot protruding from the side of his mouth. "I reckon we get there before sunset, eh?" he asks, looking at the wrinkled map handed to him two days ago by an instructor. He snaps off the foot in his mouth and inspects it. He places it in his pocket, likely seeing some future use in the clawed toes.

"Yep, yep," Singer says, smiling at his friend.

Galip takes his pile and stuffs the entire handful into his mouth, crunching on the hollow bones with head tilted back, eyes closed in bliss. Singer and Duyal shake their heads, shooting identical glances to the other, one eyebrow raised. Singer smiles broader, appreciative that their communication needs no words, glad their opinions are often identical, thankful his friend was given back to the tulb.

He had thought his friend was lost to them. Death or expulsion from the citadel had seemed Duyal's fate. Most had given up hope long ago that he would return. When his emaciated friend entered the barracks unannounced three moons past, he was smothered by his fellow novices. Wrestled to the ground, several grabbed Duyal's hair to look into his face, as if to verify that the figure before them was truly he and not their friend's ghost. Never had there been such noise in the barracks. Even Cenk left the tulb unmolested to celebrate their friend's return.

How or why the command placed Duyal back into Tulb Nine has been kept a mystery to them. His friend seems bound by some strange bargain, forced into silence on the topic. "By the grace of God, they changed their minds," was Duyal's standard answer, when asked anything of it. Singer saw the scars upon his friend's legs and buttocks. He knows Duyal's stay in the cell was not a pleasant one, that he kept his promise to them. Ultimately, he does not care what happened, why they chose to release him. His brother is out of the hole and back where he belongs. This is all that matters.

Galip, now grinning from the immediate benefits of the flesh, says, "At this point, I think we could hit these posts hopping on one leg if we had to. I can smell this one near."

Duyal smiles. "Hope so."

For most of the past moon, they had found every checkpoint required by their instructors. Some points had been only a half day's march apart, requiring great speed to reach by the assigned deadlines, while others required consecutive day-and-night marches for a prompt arrival. No novice knew when this final event would end, or where; perhaps only Aqtay or Safir possessed such knowledge. What the recruits did know was that all teams in the tulb shared the final checkpoint, and that each would arrive at it from a different direction.

On the coldest days, they had traveled at night, navigating by the stars and catching some sleep in the warmer midmorning hours, if possible. They had often relied on at least some moonlight to aid their passage, yet a new moon last evening and fatigue had stopped them early, the three huddling in a shivering mass all night.

As the days and weeks passed, the assigned terrain had only become steeper and more treacherous, the paths less defined or nonexistent. Increasingly their routes were shared with an assorted collection of traders and bandits. Unarmed and most often unable to distinguish who was friend or foe, the novices chose to steer clear of all they encountered.

Chewing absently on the tough skin, Singer ignores the irony of it all: that their Mamluk seniors had spent the last eighteen moons beating and brainwashing the Kipchak out of them, only to have their final test be one requiring a keen Kipchak to excel. Also, the instructors had methodically polished the novices' weapon and riding skills, only to send their pupils into the hinterlands unarmed and on foot. He chuckles to himself. Just another gut check. All that counts is reaching the next checkpoint.

And while not easy to find, at each terminus was always a numeral carved into a large wooden post and a metal plaque etched with a verse from the Koran, the words not scribed in the usual Arabic, but in their native Turkish. At each, they marked the numeral onto the single scroll they carried, the ragged parchment covered in oil cloth. At times, an instructor was camped at the marker when they arrived, as those men not slated to deploy with al-Salih to Diyar Rabi'a in support of the sultan's campaign in Damascus and Homs had been tasked with roving between the markers on horseback.

The instructors often stayed the evenings with host families, mostly large herders or merchants whose loyalty had been bought by al-Salih. Yet the instructors were required to pass some time each day at hasty camps made at the markers, in order to verify the arrival of expected teams and make observations of each team's conduct that would be of interest to the command. This was boring duty for them. Yet it was preferable to an empty hippodrome, as both junior tulbs on hand were in their first phase of training, the novices' full attention on the Koran and the holy men, not the weapons of the Mamluk.

"We best go," Duyal says.

They rise on sore joints to shoulder their bedrolls and step off to the north in file, letting Galip take the lead. They strain to keep pace with the long-legged novice, the jagged peaks of the Karasu looming in the distance, their white tops bisected by the rising sun. They climb, the patches of sprouting goosefoot at their shins soon replaced by sharp stone, ice, and brown traces of last year's weed. They struggle to keep their feet across the slick rock, timing their steps to hit patches of grass and clumps of purple crocus, some of the flowering heads punching through pockets of crusted snow.

They walk in silence, Singer and Duyal stretching to match the footholds made by Galip. This unspoken game is enough to block the pain in their feet, the exertion from the march sufficient to keep the cold from their minds. They lean into a goat trail carved on the side of a cliff, using the hand-worn branches on the odd cedar and black pine to check their steps on the sheer sections.

Singer thinks of the finish. The sweetness of the tulb arriving at the final checkpoint, three at a time, the relief in knowing his friends are safe and will soon be graduating together. "You think they will keep us in the same unit?" he asks.

"The three of us, or all of us?" Duyal asks.

"All of us."

"Needs of the corps, my friend," Galip says, mocking a phrase heard repeatedly from their instructors.

"The last two classes... they stayed together," Duyal says.

"Yeah, well, I think they expect unit-wide losses in Diyar Rabi'a," Galip says.

"Right, right," Duyal says.

"And we might have Damascus right after and that won't be pretty," Singer says.

"Nothing like jumping right into the fire," Duyal says.

"Yeah," Singer says.

The sweat across his shoulders revitalizes the smell of horse from the blanket. This musk meshes with the sour rank from his tunic, providing him a comfort that comes from familiar scent. Under his breath, Singer hums a Kipchak tune pulled from the depth of his memory, a song he believes he heard once at a wedding.

Back down they plod, across a high wadi, where layers of hard rock turned sideways project at angles both bizarre and precarious. They climb, stopping at a crest to view the expanse before them.

The basin of dense oak shrub and juniper darkens before them. The sun is a full fist above the mountain, yet has become obscured by a gray-yellow haze. The horizon glows an abnormal bronze, flanked on its edges by a dull brown. The breeze in their face stiffens.

"What do you make of that?" Galip asks.

"Just what we don't need. Let's beat feet for some shelter," Duyal says.

They resume at a quickened pace, eying the tan landscape for a suitable place among the cliffs. Duyal points up to a shadowed area between massive rocks. A cold waft hits their faces, each successive squall gaining in strength as they pick their way through the boulders.

"I see nothing better. What do you think?" Duyal asks.

They nod, follow him inside the small cavern. They remove their sodden tunics and wrap the blankets about their shoulders as they sit. Singer leans out the entrance, pulling his hat tightly to his head and squeezing his tunic between his knees to keep the wind from taking it.

The burnt sky is quickly swallowed by a dirty vapor. Grains of sand peck his cheeks. He retreats back into the cave, pulling the blanket over his head, annoyed at the whistle that swirls through the cavern.

Damn wind. For as long as he can remember, he has abhorred it. Perhaps he associated it with no food, pitiful looks of hunger from his young brother and sister, his inability to provide. He recalls the gales in the Ural country. The winds, which not only forced most animals to bed down, but also pushed his arrows away from the cautious game he did find.

Maybe it was purely the wail, the bluster that dulled his own senses, making him less capable of protecting his siblings from the raiders that lurked in such weather. Crooks—desperate thieves of necessity, no different than he once was. But ultimately, strong wind meant a loss of control to him, rising in proportion to the strength of the gusts.

But he supposes the aversion, the anxiety, all run deeper than that. He has blocked it out for so long, yet knows exactly where the angst originated. He shakes off the thoughts, pressing the tunic to his face and tying the sleeves behind his head to keep his lungs free of the dust that now twirls about their sanctuary. His fellows have done the same.

The shrill in the cave turns to a roar. He shivers, then brings his legs to his chest and mashes his hands to his ears. He doubles up the material over his mouth and nose, but it does not stop the sting in his chest. He closes his eyes, the tower of blowing sand outside transforming in his mind to sideways sheets of snow across a steppe, years ago...

> *His father paced about their ger, the shelter chilled, despite four layers of felt that swathed the creaking willow frame and a fire stoked hot with burning cow dung. He then sat, elbows buried in his thighs, bent over, the characteristically tranquil face showing droplets of sweat high on his windburned forehead.*
>
> *Again to his feet, he pulled the felt flap aside to peek out, as if somehow repeating this action enough times would make his wife and livestock reappear. Sensing their father's unease, Nergis and Baki dug deeper under Singer's arms on the opposite bed.*
>
> *The blizzard had come up quickly over the mountain, and surely their father regretted allowing his wife to venture off alone to bring their wandering sheep and goats back to the stable. But their mother was stubborn, having no tolerance for the loss of even one animal. She had not asked his permission and left in a rush.*
>
> *His father sat with fingers laced. He pushed the felt slippers from his feet and pulled on his high boots. He looked hard at Singer and then at the younger siblings on either side. Moments passed.*
>
> *Eventually he rose, pulled on his fur hat and calmly said his last words to the three. "I'm going to find your mother. I'll be back soon."*

Years later, Singer rolled through his own mind what had to have been in his father's head that evening. Should I leave my children to find their mother? How many animals can we afford to lose and still survive the rest of the winter? Should I wait until morning, or would my wife and the small flock be too spread out or frozen by then? If I should become lost and their mother is dead, is my eldest son capable of protecting the young ones?

The haunting wind and heavy snow did not let up that night. They awoke the next morning to silence. Singer pulled open the flap to find their ger buried in snow drifted chest-high.

There were no tracks to follow, so he zigzagged his way downhill and downwind for half the morning, figuring the flock, and subsequently his parents, would have likely traveled this route. His heart sank when he came upon the leather-wrapped handle of her staff sticking out of the snow. Singer dug down and found his mother lying stiff, her hands crossed over her breast. She had known her fate, had embraced the elements.

It was not until the first thaw that he found the body of his father, not mentioning this to his brother or sister. His father had likely dug a snow shelter that night, once becoming disoriented, yet it was not enough to keep the hearty man alive.

Every sheep was dead. The wolves found most of them, the sharp-nosed canines able to detect and unbury the scattered stock better than he. Fortunately, one of the family's cows survived, having plowed its way back to the stable that morning.

It was from this night forward that Singer became both mother and father to his two siblings. He was but eleven.

A nudge from his friend awakens him, disoriented and cold. The wind has stopped. He looks down to the sand holding in the folds of his blanket, licks the grit from his lips. He stretches to see the sun's position from the cave. He shakes the sand from his blanket, brushes it from his clothes and hair. They must move quickly now, as the amir at their next station will listen to no excuse.

"Glad we weren't caught in the open," Singer says, his head sideways, clawing sand from his ear.

"Yeah," Duyal says.

They continue, the sun dipping in a stunning blue sky, the path before them void of any track, as if no other animal lived, as if they were the first humans to walk this barren country. A pale dust covers the leaves on the oak shrubs, and every bloom in the valley has taken on the dull brown aspect of the hills.

Nearing their objective, they spot a cluster of pine and three specks of white huddled beneath the nearest of them. They lengthen their stride, certain this must be their navigation post, curious which trio of mates also shares the same marker.

The other threesome meets them on the thin path, just shy of the trees. The two groups stand before each other in silence, wondering which would be first to break the instructors' rule and speak to the other. Perhaps this is another test, another way to fail.

"Looks like you have found your next checkpoint," Ox says, motioning back to the trees.

"I suppose we'll find out soon enough," Duyal says with a grin.

"We all best move on," Singer says, figuring an instructor could have eyes on them right now.

Ilker and Demir look down to the ground, Ox shifts his weight to his other foot and looks to the high ground around them.

"No instructor here, eh?" Duyal asks.

Ilker's bottom lip trembles. He bites it down. Demir rolls down the sleeve of his tunic.

"What's wrong?" Duyal asks.

They all look at Ilker. The sides of his mouth quiver.

"Ilker, what have you done?" Singer asks.

Ilker looks away, eyes half closed, mumbling.

"Listen, here's the number off that post. You guys can't go any farther down there," Ox says, handing Duyal his scroll.

"Don't touch it," Singer says, looking to the trees for sign of an instructor.

"We're here early. We don't need the help," Duyal says.

"Let's go," Singer says, taking a step past them.

Ox grabs Singer by the shoulder. "You're not going down there."

Singer scowls.

"What's going on, Ox?" Duyal asks.

Singer knocks himself free of Ox's grip and takes a step back. "What have you done this time?"

Ox curls his lip and then meets the eyes of his three comrades. "Ekrem is dead."

Demir and Ilker look up at their friends, their look confirming the words.

"Dead?" Duyal asks.

"You killed him, didn't you?" Singer asks Ox, his eyes quickly leaving the giant and blank face of Demir to rest on Ilker.

Ilker has removed his hat. He scratches the receding spot on his head. He looks down and begins digging the funk from his fingernails with his thumb. He slowly nods his head.

"We brought revenge for Ichami's death," Ox says.

"Then you're certain it was Ekrem?" Duyal asks.

"We know he was the one," Ox says.

"You know?" Duyal asks.

"I know what I heard that night," Demir says.

"But you saw nothing. No person. You really know nothing," Galip says.

"We didn't need to see anything else. I know that Ekrem raped the unwilling boys from other tulbs—that he would've never stopped, never been punished. How many times did that snake cozy up to our mates, using his position, his reputation to get close to the most vulnerable of us?" Ox asks.

"You fool," Singer says. He lunges at Ox, yet the giant anticipates the move, his dark-haired fist crashing into Singer's forehead with a dull thud. Singer crumbles to the dirt.

Singer tries to rise to his elbows, but is unable. He looks forward. The horizon twirls. His ears ring. He sees the blurry figure of Duyal being held back by Demir and Ilker. He senses those about him screaming, but he hears none of it. He feels his lungs empty and buries his head in the crook of his arm.

He eventually pushes himself up to his butt, rubbing his hand across the knot that has formed above his eye socket. Duyal reaches out and pulls him to his feet.

Ox has his hands outstretched. "What in this life is perfect? You think the evil ones ever expose themselves completely? No, they don't... we know enough to reckon it was Ekrem who jumped Ichami," he says, summarizing what was likely a lengthy conversation between them.

There is a moment of silence, eyes meeting eyes, disbelief on some of their faces.

Galip steps before Ox. "You won't get away with it. They will catch you. You..."

Ox grabs him by the throat with one hand. With the other, he calmly points his finger into Galip's face. All move forward, yet hesitate at the calmness of Ox's voice. "They won't catch us... and *we*... all of us... have no choice but to get away with it."

Galip's eyes grow large and watery. He slowly drops his hands from the rippling forearm. Ox nods and gradually releases his grip, his eyes not leaving Galip's.

"We won't be pulled into this dung pile. We had nothing to do with this," Duyal says.

"Now you do," Ox says.

"You're an idiot. Ekrem taught us everything. He was the best of them," Singer says, his neck craning to meet Ox's face.

"Tsst. He was the best archer. As a man, he was the worst of them. If Ichami were alive, he'd tell you the same," Ox says.

"You're crazy," Singer says.

"No," Ox says.

Silence.

"Where's the body? Where's his horse?" Duyal asks.

"He's at the trees, by the marker. We smacked his horse on the ass," Ilker says.

"What of his gear, his weapon?" Singer asks.

Ilker removes the blanket from his back, unrolls it, exposing Ekrem's purse and bow snapped in half.

Duyal groans, rubbing his temples.

"We're not taking them—we'll bury them far from here. Nobody'll find them," Ox says.

"Or this," Demir says, pulling the crimson-stained training dagger from his blanket.

Recalling the dagger Ilker had taken from citadel during Erol's foot injury, Singer looks to Ilker. Ilker anticipates the eyes and averts his own. Singer wonders how they could have hidden the weapon. It does not matter now. He shakes his head.

"When Ekrem does not return, they'll come for him. They'll find his horse. They'll see our tracks. They'll know we were the last groups here," Duyal says.

"Oh, they'll come. But all they'll find is a dead instructor on his cot, murdered by a dagger, the area swept clean of prints by the wind and rain. They might find his horse, his gear missing—his only weapon, the bow, taken by the bandits who killed him... and they will question our two groups and others, novices without a real purpose or weapon to commit such a wicked act. Remember... Ekrem was a *Sayfiya,* a stray dog in the regiment. He has no brothers in training anywhere near who'll seek revenge. The citadel will only mourn, my brothers, not investigate," Ox says.

With these words, Singer's head begins to ache. He looks down to the path beneath their feet and back toward their approach. Rock. They have left not even a heel mark. He looks to the uniforms of his mates. No blood, no cuts upon their arms, no stains upon Demir's blanket.

"Both our teams arrived here last night before dark. We never saw each other. You saw no instructor, recorded the number and moved on," Ox says.

Duyal sighs.

Ox squares on him. "Don't look on us as if we are assassins of our own kind. You didn't see Ichami strapped on that cross—prey executed in place of the predator. Ekrem—he's why the eunuch killed our friend." He turns to glare at Singer with tears in his eyes. "You don't forget... this was for Ichami, the best of us—that's it." He waves his sausage-sized finger across the front of them and looks each in the eye once more. "For the *Khushdash*."

The novices look at each other again for a long while, from long face to long face, as do those bound by a dark promise. Then, as if on cue, they stoop to grab their things and step off in opposite directions.

CHAPTER
42

Ox
The Amir's Mess, the citadel, Hisn Kayfa
March 27, 1238

Ox stacks a third plate in the crutch of his arm, careful to avoid the tender stitches that darn the smiling cut along the base of his bicep. Through a film of lamb grease, he admires the ornate drawing of an Arabian in the plate's center, dressed in rings of blue and black about the rim. Beneath the horse on each piece is the identical inscription: "al-Salih—Warrior of the frontiers."

He examines the quality of the enameled glass and grins, satisfied that finally he also is permitted to eat from such plates, never again having to take meals off the splintered wood slabs in the novice chow hall. He reaches between two scarlet shoulders to snatch an opaque flask from the table, the vessel wrapped in a hand-painted web of vines and red blooms. He moves toward the galley, dodging other junior Mamluks who clear the bowls, platters, and goblets, also glazed in radiant colors.

With the last of the dinnerware removed from the tables, he takes a deep breath and walks with several others to a long bench, where stacked pairs of lidded pots sit staged. Steam ascends from the spout on each, like spirits stirred from their asylums. Some of the mist slowly forms into gray skulls against the dark wall, their deep eye sockets and tapered nasal passages elongating peculiarly before fading entirely, the ghosts seemingly free now to conduct their dubious craft unseen. An illusion. He tells himself it was just an illusion.

He nods gravely to Demir, as the lad grabs the handles on both pots and steps off toward his assigned tables. Ox takes another pair to his, where amirs chat, sitting on thick-legged chairs angled toward each other, the reverberation from their undertones amplified by the rock-arched ceiling.

From the top pot, he fills the cup of the man most senior, the design on the Mamluk's mug depicting a falcon returning to his owner's arm, a rabbit clasped in its talons. The amir nods in appreciation, holding his hand over the cup. With the smoky-sweet smell of Turkish *cay* in his nostrils, Ox takes a sidestep left.

The amir looks up. "Just a little water with it, please."

"Of course, my Amir," Ox says, filling the cup three quarters full from the upper vessel and then topping it with hot water from the bottom pot. He continues around the table until the vessel is nearly empty. He glances across the room.

Demir tilts the last drips into Amir Aqtay's cup. They meet back at the bench, where they find another stacked pair steaming. His friend snatches the pots and shoots him a sideways glance, his top lip twitching ever so slightly.

Ox stands formally with cupped hands resting atop his rump. He scans the place. Straight-backed men in red speak solemnly, their folded hands atop mustard-colored tablecloths. A few nod in agreement on points deliberated, while stroking beards of blond and red. Weighty looks occupy some faces, all amid the low buzz of their garbled words.

The command has dismissed the regular servants of the mess this day, the amirs wanting nothing but Mamluk ears in their mess this evening. New graduates continue to duck in among the tables, filling and refilling cups of tea.

He wipes the beads that form on his brow, recalling the veiled hag at the river's edge many moons ago:

> *"Just dump it in the drink, he'll taste nothing," she croaked in a voice not her own, handing him the vial amid the wad of dripping gray tunics.*
>
> *"She's been paid?" Ox asked.*
>
> *She nodded, the cloth across her face calling to attention dark, cunning eyes above bags of skin. "Any of you snitch on her or me and you'll not live long." The force of her threat caused the woman in rags to abandon her faked voice, bringing forth an accent matching the sailors who brought him here so long ago.*
>
> *He turned from her and stumbled over a rock on his first step back toward the citadel. Then up the steep stairs without looking back, the laundry dripping on his thighs, the vial held tightly between his fingers underneath.*

Feeling Demir's stare, he pulls in a deep breath and takes a final survey. He tells himself that all is normal. Satisfied, he raises his right hand to the callus on his ear, still watching the men in red coats.

Demir's eyes leave him. He looks down, pulls the stopper from the vial banded about his arm and dumps the contents into the spout of the top pot, his back to the room, his sleeve mostly covering his work. He replaces the cork, picks up the pots and heads back to his table.

Feeling more at ease the farther his head turns, Ox halts when meeting a pair of familiar eyes at a far table, the only man in the room not absorbed in discussion. Cenk smiles, raises his black eyebrows and tilts his head, as if somehow impressed. He leans forward, shifting his gaze from Ox to Demir, as the ape-armed boy fills Safir's cup. He then leans back, again nodding slowly in a contented manner, his dark eyes squinting, assessing.

Ox swallows hard, his knees go wobbly. A buzz takes over his head. His throat begins to burn. He turns in the direction of his friend.

Demir strides toward the galley, eyes locked forward, eager to dump the pot before another amir signals him for a top off. Slowly, Ox forces his head to turn once again toward the far corner.

Cenk watches the lad until he is out of sight, his forehead rumpled in calculation. Nausea pushes up in Ox's stomach, bringing spew to his throat. He forces a gulp, rubbing the puckered stitches on his bicep, waiting for his former *Muallim* to rise from the table and notify the others of what he has seen, for Ox's life in the regiment to be over before it starts. But Cenk leans back in his chair, sitting more comfortably than before.

He must do something. Anything. He looks to the bench, where a lone pair of pots sit.

He wipes his brow and goes to them, wandering between the tables mindlessly refilling cups, yet avoiding the corner table.

Aqtay pushes his chair back and nods to a Mamluk near the door. The clunk of heavy wood on frame and jangle of hardware cause the hum in the room to diminish. Chairs yelp on the stone as they orient toward the head table. The drone in the room falls off to an eventual silence, as more eyes move toward the only man who stands, his hairy knuckles locked atop his chair, as if it were a podium.

With no emotion, Aqtay speaks. "I will bypass the formalities this evening and get immediately to the matter at hand. Last night, I received a scroll from our emissary in Damascus. The sultan has died. The sickness al-Kamil has been fighting took him in the night three days ago."

Silence. Some amirs turn to read their friends' faces.

"The sultan's senior amirs formed a junta. Included is 'Izz al-Din from the *Ashrafiyya* Regiment."

A grumble grows about the tables, men shift in their seats. "This a reward for his brilliant inability to defend Damascus?" an amir calls from the front table.

"Enough. There'll be time later for your views. As expected, the assembly honored the sultan's clear wishes and confirmed al-Adil II to succeed as the sultan and ruler of Egypt. Our prince will maintain in the Jazira."

More muttering among them, but quickly they move to a nervous hush.

"Our emissary sent word of al-Kamil's death to our prince in Raqqa, where he's said to have raised the siege and made his way northeast toward the fortress at Sinjar. Al-Salih, of course, will not recognize the succession of al-Adil II to the sultanate."

Some amirs sit up even straighter in the high-backed chairs at just the mention of their prince's name. Others lean over to whisper toward a comrade.

"The situation in Damascus is thornier. The assembly of amirs has decided to support al-Kamil's nephew, al-Jawad, as opposed to the sultan's other nephew al-Nasir Da'ud of Karak."

An older amir sarcastically pipes in, "Governorship to the highest bidder, was it? The easier of the two to influence, my Amir?"

Aqtay scowls.

The room erupts in conversation among the tables. Another amir stands and speaks above the crowd. "And what of our father? Al-Salih has but few of us with him and the Khwarazmian allegiance rests only upon receiving their promised booty. With Raqqa not fallen, what's to keep the self-serving bastards from falling on him and our brothers?"

The room again flares up, some amirs nervously stroking their beards. Several wearing scars on their necks and arms from not-so-distant skirmishes with the menacing Khwarazmians shake their heads in disgust. Amid the din, Safir rises from his chair, places his hand on Aqtay's shoulder, bends to his ear and then moves toward the door bent in discomfort, his face turned grayish.

Ox looks to Demir. Expressionless, his friend watches Safir unlatch the door and quietly close it behind him. Ox tells himself to act naturally. His fingers begin to tingle. He takes a breath and then looks over at Cenk. The dark man has been staring at him, his elbow resting on the table, his index finger bisecting his nostrils in thought.

Aqtay raises a hand. "Quiet! Quiet! Our emissary wrote that our master is safe. He'll remain in Sinjar for only a short while. We'll assemble a reactionary force and have them ready to move if needed. Otherwise, we'll do nothing until we receive the message from his pigeon…"

CHAPTER
43

Duyal
The Polo Field, the citadel, Hisn Kayfa
Feb 4, 1239

The carved chunk of willow root skips across the frozen turf, slowing to a lazy roll. Beating hooves bear down on it, the dual-toned hammer resonating in the open air. Forked plumes of breath expel from the horses' nostrils. Clods of frosted turf fling in the air, divots peppering the white-dusted field.

"Your line! Your line!" his teammates sound.

"Nearside!" Duyal yells, putting one leg to his Arabian, angling his approach to intersect his opponent. Coming alongside Demir's mount, he nudges his horse's shoulder into his friend's.

Demir leans over the neck of his animal and raises his mallet to hit the wooden ball, yet Duyal "hooks" him, coming down with his own, using the stick's head to restrict his friend's swing. The ball comes to a halt as both riders rumble past it.

"Eat dung, mongrel," Duyal says, grinning, swinging the mallet twice about the strap on his wrist for effect.

"Goat sticker," Demir says.

Singer, his team's midfielder, swoops in behind them and cracks the ball down the far side of the field. He follows his shot at the gallop. As the opposing forward, Demir circles his bay and gives chase, the doubled-over braid of tail smacking his horse's buttocks.

Duyal reins in and returns to his defensive zone. He pats the mare's steaming shoulder. He leans to her ear, taking in the pleasant scent of straw, dust, and horse. "Nice work, girl. Nice work."

Watching the action downfield, he slips his hand under the browband of her tack and rubs the white patch on her forehead. He scratches her withers, bringing forth a groan and an elegant arching of her neck. He recalls a conversation at the stables with a young Bedouin: "The high crest means a horse of high courage, you bet on this," the Arab had said. Duyal hopes so.

He has named her "Moonshine." He knew Ishak, the elder in the stables, had chosen this mare specifically for him, Duyal recalling the old man's smile as Duyal heaped praise on the animal's composition so many moons ago. The old man had watched him visit with the horse those evenings, after his chores were done. Ishak had remembered, had done this for him.

She is six years old and moves with the smoothness of a wide river. All summer and fall he trained on her, both rider and horse acclimating to the other's quirks and habits. His glossy chestnut tops sixteen hands, a full four hands taller than the last animal he called his own, nearly three years past on the steppe, so far away.

His own. He beams, still trying to wrap his mind around this concept and all the changes that have occurred since his tulb's manumission, the professed ending of their enslavement to al-Salih. As expected, the ceremony consecrating this event had been grand. Every Mamluk not away on campaign was on hand, a throng of scarlet and gold behind them to view the long-held custom: marching and formations; respects paid to heroes long deceased; seniors' speeches on the future of the corps and the honor in serving their prince.

A majority of his instructors had been there, most of them pleased to review the fruit of their efforts. A notable exception was Safir, the eunuch having fallen ill last spring. Quarantined for weeks with the young novices infected with the fever, Safir finally succumbed—his diarrhea turning to vomiting, then to violent convulsions and death. Too much interaction with the town's vendors, or one too many visits to the barracks of doomed novices, was the consensus. So ironic the amir would die himself of the illness that he tried so hard to keep outside the walls of the citadel.

It had already been eight moons since Safir's funeral. The turnout was heavy, yet the event had a feeling of warriors on hand out of obligation, not as a sign of respect for the man, or grief for a friend. Amir Aqtay and al-Salih, of course, were troubled, the two struggling to hide their emotion. Yet the event felt odd, forced. One would have imagined a solemn affair, a ritual with a feeling opposite the manumission certainly, but in reality the memorial service lacked any substance at all.

Then again, their manumission, despite all of the formal trappings and anticipation, actually also meant very little to him, in essence. It was a rite of passage, a show indicating they had met the requirements. Certainly the obligation to serve his master had not changed. They owed al-Salih everything. Indeed, no graduate would be riding his newly won steed out the gate for any reason other than executing the prince's will upon his rivals.

And Duyal remains keen to execute any task his prince assigns, travel to any place, fight any enemy. Despite al-Salih's initial desire to place him in the vanguard unit, the command instead assigned him to an amirate of regulars, along with the rest of his training tulb. Not another word of the reconnaissance team was mentioned to him. While it would have been a great opportunity, Duyal somehow feels he is better off serving away from his brother right now. Perhaps the amirs felt the same. He wishes to prove himself, prove his worth to the corps among his brothers in training, rather than having to perform in the shadow of Gozde.

Rumor was that Gozde and his fellows had been in the vicinity of Damascus for a moon or more, acting as the eyes and ears for their prince. If Duyal had been with them, he would not have had this opportunity to familiarize himself with Moonshine and the new gear he now bears.

He pats his horse. A blaze of pride runs through him. He cannot wait to prove that his prince's faith in him was not an error. And surely faith al-Salih must have—in all of them. Why else would he have bestowed such favors? Surely their prince knew his gifts would only act to tighten his grip upon the newly graduated tulb. For not only has al-Salih provided them with fine horses, but also every manner of custom-fit gear and weapons they will need, sparing no expense. Duyal knew this had been the case with every finishing class, but to have watched it materialize for his own tulb had been overwhelming. When Duyal awakens each morning, his first act is still to reach below his cot to check his kit, ensuring it has all not been a dream.

A Mamluk cracks the ball across the field, others give chase.

His mates sit atop saddles of fine wood, crowned with yellow padded seats of tooled leather, their feet resting upon ornate stirrups of crafted bronze. Upon the riders' heads are new helmets, lamellar leather coated with shiny layers of red and black lacquer. Embossed on each side is the lioned heraldry of their master.

Closest to their skin, they wear fine silken tunics and chain mail hauberks, acquired by al-Salih from the Italians, the infidels selling to the knights of Islam despite the papal ban. Covering the mail are their long coats, the scarlet *qaba* of winter. Over these each Mamluk shoulders a new *jawshan*—a hardened leather cuirass, constructed by the time-consuming method of stitching together overlapping layers of fire-dried squares of thick hide. Gone is the hooped armor used in training, which for years snagged their bowstrings when shooting.

Their winter trousers are stunning—quilted, silk-lined and tinted mustard. The fine wool blend is stitched with a crescent design, centered between vertical stripes and connected with triangles laid in luxurious form. Strapped to their shins are gaiters of strong cloth, stuffed with cotton plant and edged with heavy strips of leather. The gaiters too are ornamented with the insignia of al-Salih. Their new boots fit perfectly, stiff-soled, yet with soft leather uppers that lace behind their calves.

And their weapons... he will never forget his mates' reaction when the cherry overlays were pulled away in unison, new Mamluks staggering in disbelief between tables to find the parchment tab that corresponded with each man's gifts. He had rarely seen his friends cry, yet tears streamed down the faces of nearly every graduate as each discovered his name in Turkish text and fondled these most cherished pieces for the first time.

As expected, their prince had provided only the finest wares. He hired the best bowyers in Anatolia to construct bows of hardwood, horn, and wild tendon. A Damascene craftsman, brought to Hisn Kayfa by al-Salih years ago, crafted the graduates' swords. Weeks before manumission, his mates had heard the ring of hammer on wootz steel from their guard duty perches high in the towers, the clangs bringing confidence, audible proof of the preparations being made for them.

While al-Salih's "Master of the Robe" ensured their gear was built to fit each graduate, his instructors took the personalizing a step further. Embroidered onto cloth, burned into leather, engraved into metal are bountiful dedications to their prince, accolades to their father. Inside the bowl of every shield, the identical writing resides: "Defender of the Faith." Upon Singer's gaiters—"Father of the poor and miserable." Etched into Demir's dagger scabbard—"Reviver of Justice among all."

Further, for every graduated novice, the instructors also chose Koranic verses, which characterized each young man, or selected passages known dear to a certain individual. To confirm their own impressions, instructors interviewed novices' mates, and eunuchs dug up scribbled notes taken years ago during religious training, finding words from the Koran that were instrumental in a novice's conversion to Islam.

It was the most agreeable of paradoxes. That these instructors, who for endless moons had scolded and beaten the individualism out them, who had condemned those novices that thought themselves in any manner special, now went to great lengths to celebrate each young man's uniqueness.

Hence, born upon their saddles, armor, and weapons are phrases that bring instant motivation to each new Mamluk. For Duyal, a craftsman had split his favorite verse into three sections. Across the neck guard of his *jawshan*—"And be not weak-hearted in the pursuit of the enemy." Down the length of his left gaiter—"If you suffer pain, then surely they too suffer pain as you suffer pain." Down his right gaiter—"And you hope from Allah what they do not hope; Allah is knowing and wise."

He adjusts his belt buckle, feeling the smooth metal surface and jutted legs of the lion. He rubs his hands across the rumpled flesh above his forearms, where Ilker had stitched the slashes. He recalls the day both symbols were granted.

Cenk ran his finger down the battered scroll. Satisfied that the numbers matched his key, he moved to their packs. Dumping the contents upon the rocks, he squatted in the faint light, sifting through their kit, ensuring nothing was missing, searching for the smallest shred of forbidden gear. He rose to his feet and slowly turned to the filthy novices before him. Chiseled into their foreheads were white creases of worry, much too deep for faces as young as theirs.

Then a peculiar calm fell upon their instructor's face. He looked at the three as if he had never seen them before, as if they were just then no longer subhuman. He tightened his lips and nodded, then resumed his nervous pacing, eventually turning his salt-stained back to them, his hard eyes directed to the wine-tinted horizon.

Duyal and Singer looked at one another, a smile forming on their faces at the identical instant. They embraced, tears smearing their sooty faces.

With free hands they pulled in Galip, the smell of greasy hair and grubby wool set in their nostrils. They had passed the final exercise. They had made it. They joined the others, who stared nervously westward.

The last team materialized on the horizon, first as white flecks against the brown mounds, then closer as shambling ruffians, hands grasped to tunics, pulling each other toward the swarm of them gathered about the final navigation post. As the trio dropped over the last rise, a cheer erupted, some of the novices running to them with shouts of encouragement, their eyes turning back to the opposite horizon glowing gold.

Reaching the post, the team was swallowed in a mass of bouncing gray, chanting, "Nine! Nine! Nine!" Their tulb number. One of them scrawled the post number and handed the scroll to Cenk, just as a sliver of sun crested the jagged landscape. They had met the time limit. A new day had dawned.

Cenk then assembled the tulb, cutting short the last of their merriments. With bodies locked, they fastened their eyes upon the man.

"Stand at ease," Cenk said calmly.

He paced before them, fingers locked behind his back, as always. He then spoke earnestly: "There are no more tests, no more games. You've met the requisites and have now earned your positions as true defenders of Islam. You're no longer nomads, captured enemy, slaves. In the coming days, years, you'll own horses, uniforms. For some of you, even fiefs in far-off lands . . . but . . . but all of this is worthless, compared with the title you will soon bear—Salihiyya Mamluk."

He brought his gaze off the mountain behind them and met their eyes to see if they sensed the enormity of their newly won positions. Goosebumps stood the hair on Duyal's arms erect; a shudder crept up his spine.

"But this is not a day for long-winded speeches. You'll hear enough of those at your manumission." He turned to Singer. "Guide on."

Singer took a step back and departed ranks, retrieving his instructor's pack. He unbuckled the straps and took a position to the left of his Mu'allim. Cenk moved to the first novice, looking thoughtfully at Ilker for a few moments. Reaching into the pack, he retrieved the bundled cloth, unwrapped the Mamluk insignia and pushed the belt buckle into Ilker's right palm.

When he had covered all three ranks, he again centered himself before them. "Circle up. Roll up your sleeves."

He then removed the dagger from its sheath and handed it to Singer, ducking his way outside the circle they formed. Singer took the blade and with no expression opened a deep gash across the base of each bicep. With blood coursing to his fingertips, he handed the razor-sharp weapon to the next man, who did the same. Down the line the dagger went.

As Duyal felt the ice-cold bite of steel, his heart hammered on breastbone. With a slosh, he locked arms with Ilker on his left, Galip on his right. Dehydrated and famished, his head went woozy.

When all thirty-four were hinged, he sensed nothing but heaving chests, their combined pulses and the two-toned calls of nearby chickadees, the birds indifferent to the ritual below them. They stood in silence, the novices' blended lifeblood dripping from elbows, forming a circle of ruby upon the tan stone. Each before him was now his ikhwa, his blood brother. There his mind swam in unspoken vows of fidelity to each.

He would live with the regret of not taking more action to save his own family, but knew at this moment that he would not make this mistake with his brothers before him. He would die before leaving a single one of them on any battlefield, anywhere.

He found the sober faces of Ox and Demir. Their eyes were upon him, reading, analyzing. It was then he realized that this ceremony had also a second, less tidy purpose. It would serve too as a blood-tainted muzzle. The tacit oath of fidelity between these brothers, sewn in sweat and toil, was now further sanctified, not only in each other's blood, but also in that of their slain instructor, Ekrem. Six within this circle would take that secret to their graves.

Cenk orbited the formation, finally speaking. "This consecrates your Khushdash. Blood brothers you'll always be... yet as you go forward, wearing the scarlet and gold of our regiment, keep in the front of your mind the valor of those Salihi who fell in combat before you. In all that you do, act always to not disgrace these men who died on the field, wearing the same lion of our master at their waists, bearing like scars at the crook of their arms. *For they watch us from above. Believe me, they still observe their fellow Mamluks, those serving under the red-lioned pennant."*

With this, he turned and moved away from them. He climbed a hilltop and stood gazing at the golden radiance spreading upon the barren landscape, his hands now clutched loosely behind him like an old man, his shoulders slumped in contented exhaustion.

The horse jerks the reins in his hands, likely aware of his rider's inattention. The pounding of hooves enters the edge of his zone. He squeezes his calves, feeling the animal quicken to the canter. He wonders how Moonshine will respond when her rider carries not a cane shaft and hard-wooded head in game, but Mamluk bow, sword, and lance in war.

He slows his horse, positioning her to protect their sector, watching his teammates push the attack up the field. Several leave their zones, their desire for the ball taking them a few paces out of station.

On the field's edge, Aslan, the lance master, wears a frown in reaction to the minor lack of discipline he now sees. "By Allah, keep to your lanes!" He puts his fingers to his mouth, whistles loudly twice.

The Mamluks turn from the ball and halt their horses, heads snapping to him. He crosses his arms, then pats each shoulder. Upon the signal, they race to execute the steps that have long become muscle memory.

Duyal removes his helmet, placing it on the embroidered pommel of his saddle. He sucks in his breath, grasps the shoulder straps, and in one motion, bends forward to pull the stiff armor over his head. He secures it with one hand to a rawhide strap on his saddle, while gathering and folding the front hems of his hauberk with his other hand, suspending the heavy material atop his helmet's crown.

He unfastens his belt, allowing the exact overhang, which balances the stiffened leather and scabbard across the cantle. He grasps the rear of the chain mail armor, again bows his head and pulls the garment over his upper torso in one tug. Lashing it down with his left hand, he pulls around the head of his horse to see the progress of his mates. A fine vapor rises above the heads and shoulders of each man. Their sweat-soaked tunics cling to abdomens tight and rippled, backs thick with muscle.

"Quickly, quickly, quickly!" Aslan yells, a smirk emerging on his face.

Those with stowed gear immediately rush on the ball at midfield to take advantage of the momentary inaction, Galip among the first to arrive. Aslan's grin turns to tight-lipped seriousness, as he observes a few of the riders still struggling to pull the armor over their heads.

"By Allah, what good will you be to our prince if shriveled like a raisin?"

Duyal grins. Since moving into the quarters on the east side of the citadel, their relationship with Aslan and the other instructors has changed. These seasoned Mamluks are now much more the big brothers, or at least tactical experts, much less the intimidating authorities they were just several moons ago. While still devoted to correcting flaws in the young warriors, they now sprinkle more jokes and kinder tones into their tutoring. Yet the lance master cannot let this defect pass, as every Mamluk knows that even the seemingly simple skill of removing their mail while on the move can become a burden to fatigued men.

"Your blessed hauberk—it'll be the preserver of life when arrows fill the air, and the snuffer of it when the desert starts cooking!" Aslan booms.

How many nightmares had they heard of men slow in donning their armor being the first to fall, as the arching rain of arrows fell upon them in combat? They would not always have adequate warning. And during a hasty retrograde, when speed was essential, the expedient removal of mail was key. Doing so swiftly, while moving on horseback, frequently meant the difference between living to fight another day, or allowing the sun on chain to bake all the moisture out of men—soldiers already parched and exhausted after the rigors of battle.

Battle. It is not a matter of if, but when for Duyal and his mates. Many of the citadel's Mamluks could be in the fray at this very moment, as al-Salih had taken them to Damascus, following the predictable drama between the Ayyubid princes since the death of al-Salih's father, al-Kamil.

Damascus under al-Jawad was a debacle. Emboldened by a recent victory in Palestine against a rival prince, al-Jawad gave indication one Friday sermon that he was ruling the dominion via his own right, not merely as a subject of the new sultan, al-Adil II. The sultan was furious. Some in al-Jawad's army abandoned him. This was the break the *Salihiyya* had been hoping for.

With his treasury in ruins, the populace hostile toward him and his forces fleeing in droves, al-Jawad offered his cousin, al-Salih, a most tempting deal: Damascus, in exchange for several of al-Salih's territories in the Jazira. It seemed to Duyal and the other Mamluks that al-Jawad was motivated to put another ambitious prince into Damascus to distract the angry sultan and then slink northward to the less provocative, more distant possessions of al-Salih's.

Having waited patiently for many moons, al-Salih decided he would swoop in and snatch Damascus, the second most important city in the realm. Bringing most of his Mamluks, a detachment of regulars from Mosul, and forces led by the prince of Hama, al-Salih had left this past moon to execute the terms of the deal with his cousin.

Yet here at the citadel the rest of al-Salih's troops sit, agonizing over their prince's safety, al-Jawad having proven himself untrustworthy to nearly every relative during the last year and al-Salih traveling with a force likely inadequate to topple Damascus. Further, the newly allied powers of Aleppo to the south and the Rum Seljukids to the north unquestionably had ambitious eyes for the Jazira. Would they choose to attack while al-Salih's defenses were halved?

Duyal tries to push out the negative. Al-Salih was not just a warrior, but also a skilled diplomat. He would find allies among the other princes to secure his position in southern Syria. Many within the walls speak of a day soon, when word will come for the remaining Mamluks to abandon both Hisn Kayfa and Amid all together. They, too, will make for the citadel in Damascus.

A single whistle blast from Aslan. The period of play, or *ara*, has ended. The riders rest their horses, most walking them toward the edge of the field.

"My set of armguards that we'll still pull this game out," Ox says to Demir, turning his big gray so that all could hear his challenge.

"Whoa, ho, ho," Ilker says, followed by a chorus of snickers and insults from the competition.

Demir looks down and shakes his head, watching his horse tear at the nubs of frozen grass.

"Take his bet, we've got this thing," Galip says, steering his mount toward Demir.

"You're up two. Afraid you can't hold your lead against this pitiful band of rogues?" Ox asks, waving his arm toward his own teammates.

More laughter.

"Shit," Demir says.

"Who would want your armguards anyhow, unless they needed cover for their shins?" Singer asks, complimented by a bawl of chuckling from his teammates.

"You could melt them down for horse armor," Duyal says.

They all laugh, some resting elbows on pommels, others turning in their saddles to catch the reaction of friends.

Aslan whistles three times. He swings his arm across his chest. The lance master knows that an enemy may one day surprise these Mamluks in camp, while the men rest, while the horses graze. They must be ready for anything.

Mamluks jump from their mounts, fingers nimbly untying the lashings that hold their armor and weapons. Upon their longcoats, they place their kit in identical fashion on the turf. Returning to their horses, they unbuckle saddle and blanket straps, tugging the wood and leather free and flopping moist blankets over their shoulders. Holding the saddles high to keep from tripping on leather fastenings, they waddle to their kit and gently lay the steaming load beside their piles. They snatch only their mallets.

Unburdened, they run to their Arabians, the young Mamluks springing atop their barebacked mounts like a pack of coyotes bouncing through the high grass. Duyal smiles as he lands lightly upon Moonshine's back, immediately grabbing the crest of her mane while wrapping his legs loosely about her flanks.

He turns her head and gives her some leg. They are off to the ball on the far side of the field. The thump of his horse's hooves on hard turf joins the others in the thunder of a full gallop. With six of them bunched up, Galip reaches out with his mallet and pops its head against Ilker's shoulder, half-heartedly trying to dismount him. Those nearby let loose boyish giggles. Singer flashes Duyal a grin, before burying his head in a tuck.

Their horses bear only bridles, with iron bits and long cheek pieces. Separate leather collars hold the Arabians' only remaining adornments, simple bronze holders, sprouting thick tufts of red-stained horsehair at the horses' throats. These tassels now swoosh in the wind, pulsating in time with their hoof beats.

The rush of cold air permeates his damp tunic, invigorating him. He leans forward. Free of his armor and gear, Moonshine reaches a swiftness Duyal has yet to experience. He has almost forgotten the sensation of a horse's shoulder and rump muscles expanding and contracting against his own body. This and the drumming of hooves, the rise and fall of his horse's lungs and feel of his animal's hip points against his own buttocks take him away from the place.

He floats, at first rising high above the field, until he can no longer see it, nor the river or shack-covered mountains. His memory then catches the south wind, taking him blindly through a wall of dark clouds, faster and faster, the whirling mist wetting his hair and cheeks.

Far north he flies, the sky clearing as he reaches the steppe of his childhood. He drops through a thin puff of cloud, rushes over the familiar contour of grays and browns and snow-blotched whites. Several specks catch his attention below.

His speed slows. He moves nearer. The figures transform into fur- and wool-clad boys on ponies, three lads racing fearlessly across the frozen grassland, pushing their ponies up the hills, leaning back on the downhill slopes, applying reins only to navigate the mounded frost heaves that pock the swamplands. Two ponies show scars through their thick winter coats, dark nicks and healed slashes against coats speckled with spots of brown and white. The trio reaches a high flat. Silver-tipped grass for as far as he can see, interrupted in stretches only by a splattering of craggy boulders, smoke-belching gers far in the distance.

From above, he closes on them. The wind pushes the dusty blond hair from their faces, parts the mottled fur on their backs. The biggest of the nomads chuckles to the rider at his side, points ahead to the lightest of them, the younger one who begins to pull away. His mate returns the smile, shakes his head. This boy then extends his arms to accommodate the stretch of his pony's neck. He slides his butt up, raises his knees and ducks his head even tighter behind the neck of the stout-legged animal.

Duyal is lowered, spun to face the trailing riders. He is startled, recognizing them as Gozde and himself. He stares at his brother for a long while and then at the younger him.

The boy smiles with eyes closed, having become one with the four-time gait of the gallop—near hind, off hind, near fore, off fore. In a subconscious bliss, the boy absorbs the pony's movements in complete fluidity, collecting the force at the stallion's high point, remaining feather-light at the bottom.

Remaining unnoticed at the boy's side, Duyal smiles at his own youthful form. Surely that must be what Allah has in mind for him and his brothers in heaven one day. That must be heaven.

ACKNOWLEDGEMENTS

I recall a line on the "acknowledgements page" of a friend's New York Times Bestseller: "Writing a book is no more solitary than fighting a war." True. But I think my friend would also agree that without key allies in "the war" to finish a book, there will be no book. The enemy, as writer Steve Pressfield reminds us: "Resistance"—that relentless, multi-faced demon, hellbent on keeping our art from taking form. So with heartfelt appreciation...

First, I thank Linda—for dealing with the daily, 5 a.m. alarms and this hermit's key-pounding obsession. Without her continuing support and understanding, I fail.

"Semper Fi" to Steve Pressfield, to whom I naively recommended a decade past to "write some fiction on these Mamluks or Mongols." His response: "That book would take me five years to write. Why don't you do it?" Thanks for that initial challenge and encouragement ever since.

A tip of the hat to my publisher, Mike Sager, for his patience, his expediting skills, and for staying true to his unit's mission. Stay "real," Mike.

Thank you, editor John Pahl—for sniffing out weaknesses in tale and prose; for your tactful, energetic assistance. And credit to editors Scott Couturier and Jean McDonald—dedicated pros, who also cleaned up the work.

Gratitude to the "Yooper" brain trust—Eric Palo and Dave Murphy—for their ideas, aid and novel approach to the subject.

A nod to early readers Steve Rose, Amy Gaudard and Jeff Graft. And to Mike Franzak, my friend and fellow devil dog in the fighting hole—"Wolverines!"

A cup of airag raised to Nergui and Gana for tolerantly answering my endless questions. To my Mongol pony, "Moonshine"—cheers for sparing this unskilled horseman. To the desert-scouring, history guru, Gidon: "Shalom, shalom, fellow warrior."

Gratitude to Bill Gracie for stoking that desire to "write well" in the 80's. Thank you Nate Fick, Doug Weaver, Jen Thomas, Steven Novak and others I foolishly overlooked. Last, nameless recognition to dozens of scholars, whose works I brazenly, yet adoringly, pillaged for years. Without their many studies and translations of Arabic works to English, I was lost.

ABOUT THE AUTHOR

Brad Graft is a businessman who runs a national chain with his partners. A former U.S. Marine officer, he helped develop a military program that assists wounded servicemen and families of the fallen. He continues to steer fundraising for charities serving this cause. An avid fly fisherman and hunter, for decades he has pursued gamefish and predators in remote places around the world. Also a history buff, his research on the *Brotherhood of the Mamluks* series took him to the Middle and Far East, where he studied Medieval-era routes and fortresses and trekked the Mongolian steppe on horseback, learning the ways of native hunters and nomadic herders.

ABOUT THE PUBLISHER

The Sager Group was founded in 1984. In 2012 it was chartered as a multi-media artists' and writers' consortium, with the intent of empowering those who create art—an umbrella beneath which makers can pursue, and profit from, their craft directly, without gatekeepers.

TSG publishes books; ministers to artists and provides modest grants; and produces documentary, feature, and commercial films. By harnessing the means of production, The Sager Group helps artists to help themselves. For more information, please see www.TheSagerGroup.Net.

Printed in Great Britain
by Amazon